Revenge
of the
Golf Gods

HOWARD JAHRE

Revenge
of the
Golf Gods

REVENGE OF THE GOLF GODS

iUniverse books may be ordered through booksellers or by contacting:

iUniverse
1663 Liberty Drive
Bloomington, IN 47403
www.iuniverse.com
1-800-Authors (1-800-288-4677)

ISBN: 978-1-4917-5180-0 (sc)
ISBN: 978-1-4917-5181-7 (e)

Library of Congress Control Number: 2014920542

Print information available on the last page.

iUniverse rev. date: 04/13/2016

Acknowledgments

THE PUBLICATION OF MY first novel, Revenge of the Golf Gods, a labor of love, and a lifelong ambition, would not have been possible except for the following people, all of whom contributed in their own unique way.

To my wife, Elizabeth Helke- you were an invaluable ally during my most frustrating hours.

To Lisa Cerasoli and her team- your personal approach in editing my manuscript far exceeded my expectations.

To Dr. Bruce Leuchter- an aspiring golfer and former Director of Clinical Neuropsychiatry at Weill Cornell Medical College.

To Kenneth Zakin- an avid golfer and a friend for over fifty years, who took the time from his hectic schedule and painstakingly plodded through an earlier manuscript.

To my many friends at Fresh Meadow Country Club–your encouragement to write this book will never be forgotten.

Chapter 1

GORDON HOWARD DROVE HURRIEDLY along the Long Island Expressway in his java black Range Rover sport coupe, unmindful of the clearly posted exit signs, anxiously preoccupied with a rapidly unfurling crisis. Beads of cold sweat trickled down his forehead.

He passed Creedmoor State Psychiatric Hospital. Its dilapidated, barred windows stood out as a painful reminder of his one week incarceration. The incessant rants of the crazies echoing through the squalid labyrinth of dimly lit hallways reverberated in the recesses of his mind.

The episode occurred shortly after he started working at his father's mega hedge fund, AH Advisors. He vividly remembered the oozing blood, wrapping a homemade tourniquet around the self-inflicted razor wound, and then calmly driving to Creedmoor to officially admit himself at 3:17a.m. Yes, he remembered the time that was scribbled on his "chart." A small scar on his left wrist remained permanently visible. He intended to inflict just a nick, but had too much to drink and lost control of his hand.

He had waited until his father was away on business, instructing the hospital to call Alan Howard's cell phone, hoping he would cut his trip short.

The staff psychiatrist diagnosed it as a one-time immature event, treating him with some counseling and a regimen of mood stabilizers before officially releasing him.

The rambling goodbye note still lay starkly on his pillow when he returned home, the final reminder of how his fake, attempted suicide was just one more botched attempt at success.

He was certain his father got those messages. But why couldn't he have mustered the courage to call him directly that night? Maybe he was afraid? After nine years, the nagging questions still haunted him.

Gordon Scott Howard, revered early on as a "freakishly talented wunderkind," was destined for superstardom. Or so he deep down believed. He was named collegiate All American three years in a row and was runner up in the US Amateur, a short game wizard who nonchalantly reeled off five consecutive birdies in an NCAA match, holing out twice from the sand while draining three slippery downhill twenty-five-foot putts.

But fame had been, at best, just a fantasy.

Although he drove past it on every workday, today he dwelled on his stint at Creedmoor, even though it was a near decade later. It was all about regret, the reason that got him there in the first place. He couldn't stand himself for not making any attempt to play golf professionally. He asked himself why, struggling for the answer, wondering if at this point of his life, self-sabotage was his middle name. It was frightening.

Snake Hollow Road appeared suddenly. He stomped on the accelerator, the inertia pinning him flush against his seat as he recklessly barreled past an eighteen wheeler, oblivious to the piercing honk of its foghorn, cutting the trucker off while nearly caroming into the steel dividers that separated the highway from the exit ramp.

Speeding onto the service road, he daringly shot through the yellow light at the intersection, hung a sharp left turn, and hurried north. He was just two short minutes from his highbrow country club.

The wailing siren startled him as the police car nosed up directly behind. "Pull over to the side of the road," a voice blared through a loudspeaker. The patrol car's headlights flashed ominously in sequence to its rotating red and blue alert bars.

Gordon brought the Range Rover to a halt on a small patch of grass, and sat silently as the officer sauntered over and motioned for him to roll down the window. He could see exactly what the officer was thinking —*I gotcha, smart-ass*—it was written all over his face.

2

"Shut off your engine and step out of the vehicle." His voice was monotone but commanding.

Gordon wiped his brow as he faced the officer.

"Your license and registration," the cop demanded, eyeing his suspect with a cold stare.

Gordon yanked out his wallet and silver billfold, flashed a roll of hundreds, and awkwardly groped for the documents—a maneuver he had learned from his father. He knew instantly the cop wouldn't take the bribe, and sheepishly handed over the identification. Sometimes it worked, sometimes it didn't.

The officer was a portly man of average height, his right cheek on his pock marked face marred by a deep scar. Polyester stretched pants were neatly inserted into his militia boots. His bronze badge was displayed prominently on his jacket over his left breast:

Police
Sgt. D. Riley
#3216745
Nassau County, NY

"I've been tailin' you—saw how you cutoff that eighteen wheeler. I clocked you at over ninety. Are you crazy or somethin'? Wanna get killed? I got a son your age, you got parents?"

"Just a father," Gordon murmured.

"How do you think he'd take *that* phone call?" Riley chastised him, not expecting an answer.

Gordon's head hung low, thinking whether subconsciously he harbored a death wish.

"Sit in the car and wait."

"Yes sir."

Gordon shut the window to drown out the intermittent squawks from the police radio. Then he instructed his hands free cell phone, "Call club."

"Pro Shop, can I help you?" Charlie Evans, the head professional, answered the phone.

"It's GH, Charlie," he said, trying to sound upbeat. "I'm running late. Can you meet me on the range at eleven thirty? And bring the Sony. I need to check out my swing, hitting it sideways these days, working on a new move."

"No worries, GH," Charlie replied. "If I could hit it sideways like you, damn, I'd stop givin' lessons to these rich bitches and would hit the tour." Charlie never understood Gordon's whimsical approach to the game, how he had so nonchalantly squandered his abilities—a guy with more talent than some touring pros.

"Thanks Charlie, let's play sometime. I'll spot you two shots a side, need the starter real quick." Charlie transferred the call.

"First tee, this is Jimmy."

"Hey Jimmy, its GH—I got two guests today, probably the usual hackers. I figure around two o'clock; need a cart and two caddies. Is Swifty around?"

"No problem, GH, Swifty's waiting for you, course is wide open."

Riley returned just as Gordon finished the call, motioned to open the window, and handed him back his license and registration. "I'm writin' you up for reckless speedin'. Got you on scope, gonna lose your license."

The officer was filling out the summons when Gordon reached into his back pocket, pulled out his wallet, and flashed a silver and gold badge:

Police Benevolent Association
Alan Howard
Assistant Deputy Commissioner
For Your Generosity in Support of our Members and their Families
Robert Burton
Nassau County District Attorney
June 15th, 2009

Riley scrutinized the inscription.

"Alan Howard's my father, you need proof, take me two minutes."

Riley walked over to his patrol car, turned off the flashing lights and alert bars to speed up the traffic—the ever so curious rubbernecks.

"Let's get to a quieter spot." Riley spoke as if they were new-found acquaintances. "It's tough to do business here, meet you by the lower lot."

A WEATHER BEATEN SIGN, *Old Point Country Club—Private—Members only,* hung inconspicuously from a hinged post. Gordon proceeded up a long tree-lined drive and abruptly turned into the employee lot. Riley arrived a few minutes later, feigning a routine patrol.

The two men walked over to a small bench directly behind their cars, concealed from any onlookers.

"A joint like this must cost a mint," Riley said as he stretched his legs.

Gordon opted to lean against the side of the patrol car.

At six feet, two inches, Gordon sported a fit and toned physique; wavy unkempt light brown hair swept behind his ears and nearly grazed his collar. Athletically handsome with an aquiline nose, strong jaw line, and blue-gray eyes, he donned khaki Bermuda shorts with a brown braided rope belt and leather driving moccasins. A pristine white unbuttoned Izod polo shirt exposed a tuft of his chest hair, which drew the eye up to his unshaven face.

"I love to play, but gotta get up real early in the morning, haul my ass down to Bethpage to get on the list. We got a group of guys, take turns. Sometimes we slip the starter a fifty. He knows we're cops, so he bumps us up. Still real crowded and takes at least six hours, not includin' waitin' to tee off." Riley made an imaginary swing. "I suck, only broke a hundred once, can hit the mother three hundred, but it ain't always in the fairway."

Gordon didn't see any purpose in letting Riley know that he was the de facto club champion, carried lower than a scratch handicap, and was hell bent on turning professional.

"Christ, I remember golfing here in some charity deal; this

place is first class. Your dad springs for big bucks every coupla' years for the PBA, probably a hundred fifty guys, all kinds a judges, police commissioner, Nassau DA. One year he had the frickin' Mayor of New York City and Senator what's his face? They had a big limo waitin' outside. Young broads walkin' around servin' everyone booze, like I died and went to heaven; lobsters, steaks, shrimps as big as my goddamn fist, barbecued ribs, burgers and dogs, big salad bar for the health fags. Real nasty desserts too—frickin' hot fudge sundaes, even my favorite—butterscotch."

Riley smiled as he rubbed his protruding stomach, which hung heavily over his belt. "Shows, don't it?"

Gordon tried to hold back a smirk.

"Tell ya, your dad's a real sport, bet it cost him at least twenty grand. We appreciate it, figurin' on what we get paid."

Riley spewed on as Gordon listened, not quite sure how much of this drivel was part of the negotiations, how much for real.

"My kid had some goddamn blood disease, always ragged out." Riley volunteered, bearing his soul. "Frickin' insurance didn't cover his medical bills, would have taken every nickel I had. What your father built for the PBA over at North Shore Hospital—was like Jesus answered our prayers. They thought leukemia, but was some crazy virus, might come back, not sure. Now he's fifteen and plays defensive end over at Roosevelt. The coach thinks he's scholarship material. I'm keepin' my fingers crossed since his grades ain't that great."

Gordon looked at his watch. *Running late, damn it!*

He noticed Riley's misty eyes, and couldn't help but sympathize about his son. Those were headaches nobody deserved.

"I'm rooting for him."

Riley acknowledged Gordon's heartfelt honesty with a nod of his head.

"Sorry about the speeding, Sergeant Riley, not like me, would appreciate some consideration. How about I make a donation to the PBA?"

"That ain't necessary, your father did enough."

"I insist", Gordon said, somewhat emphatically. "Just give it to your son, some extra spending money."

Gordon turned his back and counted out three crisp one hundred dollar bills. They shook hands, the tightly folded contribution finding its way into Riley's right jacket pocket.

"Better you should leave first, I'm gonna wait a few minutes so as not to cause suspicion."

Gordon got back into the Range Rover and inadvertently gunned the engine, leaving rubber tread marks and a loud squeal. He slowed down for the *golfers crossing's* bright yellow warning sign, and was momentarily calmed by the vista of the exquisite panorama of lush green sweeping fairways isolated by towering trees. He continued around the circular drive, which framed the putting green, stopping underneath the portico at the clubhouse entrance.

The valet, a student from Mumbai, neatly attired in a light khaki uniform, spoke just enough English to service the club's finicky members. He parroted his standard greeting as he promptly greeted Gordon and opened his door.

"Good morning, Mr. Howard, how are you today?"

"I'm OK, I guess."

"Very good, sir," the valet smiled.

Gordon, dispirited, walked into the clubhouse, dreading the damn day more than ever.

Chapter 2

"Hey Danny, what's the latest?"

Gordon's lifeless voice was not looking for an answer from Danny Anderson—head men's locker room attendant. Danny stood in his cubicle working on a pile of member's golf shoes—cleaning, polishing, and fixing spikes, whatever needed to be done.

"There's nothin' new since I last seen you, GH, which was yesterday, huh." He laughed heartily. "Who you gonna take apart today, Tiger Woods, huh?"

Danny would always add a "huh" at the end of a sentence, arch his bushy eyebrows, and flash a wry grin. He spoke with a tinge of sarcasm, always to the point, but not mean spirited.

"I think I got a better shot against Arnold, the way I'm hitting it," Gordon replied half jokingly.

"Well, if Palmer comes around looking for a game, I'll come get you, how's that, huh?"

"Cut the crap, Danny, it's a work day, two guests, the usual routine."

"What's with the long face, GH, huh?"

"Not sure, can't explain it, just in a lousy mood."

"Lady troubles, huh?"

"It's nothing to do with Liz but thanks for asking."

"You'll feel better once you hit the course, huh."

"Hope so, I'm range bound, running late. Set them up in the old section; I don't have the head to be sociable today."

Danny worked hard, and Gordon always took care of him, a hundred here, a fifty there, their own private arrangement, strictly against club policy.

Gordon watched as Danny finished off the last three pairs of shoes and put them in the shoe cart, which he wheeled up and down the aisles, placing the shoes in the appropriate lockers, treating them as if they were fine pieces of jewelry. He yelled over at Gordon. "Never know who's gonna show up lookin' for their frickin' shoes, huh."

Gordon laughed to himself. *God forbid a member couldn't find their precious golf shoes.* Gordon would bet the ranch that Danny knew where they were. And when he found them, they were returned with a sincere apology.

Danny assembled two sets of amenities along with a full length fluffy robe adorned with the Old Point Country Club crested emblem, which he placed tidily on the bench adjacent to two empty metal lockers, far away from Gordon Howard, as instructed.

GORDON OPENED HIS CHERRY wood locker, grabbed a pair of golf shoes and tossed off his loafers, which Danny would polish while he was out on the course. He checked himself out in the full length mirror at the end of the aisle—*today would be a struggle*—then walked forlornly down the hallway, through the double doors, down to the bag room.

Grabbing an open cart, he made a quick U-turn and scooted along the path past the tenth tee, narrowly missing an oncoming caddy shouldering two bags, then over to the range, where Charlie Evans was patiently waiting for him.

"Sorry I'm late, Charlie. Did you bring the Sony?"

Charlie wasn't upset, as they had a good working relationship, especially at three hundred an hour—double his normal rates.

"Yep, GH, all ready to go, downstairs, nice and quiet."

Just being on the range with Charlie lifted his spirits.

Gordon was finicky about his golf lessons. He always worked on the lower level, on the far left side, away from the hackers and gawkers who would ooh and ah watching his prodigious drives sail deep into the woods, twenty yards beyond the driving range.

Everything was in place; Gordon's bag, Charlie's big leather professional Taylor Made bag with his name emblazoned on the side, the Sony recorder, an ice bucket with cold water, and two pyramids of balls stamped Titleist Practice. A lone tractor at the far end of the range was doing some house cleaning.

"Hey, GH, congrats—heard you qualified for the Long Island Amateur over at Maplewood. Good work. Tough little course when the wind blows. At least two shots harder than this place. What was the cut?"

"Yep Charlie, could be a great tract but needs work. I had a bunch of matches there in high school. Greens are tricked up, bunkers full of silt; tough to get a good spin on the ball. I played horribly, shot even par. Drove the fourth hole and drained a tricky fifteen-footer for eagle, then double bogeyed fourteen when the caddy lost my ball. Had a couple of birdies and a few bogies, hit only nine greens but got it up and down. The cut was eight over. I was low medalist, no big deal."

"Who're you playing in the first round?"

"Already did, some college kid. I had him three up after fourteen, then he goes birdie, birdie, birdie, and knocks in a lucky forty-footer on seventeen. We halve eighteen, and then I duck hook it into the water on the first extra hole."

Charlie grimaced hearing another one of Gordon's woeful tales. He thought Gordon was a real head case. As good as Gordon was, especially his short game, he never gave himself any credit, only seeing the dark side of the game. He was constantly self-berating, throwing clubs and cursing, unable to withstand the competitive pressure of a real tournament with very good players—not the hackers at Old Point.

He remembered what Gordon's father told him, just last month, after a few martinis too many at the bar in the men's grill room. "Listen Charlie, straight from the horse's mouth, my son's lucky I was born before him. He's a lazy, spoiled brat. If he wasn't working for me, he'd be bagging groceries. Working! That's a laugh. I pay him half a million a year *not* to come to the office. Want to know what he does all day? My assistant sets up golf games with investors, guys who can write big checks for my fund, hackers who get all turned on watching him shoot two under. Nice work if you can get it."

GORDON WAS A PROBLEM child, a textbook case, a project. Back in junior high school, the principal had a sit down with Gordon's father, insisting he get counseling, or find another private school.

The school psychologist reported Gordon harbored deep-rooted anger, and was prone to self-destructive, addictive behavior—the result of Alan being anything but a father. He was more interested in his high profile hedge fund and gigantic ego than dishing out some love and an occasional pat on the back to his kid.

Alan dismissed the diagnosis as "a bunch of bull from a two bit social worker who couldn't make it as a real shrink." All Gordon needed was "a goddamn kick in the ass."

He finally dumped him off to Charlie Evans, as if he was dirty laundry, instructing Charlie to "clean up his act and teach him some respect; I'll make it worth your while."

Charlie played surrogate father to see what made Gordon tick, motivated by more than just the generous amount of money that Alan threw at him. It was crystal clear after a few lessons that this thirteen-year-old was born with golf in his DNA.

Some three years into the regimen, just shy of his sixteenth birthday, he busted through par, and when Charlie hugged him like a father would, a flood of ecstatic tears shot from his eyes.

Gordon was hooked, oblivious to anything other than that euphoric rush from blistering a perfectly struck iron dead at the flag.

That evening they celebrated, walking the course while sharing a fat joint packed with the best hooch Alan's money could buy. Charlie hadn't gotten high since college; their twenty-year age difference suddenly became irrelevant.

Stoned out, they gawked at the billions of stars which danced in the clear night sky. They sought out the constellations and watched blinking objects meander in and out of sight, giggling that one of them was a concerned Tiger Woods scoping out the competition from his private jet.

They rambled on with no particular agenda, until Gordon opened up, lambasting his father.

"I *despise* him, hope he dies."

"C'mon, sport, your father loves you; he's just busy with business."

Charlie dismissed it as typical teenage rebellion, until Gordon lost it, vividly describing his father's abusive browbeating and the dreaded belt floggings. He held onto Charlie, wailing like a child.

The admissions were too horribly detailed to be concocted; how he would stutter, twitch, and whoop with pain, then run into his room, lock the door, and bury his head beneath his pillows, drowning out the deafening tirades that never seemed to end.

Charlie thought he understood him. Deep down, despite his privilege, stood a genuine good guy, concerned for the less fortunate, who Gordon felt got a raw deal in life.

Charlie Evans wasn't going to get any more involved in family feuds. The club was a haven for gossipmongers, and as head professional, he needed to keep it all business, especially with a ten-year-old at home and another kid in the oven.

He was certain there were more serious issues with Gordon than what Alan had bellyached about. And how much Alan bore responsibility was anybody's guess. But he wasn't a damn shrink, yet he couldn't stop thinking about how many times he heard about some young man "with everything to live for" tragically putting a gun to his head.

CHARLIE POKED THROUGH GORDON'S bag and pulled out a five iron. "When the hell are you retiring these antiques? Wilson Staff X-31 blades are in the hall of fame, with the Bobby Jones mashie and niblick. You don't think you'd knock off three shots a round sporting some new technology?"

"It's the singer, Charlie, not the song" Gordon quickly reminded him. "I get these re-grooved every couple of years, like brand new. Handicaps haven't come down in fifty years. It's all a bunch of hokey marketing to push more gear. Crenshaw won his last Master's using Walter Hagen 1957 blades. I hit some of your new demos, and yeah, maybe my misses weren't as off line, but when I struck it pure, they didn't have the sweet feel of my forged blades. They melt in your hands and stick in your gut, especially when you knock it to three feet. It's better than sex, Charlie, much better."

Charlie knew Gordon was right, but then again Gordon hit is as pure as any pro.

"Hit me a few, let me watch."

Charlie adjusted the settings on the Sony camcorder and peered through the telescopic lens while Gordon loosened up. The Sony was specially fitted with software that allowed Charlie to superimpose his student's swing, frame by frame, against the top touring pros—more public relations than any real value. It also suckered them in for more lessons and expensive video analysis. Of course, everyone wanted to be compared to Tiger, and Charlie gave them plenty of encouragement, dropping buzz words like spine angle, shoulder turn, takeaway, torso rotation, position at the top, ad infinitum.

"OK, GH, she's all focused, where you aiming?"

Gordon pointed to his target, "the green with the blue flag, 210 yards."

Charlie hit the record button. "OK, GH, we're rolling. I'll take some from behind, then from the side."

He struck the first dozen balls with a right to left draw, the second dozen a high left to right fade, all landing within a few yards of each other.

Charlie just watched, silent, moving to a different angle and readjusting the focus on the lens. There wasn't much he could say, more what he thought.

Textbook—pure, fucking textbook.

Gordon appeared distant while Charlie fiddled with the settings.

"I'm ready to go, GH, same swing. Are you OK? You look down and out, like you just three-putted from two feet to lose the US Open."

"I just have a ton on my mind."

"Save it for later, GH, this is golf time, not a therapy session."

Charlie knew Gordon was going through a rough spell, some telling comments about his father he had made over the past few weeks, but wanted him to stay focused.

With the metronomic ticking of a finely tuned clock, Gordon repeated the exercise, admiring shot after shot, which journeyed toward the flag, mixing up draws and fades, and a final two iron stinger for good measure. It was something new he was working on, just like Tiger, which flew the green and rolled into the woods.

"OK, good work, GH." Charlie thought he saw something.

They walked over to the high tech training facility, where frustrated members could blast balls into a specially designed net. A rubber tee hooked up to a computer downloaded with special software measured an array of swing performance statistics; launch angle, spin rate, clubhead speed, carry and roll, ad infinitum. Charlie would do an evaluation—like a physician examining an ill patient. Invariably he found a cure, which was an entire set of new clubs, custom fitted with an array of expensive shafts, just like the pros. Not that such doctoring up improved their games. If anything, it just made their maladies worse, but the obscene profit margins helped Charlie make ends meet.

He removed the cartridge from the Sony and inserted it into a multimedia player affixed to a high definition monitor.

"Come sit with the doctor, GH, let's take a look."

Gordon sat quietly as the two watched the video. Charlie ran through every swing, his head perched forward cradled in his hands, uttering a few "uh huhs," nothing else. He replayed the video in slow motion, stopping at certain points, forward, then back, uttering a few more "uh huhs."

"Where did you pick up *that* move?" His eyes remained transfixed to the screen.

Gordon knew as much about the mechanics of the golf swing as most professionals, able to quote chapter and verse from any and every golf instructional book. A good part of their relationship was the banter about the seemingly endless swing theories, trying to make sense out of something that, for all who tried to conquer the game, remained a mystery.

"I've been fiddling with it for a while off and on, trying to get more consistent, tired of army golf—you know the drill Charlie, left, right, left, right. Look, I hit nine greens last week and shot one over par. All I'm doing is a reverse wrist cock, pre-squaring the clubface to the ball, pushing my left wrist down, which flattens it out, cupping my right wrist, turning my shoulders and the club is dead solid on plane, perfectly square."

"I don't mind an early wrist set, GH. Faldo won the Masters with it, Ballesteros won the British. Like everything else with this game, there are pros and cons."

Charlie fiddled with the player until he found the frame, stopped it at a precise point, and walked over to the monitor as Gordon joined him, grabbing two demo six irons that were leaning up against the wall.

"I got it, GH, saw it on the range, confirmed it right there." Charlie pointed to Gordon's new reverse wrist set in full view. "Show me what you do, start to finish, slow motion." He handed Gordon the club.

The two stood facing each other. Gordon went through his routine, stopping after each move as Charlie imitated him.

"OK, GH, look at my grip, sort of like this?"

Gordon examined Charlie's grip, like an engineer looking to make sure all the parts were properly in place.

"I want the shaft more in the lower palm of your left hand, with only two knuckles of your right hand visible at this point," he said, adjusting it until it was perfect.

"OK, I got it, GH, feels weird though."

"Not weird, pro, just different." Gordon repeated the routine, turning his shoulders while the club moved straight back and then up, with Charlie following along. "Now look at your clubface, Charlie, perfectly square to the target, not open or shut, right?"

"Yep, dead on square, GH, now show me your downswing."

Bruce Haberman—an eye surgeon who boasted a twelve handicap but played like an eighteen—suddenly entered the room, saw the two of them in their respective mirrored image poses.

"Morning, Doctor Haberman. Can you give me a few more minutes? Mr. Howard here is showing an old dog some new tricks."

Haberman checked his watch and gave Charlie a dirty look, a reminder he didn't like waiting for an appointment. He had a reputation as a rich snoot with an inflated ego and a deflated handicap, who wreaked havoc with the dining room help and considered Danny to be his personal servant—a nightmare for the caddies who had to lug his oversized bag, debate every shot, triple read every putt, take undeserved blame for his lousy performance, then get shortchanged on tips.

"What's *a few more minutes* mean?" he asked snidely.

Gordon wasn't in the mood; he couldn't stand the guy and didn't appreciate the interruption.

"Hey, Doc, go over to the hospital and get your eyes fixed, don't know any twelve handicaps who think five-footers are gimmes."

Charlie cringed at Gordon's remark. Haberman and his wife spent too much money to risk alienating him.

"He's just in a bad mood, Doctor Haberman. Can you please give me fifteen minutes? Lesson is on me."

"You got it, Charlie, fifteen minutes, on the house." Haberman glared at Gordon.

"I know about you. I have money with your father. He'll hear about this, as will the grievance committee." Haberman stormed out.

"Screw him, Charlie. I got the lesson covered."

"GH, these people pay my bills. You gotta do me a solid and

keep your opinions to yourself. You know how this place works, unless you want to book me for the whole season?"

"I'm probably half of it anyway," Gordon reminded him. Charlie acknowledged that appreciatively with a smile.

"OK, back to business, GH. Show me what you do to initiate the downswing."

Gordon placed the club perpendicular to his shoulders, his torso wound tightly. Charlie imitated the position, facing each other.

"At this point, Charlie, all I can feel is the tension in my body. My left wrist is slightly bowed out, a strong position, the club feels light. My first move down is a slight shifting of my weight to my braced left leg, from the ground up. Then I kick in my right knee and turn my hips straight left. I feel like it happens simultaneously, my arms are pulled down into the slot and the clubface returned to the ball—almost automatically—a passive move, nothing forced. I can increase my clubhead speed by turning faster, where all the power is generated from my rocking shoulders and my rotating torso. At impact, my head is almost behind the ball, all my weight is left, and my hands are…."

"Quiet?"

"Exactly, but strong and powerful, almost like they were molded to the club, it's tough to describe."

"I got it, GH. What you're doing is pre-setting a square face, taking your hands out of the swing, allowing your big muscles to control the shot. It eliminates the flip, or the push. You don't have to think about it, which is what we all strive for. But foolproof it's not. If you don't start your downswing with your legs and hips, your arms take over, the clubface shuts, and that ball goes left of left. Don't get me wrong, there were plenty of guys who could use their hands like magicians. Hogan for one—he opened and closed the damn clubface on purpose. But he had a different problem, a real bad case of the hooks. That move allowed him to fade the ball, his so-called secret, which was just a cupped left wrist on top, supinated at impact. He never admitted it, but that's what the pundits claim."

Charlie swung his club in slow motion, trying to imitate Hogan's unique hand action, and then continued.

"Point is there's no perfection in this damn game. Hogan said he hit one, maybe two, perfect shots a round. All the rest are good misses. Then it's a question of your head, confidence under pressure. You want to see perfection in golf? Fly out to Callaway or Taylor Made in California and watch Iron Byron, the machine they use to test new gear. Every swing is exactly the same, dead center perfect. But then again, it's got no brain, no heart, and no emotions."

"You know," Gordon said kiddingly, "not so bad you were leading the US Open in the first round back in 1983, missed the cut and wound up here. Look at what good times we have."

"Cut it out, GH. That's hitting below the belt. Give a guy a break, I still have nightmares."

THERE WERE DIFFERENT STORIES of what happened. The official Charlie Evans version, right from the horse's mouth, was that an ex-girlfriend—who broke his heart when she jilted him for another guy—went to the Open and watched Charlie birdie the seventh hole to take the lead. Then he saw her holding hands with her new beau, she waved, and it was downhill from there.

Gordon reached into his pocket, took out a wad of cash, peeled off a hundred dollar bill, and shoved it into Charlie's back pant pocket.

"The Ben Franklin is for Haberman. Make sure you bill me for the lesson, add an extra hour for the wisecrack. What the hell, I can handle it. And keep those videos in my folder. Have fun with the Doc, Charlie."

"Thanks, GH, try enjoying yourself today, no club throwing. Build your confidence; work on that new move, old habits die hard."

"I'll try," Gordon replied soberly, his head in a fog, as he trudged back to the clubhouse to meet his guests.

Chapter 3

"You're guests are here, Mr. Howard. I sat them over by the window, your favorite table."

"Thanks, Lori, I'm late, just tell them I'm on my way."

"Will do, and by the way, we have black bean soup today, your favorite."

Lori Larsen had the unenviable job as head hostess in the men's grill room—sectioned off from the rest of the dining room—a place to tell off color jokes, watch one of three humongous high definition televisions, drink at two bars stocked with an assortment of nuts, or play high stakes gin rummy in a separately staffed card room. Overall, it was a cherished haven away from the wives.

Women members were not permitted to enter the men's grill, persona non grata, with dire consequences; forty lashings, solitary confinement, or execution by lethal injection. At least some of the men had discussed this; some jokingly, some seriously.

The men's grill was quiet. It was a Wednesday, when most of the members were at work—a cadre of attorneys, real estate developers, investment bankers, business owners and hedge fund managers—men who worked hard and made big bucks.

Gordon approached the table along the large panorama of windows overlooking the ninth and eighteenth holes—the primo spot to enjoy lunch and watch an occasional golfer hit into the green.

"You guys are early or I'm late, we probably got our wires crossed."

"No problem, you must be Gordon," replied Ed Sobel. "These things happen. Say hello to my son, Stuart."

They all shook hands.

"Hope Danny took good care of you guys?"

"Everything's copacetic. Your father's a living legend; you have some big shoes to fill."

Gordon ignored Ed's comment.

Ed Sobel, balding and short, carrying a pregnant looking pot belly, appeared to Gordon around sixtyish. His son Stuart was his spitting image. Neither resembled athletes.

"Everyday's a great day on the golf course, right guys? Let's order up, we can hit some balls and then tee-off. What are your handicaps?"

"My handicap is my game. And my son here, his handicap is his wife."

The two of them guffawed. Gordon didn't find it funny, having heard this inane dribble umpteen times from the hackers he was obligated to play with.

"No worries, food's great here. We can order off the menu or grab a salad."

Over lunch they made conversation, mostly small talk. From what Gordon could gather, Ed Sobel had sold his family's fragrance manufacturing business to International Flavors and Fragrances, a New York Stock Exchange company. Sobel made it perfectly clear between bites the number was two hundred million, all cash. They were considering investing with AH Advisors, a small allocation at first, around five million, and once they felt comfortable, they would add.

Gordon heard only snippets, his mind a million miles elsewhere.

"Time to hit the links; I'll give you the nickel tour after the round." Gordon stood up, gulped down his water and left the table.

"Hey, Lori, charge it to my account," he said, marching past her, through the front door, and over to the starter. The Sobels tagged along like obedient puppies.

"Gotcha all set up, GH. Your guest's are on an open cart. Clarence will go with them, and you got Swifty on the bag."

"Thanks, Jimmy, let Clarence take them over to the range. I'm gonna hit the putting green, then tee off in fifteen minutes."

At just about 2:00 p.m., they all stood on the tee of the first hole, a four hundred forty-two yard par four. After Ed and Stuart Sobel took their first practice swings, Gordon muttered *fuck* under his breath.

"Hey guys, the course is long, no sense in torturing yourselves. Why don't you hit from the red markers. I'll play from the blacks or the stakes, whichever is further back. Let's make it interesting, your best ball against mine. I'll spot you each a shot a hole—small stakes, a buck a man."

Ed Sobel had to confer with his son, as if it were a major financial decision.

"How about we go five dollars a man?" Stuart Sobel countered with a wide grin.

"Now I'm scared, but what the hell," Gordon replied, as he waved them over to the side of the tee box. He walked back to the black markers, teed up a brand new Titleist Pro V1, took a few practice swings, addressed the ball and checked his alignment. The crack of the driver broke the silence as the ball took off low, then rose higher, with the wind pushing against it, until it landed some three hundred plus yards down the fairway, dead-center perfect.

"Wow, that's amazing!" uttered Stuart Sobel.

"Jesus Christ!" added Ed Sobel.

Gordon ignored the accolades, picked up his tee, pointed to the red women's markers, and pranced down the fairway, turning around every so often to watch them dribble their drives into the rough. He knew Clarence would take care of them; point out the water hazards, the out of bounds, read the greens, help them with their swings, replace the divots, fix ball marks, keep score, show them a good time.

They were incommunicado for the front nine, chopping up the course, straying into the woods, making a mess of the sand traps, four and five putting the greens; all in all they didn't belong on a golf course. Gordon suspected it the moment he met them with their asinine remarks about their handicaps. And then he knew it when he witnessed their hideous practice swings. He didn't care. It gave him time to hone his new move, hitting three and four balls into the greens; fades, draws, and punch shots, with Swifty carrying his bag and chasing down the balls, getting Gordon all pumped up.

Swifty had always caddied for Gordon, some fifteen years, at the club, in tournaments, wherever. He knew his game and his temperament. They were a good team, and Gordon took special care of him.

"Great shot, Mister Gordon—super right there, she's two feet, Mister Gordon—in the bunk, Mister Gordon—great up and down, Mister Gordon. That drive there is three twenty-five, Mister Gordon."

Some four hours later they all met up at the eighteenth tee. Clarence looked haggard, the Sobels more so.

"Where've you guys been, trying to avoid me?" Gordon fed them a bunch of obvious bull. "I thought you fell into the lake over on fourteen. I called Jimmy, you had me worried."

Ed Sobel looked at his watch.

"Thanks for having us. We're running late. Clarence will take us in."

Nobody shook hands, or said anything more for that matter. They just left.

Gordon slipped Clarence a fifty dollar bill for keeping the Sobels out of his hair, waited until they were out of sight, and then pummeled his driver way over the fairway bunkers. He walked with Swifty down the eighteenth fairway, toward the clubhouse.

"You OK, Mister Gordon?"

"Not really, Swifty."

"I can tell—there's somethin' with your father again?"

"The usual stuff, I'm just feeling a lot worse today."

"I know you for a long time, don't I?"

"Sure do, Swifty, why?"

"You want my honest opinion, Mister Gordon?"

"Yeah, go ahead." Gordon arched his eyebrows, curious what was on Swifty's mind.

"The way you treated them business guests. As long as you're workin' for your father, and collectin' a check, then the way I see it, you got an obligation to do the right thing by him. There are a lot more important things to this damn life than golf. And treatin' people with respect is one of 'em."

Gordon wasn't surprised at Swifty's comment. He knew he acted like a complete jerk.

"So now you're a philosopher," he replied, half jokingly.

"No, Mr. Gordon, I ain't a philosopher, just a person, blood runnin' through my veins, same as you, just my skin's a different color, that's all."

IT WAS CLOSE TO 5:30 when they walked off of the eighteenth green.

"I got your clubs, Mister Gordon. I'll clean 'em up and they gonna be in your rack for tomorrow."

Gordon pulled out his silver billfold and peeled off a hundred dollar bill.

"Thanks, Mister Gordon, I see you tomorrow."

He looked at Swifty; his ragged clothes, mismatched socks, and second hand sneakers laced together by different colored shoelaces; his craggy weather beaten face, curly gray unkempt hair, fingers yellowed from years of cigarette smoking, his toothless smile—he was one of the only real friends Gordon had.

Gordon shoved another hundred into Swifty's shirt pocket. "Get yourself some new sneakers. We gonna be doin' some serious walkin' together, you know what I'm sayin'?"

"Yes sir, Mister Gordon. Are you makin' fun of me?" He wondered if Gordon was serious this time, about leaving his father, and attempting to turn pro.

"Hell no, I'm just imitating you. It's flattering."

"Same difference ain't it?"

Gordon pondered Swifty's retort, and walked into the clubhouse, where Swifty and his ilk weren't permitted.

"Hey, GH, what the hell did you do to those guys, huh? They bolted; no shower, no steam, didn't even let me clean their shoes, real pissed off, huh. How many times I frickin' told you, when its business, let 'em win a few bucks, huh. What'd you fleece em for, couple a grand, huh?"

"No way, just sick of this, wasting my life. Its hard work, Danny, believe me. What's it been, eight, maybe nine years, just to please my damn father."

Danny felt sorry for Gordon. Sure, he was a rich kid who lived the life most people only fantasized about, not a care in the world, other than keeping his golf game in good form, to show up for his business appointments, and act reasonably civil. But the privilege had strings attached. Danny knew he had serious father issues. Charlie kept him in the loop.

"So just tell him to shove it, and work here with me. I'll teach you how to clean the frickin' toilets and kiss ass, huh."

"OK, Danny, cut the bull; you know where I'm coming from."

"Gus is ready for you, GH. You need to chill out. Go get yourself rubbed down, relax your head, sweat it out in the steam room, and chug down a cold one for the road. You'll figure it out, GH, huh?" Danny chuckled in his inimitable way, and grabbed a mop to clean the bathroom floors.

Gus had been rubbing Gordon down for as long as he could remember. He knew every nook and cranny of Gordon's torso.

The club hired him full time when he came over from Greece, enrolling him in masseuse school. Gus lived in the upstairs dormitory the club maintained for the hired help. In the winter he travelled to Florida where he set up shop in a spare room in one of the billionaire member's oceanfront Palm Beach estate. Most of the members travelled to Palm Beach in the winter—their second homes—and belonged to snooty country clubs like The Palm Beach Country Club, where Bernie Madoff used to be a distinguished member, and the recipient of a good chunk of their money.

This wasn't just a simple massage. Gus stocked a full assortment of sweet almond, apricot kernel, and grape seed oil, which he mixed with lavender, bergamot peppermint, and eucalyptus. It was blissful heaven; the soft music, scented candles, and Gus's strong hands, lulling Gordon into a state of nirvana, expunging whatever stresses that could possibly irk him.

Gordon was Gus's meal ticket, and Gus was Gordon's therapist, for his body and his psyche, listening to his problems and allowing him to cathartically emote in the privacy of the massage room. Gordon trusted Gus; he was a good soul, a straight shooter.

"Mister Gordon, wake up, you fell asleep on me."

"Thanks, Gus, tough day today," as he slipped him a gratuity.

Gus had also heard about Gordon's issues with his father.

"Mister Gordon, you know you can tell Gus whatever you want. I never say anything to anyone, just me and you."

"Yeah, I know Gus, thanks."

"See you tomorrow, Mister Gordon."

AFTER A HOT STEAM, shave, and shower, Gordon dressed into dark blue jeans, an Egyptian cotton long sleeved white shirt, brown leather belt, and rubber soled moccasins.

A few members were sitting in the men's grill, having drinks, helping themselves to the assorted hors d'oeuvres kept warm in bains-marie; chicken wings, pigs in a blanket, egg rolls, and small pizza squares. Gordon perched on the bar stool, staring blankly at the 6:00 p.m. evening news, absorbing none of it.

"Can I get you something, Mister Howard?"

"What's on tap tonight, Fred?"

"I got Stella, Brooklyn Lager, and Heineken."

"OK, Heineken, real cold."

Fred reached down and pulled out a frosty beer stein. "Feel this, cold enough for you?" Fred smiled accommodatingly.

"Perfect." Gordon munched on a batch of assorted nuts while Fred filled the chilled stein with the sudsy brew.

Fred knew how to run a bar; a splash of cranberry, a dash of vermouth, the little touches of lemon and lime twists slightly rubbed around the edge of the glass, an extra orange slice, and the olives- plain or stuffed with pimento and blue cheese. Each drink was a work of art, to be handled delicately, to swirl in your mouth and admire.

Gordon guzzled it down.

"How about a refill, Mr. Howard," he asked obligingly.

Gordon looked at his watch; he needed to be in the city by 7:30.

"Yep, one more, thanks."

Fred filled a fresh frosty mug to the brim and slid it over to him. Gordon chugged it, eliciting a small belch, and a real good buzz.

"Just bill it to H–3, Fred."

"I got your number, Mister Howard, no problem."

He walked through the front entranceway and underneath the portico, prompting the valet to hustle down to the member's parking lot.

"Have a nice evening, sir." The valet hopped out of the Range Rover, waited for him to nestle into his seat, and gently closed the door.

"Thanks, you too," Gordon replied, as if it were an effort.

He proceeded down the sinuous drive, turned left onto Snake Hollow Road passing the spot where Riley had pulled him over, and then headed west onto the Long Island Expressway. He in- structed the hands free telephone, "call office," and switched on the speaker. He waited as the phone rang until a man answered who recognized the incoming number.

"Yes, Gordon, what is it?" The man sounded annoyed.

"I'm just checking in."

"So how did we do today?"

"I shot three under," Gordon answered, intentionally snotty.

"Not your goddamn score!" Alan Howard shot back angrily. "Money, how much are they allocating? It should've been a layup with these guys. They spent three, maybe four hours with Jeremy yesterday. I met them. They were talking five million to start, maybe more."

Jeremy Chang was Alan Howard's right-hand man. A Harvard graduate with a Stanford MBA, Jeremy knew each and every strategy comprising AH Advisors—the hedge fund Alan Howard inherited from his father and ran with an iron fist.

Gordon had Jeremy's position right out of college, but he couldn't cut the mustard. As he saw it, his father was a tyrant and expected perfection. Alan had a different opinion. They battled bitterly. Jeremy was Alan's fair-haired boy, a non-family member destined to run the business.

"I have no clue, maybe five, maybe zero."

"No clue?" he snapped. "After four hours pouring on your inimitable charm and wowing them with your Tigeresque drives, that's how you answer me!"

"Yeah, you got it, no damn clue. Maybe you need Jeremy to close these deals. He does everything else for you, and you think he's God, so there you go."

"OK, I got it, crystal clear. It's all about Jeremy, and you're still bent out of shape. When the hell you'll start being accountable to yourself, and to me, is a goddamn mystery. Half a million bucks a year for a stupid public relations gig and you're giving me lip? Do you know what the word respect means? Do you?!"

Gordon just listened, waiting.

"Answer me!"

He couldn't.

"I'm counting to three, and then...."

"Go to hell!" Gordon hung up. The feud was long coming to a head. The alcohol didn't help, or maybe it did.

The phone rang. He expected it.

"Gordon Howard," he answered curtly.

"The next time you hang up on me will be your last, do you understand!"

"Sorry, have a bad connection, who's this?"

"It's the guy who signs your paychecks! Is the connection better now?"

"I hear you, Mr. Chairman. What's on your mind?"

"Listen wise ass, I want you in my office tomorrow morning, nine o'clock sharp, not ten, eleven, or high noon. And then you'll hear what's on my mind, loud and clear!"

"You got it." Gordon hung up, emboldened, ready to finally confront his demons.

Chapter 4

GORDON PULLED INTO THE underground garage beneath his terraced co-op duplex penthouse on the corner of Seventy-fourth and Park Avenue.

"I'm in for the evening, won't need it tomorrow."

"No hay problema," uttered the attendant, dressed in his work uniform—a white tag with *José* affixed to the front breast pocket.

Gordon didn't wait for the elevator, and was in no mood to make small talk with the lobby concierge or the nosey doorman. He hiked up the garage ramp onto Park Avenue, to Seventy-Fifth Street, then over to Madison.

He loved that block, its serenity speckled with stately townhouses, some partially camouflaged by the late summer foliage. Well dressed men walked to and fro as black limousines dropped off important passengers, while the private neighborhood Community Watch patrol car scouted for suspicious characters.

He checked his cell phone for messages, and then speed dialed Liz.

"Hey handsome, where are you? Just sat down, kind of crowded tonight; they're pouring the Grey Goose as we speak, twist or olive?"

"Rough day today; twist is fine, make it a double."

Liz had a sneaky suspicion about what happened. "I'm all ears, don't freak, hon."

"See you in a few, just two blocks away."

THEY HAD MET AT the concession stand during the practice round of the US Open golf tournament at Shinnecock Hills in 2004.

It took just one look from Liz for Gordon to come on to her.

The epitome of a Ralph Lauren girl, she stood five foot seven with blue eyes and high cheekbones. Athletically thin—her body was perfect. Her chestnut hair was pulled back in a ponytail; she wore hooped earrings, khaki shorts with a braided brown belt, a black tank top, a Swatch watch with a leather band, and a pair of white Nike tennis sneakers. She had small, firm breasts, and there was hardly a trace of makeup on her fresh face; her tanned legs were lean yet shaped, her shoulders smooth, her skin flawless with a faint scent of some unique eau de toilette.

She stood ahead of him, waited in line, and ordered a Heineken, as did he.

"Can you please make sure it's cold," were the first words he heard, a deep sultry voice enunciating each word, the type that could host a radio jazz station.

She had taken the Long Island Railroad from New York City to the course—a two hour jaunt, and walked all eighteen holes. An autograph hound with bounding enthusiasm, somewhat of a tomboy, she could whistle with the best of them, two fingers in her mouth.

He invited her to sit with him in the AH Advisor's corporate tent.

She told him she was from Sturgeon Bay, Wisconsin, graduated from the University of Minnesota with a major in journalism and minor in philosophy, and worked for a small public relations firm in Tribeca. Her parents had divorced when she was thirteen.

She took up golf in high school as a lark, made the school team, and became hooked. She broke eighty consistently, and was good enough to play on her college squad, until a skiing accident dislocated two discs, and her golfing days were over.

She lived on the West Side, near Central Park, and enjoyed riding her bicycle to work along the path off of the West Side highway. She possessed a killer smile—which lit up the small dimples on her cheeks—and loved to laugh.

By day's end Gordon was head over heels. She was standoffish. He drove her back to the city in his Porsche. She wasn't impressed.

The Sunday night stop and go traffic gave them ample time for chitchat. He told her how badly he felt about her accident, which she dismissed with a sigh and, "That's life, Gordon."

And then she philosophically opined why her infatuation with the game never ended. "Golf's inner beauty, the myriad of mysteries that make it so addicting, a microcosm of life; saddled with elation, depression, joy, sadness, obstacles, determination, honor and respect—the mere thought of cheating repulsive and a sacrilege to all those who play by the rules. The graciousness of both winning and losing…. It's a game never owned, just borrowed for a brief while, and then returned to the Golf Gods, who lurk in the majestic surroundings of the transcendental serenity."

"Where did you come up with that?" he asked her, intending a back-handed compliment.

"I'm a journalist, not a *plagiarist*" she said emphatically, clearly miffed at his comment.

"Sorry, didn't mean it that way" he apologized sincerely, obvious he had struck a sensitive spot.

Whew! Gordon knew immediately that this was one interesting woman, an unexpected and long overdue turn on. *And who were these Golf Gods?* He was embarrassed to ask her, as their significance eluded him.

The next day he sent her flowers, with a note:

Liz, I hope you enjoyed the day as much as I did.
Gordon

They dated. Their personalities were complementary and their backgrounds dissimilar, she a Lutheran, he Jewish, although neither cared. She preferred Jewish men, and he avoided Jewish women, figuring they were just after his money.

She deliberately made him wait before they slept together. He never pressured her. She moved in one month later, along with Sabby, her Himalayan cat, short for Sabatchna.

GORDON HAD BEEN A regular at Mario's for as long as he lived in the city, some nine years. Situated mid-block on Madison Avenue off of Seventy-Eighth Street, it boasted an outdoor café where dining patrons could take in the scenery, and rich older men could ogle the eye candy. The food was good, expensive, and the portions small. Reservations were required, except for Gordon, who always took care of Mario.

"Mister Gordon, buongiorno, so nice to see you. Miss Liz is waiting, your favorite spot."

Gordon shook Mario's outstretched hand, slipped him a twenty dollar bill, and walked inside to the last table on the left. It was the banquette with two seats side by side, and the picture window had a stunning view of Madison Avenue.

"Hi beautiful, how was your day? Mine sucked."

"Did you forget something?" she said, her eyebrows arched, her finger touching her lips.

"Sorry." He planted his lips on hers.

The waiter came over with a double Grey Goose vodka martini, a glass of Pinot Noir, a loaf of warm Tuscan bread, and a small dish of extra virgin olive oil, heart healthy. "Good evening, would you like to hear our specials?"

"Give us a few minutes," Gordon responded.

All of the waiters at Mario's spoke with accents. They came mostly from Italy, Slovakia and Romania, their phony suave elegance adding a touch of Euro trashiness, which bumped up the prices.

Gordon took a healthy gulp of the martini, the buzz from the beer still lingered. She sipped her wine and picked at the bread. She knew something was wrong, just the way he was tapping the table, staring into space, unusually quiet.

"OK, hon, what happened, your father again?"

"Yep," he replied, before swallowing the remainder from the chilled glass.

"Gordon, you're not a baby, and this isn't a quiz. What the hell happened?"

Before he could answer the waiter reappeared. Liz knew that Gordon was in no mood to hear him regurgitate the list of specials.

"Two Mario salads, linguine white clam sauce, vegetable lasagna, vinaigrette on the side."

"Yes, signora," the waiter replied as he jotted down their order.

"And another martini," Gordon added, as he lifted his empty glass and looked at her for approval.

Liz had put a stop to Gordon's excessive drinking, which brought out his ugly belligerent side, although never physically abusive. She blamed her parents' divorce on her alcoholic father, and threatened to leave him. She had packed her bags and said, "It's me or the vodka."

Gordon finally broke down and begged her to stay.

"Just one more, hon, I promise."

"OK, but you have to talk to me. This is no joke Gordon. I know you, and I love you. Something is really wrong. Whatever it is affects both of us."

"I told him to go to hell."

"He yelled at you again, didn't he?"

"The usual, I just lost it today, fucking Jeremy!" as he pounded the table.

"Gordon, either you control yourself or I'm—"

"Sorry."

The waiter brought over the second martini. Gordon started working on it, taking a few sips, and then let it sit.

"All of a sudden it's about Jeremy? He's been there for years, a superstar, and you know how much Alan depends upon him. You guys are lucky to have him."

"He just worships this guy—Jeremy this, Jeremy that. I'm sick of it."

"Want to know what I think, handsome?" Liz had a way of

pacifying him when he got into these moods. She put her arm around his shoulder and kissed his cheek.

"What?" He looked at her.

She could see his moist eyes; an errant tear trickled down his face. "I think you're just jealous. Not everyone is cut out for business. The truth is that if Alan wasn't your father, and you had to interview for that job, you probably wouldn't have qualified. You had your shot and it didn't work, so grow up and stop crying over spilt milk."

"Listen, I'm a classic underachiever," Gordon replied. My SATs were 1500, but my grades, well; let's just say I made the top half of the class possible."

"Very funny, wise guy, that's a new one."

"I could've grown into it, Liz. What Jeremy does is not rocket science. It's mostly statistics, just analyzing a money manager's returns, and working up a risk volatility profile. All these formulas sound difficult; Sharpe ratio, standard deviation, alpha and beta, but bottom line they're just numbers."

They dug into their salads. It was a lot more than that. Gordon had never told her the entire, unadulterated story.

He mused about what had transpired when he started there, fresh out of college and wet behind the ears. At the time, the firm was managing some two billion dollars. Gordon was the guy who allocated the firm's capital to the various AH Advisors money managers—MBA graduates of the best schools, highly competent and well compensated—earning seven figures a year, plus bonuses.

Gordon had more than a cursory understanding of the dozen or so of the firm's investment strategies, but he wasn't in the same league as these money managers, not even close. Eventually, Alan Howard was given an ultimatum by these men and women who made the firm oodles of money, and resented Gordon and the flagrant nepotism. The boss took action, replacing his son with Jeremy Chang. It was a bold stroke, which immediately bolstered morale.

Gordon was promoted to Vice President of New Business Development. Alan tossed in a hefty salary increase, corporate credit cards, and a company car. A trumped up press release appeared in *The Wall Street Journal*, something Gordon insisted upon to assuage his wounded ego. He could see the article, and remembered every bogus word of it, which resounded in his head with the resonance of a chiming bell.

AH Advisors Expands with Key Promotion and New Hire

Alan Howard, managing director of AH Advisors, a two billion dollar multi-strategy hedge fund, announced today the promotion of Gordon Howard, his son, to the position of Vice President of New Business Development.

"Gordon has done a yeoman's job over the last two years allocating and monitoring firm capital to the multiple strategies we deploy on behalf of our institutional investors. We are grateful for his arduous work and dedication. He leaves behind a solid infrastructure, which will enable us to increase our assets more quickly than anticipated. We expect Gordon to contribute to the growth of our fund with the same successes he has achieved. Jeremy Chang, a Stanford MBA, comes aboard from BLS Capital, where he was responsible for risk and capital allocation, overseeing more than five billion dollars in client assets. Jeremy will assume Gordon's duties, effective immediately."

"HEY GORDON, ARE YOU with us? Gordon!" Liz waved her arms back and forth, as if he was in a trance.

"Sorry, just thinking, forgot what we were talking about."

"We were talking about your screwed up relationship with your father and how you have a bug up your backside for Jeremy."

"Right, so what do you think?" Gordon tried to focus amidst the clutter of too many thoughts.

"Maybe your father's just a miserable bastard, and you're his whipping boy, his scapegoat. He figures blood is thicker than water, so he takes his stuff out on you. What's that word you guys use, mish...."

"Mishegas, it means craziness."

"Right, and me, I'm a shikseh?"

"Totally a shikseh, thank God!"

"What is it with you Jewish boys and us shiksehs?"

"It's a long story, and besides, only shikseh goddesses, so consider yourself lucky."

He got a real kick out of teaching her some Yiddish, snippets he picked up from his grandparents.

"But look Gordon, be honest with yourself. Nobody forced you to take that job. You did it because it was easy, pure nepotism, and maybe your dad shouldn't have given it to you. All you rich guys have so much money, and so many issues."

Gordon listened; she made sense, and had a good head on her shoulders.

"I wasn't born with a silver spoon in my mouth, and never knew about the expensive country clubs, the fancy cars, the yachts or inherited wealth, until I met you. And the last time I checked my last name is Stuart, not Rockefeller. Sure, my family was a bit dysfunctional, but that's par for the course, no pun intended. My dad owns a furniture store. It's a living. He tells me the property is worth more than the business, but I'm not rooting for him to die. I was brought up with a strong work ethic. I always took risks and had big dreams. I wanted to be a TV anchorwoman or magazine editor. And then reality set in. But I'm not throwing in the towel; surrender is not in my vocabulary. Yet I'm pretty happy with my life. And marriage was never a priority."

"Why did you bring that up?"

"What, about happiness?"

"About marriage, trying to tell me something?" His voice quivered.

"Don't freak, Gordon. I never said I wouldn't marry you. But unless you find yourself, marriage will be one huge mistake. You have to dive inward to discover who you really are, or who you're not."

Her telling comments about taking risks and having big dreams struck a sensitive nerve and gave him food for thought.

"I don't care what you do, but there's no way I'm spending my life with an angry guy who chooses to live in his father's shadow. And I'm not interested in your money or that ridiculous club with those horrible people who have nothing better to do all day than complain that the salmon is too poached, or their omelets too runny, or the dill dressing a wee too spicy. The way they treat the help is a disgrace, like they were indentured servants."

Gordon found Liz refreshingly different, as her middle name was Ann, not *Entitlement*, like the Jewish gold diggers he had used just to get his rocks off. She was a woman who would walk five extra blocks to save two dollars grocery shopping, and would rather cook than blow money on overpriced restaurants. She had it down to a science; she knew *exactly* how much they would save eating at home. Calling in sick at work was verboten. Hiring a cleaning woman was a waste of money, figuring she could do a better job, especially scrubbing the bathrooms. And other than her bicycle, she always rode the subways, and would bombard him with a constant nagging reminder; "Gordon, it's clean, cheap, and fast, it's ridiculous that you only take taxicabs."

"So what are you doing with me?" he asked, hoping for a few compliments, a little boost for his ego.

"Because you're great in the sack," she replied, trying to keep a straight face. "And I love your short game; gets me all excited," she laughed.

He figured she would make light of it.

"C'mon, Liz, I'm serious. Stop with the jokes."

"OK, you poor soul," Liz replied soothingly, as she put her arm around his shoulders and snuggled real close. "Why do I love thee? Let me count the ways; handsome, athletic, funny, ballsy, traditional, caring when you want to be, a champion of the underdog, and last but not least, a trust fund baby!"

"I'm seeing him tomorrow morning—a showdown. And you know what?" He gulped down the rest of the martini.

"What?"

"I'm resigning, gonna tell him to shove it. I don't need his money. The duplex is worth a few million, and I got enough socked away. It's not *fuck you* money, but that's gonna come. He'll go ballistic and threaten to cut me off. I'll paint a picture that it's his fault, just to lay on a guilt trip."

"What kind of guilt trip? Alan's a heartless sonafabitch. You can't go in there as a wimp, Gordon. Stand up for your rights and be aggressive. He needs you more than you need him."

Her words empowered him. She was terrific like that.

"Let me worry about it," he said reassuringly, while trying to muster up some courage. "You OK with this?"

"Are you kidding me? It's music to my ears. With your rolodex, tons of hedge funds would hire you in a heartbeat."

"My employee days are *over*," he told her brusquely.

"I'm listening," she replied, unsure what to expect.

"I'm going pro, Liz, one hundred percent dedication. Half these hotshots on tour I beat in college. I should've done it when I was twenty-one, after graduation. I can see the headlines now; tell me how this grabs you-family feud with prominent hedge fund titan prompts new golf superstar."

"Gordon, is that you or the Grey Goose I hear?"

"You think I'm crazy enough to do this just to get even with my father? What's that complex again?"

"Oedipus, but he killed his father, unless you're planning something really dire."

"The thought crossed my mind," he immediately answered her, his tone spookily serious.

She noticed that, but fluffed it off. "People do things for crazy and inexplicable reasons. You need to really think this through." She knew it was just a fantasy, making it as a touring professional, but wouldn't dare discourage him, not now.

"C'mon Liz, I tried the therapy gig. If I sat and analyzed every move I made, I'd be schizo. It feels right, in my heart of hearts, in my gut. That should be good enough."

"I would love to be a fly on the wall tomorrow morning."

Gordon held up his right hand. "Scout's honor, you'll be the first to get the blow by blow description."

He signaled for the check. She checked the math, as she always did—another one of the little things that made her special. Mario's had a reputation for making mistakes, usually in their favor.

"Let's go, I have a big day tomorrow."

"*We* sure do."

Chapter 5

At 9:20 a.m. the following morning, Gordon Howard entered the hallowed premises of AH Advisors LLC, which occupied the entire top floor of the IBM building on the corner of Madison Avenue and Fifty-Seventh Street. He was dressed in a lightweight Brooks Brothers blue suit, button down white shirt, yellow and blue striped tie, and cordovan Alan Edwards classic winged tip shoes. The outfit was Liz's idea, figuring it would give him a sense of professionalism, and the intestinal fortitude to do what needed to be done.

"Well, hello, Mr. Gordon Howard. And don't we look spiffy? I never saw you so dressed up. Your father has been expecting you. Getting ready for some golf this weekend? Labor Day, thank God, I need the rest."

Shirley Fornelli, the receptionist, while eyeing him, held up one finger as she attended to the switchboard.

"AH Advisors, may I help you? Sorry, Mr. Howard will be tied up for a while. May I take your name and number? OK certainly, let me put you through to Jeremy. You're welcome."

"I remember when those calls went to me, don't you, Shirley?"

"Sorry, Gordon, I'm a crazy person here. The phones don't stop, I can't even go to the bathroom, and you know how your father can be. My mother always said, 'Que sera,' *whatever will be*—you know what I mean?"

"Yep, sure do, from the Alfred Hitchcock movie, *The Man Who Knew Too Much,* Jimmy Stewart and Doris Day. I've seen all of Hitchcock's flicks."

"You always had a great memory, I never knew about any

40

movie. Who's Hitchcock? I can't remember what I had for dinner last night."

Gordon laughed to himself. That was highly unlikely. Shirley loved to eat, and it showed.

The phones lit up. Shirley juggled them like the professional she was, and mouthed "good luck" as Gordon walked down the hallway.

ALAN HOWARD'S OFFICE REEKED of money. The stained wood flooring was elegantly covered with a French Aubusson tapestry rug, its gold weft weave interlaced against a moss green warp. A rectangular, hand carved, rosewood desk offset a tan leather high back executive chair, accompanied by matching club chairs. Above his desk hung a hand blown beveled glass light fixture, suspending three glass shades with swiveling down lights, accented in a leafy, frond motif. The chandelier was supported by two elongated brass chains firmly upheld from an ornate bronze canopy. Crown moldings on the ceiling, painted gold, matching the carpeting, finished off the space.

Alan Howard could well afford his huge ego. An avid art enthusiast, the walls were graced with his latest acquisitions, all purchased at auction from up and coming artists de jure. The floor to ceiling windowed north wall offered spectacular unobstructed views of Central Park and beyond.

Behind the desk stood an important antique credenza purchased at a Sotheby's auction, the bottom serving as a mini-bar, the top a repository for the plethora of his achievements and awards. Bereft of the usual personal memorabilia—the precious family photos—made the office, all in all, cold and austere.

AS MOST IMPOSING FIGURES, Alan stood well over six foot with broad shoulders, a thick chest, and muscular back and arms. He resembled Gordon, or vice versa; the same blue-green eyes, aquiline nose, and strong chin. His full head of wavy salt and pepper hair—which brushed his ears—made him look considerably younger than his sixty years. A personal trainer kept him in shape. A private gym, steam and shower, abutted his office.

With the door ajar, he sat at his desk, but was hidden behind an opened *Wall Street Journal.*

Gordon strolled in and plopped himself down in one of the two tan leather club chairs.

"You're a half hour late; I said 9:00 a.m.!" Alan Howard's voice boomed from behind the newspaper.

"Big deal, didn't know this was the Marine Corps. Want me to drop for fifty push-ups?"

Bolting from his chair, he marched across the room and violently slammed the door shut, which jingled the delicate light fixtures.

"Going somewhere? Last time I saw you in a suit was your Bar Mitzvah, which you screwed up royally."

"Yeah, I got a few interviews," Gordon answered snidely.

"That's legit. Just remember the agreements you signed; don't give my competitors any trade secrets." Alan spoke in the haughty tone that defined him as he walked backed to his desk. "What's gotten into you? Your attitude stinks, like you got a stick up your ass. If you were working for a stranger, they'd throw you the hell out."

"And if I weren't your son you'd cut me some respect."

"I'm listening," his demeanor was condescending—the way he leaned back in his chair.

"Jeremy for one," Gordon quickly professed.

"What about him?"

"I could've handled that job. Maybe it would've taken me a little longer, but c'mon, what he does is not rocket science."

"Really now, and how did you come to that brilliant conclusion?"

"I'll go toe to toe with him anytime on statistics."

"Right," Alan retorted sarcastically. "And I guess you believe in the tooth fairy, or you can beat Tiger Woods spotting him two a side."

"I don't find that very humorous."

"Wasn't meant to be, you just sound asinine, as usual. Maybe you forgot, but there were a bunch of pissed off people around here."

"I was getting the hang of it; you should've had more patience, stuck up for me."

"I thought I did. That glowing press release I let you write for *The Journal* was a bunch of bull."

"C'mon, Dad, that blurb was as good for you as it was for me, so cut the crap."

"It's old news, beaten to death. No way in hell you could've handled that job. It's more than just numbers, a lot more. Not that you had such an in-depth understanding of our strategies."

"Cut it out, I don't want to hear it."

"I didn't know you were so sensitive."

"Go ahead, I'm listening."

"Let's call a spade a spade. Balancing the portfolio is a goddamn headache. Reallocating capital to smooth out the returns requires more than just a bunch of performance ratios. You need a macro view of the world; political unrest, interest rate fluctuations, sovereign debt devaluations—everything is interrelated today. And it's not nine to five, its twenty-four seven. This kid has a Bloomberg machine in his bedroom, glued to the overnight trading session."

"So?"

"That's not you, Gordon, never was, and never will be. You are what you are."

"What the hell does *that* mean?" Gordon's question stung with belligerence.

Alan Howard leaned across his desk, crossed his arms, and stared at his son. "I graduated Penn cum laude with an MBA from Columbia. You screwed off for four years in Arizona playing golf and getting laid. You didn't give a damn, figured you would just coast through life, money never an issue. So tell me, why should I even think about getting you involved in this business, so you can goddamn run it into the ground, have your grandfather roll over in his grave? What he left me was a pittance compared to where it is now. I'm not managing six billion dollars because of my good looks. Sorry pal, you made your bed, now you sleep in it. Don't blame me for your shortcomings."

Gordon stood up and removed his jacket, unbuttoned his shirt cuffs and rolled up his sleeves. He paced back and forth, as if he were addressing a jury.

"I know the story, heard it a million times. You're larger than life, a living legend; congratulated for your charity, counseled for your wisdom, courted for your wealth—a financial savant extraordinaire who turned millions into billions."

Gordon pointed his finger directly at his father's heart.

"There they are, right behind you on the credenza. Look at them, all the hyped up articles; Forbes, Fortune, Business Week. What did they call you; a self-made rag to riches icon? Are you kidding me! It's all a crock, what you want people to think. I applaud you; kudos for building assets, you and all your competitors, thanks to a sick bull market, a no brainer, like a one-foot putt. And believe me, I know what I am, and always was—Alan Howard's personal goddamn punching bag. Funny how you kiss Jeremy's ass, but whatever I do is never good enough. But it's not too late. I've got big plans, and you're not part of them; no way will I let you destroy me anymore, no goddamn way!"

Gordon felt uplifted, as he had finally got most of it out, including the perspiration that dripped from his forehead onto the precious carpet. As much as he was prepared, he vacillated bringing up the Creedmoor incident. Emotionally drained, he sat back down in the club chair across from his father's desk.

Alan had heard some bits and pieces of Gordon's harangue before, just more sanguine versions. "Sounds like your smart shikseh gold digger journalist girlfriend wrote a pretty eloquent speech for you," Alan said belittlingly.

"Shut up!" Gordon snapped back. "You know how much it pisses me off when you call her that. Keep your goddamn opinions about Liz to yourself."

"OK, now it's my turn." Alan jumped in, seemingly unfazed by Gordon's hostility.

"Nobody put a gun to your head. You chose to work here, and now I'm the bad guy, and you're blameless. It's easy to pass the buck, something you've always been pretty good at. And who gets paid ridiculous money for the goddamn privilege of your torturous work schedule?"

Gordon posed a glaring stare as his father continued.

"Don't get me wrong. It takes a lot out of you to drive out midday in a fancy new car to an exclusive country club, be served a gourmet lunch, and take a leisurely walk around a drop dead beautiful golf course with a prospective client or two. And then you suffer through a brutal massage and a piping hot steam, haul your royal ass into the shower, hit the bar for a cold one, and go home by whenever the hell you feel like it."

"Stop the bullshit," Gordon shot back. "You never gave me a dime's worth of charity. I earned every penny of it. How much money did I raise for your firm playing golf with these clowns? Does five hundred million sound about right? Whatever you paid me was a fraction compared to what *you* made. If you think what I did was enjoyable, you need to have your head examined. How about pure torture? And guess what? I'm done with it. Good luck in finding someone else like me to do your dirty work. It won't be easy, and then you'll realize how valuable I was."

Gordon suddenly became sullen. "How come you never came to visit me when I was in the hospital?"

"What are you talking about?" Alan sounded surprised.

"You knew I was at Creedmoor, I made sure of it. You could have at least called me there."

"What! You were in a mental institution? Is this a joke, Gordon? If it is, I don't find it funny."

"It's not a joke. I can't tell you how much that hurt me." Gordon's eyes welled up with tears.

There was a sudden knock on the door.

"Come in," Alan barked, as Jeremy Chang entered the room.

"Sorry to interrupt, I can come back if…."

"Talk to me, Jeremy, what's up?"

"You know those Sobel guys I've been working for a few months? They like our fund, especially the way I diversified the risk. We were competing with Whitehaven for their allocation, five million minimum to start."

"Yep, know all about it. Einstein here had them out at the club yesterday. Are they coming aboard?"

"Can we speak privately, Mister Howard?"

Jeremy avoided any eye contact with Gordon.

"Stay put," Alan ordered him, as if he were a dog.

The two of them walked outside and shut the door. Gordon knew what was coming next; his father's ranting was crystal clear, with Jeremy getting him all worked up.

"Good," he murmured to himself.

Stone faced, Alan walked back in and sat down behind his desk. "Let me understand this, and correct me if I happen to veer offline."

"No problem, shoot."

"So these Sobels sell out for a couple of hundred million, all cash, correct?"

"Yep," he responded.

"And Jeremy works his tail off and gets them all hopped up, competing with Whitehaven for an allocation, minimum five million, with more to follow if we perform, right?"

"Supposedly," he answered snidely.

"And all they want to do is meet my brilliant son, get treated to a swell day out at the club; a little lunch, some golf, a few drinks, correct?"

"Sounds right," he replied sarcastically.

"And all you have to do is be civil for a few lousy hours, show a little interest, and maybe help them with their swing, just some public relations, right?"

"Correct."

"But you ignore them, insult them, show up late, treat them

like trash; they're not good enough for you, because all you care about is your goddamn golf," his voice growing noticeably louder.

"That's not my problem anymore, remember?"

"Listen to me!" Alan shouted. "You're finished, kaput. Your salary will go to the homeless, every stinking penny. I want your company credit cards and the keys to your fancy company car. You can kiss your club membership goodbye. You're on your own, and when your money runs out, don't come crying to me, because you're getting squat while I'm alive, and less when I'm dead!"

"Have any other words of encouragement before I venture out into the real world?" Gordon spoke contemptuously.

"Yeah I do, smart ass. If you think you have a snowball's chance in hell making a goddamn living playing golf, you're crazy. Maybe you do belong in Creedmoor."

"I figured you would say that, you fucking sadistic bastard!" Gordon bolted around the desk, grabbed his father's shirt at the throat and yanked him upward, their bodies touching, his right fist clenched.

"Go ahead," Alan egged him on, his arms at his sides. "Throw the first punch. You know you've been dying to for a long time."

He delivered it quickly and decisively, a right cross pummeled squarely against Alan's left check, whose knees buckled as he toppled to the floor, the knockdown accompanied with a pronounced thud.

Alan quickly stood up with his fists poised, their eyes locked in sullen stares of indignation, silently speaking words that only a father and son could hear.

The melee reignited for Gordon the vivid images of the brutal beatings he had suffered as a kid.

"Now you know what it feels like!" Gordon shouted angrily.

Alan heard him loud and clear. He retreated to his desk chair, and quickly called security.

"Joe, this is Mr. Howard, no, Alan Howard! I want you in here, immediately!"

It didn't matter. Gordon was gone, minus his corporate credit cards and keys to the Range Rover, left on his empty chair.

Alan Howard sat back in his desk chair and massaged his throbbing cheek, beaming with the pride that only a father could understand.

GORDON WALKED DOWN THE entire fifty-two flights in the stairwell, avoiding the schadenfreude of the wolves who had gathered at the front door. As he left the building into the hustle of Fifty seventh and Madison, he speed dialed Liz, who answered immediately.

"How did it go? Are you breathing? I'm sitting on pins and needles."

"Yeah, went great, I guess. Feel sort of sick, like I want to throw up."

"To be expected, Gordon. It's a traumatic experience to cut the umbilical cord; it just took you a little longer, like thirty years. How did he take it when you resigned?"

"He took it on the left cheek, one punch in the first round."

"You guys got into a fight?"

"He egged me on and I lost it. I could have taken him apart. But at least I told him what I needed to. He needs me more than I need him."

"Exactly Gordon!" she said emphatically. "And what was his reaction?"

"He tossed it back in my face, basically disinherited me; the car, the credit cards, everything. But I'm OK, we're OK, right?"

"So he fired you? Don't assuage me with *disinherit*, tell it like it is."

"He had to have the last word, but I told him I was history. So he threw me out on my ass, which probably made him feel better."

"Why don't you chill out, grab an omelet and a double shot Bloody Mary. We can strategize later. You need a plan, and if anyone's organized, it's *moi*. Get used to my cooking; we need to watch expenses. How about we have my famous baked chicken with a nice healthy salad and a cheap bottle of wine for dinner?"

"Liz, the word is inexpensive. I don't drink cheap wine, never did, and never will. It's just against my upbringing, *capiche?*"

"Sorry your majesty, inexpensive; see you later."

Gordon walked aimlessly around the city, beset with terrible thoughts, thinking that the acrimonious confrontation with his father was a colossal blunder, and direly afraid of what he might do next.

Chapter 6

FROM HIS MANNER OF speaking, a gruff voice with a distinct Bronx accent, one would never surmise that Norman Berger was intelligent, with a preternatural penchant for biology and physics. Born with Scheuermann's syndrome—a permanent deformity of the spine—he was far from a regular guy, not a man's man, or a woman's man, with more than his fair share of oddities besides his appearance.

Nicknamed Quasimodo and Midget, girls would run away from the hideous looking hunchback, a social misfit who found solace peering through a microscope at the DNA of a fruit fly.

MERCK, THE PHARMACEUTICAL CONGLOMERATE, thought hiring Norman Berger was tantamount to finding the proverbial needle in a haystack.

A rapid series of promotions catapulted him to top dog, accompanied by a brusque, haughty demeanor that bellowed, "I'm brilliant and you're an idiot!"

His immediate superior, the very "corporate" Dr. Kenneth Mintz, notated in Norman's employee file: *loner, weird, intellectually superior, intolerant, delusions of grandeur.*

Norman's colleagues complained about him like a gaggle of catty women.

Management called an emergency meeting. Jim Frazier, executive head of human resources, summoned Mintz in for a powwow.

"Ken, your boy Berger is poison. You hired him—what the hell were you thinking?"

"I know, tough to work with; but he fast tracked high school, full scholarship to Penn, came with references up the ass; Phi Beta Kappa, Magna Cum Laude, double PhD in psychomotor neurology, and, get this—molecular pharmacology. My contacts at Penn swore up and down he's the real deal. Last thing I wanted was to lose him to the competition. And look what he's accomplished, ten years in this business flies by too damn quickly."

"Yep, I got it, except one bad apple...."

"Cut the life lessons, Jim, we need a grand slam, there's squat in the pipeline."

"Got any ideas? The boys upstairs think he's a cancer that needs to be cut out, ASAP."

"Funny you should ask."

"Tell me."

"OK, we get the best of the best and set up a top secret facility. The game plan is a full scale blitzkrieg on Amyotrophic Lateral Sclerosis."

"You mean Lou Gehrig disease?" Jim asked skeptically.

"Exactly, it's right up Berger's alley. He's an egomaniacal control freak, and will keep them all tight lipped. Last thing he wants is the competition to get a whiff of what he's doing. His old man got slaughtered by ALS, and I know for sure he's got a fuming personal vendetta."

"And Berger is the captain of this ship?"

"Corporate was all pumped up when I landed him, had all these plans, Berger this and Berger that. I sat in on the meetings, Jim. They were talking a billion bucks, whatever he needed. But as usual, they screwed it up, got lost in the bureaucracy with the other best laid plans of mice and men that often go astray." Ken Mintz felt like the cat's meow—sticking in that famous literary reference.

"Continue, Mr. Steinbeck," Jim acknowledged the quip with a smile.

"You know what a cure for those death warrants is worth?"

"Sorry Ken, I can't count that high," Jim responded, somewhat facetiously.

"Exactly," Mintz continued, "so we sit him down, dangle a bunch of money, and let him pick and choose his team. Everyone shares in the pot of gold, the best incentive to put up with his crap. What the hell is ten, twenty million—if Berger finds a cure?"

"And if he doesn't?"

"C'mon Jim, we're in the biotech business. What do you think we do here all day, pick lint out of our navels?"

"This isn't an overnight gig, Ken. And it's gonna require a boatload of capital from corporate."

"I wasn't aware of that, so thanks for the heads up."

"OK, Ken, save the sarcasm. Berger's gonna be privy to a slew of proprietary info. Are all the legal docs in order?"

"Yep, he signed his life away back when he came aboard."

"All right, you gave me enough ammo; I think I can sell it, I'll need a few days."

"I'm counting on you, thanks, Jim."

THE PROJECT WAS A debacle, as the number crunchers eventually waved the red flag, and Merck pulled the plug after a decade of hemorrhaging.

Norman approached Ken Mintz after he received the news.

"I was making progress, Ken. The inoculated mice with impaired motor functions identical to ALS showed improvement. Another year or two was all we needed. What the hell happened?"

"It came from upstairs, Norman; whatever you gave them just didn't cut it."

"I understand, what's done is done. But I need to keep working, at least until my pension vests next year."

"Ok, take a few weeks off. When you come back, just make yourself scarce, and get lost in the shuffle. A year around here goes by like *that*." Mintz snapped his fingers.

"Fair enough, Ken."

Norman briskly walked home, anything but upset. He revered in his cleverness, how he had orchestrated a first class ruse, cajoling

Merck into keeping the project alive years beyond its useful life, slyly baiting them with a slew of half-baked promises, feeding them just bits and pieces, stringing them along and tossing them scraps as one would placate a hungry dog, while he surreptitiously secreted away a treasure trove of proprietary information, all for his self-serving use.

He ruminated over how many nights he had lied awake, convinced he alone was *ordained* to save the world from the nefarious ALS, smugly confident he was getting close to discovering the formula. It would take a year, maybe less. He could see it now, crystal clear in his mind's eye; FDA approval, fame, fortune.....*a Nobel Prize.*

Chapter 7

Norman Berger's diminutive apartment reflected the thumbprint of a megalomaniac. It was anything but a home, with every nook and cranny strewn with medical case studies. Mountains of scientific articles were stacked against barren walls, research dissertations were scattered on dilapidated furniture, while whiteboards crammed side by side were saturated with important protocols culled from the tsunami of data he had so brazenly stolen.

Erotic magazines littered his unkempt bed.

The telephone rang early the next morning.

"Norman Berger," he answered curtly.

"It's Ken, we have a problem," he spoke urgently.

"What is it?"

"You never signed our nondisclosure and confidentiality agreement. Without it they'll bust a gut. They'll toss you out of here how you came in–with zero, including your company apartment. I'll have no leverage, and you'll kiss that fat pension goodbye."

"Sure I did," he lied.

"Got a copy?"

"Are you kidding? It was forty years ago! What the hell are they concerned about? I'm getting ready to retire, for Christ sake, you sure about this?"

"Positive, you have a problem with it?"

"Course not; I just think it's an insult."

"It's not negotiable."

"Email it to me, let me read it over."

"I need it signed and returned pronto."

"OK, Ken, understood."

Norman wondered—*what did Mintz know?*

Suddenly he felt everything change, threatening his grandiose plan, turning it topsy-turvy, his raison d'être swirling in an existential nightmare, with time now parading around that nightmare like a mortal enemy.

He slaved without the luxury of sleep, energized by pots of black coffee and sheer adrenergic rush, analyzing ad nauseam the formulaic whiteboards, cocksure there was a common link that would unravel the elusive ALS mystery.

A week passed quickly.

Ken Mintz sat opposite Jim Frazier, his immediate boss.

"How the hell did you let this happen? I goddamn asked you if Berger's legal documents were in order. This fiasco was your idea, not mine. I went to the board and got their approval, now it's *my* ass in a frickin' sling!"

"I'm sick about it, Jim. It's standard operating procedure; somehow, Berger fell through the cracks. I think he strung us along just to keep getting paid. Maybe I'm paranoid, but I just don't trust the sonafabitch. Berger knows we need that agreement. I used his pension as a bargaining chip. There's no way in hell he walks away from a million bucks, not at his age."

"Where is he?"

"I gave him a few weeks off, can't stand the sight of him anymore, and I'm fed up with his holier than thou attitude. He's probably holed up in that stinking one room he lives in, doing God knows what."

"Well, he can't do any damage over a few weeks; let's get that NDA, put this damn fire out."

"OK, Jim, agreed, I'm on top of it."

Norman dozed for a few hours, awakened by a dream he had seen something on the third whiteboard, only to be greeted by disappointment. Moments of elation, when he thought he had discovered it, were tempered by defeat, as each ensuing attempt was sabotaged by failure, while his ability to reason became increasingly clouded.

Ken Mintz hounded Norman with telephone calls, leaving a barrage of threatening messages on his answering machine, pressing for the non-disclosure documents. Norman ignored them, sending Mintz an email——*my attorney is looking over the document*—trying to buy time which was ticking too quickly

Frustration morphed into despondency, and then into hallucination, as the animated whiteboards jeered him, their haunting voices reiterating all of their ballyhooed scientific jargon; *mitochondrial energy factories, SODA1 protein, TPD43 protein, ISIS-SODA2-RX, catechol-o-methyl transferase enzymes, mirror neurons....*

It was there, but he couldn't see it, so deftly camouflaged, hidden amidst a convoluted jigsaw puzzle of oddly shaped pieces.

Norman stalked the room, and then he panicked, berating himself, screaming at the frantic ringing of his telephone and Mintz's dire ultimatums.

Suddenly, he was jolted by a notion, unsure whether it was an epiphany or a delusion. He cautiously approached the second and fifth whiteboards, his hand trembling as he made the erasures and modified the chemical compositions, stepping back for a full view.

"Eureka!" he shouted; he scampered about in a cathartic shrieking of emotion, and then he kissed the whiteboards—triumph.

Now he needed to prove it.

KEN MINTZ KNEW NORMAN was odd. He was flabbergasted when he suddenly quit Merck—walking away from a seven figure pension—until he realized what had happened, and got sick to his stomach.

Packing his bags, and his invaluable discovery, Norman headed for Triangle Park Research Institute just outside Raleigh, North Carolina—a haven for cutting edge biotechnology companies, especially one, Whitcomb Pharmaceutical.

His first order of business was with a patent attorney.

Chapter 8

Dr. Blair Whitcomb, a somewhat successful neurologist, wasn't cut out to be bogged down in regulations, paperwork, and the daily grind of longer hours with less to show for it. He was looking for the big score, the blockbuster drug with "permanently gone golfing" written all over it.

At forty-four he dumped his practice to his partner, and investing a good chunk of his net worth into Whitcomb Pharmaceutical, a biotech company working on a cure for ALS.

As glamorous as it sounded, the odds were stacked against him. After six years, he became increasingly despondent with his lack of progress, which tempered his exuberance, second thoughts that gave him the sweats, and kept him awake at night. A twenty person staff of research scientists had dwindled down to a skeletal crew.

While the business hemorrhaged, he struggled to get out of bed in the morning until he finally lapsed into a full blown depression. His concerned but constantly nagging wife insisted he seek professional help. A psycho pharmacologist bombarded him with the usual stable of medications, until they found the right combination, which at least allowed him to somewhat function.

Blair knew only too well that these antidepressants were not cures, but only masked the symptoms, deathly afraid that any more bad news could trigger a complete nervous breakdown.

He was sitting in his office, flipping through golf magazines, when the phone rang. He noticed the name on the caller ID— Merck.

"Blair Whitcomb," he answered, curious as to whom it could be.

"Hey, Blair, its John Nozenski, remember me?"

Blair's memory was not in the best of shape, considering the anti-anxiety pills he scoffed down as if they were chocolate candies.

"Sorry, had a long day, remind me."

"C'mon, Blair, I was one of your first hires at Whitcomb. I did all the research on your protein chaperone theory. You were gung ho on it as a possible bullet against ALS."

"Jesus Christ, of course, we nicknamed you Nose, right?"

"That's me, the Nose knows what the Nose knows, remember?"

"Yep, I hated to lose you—thought you knew your stuff—but a man's gotta do what he's gotta do. How are things at Merck?"

"Not bad, Blair, I have job security, so the wife is happy. It pays the bills and the benefits are generous. Sure, I miss the entrepreneurial spirit, but security goes a long way. Maybe I'll never be rich, but I needed to be realistic. I guess I'm not a gambler, and I know you are, which is why I called."

"Don't remind me, Nose. The grass is always greener. I found out the hard way that this business is brutal. You get ripped off by the charlatans who doctor up their results just to keep the funding flowing, or the back stabbing employees who steal your formulas and start up on their own. The NDA's aren't worth the paper they're written on, unless you're sitting on a war chest to feed the high priced attorneys who suck your blood dry."

Blair sighed, trying to remain focused.

"And if you win it's a Pyrrhic victory at best, because you're already broke."

"I know you're going through some rough times, Blair. It's a small community when it comes to ALS. And there aren't too many secrets—everybody likes to gossip. But if you figure out ALS, then Parkinson's becomes a no brainer, and you're talking billions with a big fat "B.""

"So I guess you called me out of the goodness of your heart because you stumbled over the cure on some mad scientist's blog and wanted to repay me for such a great boss I was?"

"At least you still have your sense of humor, Blair. You did right by me and now it's my turn for a payback. I've been working on a top secret project up here at Merck, an all-out assault on ALS. I came in right in the middle. I did some quick math, and figured over the last ten years they went through seven to eight hundred million. Just a week ago they pulled the plug. I was working for the guy who ran the damn thing. His father got nailed with the goddamn disease and he was obsessed with finding the cure. He's been here forever, just a year away from a seven figure pension. You'd figure he would just go through the motions and retire. But he tells Merck to stick the pension up their corporate ass and then he quits, like it was no big deal."

"What's his name? I know most of the ALS guys."

"Norman Berger."

"Dr. Norman Berger? The guy's a legend—supposed to be *the* man on psycho-motor disorders."

"It's better than that, Blair, much better. The guy's a genius; I mean his IQ is in the stratosphere. And he lets you know it. He's got zero patience for people. I'm not a shrink, but he would have you believe he was hand-picked by the Almighty to save the world from ALS. He's been plagued with Scheuermann's syndrome all of his life, not exactly a matinee idol. I felt sorry for him, tough thing when you know people avoid looking at you because it makes them uncomfortable. For some reason he took a liking to me, at least as much as he could like anybody. He made me his assistant on the project. Sure I knew my stuff, which helped."

"Why did Merck bail? Was he accomplishing anything? Eight hundred million for them is a drop in the bucket."

"So here's where it gets interesting, Blair, and the reason for the call. I know for a fact that Berger was playing games with the research. I prepared the monthly memos for corporate from the information Berger gave me. A slew of novel protocols the researchers developed weren't included. I asked him about it once, and he said they were worthless and not to concern myself with them. But I know for sure he stored them on his laptop. Berger started acting funny the last two years. He would hole himself up in his office with his computer and hardly had any interaction with the research team. And every month we went through the same drill with the memos to corporate, and he would secret away anything he found interesting. Everything was cloak and dagger, mysterious, almost like corporate espionage. And I think he's real close to figuring out what makes ALS tick, which is why he quit after we got shut down. I wouldn't blame him, considering he could set up his own shop or partner up with a guy like you."

"So Merck got all the leftovers, and he kept the prizes. No wonder they dumped the project. He's a corporate thief, nothing new in this biotech game."

"Call him whatever you want, Blair. But somebody is going to make a deal with him, and if he finds the cure, we are talking a whole lot of money."

"Do you know where he went?"

"When he left he told me he was heading for the research institute down there, which is what I suspected, so I gave him your number, and told him to give you a call. I figured you can bring him on and work something out. He's a royal pain in the ass, a real weirdo, strange as hell. He would spend hours playing with his mice. His personality is for the birds, not the kind of guy you want to grab a few beers with. He thinks he knows it all, and doesn't like being challenged. But if anyone can lick ALS, it's him, no doubt in my mind."

"He sounds like a wonderful human being."

"Save the sarcasm, Blair. He is what he is. Nobody's perfect."

"And Merck has no clue about this?" Blair asked with a keen interest. "I'm not looking for any lawsuits."

"I don't know what Merck knows, or whether Berger signed any confidentiality agreements. Maybe there's risk, or maybe there's not. You're the gambler, Blair, remember?"

"OK, Nose, this is real interesting. If things work out I want to take care of you."

"Whatever you think is fair, Blair. I didn't call you hoping to get a finder's fee."

"Thanks, Nose, and one more thing."

"What's that?"

"Do you have Berger's cell number?"

"How does 919-544-9878 sound?"

"Perfect, I'll be in touch."

Blair ended the conversation, wrote down the number and hung up the phone, thinking.

Chapter 9

DR. BLAIR WHITCOMB SAT across from Norman Berger. Nose's story sounded too good to be true. He hoped that the miracle he had been praying for to save his failing company was not just another wild goose chase.

Whitcomb Pharmaceutical occupied a three thousand square foot facility within Triangle Research Park, one of a few dozen cookie cutter buildings abutting each other in a semicircular atrium, peppered with pre-assigned parking spaces, the starkness softened by shrubbery and a small gurgling fountain.

Blair Whitcomb was neatly dressed in cuffed khaki pleated cotton slacks, a crisp white oxford button down, argyle socks, and brown penny loafers. He appeared in sharp contrast to Norman's wrinkled black shiny trousers, black laced scuffed shoes, white socks, and polyester green shirt with half knotted red tie. Blair ascribed Norman's outfit as the tell-tale sign of a mendicant, a mad scientist, or both.

With his chiseled, handsome face, blue eyes, and full head of blond hair combed straight back, Blair resembled a Ken doll.

"So what exactly do you do here?" Norman spoke first, his tone condescending.

"You get right to the point, don't you?"

"Time is money, Mr. Whitcomb. What I have is invaluable. I don't need a friend, a dog, or a wife. Either we have a fit or we don't."

"Call me Blair. It's not so official around here."

"OK Blair, John Nozenski said something or other with Amyotrophic Lateral Sclerosis."

"You're the guru on ALS; at least that's what our mutual friend told me."

"I'm always interested in learning something new."

Blair figured he would test Norman, to see what he really knew.

"Well, it's no secret the root cause of ALS is the inability of the body to control the mechanisms in normal cells, resulting in neuronal death, and the complete breakdown of motor functions. But here's the difference. I'm convinced there are underlying infectious proteins, possibly a genetic aberration of prions, which initiate the cell mutations. I'm betting we can design cutting edge novel drugs to act as a chaperone and enhance the body's natural protein chemicals."

"And the result is, if you don't mind my asking?"

"I'm substantially prolonging their lives with milder debilitating symptoms."

"If you say so, Blair," he spoke dismissively.

"Let me ask you a stupid question, Dr. Berger." Blair sounded annoyed.

"Call me Norman."

He didn't.

"Why the hell would anyone sane leave Merck after thirty years? Lifers there get stock options, hefty retirement plans, free housing, health benefits, and…their own private golf course. Not too shabby a life."

"I resigned." Norman replied matter-of-factly. "And I have zero interest in golf."

"Just so you know, I'm a golf fanatic, but I won't hold it against you."

He pointed to the collection of trophies that graced his desk and autographed photographs of him posing with famous professional golfers that dotted his walls. Spewing on about each picture, Blair dropped names like Sir Nick Faldo, Johnny Miller, Ben Crenshaw, Tom Watson, sounding to Norman as if these men walked on water.

"I never met Jack or Arnie, maybe one day if I'm lucky—would be the greatest thrill of my life."

Jack Nicklaus and Arnold Palmer were golf royalty, even nerdy Norman knew that, not that he gave a hoot. Had he his druthers, he would do handstands to meet Louis Pasteur, Alexander Fleming or Jonas Salk—to peer into the minds of scientists who changed the world.

"It's tough to relate unless you're into golf." Blair carried on, "better than sex, much better."

AN ASTROTURF CARPET RAN the entire length of the wall, some twenty feet long, three feet wide, with a two-inch round hole at the far end cut down into the flooring. Leaning against the near side were a dozen or so different style putters, one considerably longer than the others. An assortment of Titleist golf balls speckled the carpet.

Blair poked through his collection, grabbed his Wilson 8802 blade putter, and lined half a dozen balls next to each other, proceeding to stroke them, holing two. He reached for his long putter, which resembled a broomstick with a metal shaft and mallet face. Reversing his hands, he hugged the handle against his upper chest, took a few practice strokes, and with a pendulum type rocking motion of his shoulders stroked the remaining balls. He again holed two, the other four just short, but dead on line.

"Christ!" Blair moaned. "You know what they say; a hundred percent of the putts that don't reach the hole don't go in."

Norman thought the remark was idiotic

Blair spouted on about persimmon wood and metal head drivers, sand wedges with their various degrees of bounce, and the infamous Lee Trevino anecdote that "Only God can hit a one iron." Then he proudly unveiled an assortment of relics encased in glass, mounted behind his desk wall, as if they were precious museum pieces. They had strange names like Brassie, Spoon, Cleek, Benny, Spade, Mashie, Niblick, and Jigger.

He picked out a Macgregor persimmon wooden headed driver, the Jack Nicklaus VIP model, and stood alongside a floor to ceiling mirror taped with black strips running vertically, horizontally, and perpendicularly, intersecting to create various angles. Gripping the club, he took his stance, turning his shoulders back and forth, fiddling with his hands, adjusting his torso until it was perfect. Then he made a full backswing.

"See that, do you see it? Stand alongside of me, look into the mirror, see it now?" Blair held the pose as if he were cast in stone.

"Do I see what?" Norman thought he was dealing with a wacko, a nut job.

"The shaft angle, the clubface, right on plane, pointing straight down the target line, how beautiful is that!" Blair was grinning like a Cheshire cat.

Norman walked a few feet closer. "Move the club, let me watch."

Blair dropped the club down an inch, then up an inch, then back to where the club was on plane, with the tape hidden behind the shaft.

"Yeah, you're recreating the angles of the tape with your arms and the position of the club. When you move the club I can see the tape, the shaft is above or below the line, the wooden piece points to the right or to the left. Is that it?"

"Yes! That's it, Norman," acknowledging his name for the first time. "The wooden piece is called the club head."

"And I assume the trick in this ridiculous game is to place the club along those mirror lines and then just spin your body to the left, which will pull the head down into the ball, propelling it straight down the line, correct?"

"That's exactly right, Norman! How did you know? We say rotate, but spin is almost the same thing."

"It's a simple law of physics" Norman proffered nonchalantly, "the conservation of angular momentum, based on Newton's Second Law of gravity and force. Objects in motion stay in motion. If you want the formulas, I can write them out. There's also centrifugal force and centripetal acceleration—the radius of the swing path, but that's enough. It's just the inside moves the outside, not the opposite. The arms and hands are passive and controlled by the rotation of the muscles in the torso and shoulders. And the longer you can hold the angle into the downturn—the one between your left arm and the club shaft—the more force you will generate, because...."

"Downswing, not downturn," Blair interrupted him.

"OK, downswing, club head, who gives a damn!"

Blair couldn't stop, especially with this new cool sounding conservation of whatever he just said, all in all flabbergasted with these scientific nuances of the golf swing that Norman so readily expounded.

"I'll tell you who gives a damn," Blair rambled on excitedly. "The millions of golf junkies addicted to this game, beating balls for hours on the driving range, dissecting instruction articles from golf magazines, scrutinizing the internet for free golf lessons, fantasizing morning, noon, and night about every great shot they ever hit and will hit someday."

He caught his breath and continued. "There are guys who piss away thousands to have their swings analyzed by ridiculously expensive computer programs, lunatics who study the shapes of their divots, their ball flight, launch angles and spin rates. And when they think they figured it out, they take it to the course, confident, ready to shoot par, like they discovered the Holy Grail. But they're only kidding themselves because it never happens that way. They gyrate between depression and elation, suicidal after a lousy shot, then ecstatic after knocking the next one two feet from the hole."

Blair stopped for a moment to catch his breath again, as his voice turned somber. "Men wreck their marriages because they love the game more than their wives. They sleep with their precious putters. Maybe it sounds ridiculous, but believe me it's true. They neglect everything; their careers, their businesses, their kids. They're obsessed, chasing perfection in a sport that can't be conquered, ever."

Norman knew that Blair was speaking about himself, just from the way the words flowed so naturally.

"Every man sleeps with his putter, Blair, nothing so remarkable."

Blair didn't acknowledge Norman's quip. He wasn't listening, too entrenched in his own psychoanalysis. "All I want to do is to swing the club the same way, in the same slot, like a machine, which is impossible."

Blair remained posed in front of the mirror, the club still perfectly aligned against the black tape.

"Take a little advice," Norman piped in. "Never use the word *impossible;* it's not befitting for a man of science, difficult perhaps, but never impossible."

Blair walked back to his desk, plopped down in his chair, holding onto the Macgregor driver. "Norman, if I could automatically reproduce my best swing at will, if my muscles could just remember on their own, without my stupid brain screwing it up, I would turn professional. Maybe my short game needs a little work. I can see it now, the US Open, eighteenth hole, the applause deafening as I march up the fairway, tipping my cap, acknowledging the roaring crowd, waving, fighting to hold back the tears."

Norman surmised from the exuberance in Blair's voice that he would have given up everything, his medical degree, his business, his family, the whole shebang, for that one moment of crowning glory.

"Of course," Blair added, "the Golf Gods would have to cooperate."

"Who are they?" Norman asked curiously.

"It's nothing religious, more transcendental, sort of like an invisible power that determines whether you'll have good luck or bad luck, especially on the golf course. They're elusive and mysterious, and they work in strange ways, but there are lots of believers, including me."

"You sound more like a superstitious soothsayer than a scientist," Norman remarked cuttingly, "black cats and Friday the thirteenth."

"I never thought of it that way" Blair replied, as his voice trailed off. "Golf is more than just a game…. a whole lot more."

"And the other thing you did, with the carpet, that's just your hands, what did you call it again?"

"It's chipping and putting, Norman, what's known as the short game. Believe it or not, that's how tournaments are won or lost. All the pros have great swings on any given day, but the guys who can get up and down from the bunkers and have hands like magicians take home the bacon. It's the old saying—drive for show and putt for dough." Blair grinned, as if he had been the author of this hackneyed quip.

Norman didn't know anything about the short game, and glossed over it.

"But that's a whole different ball of wax, nothing to do with perfecting my swing and…."

"Muscle memory, I got it, Blair, enough."

NORMAN MADE A MENTAL note about Blair's *muscle memory* as he steered the discussion back to the business at hand. "You asked me about Merck, why I left."

"I think it's a fair question."

"They wooed me from Penn, needed a blockbuster drug, made me head of a top secret unit overseeing some twenty researchers. We were making progress on ALS. I was *this close* to a cure." Norman held his thumb and forefinger narrowly apart.

"So what happened?" Under any other circumstances Blair would have dismissed Norman's boasting of a potential cure as just that: braggadocio. It wasn't uncommon among certain egomaniacal breeds of scientists, although something in Norman's voice said he was telling the truth.

"The bean counters cried uncle, too much money down the drain and not enough to show for it, at least in their opinion. After ten years all that information I had was invaluable. For some reason I never signed any confidentiality agreement, it fell through the cracks, and figured I was sitting on a goldmine, better to keep it for myself."

"What about your pension. It must have been substantial?"

"I forfeited it, over a million bucks."

"That's some story, Norman, took guts."

"And just so you know," Norman veered off in a different direction, "you're wasting your time."

Blair looked at him quizzically.

"Your approach to the ALS dilemma-it won't work."

"I'm listening." Blair was anxious to hear Norman's pearls of wisdom.

"Simply put, the protein chaperone therapy you've bet on is just another hyped up protocol from imbecilic research scientists who have nothing better to do all day than write this malarkey, publish it in the usual journals as if it was gospel, and stir up the pot. Why are you so cocksure that genetically aberrant prions initiate the cell mutations?"

"Well it just seems—"

"Exactly, Blair, it *seems*, because it's convenient, and gives you a reason to get up every morning. It's no different than all the hoopla with Resveratrol and red grapes, which supposedly reverses the aging process. Now everyone is gung ho guzzling red wine as the fountain of youth. Great news, except the alcohol destroys their liver. And back to your chaperone therapy. Which prions are the culprits? They're composed of different RNA and DNA nucleotides which multiply into an infinite amount of strains, like one trillion different locks looking for one key, or vice-versa, but either way it's a guessing game at best."

Blair sopped up every word. *This guy knew what he was talking about.*

"But if I can find a better way to moderate their symptoms and extend the quality of life, then maybe ...."

"Big deal, Blair, you've accomplished nothing," Norman interjected, purposely cutting him off. "Sooner or later they're on the phone making funeral arrangements. I should know—my father had it. I watched the man die."

"I'm sorry, Norman, must have been...."

"Don't pity me, Blair. I'm not here to add a few more lousy months, a year if I'm lucky. If that's your agenda, good luck. I'm in this for a cure, that's the big money."

"But you're talking about the...impossible, aren't you?"

Blair realized his mistake immediately.

Norman exploded as he stared Blair down. "What did I tell you, are you deaf? There's no such word as impossible, listen to me, NO SUCH WORD AS IMPOSSIBLE!"

Blair cowered as Norman banged the table vehemently with each utterance. It was obvious to Blair that Norman was an arrogant, in your face, know-it-all. But everything else Nose told him about Norman Berger's genius was dead on, which lifted his spirits with more than a glimmer of hope.

Norman signaled for Blair to come real close, and whispered into his ear, "Can I trust you?"

"One hundred percent," Blair answered excitedly.

"I swear to you on my father's grave, may he rest in peace, I found the cure."

A mind boggling, seismographic, off the Richter scale statement, spoken with bone chilling confidence, Blair Whitcomb suddenly forgot about Nicklaus, muscle memory, and everything else, as if Norman Berger was the Messiah.

"Assume a regimen of a four to twelve month treatment, depending on the progression of the disease," Norman continued. "What's that worth per patient? I figure two thousand if I get them early, six when they're totally incapacitated, average it out to four. Do the math, Blair, a three hundred million dollar business, at least half to the bottom line."

Blair Whitcomb sat mesmerized.

"And I didn't figure the existing cases, the ones still alive, just icing on the cake. What's the value, with a seventeen-year patent protection? The greedy bastard suitors will be pounding down the goddamn door, the Wyeth Labs, Amgen, Pfizer, you know all the players. And for this kind of cash flow, plus their marketing muscle, five times sales is a no brainer, closer to ten, I figure."

Blair did the math in a nanosecond. "It's worth north of a billion dollars, for Christ sake!" He shouted with the exuberance of a man who had just hit the Powerball lottery, or won the US Open.

Norman knew it–Blair Whitcomb was officially hooked.

Chapter 10

NORMAN BERGER WORE A smug grin while Blair studied him; barely five foot, bald, a graying goatee, deep set beady eyes, resembling more the devil than a scientist. Extremely poor eyesight required a thick set of wire-rimmed glasses. He carried a magnifying glass to read small print.

"Nozenski told me you were looking for a partner," Blair said.

"That's true," Norman curtly responded.

"Well guess what- you're looking at him." Blair smiled.

"That depends upon the deal, Blair. I can go anywhere with what I have. Why should I get involved with you?"

Blair tried to put his best foot forward, although his guts were in turmoil. "We're all set up and ready to go. I have money in the bank, a fully functioning lab, and some smart researchers on staff."

"Got a financial statement I can look at?"

"Why do you need that?" Blair said defensively.

"To see your cash on hand and monthly expenses, that's why." Blair could feel Norman's annoyance. "Can you survive another year or is the undertaker making bankruptcy arrangements?"

"I think enough for a year, maybe more, really not quite sure," Blair answered dishearteningly.

"Not quite sure? That doesn't work. I need to know exactly to the penny, no maybes, no hemming and hawing, no pipedream stories about who promised to put in more capital, not tomorrow, now."

Blair fished through his drawer and handed Norman a sheet marked "accounting." "These are the expenses, some paid quarterly, but accrued monthly."

Norman studied the numbers with his magnifying glass, his face flush up against the paper.

"So your monthly burn rate is forty-five thousand," Norman muttered as he went through the expenses, while Blair just sat silent. "What the hell is this?" Norman looked up, puzzled. "Seems like four thousand a month on travel and entertainment?"

Blair was afraid to answer, or too embarrassed, hoping Norman wouldn't want to see the actual receipts. But first class airline tickets to Saint Barts, five star restaurants, overnight jaunts to The Plaza Hotel in New York City, the best seats at the hottest Broadway shows, and the requisite jewelry, lingerie, and other accoutrements of an extra marital affair comes with a hefty price.

Norman smugly knew that Blair Whitcomb was at the end of his rope. And if he wanted to salvage his investment, and probably his sanity, he had no alternative except the brain power of the hunchback scientist who was sitting smack dab in front of him.

"How much cash does the company have?"

Blair proffered the most recent bank statement and a separate ledger with the past due bills.

"Five hundred thirty-five thousand is your bank balance," Norman indicated, stroking his goatee. "Looks like you owe three months to the landlord and utilities, two months to the phone company, and...twenty-two thousand, four months past due on an American Express credit card?"

"If you say so," Blair responded sheepishly, like the kid who got caught with his hand in the cookie jar.

"So the company has half a million bucks, that's it, right?"

"Yes."

"I need to see the audited tax returns."

Blair fumbled through his desk drawer and handed them to Norman. After a quick perusal, he tossed them onto the floor as if they were trash.

"No surprise, Blair, as I suspected, your business is bleeding to death."

"Yes Sir, hope you don't think I was trying to hide something."

Norman didn't answer, except for, "stop with the Sir crap, it's annoying!"

"Yes Sir," Blair replied, grinning, thinking it was funny.

Norman didn't laugh, or crack a smile.

"Show me the lab," Norman ordered, as if he were conducting an official investigation.

A young man greeted them, dressed in a white uniform, the type one would see in a hospital emergency room. Blair introduced Norman to Ahmed Ravi. His assistant, Victoria Chang, was fiddling with papers, attempting to look busy.

"What are you working on, Ahmed?" Norman asked pointedly, as he walked around the lab, scoping out the equipment, and Victoria Chang.

"Are you familiar with protein chaperone, Dr. Berger?"

"I think so," Norman answered, seemingly politely, and then asked Ahmed bluntly, "I'm assuming you have supporting data of the molecular binding of the proteinase?"

Norman's eyes darted back and forth to Victoria as he waited for Ahmed to answer. She noticed that, which made her skin crawl.

Ahmed glanced over at Blair, who just nodded. "Well, uh, not yet, but…… I'm confident, we're confident," as he pointed to Blair.

"Yeah, I'm sure you both are," Norman said with cutting sarcasm, while staring at Victoria. He then just walked out of the lab, Blair traipsing along.

"Ahmed knows his stuff," Blair volunteered, "but he needs more help. It's tough to find good research scientists."

"No it's not," Norman said automatically. "you just need the right guy steering the ship."

Blair winced at the remark. The truth hurt. He again pestered Norman about Whitcomb Pharmaceutical.

"Ok Blair, why beat around the bush? I know what I am and what I have. People don't like me. I don't give a damn. I don't look like you, but then again, you can't cure ALS. Your company is bankrupt—not legally, but certainly its fiber, its life, its breath. So what do you have of value to me? There's money in the bank. The lab is functioning but needs work. More important, the strategy needs to be changed. And you need a permanent vacation. I come on as chief cook and bottle washer. A new broom sweeps clean. I'm not into titles but investors are, so I'm President and you're Chairman of the Board, just to give you bragging rights to your golf buddies. I receive a fair salary and health insurance, with a three year guarantee. You go back into private practice and start earning a living. As for ownership, I raise the working capital. I figure we need a twenty million dollar commitment, to be drawn down as we expand staff. I know who will write the check in a heartbeat once I get my hands into this place. It's enough to get the drug into the FDA pipeline. After early stage clinical trials, we go public. All the patents and patents pending I develop stay in my name until the initial public offering. I want nothing gratis. My ownership increases as the company grows, capped out at fifty percent. It's not negotiable—you take it or leave it."

Chapter 11

THE AGREEMENT WAS SIGNED a week later without rancor.

Blair Whitcomb returned to private practice with mixed emotions, but infinitely happier. He ended his extra marital affair and worked on getting his life back together again, eventually shaking off the depression and quitting the medication.

Norman kept a low profile, shuffling to the office early in the morning, returning to his two room flat late at night. The local gentry wondered what he did all day behind closed doors; maybe something top secret? And where was Blair Whitcomb?

Victoria Chang remained with the company. There was something about her, some sort of aberrant turn on, which appealed to Norman's dark side that lay dormant for too long. He knew it the first time he laid eyes on her in Whitcomb's lab. She was unusually attractive, of Asian descent, with smooth skin and jet black shoulder length hair, the type Norman knew he could never have, even if he weren't so deformed.

Norman sent Merck a business plan outlining his cure for ALS, divulging just enough new information to pique their greedy interests.

He also knew that the odds of any drug making it from lab studies to human testing were 1 in 1000.

DR. KENNETH MINTZ BOARDED the Merck G-4 at Teterboro Airport and jetted post haste into Raleigh Durham, greeted by a town car for the fifteen minute trip to Whitcomb's offices.

"Norman, it's great to see you; no grass growing under your

feet. We're very excited about what you're doing. I feel terrible how things ended."

Mintz was inwardly seething, still smarting from being reamed out by corporate for giving Norman free reign without any legal protection. He was certain Norman had stolen Merck intellectual property. Now he needed to suck up to him, all too aware that a cure for ALS could be a major step in attacking Parkinson's, and a huge score for Whitcomb Pharmaceutical.

"Listen, Ken, you need to understand something. I gave my life to Merck. You were ready to put me out to pasture. My work isn't complete. Signing that NDA would mean selling my soul to the devil. And just to be upfront, there are others I'm speaking with," Norman lied, poker faced.

Mintz just went through the motions, with a wink and a nod all but assuring Norman it was a done deal, as the amount needed from the pharmaceutical behemoth was no more than a rounding error on their income statement.

On his way out, Ken played the usual negotiating game. "Norman, let me bring it up at our next meeting. We would want a larger piece of the pie than you're offering." For Norman, this went in one ear and out the other.

Two weeks later he received a letter of intent from Merck, proposing a ten million dollar investment into Whitcomb Pharmaceutical for a forty percent ownership interest.

Norman purposely didn't answer, playing phone tag, taking a week off to fly to New York to visit his mother and pay respects to his father. He placed a stone atop the tombstone, a Jewish tradition, around which he wrapped a handwritten note: *I found the cure. Norman.*

He returned to a slew of phone messages and emails from Mintz, which he ignored, betting he would eventually buckle, afraid to lose the deal to a competitor.

They dickered back and forth until hammering out an agreement; Merck would invest twenty million dollars for a twenty percent stake in Whitcomb Pharmaceutical, with no board seat or voting rights, just a passive investor going along for the ride. Norman was adamant about this provision, to keep things under wraps until his patents were airtight.

Chapter 12

ALAN HOWARD RETURNED FROM the long Labor Day weekend, the first week Gordon was officially off of the payroll, starting his day in his usual manner, scouring *The Wall Street Journal*, searching for new ideas.

Biotechnology was a hot topic and a volatile market. Alan knew he had to attack it, get into a stock early on, ride it up, trade it, or put on a short position, with mountains of money to be made, especially betting on FDA approval.

One headline caught his eye, more than just a blurb; *Merck in Joint Venture with Upstart Biotech Company for ALS Cure.*

He read through the article.

> Norman Berger, President of Whitcomb Pharmaceutical Inc. of Triangle Park, North Carolina, announced Friday the signing of a definitive agreement with Merck and Co. The agreement outlines an initial funding of twenty million dollars, to be used by Whitcomb for research and development in its quest to find an FDA approved cure for amyotrophic lateral sclerosis, commonly known as Lou Gehrig's disease, or ALS.
>
> The Merck investment will give the pharmaceutical giant a twenty percent stake in Whitcomb.
>
> Berger, who had started his career with Merck three decades ago, is considered by most as the pioneer

in the study of the etiology of amyotrophic lateral sclerosis. Dr. Berger's father was a victim of ALS.

Dr. Ken Mintz, a Merck spokesman, further said, "Dr. Berger and Merck have had a long and successful relationship. As head of research for our ALS project, Dr. Berger made substantial inroads in unraveling the mystery of this crippling disease. We are pleased to be associated with Dr. Berger's company."

Alan circled the article and called in his secretary, who buzzed him ten minutes later. "I have Mr. Berger on line two for you, Mr. Howard."

"Norman Berger, as I live and breathe, how long has it been? I can't count that high. My God, what a surprise; how are you doing?"

"I'm alive, if that's why you're calling me after thirty-five years."

"Married or kids?"

"No and no."

"I have a son, Gordon. He just turned thirty. Time flies, doesn't it? What's that? No, he's not in business with me anymore."

"What does he do?"

"He's an incredible golfer, trying to turn professional. You can Google him. He was once considered to be the best amateur in the country. He hits it a mile; had a two handicap when he was fifteen." Alan spoke proudly, taking the liberty of some paternal bragging rights.

Norman knew about physical handicaps. "He's sick?"

"No, why do you ask?"

"You said he has two handicaps."

"No, Norman, in golf, a handicap is just a rating system."

"Why are you calling me?" Norman spoke testily.

"I read the article in today's *Journal*; you must have something special for Merck to get involved."

"You never paid me for the GMAT exams I took for you back at Penn." Norman quickly changed the subject.

Alan Howard chuckled, as if it were a joke. "I don't remember you having such a sense of humor."

"Do you hear me laughing? You must have called for a reason; maybe some inside information? I see your name in the newspapers, a big shot hedge fund manager. Kind of premature, considering we're not a public company yet."

"Why so suspicious, Norman?"

He ignored the question. "I dropped you a note, not that we were friends. It was just business. We shook on a deal. I trusted you. Without me, Columbia business school would have just been a wet dream. I told you about my father, how I helped him out with his hospice bills. It wouldn't have been so difficult to send me a condolence card with a check for what you owed me."

"My father died from ALS, if that's any consolation."

"Just more of a reason you should have taken care of it."

"Norman, if I made a mistake for a lousy ten…."

"Ten thousand dollars is not lousy; maybe to you and your rich friends, but not for what I do. You knew I had just enough to scrape out an education, and you screwed me, which I never forgot."

"Norman, you're making a mountain out of…."

"Drop dead!" were the last two words Alan Howard heard before the phone call abruptly ended.

He buzzed his secretary.

"Yes, Mr. Howard."

"Make out a personal check for twenty-five thousand dollars, payable to Norman Berger, and notate it as a repayment of loan. Bring it to me and I'll give you a note to enclose. Send it to Dr. Norman Berger, President, at the address for Whitcomb Pharmaceutical. You'll find it on the internet."

Alan Howard scribbled out the note on his personal stationary.

Dear Norman,

Please accept my apologies. I understand your anger and it is deserved. I am enclosing the past due amount with accumulated interest. If you ever need anything, I am here to help. Good luck in your new venture.

Sincerely,
Alan

BLAIR WHITCOMB, ENTRENCHED IN private practice, was content with things going well. His marriage was still intact, although he engaged in an occasional indiscretion, just to spice things up. Most importantly, his golf handicap was trending scratch.

He slept better these days, with no sweats or panic attacks. He tried not to think about Whitcomb Pharmaceutical, especially since Norman had let him know, in no uncertain terms, that "I hate being pestered."

Blair received a raft of congratulatory calls on his answering machine that Tuesday morning, bombarded from friends and medical colleagues with the news about Merck. He read the story on Google as the messages droned on.

"Yes Sir!" he shouted as he dialed the number, pumping his fist as if he had just drained a fifty-foot eagle putt.

"Norman Berger," he answered the phone on the first ring with his usual curtness.

Blair didn't notice it. He was too hopped up, and just closed his eyes and prayed to Jesus the article was accurate. He couldn't get the words out quickly enough.

"Norman, it's Blair Whitcomb; remember me, one of your major shareholders, the guy who made everything possible?"

"Mr. Muscle Memory, you and the rest of the addicts out there, but just for the record, if anyone made this possible, it was me."

"Saw the announcement about Merck, great news! When do you think…?"

"Relax, Blair, there's plenty that needs to get done. Go and work on your golf swing, enjoy your life, get it?"

And with that Norman Berger hung up the phone.

JEREMY CHANG HAD ALSO read *The Wall Street Journal* article, and called his sister, Victoria, at Whitcomb Pharmaceutical.

"How's my hot shot brother doing up there in the big apple?"

"Could be better," he answered, his voice dispirited. She could tell there was something wrong.

"You don't sound good. Talk to me."

"Where do I start?"

"Let's try the beginning."

"Alan's been brutal around the office, flying off the handle, impossible to deal with. Returns are down, and assets are leaving the company in droves. It's scary. We just lost the Texas Teacher's retirement plan; they had four hundred million dollars with us, and there's another few hundred million down there in local government pensions that will definitely follow them."

"I thought you had top money managers?"

"Listen sis, last year we returned twelve percent. I kept volatility to a minimum, did a great job, and received a good sized bonus. This year we took a small hit, but it's comical how people forget. Everyone wants double digit returns without any risk. Let them put their money in the bank for one percent. They're fantasizing; this business doesn't work that way."

"But Alan knows that. Is he blaming you?"

"The money managers report to me, so I'm saddled with their performance. In a good year, I'm Alan's fair haired boy, in a lousy year he looks at me as a liability, an expensive liability."

"Don't tell me he could be firing you. You've made him so much money."

"Not sure what he's thinking, or if he's even rational. He and Gordon had it out. I walked in on the tail end of a ballistic conversation you could hear at the other end of the office. I don't know what prompted it, but it was intense. I think they came to blows, and Alan got nailed."

"C'mon Jeremy, from what you told me, Gordon was always a thorn in his side."

"I know. He told him to pack his bags, and then cut him off.

But for whatever reason I think he regretted it, and maybe blames himself. I just know he's hurting, and seems I'm getting the brunt of it."

"That's so unfair. Why don't you leave the company and work somewhere else? With your credentials you'll find something in a heartbeat."

"I wish it were that simple. Alan's shrewd. He made me keep all my bonuses invested in the firm, so I own a percentage of AH Advisors. I would have done the same thing; always better to have your number two guy with money on the line. And if I leave, or he fires me for cause, I forfeit all of it. Besides, he pays me double what the market commands. He can kick me out and allege whatever he wants. I'm not looking for a lawsuit; my legal fees would cost me a small fortune."

"This sounds intense."

"Welcome to Wall Street, Vicky, it's all about the money."

"I feel your pain. Got any good news you'd like to share?"

Jeremy sighed, loud enough for her to hear.

"OK, what else is burdening you?"

"I think Susan's having an affair."

"No way, I don't believe it!"

"I can't prove it, but the truth is that I'm married to my work, fifteen-hour days, plus weekends; we only see each other by accident."

"Did you confront her?"

"Not yet, but she's been dropping some hints; not happy, feels abandoned, wants to wait to get pregnant. Between her, work, and Alan, I'm an emotional wreck."

"Jeremy, I'm worried about you. You need professional counseling, maybe some medication to calm you down. I'm here for you twenty-four seven, but this stuff is out of my league. If I could help I would, but...."

"You *can* help," he emphatically interjected.

"Tell me how," Victoria asked, depicting a sense of urgency.

"Alan is all revved up with biotech, been talking about it

incessantly. He figures that's where the big money will be made; the company that finds a cure for cancer, Alzheimer's, or…."

"ALS?" she finished his thought.

"It's all over the financial news, Vicky. No way is Merck investing twenty million into Whitcomb unless they already know something. Berger's been with them his whole life, and then he just leaves right before retirement? It doesn't make sense. Alan knows this guy and says he's beyond brilliant. If you read between the lines, there's more to this than just a long shot."

"So what are you getting at?"

"Alan's convinced that Berger will develop a potential cure for ALS, and then Whitcomb will go public, raising capital for all the FDA trials. Maybe the drug works, maybe it doesn't. It's a gamble. But it wouldn't hurt if we had some…."

"Inside information—you want me to be your spy?"

"You make it sound so nefarious."

"Jesus!"

"Listen to me, Vicky. I'm freaking out. My marriage is on the rocks and every nickel I have is invested in that firm. Just try to get yourself in a position where you know what's going on. And call me on a disposable cell phone, just in case, so the calls can't be traced. Maybe Alan's wrong about Whitcomb, but if he's right, this could work. And I promise you'll get your share, it'll benefit both of us. What's the balance on your student loan, a couple hundred grand? MIT isn't exactly a two year junior college."

Jeremy knew his sister was swimming in debt, and would love to wave a magic wand and make it go away.

"Do you realize what you're asking me to do? Of all people, I never thought…."

"I'm not asking, I'm pleading with you!"

There was no mistaking the desperation in his voice.

"I'm not sure."

"Goddamnit Vicky, I'm your brother!"

"And I'm your sister!"

"And what's your point?"

"My point is, I just started working for this Berger guy, and he makes me really uncomfortable, just the way he leers at me. And you're talking about insider trading and that means prison time, not something high up on the list of things I need to do before I die."

"Very funny, Vicky, don't be so paranoid. There are ways of camouflaging it; you just have to be smart about it."

"Let me think about it."

"OK, when will I hear from you?"

She didn't answer.

"Vicky? Vicky!" He thought she hung up on him.

"Stop screaming, Jeremy! I'm here, just thinking."

"Sorry, I'm on the verge."

"Stop with the drama. It won't help. This is a big decision, you'll hear from me, either way."

"Love you." Jeremy hung up the phone, hoping for a miracle.

Chapter 13

ON A HOT AND humid Tuesday—Labor Day morning—Gordon Howard started cleaning out his office, three days after he was officially canned from AH Advisors. He was alone, not another soul in sight.

His shelves were adorned with all his golf trophies, the walls conspicuous with his All-American and US Amateur plaques, and a few flattering framed newspaper clippings: *When Will Gordon Howard Turn Professional? Is Gordon Howard the Next Tiger?*

Some unflattering press was stuffed helter skelter into his bottom desk drawer, as if it was cherished trash he couldn't part with: *Gordon Howard, Too Rich to Go Pro? Gordon Howard, More Scared than Talented?*

He walked over to the window, reflecting on the person staring back at him. *Who was he?* Liz said it right; his father's whipping boy. But it was more than that. He couldn't cope with the undeniable truth, that he was psychologically dependent on his father's money. He was no different than a drug addict who tries to unshackle himself from his addiction, only to succumb to the syringe to narcotize his pain in an endless circle of failure.

He broke out in a cold sweat, shaking, besieged by a panic attack. Dazed, he haphazardly tossed his personal items into a canvas cart, dropping a pint-sized beer stein, a sentimental memento given to him from his college golf coach. The shattered glass sliced into his legs with a stinging pain. Blood oozed down his calves onto his ankles.

His mood darkened. He picked up a piece of glass and pressed it against his left wrist, feeling its sharp jagged edge as he rubbed it back and forth. He wasn't afraid; he had done it before. *But this time would be different.* Liz was entitled to an explanation. His father wasn't. He hunted for a pad and pencil. Curled up in the corner, he struggled with the words, oblivious to the torrent of tears that spotted the paper.

She knew where he was, and would eventually come looking for him. He wondered if his father would find him first. He picked up the glass and closed his eyes for the last time.

HE WAS IN A strange bed when he awoke. He looked around the room-it was small, stark, the cracked walls a putrid yellow from years of neglect. One lone window barred with prison like rods barely allowed any incoming light, which gave the room a dismal and dingy visage. An intravenous drip delivered blood directly into his punctured wrist. It felt warm. He could hear intermittent shouts of men screaming from the floor above.

A man dressed in a white hospital uniform entered the room.

"Where am I?" Gordon asked.

"You are safe now."

"How long have I been here?"

"Not long" the attendant answered. His voice sounded robotic, disinterested.

"How did I get here?"

"In an ambulance-your father found you lying on the floor in your office."

"Is he here?"

"Yes, in the hallway. He wants to see you."

"Is he upset with me?"

"I don't know" the man answered. "Should he be?"

"I'm not sure," Gordon answered him, accompanied by a deep sigh.

"You should ask him directly."

"Ok, send him in."

The attendant opened the door and peered outside into the hallway.

"Sorry, but he's gone."

The attendant left the room and closed the door. Gordon could read the bold lettering on the back of the man's white jacket-CSPH. He heard the unmistakable sound of the outside deadbolt locking the door shut, and then he knew- *he was back in the insane asylum, Creedmoor State Psychiatric Hospital.*

THE SUDDEN RINGING OF his cell phone startled him. He opened his eyes. He had fallen asleep and was sweating profusely from the surreal nightmare.

He let it go to voicemail as he listened to the message.

"Hey handsome, it's me- just checking up on you, must be a tough day. Don't shortchange yourself; it took a ton of guts to stand up to your father. I'm totally in your corner and we're going for a knockout, whatever it takes. Don't forget about our appointment downtown. Call me if you need some help, love you."

Ashamed of his cowardice and assuaged by her words, he hurled the suicide weapon across the room and ripped the note into shreds. He took one final look at his vacant office, with the vista of Central Park and beyond, leaving behind his dusty, empty desk, naked shelving, broken glass, and a bunch of bent picture hooks on the walls. He removed his gold name plate from the door and then shut it, for good.

Typically he would have paid some workmen from the building to do the dirty work, while he would *supervise*, but today he needed to do it all by himself. Wheeling the cart into the service elevator, he rode down to the basement, and unloaded his belongings into a rented U-Haul minivan.

The city was desolate, with most people away for the long weekend. He drove slowly out onto Madison Avenue, then North, past the gracious Polo mansion, stopping for an occasional jogger heading for Central Park.

He passed the Whitney Museum, their occasional weekend cultural getaway, where he and Liz would brunch downstairs at Sara Beth's Kitchen, followed by a walk through the park to the boathouse. Sometimes they just sat together on a park bench, soaking in some sun, people watching.

He turned right on Seventy-Eighth Street and passed the ten million dollar plus townhouses, then swung another right onto an empty Park Avenue. He stopped at Seventy-Fourth Street, and parked the van in front of his building.

The doorman came out to greet him. "Is everything OK, Mr. Howard, you look sad." Hector pointed to his bloody leg.

"I just need some help." Gordon opened the back of the van.

Hector knew something was very wrong, judging by the tone of Gordon's voice. "You want it in the second bedroom?"

Gordon faintly muttered, "uh huh," and then shoved a twenty dollar bill into Hector's shirt pocket.

"Thanks, Mr. Howard, and don't worry, I'll take care of it."

Gordon took out his cell phone and dialed Liz.

"Be right down, everything cool?"

"No."

"They say ninety-five this afternoon. Maybe I need to shed a few articles, if you can handle it," she said playfully, hoping to lift his spirits.

Gordon hadn't slept, shaved, or showered since that final blow up with his father, donning an old pair of ripped up shorts with a perspiration stained tee shirt, his grimy hands and fingernails caked with filth, and his hair dirty and unkempt.

He was sitting stone silent on the couch in the lobby when Liz joined him.

"Excuse me Sir, but do you live here? We don't particularly like vagrants." She yelled over to the concierge, "Hey Peter, there's some bum who's molesting me!"

"At least *you're* in a good mood," Gordon muttered, his shoulders slouched with his head buried in his hands.

"Look at me, goddamnit!"

He turned to her, his eyes watery, obvious he had been crying.

"Last time I saw you cry was when you three putted from ten feet."

He didn't laugh.

"Here, blow your schnoz into this." She stuffed a handful of Kleenex into his lap, allowing herself some playful rubbing.

"Want to open your fly? I can make you...."

Gordon jumped up. He knew she was capable of such shenanigans. Running away from her clutches, she chased after him into the street, laughing, and whistled for a cab. Opening the back door, she pushed him in, nestled close, and barked out "Fifty-Fifth and Tenth" as the cabbie sped away.

"We're getting through this Gordon, whether you like it or not-whatever it takes."

"I got your message." His voice, cracking, was barely above a whisper.

She took out two bottles of cold Poland Spring water from her knapsack, handed him one, and noticed the dried blood and the gashes on his legs.

"And FYI" she said, "most people who try to kill themselves slit their wrists," as she watered down some Kleenex and attended to his wounds.

He had never revealed to Liz the Creedmoor incident, although she had once asked about the scar, which he blamed on a childhood boating accident.

"CAN I HELP YOU?" A hefty middle aged man, his hairpiece slightly crooked, took his feet off the desk, got up from his chair, and shoved the *New York Post* under a pile of disheveled paperwork. "Kinda slow today, holiday weekend and all. Most of my type customers are out at their country homes with the family and the dogs."

"You must be Roberto, we spoke yesterday. I'm Liz, and this is my boyfriend, Gordon."

Roberto looked like a car salesman, if there was such a look, dressed in black trousers and a red shirt, his tie dotted with pictures of the company's newest models in all their splendiferous colors. He pointed to his official black Range Rover *Roberto Muniz* name tag affixed to his breast pocket and cast a smile, happy to see anyone breathing walk into the showroom.

"Yep, I remember, nice to meet you, follow me." They walked into the garage and stopped next to two 2006 Land Rovers Model LR3, one Tonga green, the other Zambezi silver, both with alpaca leather interior. Each was spotlessly cleaned inside and out; no nicks, scratches, dents or other evidence they were used vehicles.

"I like the silver, how about you, hon?" She tried to engage Gordon into some conversation.

Gordon just shrugged.

"No changes on our deal, right?"

Roberto nodded, somewhat dejectedly.

With the paperwork completed, Roberto talked up the extras; a GPS system, Bose speakers, side bars, bicycle rack, on and on, all met with a smile and a shake of her pretty head until he just cried uncle.

She acknowledged his persistence with a ten dollar bill, while Gordon maneuvered the car down the out ramp, the proud new lessee of a Zambezi silver *pre-owned* 2006 SUV with 65,346 grueling miles glaring at him from the odometer.

"I love it," Liz remarked, "so roomy and understated, and we can park it in the street. It's obscene what the garage charges, five hundred something a month plus eighteen percent tax. It's not like we're millionaires, hon."

Gordon didn't respond as he headed for the FDR Drive, playing with the dials, blasting the radio, feeling the response. The speakers were adequate, the acceleration decent, but nothing about this SUV approached his Range Rover SC sport coupe. He could live with it, considering the lease was a few hundred dollars a month, but the hassle of parking on the street was an issue.

"Liz, I can't deal without a garage. I mean I'm going out to the club every day and working on my swing, a ton of practice, not to mention all the local tournaments. If I can't beat the competition, I have zero shot. I don't need more aggravation with the goddamn parking."

Thank God, Liz thought, *at least he has a pulse.*

"That's a bunch of bull Gordon, and stop whining, you know how much that irritates me. Listen, you're now a member of what we call the working class. Just move the car before eight, go out to the club, put in a full day, and come home like the rest of us."

"Yeah, what if it rains? How about in the winter? If you think I'm gonna fight those animals for parking spots then...."

"Hold on a second. Doesn't that ridiculous club have a heated indoor driving range and a gym with every machine known to mankind? Maybe you haven't noticed, but you're getting a little paunchy right there." She poked her finger into his belly. "Every day is a work day, rain or shine, snow, sleet, or hail, I don't care. And that includes cardio and strength training. Who's that guy you like from Wisconsin, he practices all winter up there, Steve something?"

"Yeah, Steve Stricker, but he's an exception, I mean...."

"What's good for the goose is good for the gander, hot shot. Either you do it right, or don't do it at all. That's what we were taught, and if you think you're going to pick and choose your work schedule, I'm history."

He knew her well enough to understand the ultimatum. She had packed her bags before.

Gordon had no trouble finding a parking spot, which, if he understood the exceptions on the *No Parking* sign, was good until Thursday. Tomorrow would be his first day on the job, although he had to attend to some details in the morning, and speak to a perfect stranger who would change his life forever.

Chapter 14

GORDON SLEPT THROUGH THE night, aided by a cocktail of vodka and sleeping pills. He poured himself a cup of freshly brewed coffee, something Liz had always made before she left for work. *The Wall Street Journal* sat crisply unopened, which Liz had taken in from the hallway before 7:00 am, after which it usually disappeared.

He contacted the garage to cancel his reserved spot, and then called Leslie Arnoff, the club's comptroller.

"Well, Mr. Howard, this is something quite unusual here at Old Point, where a member comes in from their father and then decides to change their status. I have to call Bruce Haberman, the head of the admissions committee."

"Doctor Bruce Haberman, the eye surgeon?"

"Yes, how well do you know him? He joined the club just a few years ago."

Figures, just my luck, he thought, remembering how he had mocked him on the driving range.

"I met him once or twice, that's about it. Are you positive I need his approval? I mean my grandfather was a founding member, and my father was a past president, and I've been here...."

"I realize that, Mr. Howard," she interrupted him, "but rules are rules, and in a club like this everyone is treated the same. I know you understand."

"Geez, Leslie, I can't believe that...please call me back as soon as you get the info."

"Don't worry, Mr. Gordon, *Que sera,* whatever will be."

Gordon remembered the last time he had heard those words.

Shirley Fornelli used it, and mouthed "good luck" right before the brutal meeting with his father.

He poured himself another cup of coffee and perused *The Journal*. It appeared on page three; *Merck in Joint Venture with Upstart Biotech Company for ALS Cure.*

He read through the article and tracked down the telephone number for Whitcomb Pharmaceutical. A man answered the phone. "Norman Berger."

"Is this Mr. Berger?"

"Dr. Berger, and who are you?"

"You don't know me, my name is Gordon Howard. I read about you in *The Journal*, just wanted—"

"You're Alan Howard's son?"

"You know my father?"

"Unfortunately, and if you think I'm telling you anything more than I told him, then you can—"

"Dr. Berger, I had no idea you spoke to my father, I swear to you," Gordon said, eager to know why he was so incensed.

"I just hung up with him, actually hung up *on* him, snooping around for information. Just so you know, I can't stand the bastard, and if that offends you, then…."

"We don't get along, he's impossible to deal with, let alone work for. He canned me last week, right before the holiday, if that makes a difference."

"And your call is about what?"

"It's just that my grandfather died from ALS, I saw the article, and figured…."

"I got it; my father also had the goddamn disease."

"I know, it said so in the article. What's your problem with him? I have my own issues."

Norman seized the opportunity.

"I met your father at Penn. I was in a special scholarship program, studying neurodegenerative diseases. They say I have an aptitude for science and physics. I agree with them, but big deal, I would rather be born with a silver spoon, like you know who."

Gordon wasn't sure if Norman was including him with his telling comment about privilege.

"My parents were pharmacists, and what I received from Penn was a pittance. Your father heard I was some bright kid from the Bronx, knew I was living on scraps, and figured I would jump through hoops for enough money. It's not something I'm proud of, writing his papers and taking his exams for graduate school."

"Are you kidding me?"

"How about seventeen thousand, cash, sound about right?"

"I can't believe it."

"How the hell do you think he graduated Penn top of his class with honors and got into Columbia? And guess what?"

"What?"

"He stiffed me out of ten thousand dollars."

"That's terrible. I'll send you the money, no reason why you should get screwed like that."

"Forget it, water under the bridge. I have my funding, too busy to think about it. What goes around comes around, so they say."

Gordon wondered if this Berger guy was on the up and up, to use it as ammunition against his father. But a certain timbre in his voice said he wasn't lying. He planned to confront him, but not now, as officially they weren't speaking.

Norman changed the topic. "Alan told me you're trying to be a professional golfer."

"Not trying to be, I will be." Norman sensed some hostility in Gordon's retort.

"Do you play?"

"No, never had time, the game bores me. Your father gave me the scoop."

"He probably called me a lazy good for nothing, waste of talent, that kind of stuff. I heard it before."

"Not at all, he was bragging about you, said you were incredible, one of the best in the country. He told me to Google you, sounds very impressive."

"Are you serious, Dr. Berger? My father really said that about me?"

"Why wouldn't I be?"

Gordon choked up, and took a minute to gather his thoughts as the conversation came to an abrupt interlude. Deep down he wanted to make amends, but for some reason he wasn't ready.

"Are you there?" Norman asked, wondering what happened, thinking they were disconnected.

Gordon finally broke the silence. "It's a long story, Dr. Berger. I guess whatever you have with science, I have with golf. Just something I was born with, had some instruction, but basically self-taught. Could I be a pro, yeah, just takes a ton of work, and…."

Gordon hesitated, not quite sure why, until Norman reminded him.

"You don't have muscle memory, right? Isn't that the key, to repeatedly swing the club on the same plane, at least that's what I've been told?"

"How did you know that?" Gordon was perplexed, as the question came totally from left field.

"That's also a long story."

"Plane, arc, path, yeah, you're right, it's getting total control of your swing, and it's impossible, Dr. Berger. Nobody has that, close on a real good day, but perfection, never."

"Let me give you some advice, no charge."

"Sure, go ahead."

"Impossible is not in my vocabulary. I'm a scientist. Perhaps it's difficult, unlikely, farfetched, but never *impossible*."

Gordon was taken aback by Norman's assuredness. "Sorry, I like your thinking, just that I've played this crazy game for almost twenty years and I know that—"

"How much do these golfers earn?"

"Jesus Christ, Dr. Berger, I mean look at Tiger Woods with all those majors. Just on endorsements he was raking in a hundred million a year, before the whole sex scandal. It's ridiculous, but then again, he's phenomenal, nobody like him. He's a machine, with zero emotion; it's scary how good he is, best ever, no question."

Anyone breathing had heard about Tiger, even Norman, who made a note to verify what Gordon was all pumped up about.

"What are majors?"

"You know, the Masters, US Open, PGA, and British Open."

"If I knew, I wouldn't ask. I'm a scientist, not a golf addict."

"Well, for what it's worth, I'm rooting for you to find a cure, and appreciate your honesty."

"Email me your contact info to Berger@Whitcomb.com if you want me to stay in touch." Norman hung up the phone.

Gordon emailed Norman a brief thank you note. He didn't get a reply, at least not then.

NORMAN RECEIVED THE APOLOGY letter from Alan Howard a few days later, ripped it up, and deposited the check. He thought his motive was anything but gratuitous or apologetic. As far as he was concerned, Alan Howard was history.

Chapter 15

GORDON HAD JUST FINISHED emailing his contact info to Norman Berger when his phone rang.

"Hello."

"Mr. Howard, please."

"You have the wrong number, bozo."

"Mr. Gordon Howard."

"You got him, who's this?"

"Dr. Bruce Haberman."

Damnit, how could he be so stupid!

"Sorry, Dr. Haberman, I thought it was for my father."

Bruce Haberman knew some of the details, having spoken to Alan Howard over the weekend—one of the few people he liked.

"I understand you're interested in becoming a member. As of now, your privileges have been cancelled."

Gordon hated to kiss ass, except in emergencies.

"Yes sir, I understand the situation. I spoke to Leslie who I've known for—"

"How old are you, Mr. Howard?"

"I just turned thirty, Dr. Haberman."

"For young married couples in your age bracket, admission is a hundred fifty thousand dollars. You'll need to fill out an application, supply references, and show evidence of your charitable contributions. Somebody on the admissions committee will come to your home. We want to see how you live, make sure you and your wife are suitable for our membership."

Gordon was inwardly ticked off- *suitable for our membership?*

"I'm not married, but I have a partner, a significant other."

Haberman bristled. He thought the partner reference was a cheap shot, a low blow. "You have something against gay men, Mr. Howard?"

Gordon didn't know that Haberman had a son, or that he was gay, or where this discussion was going.

"I have no idea what you're talking about, Dr. Haberman. I'm trying to be respectful, and quite frankly, I've been at that club too long and know the rules, and would appreciate if you didn't make this anymore difficult for me than it already is."

Haberman breathed a sigh of relief, thankful his son's sexual persuasion was still under wraps.

"I'll have Leslie send you the application. And since you were a former member, we're less stringent—fifty thousand dollars, payable in full, no installments. Yearly dues are seventeen thousand, club storage is five hundred, monthly assessments four fifty, and your dining room minimum is two thousand. She gets all privileges for an extra three hundred a year."

"Why do I have to fill out an application?"

"Because I said so, that's why. You need to learn a little respect son, it'll get you a lot further in life, assuming that's one of your ambitions."

"Let's do this," Gordon replied, holding back his anger. "There's no sense in making this into a federal case. Save the club the postage. I'll come out, fill out the application, and write a check for the fifty thousand."

"OK, Mr. Howard, just see Leslie, but no privileges until we have—"

"Understood, Dr. Haberman, I know the drill."

Gordon grabbed his checkbook, called the garage for his car, and got into a shouting match with the attendant. Then he realized his mistake. *It's parked on the street!*

He slammed his front door shut and banged on the elevator button, ran through the lobby past the concierge and over the two blocks where the Land Rover was parked. He reached into his pocket.

"Damn it!" He forgot his car keys.

He sprinted back to his building, impatiently waiting for the lethargic elevator. Rummaging through his apartment, he fished around for the keys. *Got 'em!*

The elevator was sitting in the lobby. *Figures!* He bolted down the twenty flights of stairs, stomped out the front door, hustled to the car, turned on the ignition, took a deep breath, and he was gone.

EXACTLY EIGHTEEN MINUTES LATER he arrived in front of the club portico, normally a good half hour ride. The valet parked his car in the visitor's area while he rushed up the stairs to the accounting office.

"Well that was quick, Mr. Howard, I heard you're going to be a professional golfer, like Tiger."

Leslie Arnoff was a fixture at the club, a spinster and professional yenta who knew everyone's business, thriving on gossip—most of which she started, or certainly encouraged—anything to spice up a boring job and mundane life.

"What's with the hard time, Leslie? You know the rules around here."

"Look, Mr. Howard, we go way back, your whole family. May your grandfather rest in peace; such a wonderful man, such a horrible death, terrible, just so terrible."

Leslie Arnoff had a way of avoiding the topic at hand by reminiscing about the old days.

"They should find a cure for that ASL thing. All the money we waste in this country, it's a shame, and you know my sister's husband's brother had…."

Gordon had heard this story too many times; she just loved to hear herself yak.

"It's ALS, Leslie."

"ASL or ALS, what's the difference, such a nice man your grandfather."

Gordon wrote out the fifty thousand dollar check and handed it to her.

"You know it's not my business, but Dr. Haberman, he's got it in for you, something last week over at the range. He was pissing and moaning. I tried to let him know you were a long and upstanding member, with your family and all, but he wouldn't listen. You want to tell me what happened? You know me, I would never—"

Gordon wasn't listening. "Where's the application?"

"OK Mr. Howard, I told Dr. Haberman there's no application. He's confused, but I straightened him out. You want me to give you the same account number, H-3? Your father is H-2 and your grandfather was H-1, and then when you have a son…."

Gordon rolled his eyes. "I'd like a new account number and a new locker, in the old section, away from my father."

"Well you know having one of those new fancy wood lockers, there's a waiting list, and I mean people have to die or quit, I wouldn't be so hasty with—"

"Just set it up, I'll get used to it. Gotta run, let Danny know, he'll switch everything over for me."

Gordon walked out, minus fifty thousand dollars, but with a bundle more worth of self-respect. He headed for the locker room, changed into his golf shoes, then marched straight out to the range, where he beat balls until his hands hurt, his first day on the job.

He was unaware of a lone spectator perched on a grassy knoll at the far end of the driving range. Swifty watched with more than a keen interest, silently rooting that Gordon wouldn't buckle under the weight of his demons.

It was late when Gordon returned to the men's locker room to change into his moccasins, tossing his golf shoes onto the floor so Danny knew they needed to be cleaned.

"You won't find them there, GH, I already moved you, back in the old section, with the rats and the roaches, huh."

Danny stood at the end of the row with a basket full of dirty

REVENGE OF THE GOLF GODS

towels, wearing that unmistakable grin; his front teeth all crooked and chipped, others were missing, his bushy eyebrows moving up and down as he scratched his salt and pepper beard and twiddled with his moustache.

"So you think it's funny?"

"I got the scoop, GH. You know what, if you want my two cents, you should've got the monkey off your back ten years ago. But hell, it's better late than never, huh?"

"Yeah I agree, hate to admit it."

"Follow me, sport. I'm gonna show you what a real locker room looks like, huh." Danny enjoyed a good hearty laugh. He walked among the maze of aisles through an old creaky door and into the remaining remnant of the original men's locker room. The club had plans to upgrade it, but until then Gordon considered it second class; cold, dreary, and musky.

"Here we go, GH. I moved everything over, nice and clean and organized, just the way you like it, huh." Danny opened the metal locker, beaming, as if he did Gordon a huge favor. "I'm proud of you, GH, real proud, huh."

Gordon sucked it up. He knew Danny was rooting for him. He changed into his street shoes, while Danny finished cleaning up from the day.

THAT EVENING OVER DINNER, Chinese food take -out, he recapped his day with Liz, a good listener.

"Do you believe this Berger guy? You think Alan would actually pay him to take his exams? That's outright cheating, Gordon, your self-righteous father, of all people."

"Probably, but I have a funny feeling that eventually it's all coming out in the wash."

Gordon took a healthy bite out of his egg roll and washed it down with a Heineken. The food was cold. He scooped it up; shrimp fried rice, General Tso chicken, and beef chow mein.

"I got it." Liz shoved the plate into the microwave and set it for three minutes.

"I'm totally into it. I feel great about what happened. Get ready for a new and improved Gordon Howard, on and off the course."

"How about in the bedroom?" she asked seductively.

"Got any complaints?"

"Not yet, but you'll be the first to know."

"And by the way, guess who found a great parking spot—good until 8:00 a.m. tomorrow morning." Gordon beamed proudly.

"Kiss me you lunatic," she laughed as they embraced, interrupted by the microwave announcing the food was sizzling hot.

Chapter 16

WITH THE STUNNING ANNOUNCEMENT of the Merck investment, Norman quickly spread the word, enticing potential candidates with employee ownership. Resumes poured in by the truckload, most of which he shredded.

The rumor mills abounded about the weird looking mad scientist who had finagled control of Whitcomb Pharmaceutical without investing a red cent of his own money, and then somehow convinced Merck to pony up twenty million dollars.

Interviews were grueling. He pounded away, hurling hypothetical scenarios, demanding logical, well-reasoned solutions, forcing them to defend their position—*why, what if, suppose, assuming*—peering into their minds with his own brand of high powered microscope.

THEY SAT AROUND THE conference table, ten superstars, five men and five women, his handpicked esprit de corps. They were all casual in shorts and tee shirts, all in their late twenties, all Ivy League brainiacs, none romantically involved. The room was surrounded by a solid wall of whiteboards; a banner, NOTHING IS IMPOSSIBLE, hung conspicuously from the ceiling.

Norman addressed them. "Let's start from the beginning. I'm not married and don't have any friends. My age doesn't matter, but Google me and you'll figure it out. I prefer to be alone listening to classical music on the radio. I'm legally blind and need a magnifying glass to read. The glass in my frames is thick enough to be bulletproof. I've heard the snide remarks all my life, some new ones when I came here; freak, mad scientist, weird, idiot savant, just to name a few—nothing I didn't expect. For all I know, some are dead on accurate."

They laughed accordingly, breaking the pent up tension.

"What you went through to get here will seem like a walk in the park. I'm a tough sonafabitch and demand perfection. I'm not on a power trip and have no axe to grind because of *this*," Norman said, as he turned around and displayed his deformed hunched back, prompting a noticeable rumbling.

"My father was buried with ALS. I promised him on his death-bed I would find a cure. I never promise what I can't deliver. I left Merck because I refused to sign their non-disclosure agreement. Rumors are I was flat out fired. Either way, I don't give a damn."

A low murmur filled the room.

"Stupid I'm not, greedy I am. I could've stayed and lived a comfortable life, but what I have here," Norman tapped his head, "is worth multiple fortunes. So what's in it for you other than fourteen-hour days, an airtight non-disclosure agreement, and an onerous employment contract?"

The brainiacs were dead silent with anticipation.

"Assuming your performance is stellar," Norman looked out over the crew, "stock options worth millions when we go public and the goddamn drug is FDA approved!"

The brainiacs hooted and hollered in a sea of approbation.

Victoria Chang raised her hand.

"You have a question?"

"You mentioned stock options, will that be in writing?"

"It's part of your employment agreement."

"And how is *my* performance measured?" she batted her eye-lashes, a wide grin revealing a perfect set of pearly whites.

She seemed to be toying with him, displaying a flirtatious pout, which everyone noticed.

"Let me be perfectly clear, Miss Chang, no misunderstandings. This is a team effort, sink or swim. One bad link can undermine the process. I've been in this business for too many years. I know what works, and manage accordingly. It gets results. You may not like it, but I call the shots. So if I bruise your sweet little ego in front of your colleagues, just suck it up, or you know where the door is. You got it?"

"Yes Sir," she answered obediently, knowing when to back off.

"And one more warning" Norman continued, scouring the room, settling on Victoria Chang, "your hormones stay out of the laboratory. Office romances of any persuasion are a recipe for disaster. They cloud judgment, invite jealousy, and detract from the battle. I won't tolerate it, understood?"

"Yes Sir!" they answered loudly and in unison.

"See me about your agreements, take them home, read and sign them. They're not negotiable. If that's a problem, good luck in your career."

Norman felt justifiably paranoid, sitting on a multi-billion dollar coup. With the brainiacs privy to sensitive proprietary information, the NDA demanded total secrecy and tight security, with emails permitted only between colleagues, and no documents allowed off premises.

Chapter 17

By mid November, Old Point Country Club resembled a ghost town. The snooty members headed south to their winter homes at the first hint of cold weather. A handful of diehards played on weekends as long as their hands wouldn't freeze. The dining room remained open with a reduced staff.

Charlie Evans was in his shop early, packing up boxes of unsold merchandise, taking inventory of the equipment he couldn't sell. Charlie stocked mostly Taylor Made irons, hybrids, and metal woods, which he could exchange for whatever new and hyped up models the company unveiled for the next season.

"Hey pro, what's the good word?"

"I'm winding things down, GH, have some nice Polo turtlenecks. It gets chilly in that practice shed, even with the heat on full blast. I'll do you seventy-five percent off list, below my cost."

"How much are they?"

In the old days Gordon would have bought them in every color at full price, no questions asked. He still had at least a dozen, some never worn, stacked in his metal locker.

"I retail them for a hundred, so figure twenty-five bucks each, take six and I can do twenty."

"OK, pro, done deal, half a dozen, smalls, no pink or red, thanks."

"Liz is a lucky girl, bet the red would look great on her, more of a crimson color."

"No thanks, neutrals, black, white, gray...."

"I got it, GH, want me to stick them in your locker?"

"Nope, gift wrapped, need a card with an envelope. Bill them to my account; they gave me a new number."

Charlie knew all the details, having heard the story from the blabbermouth, Leslie Arnoff.

"Yep, it's right here in my computer, GH."

Gordon wrote out a note and handed it to Charlie. "And by the way, thanks for letting me use the Sony, it's much appreciated."

As for turning professional at this stage, Charlie would have bet the ranch that Gordon had two chances, slim and none. Not that he would discourage him, but the guys who couldn't get their tour cards would eat Gordon alive, that's how ridiculously good the competition was.

"No problem, GH, you know what to work on. I'm around if you want my two cents, no charge. What's the plan, other than pounding balls six hours a day? How's Palm Beach gonna survive? You were a fixture there."

Gordon had spent every winter there for the past eight years in a rented beachside condominium, playing golf with wealthy investors at the snooty Palm Beach Country Club. Alan was a full member, which gave Gordon golf privileges.

When he hooked up with Liz it worked out well, flying her down weekends and holidays, always first class. She resented it, seeing no reason to squander an extra thousand dollars for a two hour trip.

In time the routine became stale, not that Palm Beach was a prison sentence. But her career was a priority, and his cavalier lifestyle a major pet peeve. She eventually stopped the weekend jaunts, preferring the eclecticism of the city to the pretense of the Palm Beach crowd.

Now they were a real working couple, which suited her just fine.

"Pro, those days are over. Gotta hop, local tournaments start end of April, will stay in touch."

Gordon grabbed the box of wrapped turtle necks and double timed to the range.

It was uncannily mild for a week before Thanksgiving. Autumn came late; the foliage still glistened through the morning sun with the autumnal hues of gold, rust, and crimson. Gordon loved the unique beauty of the course. It was an arborist's dream, boasting thousands of trees of different species; red maples, pink and white dogwoods, cherry blossoms, catalpa, and tulip trees. Groves of majestic sycamores framed the fairways and greens.

"Mornin' Mr. Gordon, I got you all set up with the Sony and cleaned up your clubs. What are we workin' on today?"

"First things first, Swifty, I figured you'll need these." Gordon handed him the gift box.

"This is for me, Mr. Gordon?"

Swifty never received any gifts, other than a few bucks tip after a caddy round, and the new high top sneakers he was wearing, the ones Gordon paid for. He delicately removed the gold foil as if it were valuable, opened the box and peered inside. He pulled back the wrapping paper and deftly opened the envelope.

Swifty,

You're going to need these. We have a lot of work to do. I can't afford for you to catch pneumonia. And by the way, starting today, I want you to call me GH.

Enjoy, you deserve them.

Your friend,
Gordon

"Go ahead, try one on for size. I like that dark green, looks cool with your gray hair, same color I'm wearing today."

Swifty removed his tattered sweater, which Gordon promptly tossed into the trash. At five foot four, rail thin, the fit was perfect. He pulled it over his head, rubbing his hands over the fine pima cotton, accompanied by a wide, toothless grin.

Gordon pounded out two large pyramids of balls, one with his woods, and the other with his irons. He was working on his reverse wrist cock, at times stopping midway to examine the position of the club, adjusting his feet, fine tuning his swing. An errant shot produced the usual profanities, some tossed clubs, anger, and self-disparagement.

Swifty recorded every swing, moving around to catch different angles.

The sky turned cloudy as the wind picked up.

"Hey, Swifty, let's go take a look."

"Sure thing, Mr. Gordon, sorry, I mean GH; I just gotta get me used to it."

Swifty hoisted Gordon's bag onto his shoulder and led the way to Charlie's indoor teaching facility. He placed the cassette into the video machine, allowing Gordon to watch each swing in slow motion on a monitor, all superimposed against straight lines representing the theoretically perfect spine angle, shoulder and club plane.

Gordon knew that no touring professional ever consistently attained such perfection.

Swifty went through several hundred swings, stopping and starting on command, which Gordon analyzed, like a radiologist looking for a tiny abnormality, jotting down notes in his daily log.

"Hey, Swifty, it's getting close to three, how about we grab some lunch and talk strategy?"

Swifty reached into his back pocket and pulled out a baloney sandwich on white bread, wrapped in a napkin.

"I can wait for you here, GH, go on up to the clubhouse, take your time."

"C'mon, Swifty, you're eating with me, but we need to spiff you up a bit first."

He followed Gordon into the pro shop. Charlie was just finishing up for the day, and didn't notice them at first.

"Hey pro, can you fix up my man Swifty here with some corduroys?"

Charlie turned around, aghast, ashen white, as if he had seen a ghost, a black ghost.

"GH, you got a minute, something I need...."

"He's my guest, Charlie."

"Hey Swifty, you know the rules, no caddies allowed in the pro shop. I could get fired...."

"Screw the rules, Charlie. If he has to resign as a caddy to enter these hallowed grounds, then fine. He's my responsibility, you're off the hook. It's not like its July 4th weekend- this place is dead."

"Yeah I understand, GH, but I never know when some cheap bastard looking for a bargain will pop in."

"C'mon pro, stick your neck out once in a while and challenge convention, it's good for the soul, might even fix your putting yips."

Charlie just smirked, not quite sure how to answer. "They're stacked over in the corner, fish through them for the right size."

Gordon thanked him as they walked over to the pile of Ralph Lauren pleated and cuffed corduroy pants, sifting through the sizes, pulling out four colors; black, tan, dark green and anthracite, a fancy term for gray.

Swifty started to undress right down to his grungy shorts, until Gordon stopped him and pointed to the men's dressing room.

"Fuck!" Gordon blurted out, loud enough for Charlie to hear, as an unwanted visitor walked into the shop.

"Hey, Dr. Haberman, I'm just closing down for the season."

"Mind if I look around, need some last minute things. Final sale is still on, right?"

Haberman and Gordon hardly acknowledged each other, while Charlie sweated bullets, knowing Haberman would revel in seeing Swifty prance around the shop trying on new duds.

"Better if you stop by tomorrow, Dr. Haberman, running late for my kid's football game and—"

"Tomorrow I'm in surgery all day," his crystal clear tone implying he would do as he pleased.

"Goddamnit, GH!" Charlie whispered emphatically under his breath. "It's my ass, not yours. Get me out of this mess!"

"Relax, pro, it's all under control. Swifty stays in the dressing room until Haberman leaves. He gets his corduroys and a new belt. Bill everything to me. We wouldn't want Swifty making an unnecessary appearance, and then…."

Charlie knew he was smack dab in the middle of a potential catastrophe, with Swifty a political football.

"Ok GH, just make him disappear, let me work on Haberman."

"Hey Swifty, do me a solid and hang out in the cubicle for a few minutes."

"Sure GH, I understand," Swifty replied, his head drooping dejectedly, the brief interlude a telling reminder of his station in life, a lowly caddie, a second class citizen, a consequence not of his choosing, but of the mysterious and unpredictable hand of fate, at times cruel and unfair.

Haberman wouldn't leave, checking every piece of merchandise, comparing the final marked down price, just biding his time.

"Dr. Haberman, I'm closing, last day is Friday." Charlie turned off the lights and locked the outside door. Haberman got the message and walked back into the clubhouse in a huff.

"Hey, Swifty, c'mon out, coast is clear."

Emerging from the cubicle, Swifty took one long look in the full length mirror, admiring the black wide whale corduroy with a green turtleneck adorned with the Polo horse. Gordon whistled and applauded, while Swifty imitated some cool Michael Jackson moves.

Charlie bagged the other three pair of corduroys. With a new Kenneth Cole leather belt and his high top Nike black sneakers, Swifty felt like a million bucks. Gordon and his guest headed for the men's grill.

Gordon laughed to himself, trying to imagine Charlie's horror when he found Swifty's filthy old pants with the baloney sandwich stuffed in the back pocket.

Chapter 18

THE MEN'S GRILL WAS surprisingly busy for off season, with no shortage of curious, murmuring onlookers, especially one, as they walked through and sat at Gordon's favorite table. Laurie Dawson immediately came over, not quite sure what to make of the situation.

"He's my guest, Laurie, any problem?"

"No sir, Mr. Howard, I just need, uh, I mean the rule, uh, you know that we, uh."

Laurie wasn't one to get easily rattled.

"You need my guest's name?"

"Yes," she answered.

"Swifty," Gordon replied, his tone serious.

"Does Mr. Swifty have a last name?"

Gordon had no idea of Swifty's real name.

"My name is Johnson William Franklin," he spoke proudly.

Laurie wrote the name on the chit and summoned for the waiter.

"Enjoy your lunch, Mr. Howard." She scurried away.

The waiter handed each a menu, asked if they would like something to drink.

"Can I get me some bourbon, GH?"

"Sure, on the rocks or with a twist?"

"Nope, I want just bourbon, straight up."

"One bourbon for Mr. Franklin, I'll have a Heineken on draft, real cold."

"Yes sir," the waiter said as he scampered over to the bar.

Swifty was visibly intimidated by the opulence of the men's grill, slumping down in his chair, afraid to be noticed.

Gordon sensed his largesse made his guest uncomfortable, a stark reminder that the rich are different. He knew Swifty would sleep in a rundown shack on the other side of the tracks, patently unfair or unlucky, but unfortunately the truth. And it bothered the hell out of him.

"Take a look at the menu, have whatever looks good. The burgers are awesome, or grab a bowl and we can hit the buffet."

"Whatever, I ain't fussy, GH, just hungry."

The waiter brought over the drinks.

Swifty took a good healthy gulp. "Now this has got to be the *smoothest* damn bourbon I ever tasted, GH," flashing a wide grin of appreciation.

Swifty was a bourbon man, had a few every night, the generic brand. Dinner was a slice or two of pizza, a big Mac, whatever was cheap and filling. He would wake up early, always the first caddy at the course in the morning. Two loops put two hundred dollars cash in his pocket. After September he was lucky to get one loop a week, and just worked odd jobs, made a few bucks here and there, until the new season started.

"There's a telephone call for you, Mr. Howard," the waiter came over, "you can pick it up at the bar."

Gordon suddenly felt anxious. He hoped Liz was OK. He wondered; *could it be my father?*

"Be right back."

Swifty had a funny feeling about the call.

Gordon picked up the phone. It was Laurie Dawson.

"Sorry to disturb you, Mr. Howard. I don't want to start a ruckus, but some of the members have already complained to me that caddies are not permitted in the clubhouse."

"That's their problem, Laurie," he replied angrily. "He's here as my guest, who just happens to be a caddie. It's more than that, believe me."

"I understand the dilemma, Mr. Howard. I've been at this club for fifteen years, and I've never been put in this position. I can't afford to lose my job, it's so upsetting."

Laurie Dawson started to sob.

The more she cried the more incensed Gordon became, not at her, but at the holier than thou limousine liberals, the phony multimillionaires with beaucoup bucks who pay lip service to the poor and the underprivileged, the guys who toss the Swiftys of the world an extra ten spot tip and expect them to bow in gratitude, all just a balm for their conscience.

"Who said something, that bastard Haberman?"

"Mr. Howard, I'm begging you, please don't make me compromise my position. You'll force me to quit before I give you any names."

He had never heard her sound so distressed. "OK, Laurie, calm down. You're too valuable, and dealing with these people is a giant pain in the butt. But understand that it's my privilege to invite my friend Mr. Franklin to lunch. He's perfectly attired, not rowdy, drunk, smoking pot, or eating with his hands, and has feelings just like anyone else."

"I understand, Mr. Howard, you make me laugh."

"So as a fair compromise, he won't be going to the buffet and prancing around the room. I'll keep it real low key, and we'll be out of Haberman's face as quickly as you can fire up those cheeseburgers and cottage fries."

"Medium rare, Mr. Howard?"

"You know how I like it, Laurie."

"Thank you, and by the way, just between you and I?"

"I'm listening."

"I can't stand the bastard either!" She burst into laughter, and Gordon cracked up, the heartiest laugh they each had in a long time.

"I GOT A SNEAKY suspicion you got yourself a problem with me, GH," Swifty remarked, as Gordon returned to the table.

"How's that, Swifty?"

"Listen, I'm no road schooler, but I know people, and that there call was about me. But lemme tell you somethin', there ain't any reason to get yourself in a dander with these folks. Truth is that I don't feel comfortable here. I don't belong, just like you don't belong in my world. It's just the way life is. We all have our places, our own way of doin things, of gettin' by. But to tell you the truth, I been caddyin' at this club long as I can remember, and I never seen more fucked up people than I seen here."

"You mean *Rhodes Scholar*, dude."

Sharing a laugh, Swifty polished off his bourbon while Gordon chugged down his Heineken. He signaled for the waiter to bring them a refill, who quickly came over with the drinks and set the lunch platters down.

Swifty doused his food with ketchup and mustard, then unabashedly took a gigantic bite of the burger, shoving a bunch of cottage fries into his mouth, and washing it down with the bourbon, while Laurie Dawson looked from afar, as did Bruce Haberman.

JOHNSON WILLIAM FRANKLIN WAS on the cusp of turning sixty, but his demeanor suggested a man considerably older. Years of two packs a day killer non filter cigarettes had affected his heart. His daily regimen of walking the course probably prevented an early burial. Without medical insurance, he was fortunate a few good samaratin physicians at the club tried to keep him in somewhat decent health.

He spoke with a throaty, raspy voice, noticeably huffing and puffing when walking uphill, at times stopping to catch his breath. Gordon had convinced him to stop smoking, but the irreversible damage had been done.

His step was a few paces slower these days, but he could still read greens with the precision of an eye surgeon. He was blessed with the uncanny ability to figure the yardages to the pin, unduly confident in his club selection, accounting for the wind, terrain, and lie, and most importantly, the adrenaline pumping through Gordon's system.

Swifty liked to bet on the majors; the PGA, the Masters, and the US Open. He would wager a few bucks on long shots, the underdogs nobody ever heard of. He identified with them; they were kindred souls. It gave him a rooting interest in the tournament and a respite from the daily grind at Old Point. He had a friend in Las Vegas who had the inside track on the odds and placed Swifty's bets.

Gordon knew about it, and over the years all of Swifty's gambling money came from Gordon's pocket, who considered it a charitable donation.

Swifty's wagered fifty dollars in the 1991 PGA Championship, betting on an unknown Arkansas pro named John Daly, whose 300-plus yard drives brought the difficult Crooked Stick golf course to its knees. At odds of 100-1, Swifty pocketed a cool $5,000. Gordon was happy for him. He never won another bet.

"Listen, GH, I gotta ask you a question, somethin' I been thinkin' about."

"Sure, Swifty, what is it?"

"Maybe it ain't my business, but why you wanna do this?"

"Do what?"

"Leavin' your father the way you did and goin' out on your own. That's a whole lot of money you walkin' away from. Everybody at this damn club knows what happened. Don't you think you takin' a big risk, least that's how I see it? What you gotta do is look real deep inside, cause if what you're doin is just to give your old man a kick in the ass, then I don't want no part of it. And don't think I'm not appreciatin' what you do for me, but I ain't a charity case. I'll bust my hump for you, GH, but we gotta be on the same page."

Gordon had to think about the question, which was unexpected.

"Well, GH, what you thinkin?"

"I'm doing this for *me*," Gordon shot back, poking his finger firmly into his chest. "My father is history, get it?"

Swifty knew when to back off. But he suspected there was more to it than Gordon revealed.

"You want me full time, then I'm your man, unless Tiger comes huntin' for me."

"Or you go hunting for Tiger."

"I ain't the safari type, GH." Swifty beamed proudly at his clever quip.

"Picture us walking down the eighteenth fairway of the US Open, the crowd roaring after I drill a six iron fifteen feet below the hole, with you at my side, toting my big bad Wilson Staff bag, sporting my Titleist cap, freaking millions glued to their TV sets, and two putts to win."

"Yeah, I can see it, GH, but more important, we gotta do our deal."

Gordon was prepared. Swifty wasn't stupid, at least as to the way life worked.

"How about two thousand a month, cash, plus ten percent of my winnings."

Swifty took a hefty gulp of his bourbon and rubbed his chin, assessing Gordon's offer. "I make that much now in a season, and have nobody lookin' over my shoulder. And unless you the next John Daly, then I need better odds, twenty percent."

"Hey, stop with the bull!" Gordon replied, seemingly miffed. "Either you believe in me or you don't. The way I see it, it's the last chance for both of us, and anytime you want to call it quits, there's always Mrs. Birnbaum, old man Shapiro, and all the other hackers to pay your bills."

If there was anything Swifty hated, it was caddying for a bunch of octogenarians who took six hours to traipse feebly around the course, making certain every ball was properly putted out, pestering him for accolades. He could hear it in his sleep, pure torture.

Now that last shot was a nice one, Swifty, don't you think?

Yes, Mrs. Birnbaum, just like I'd been tellin' you, you gotta keep your head down and swing easy.

"Listen, GH, I always been honest with you. Do I think you're gonna win the US Open? I'll be kind and say you're a long shot. I'm all hopped up cause you finally gettin' out from under your old man's shadow. Every man gotta find his own way in this damn life, and it make no difference what he does, long as he's honest with himself. And if totin' your bag is gonna push you to be your own person, to find whatever you're lookin' for, then I know I done a good deed."

The tone of Swifty's voice suddenly turned more serious. "You gotta promise me we gonna hit the gym every day, GH. You gettin' flabby in the belly and you ain't as long as you used to be. These kids got youth and power, three hundred yard drives ain't a big deal, and that there is with a damn three wood. You ain't a spring chicken no more. You gotta work on your stamina, your legs, build them muscles, cause without that, we're both wastin' time."

Gordon knew Swifty was right. Liz had needled him about his abs losing their tone, the beginning of some unattractive flab. He never had a weight problem, and had always avoided the gym. But he was losing distance as he aged, and knew that things needed to change quickly if he wanted to compete.

"And this business of cussin' after you messes up, throwin' your damn clubs, actin' like a spoiled brat. There ain't perfect in this game, and you're not a damn machine, somethin' you gotta learn. Maybe you got game, but not between the ears, not yet. You were better on the range today, but it's a different story on the damn course. I'm gonna calm you down, get your head in the right spot, no extra charge."

"I totally understand," Gordon replied sincerely.

"And one more thing you gotta know, GH."

"What?"

"I got no kinfolk anymore, just me and this club. And don't think I don't trust you, but business and friendship sometimes can be like oil and water, so...."

"Our deal is in writing, strictly by the book. Give me a few days to work on it, and then read it over, make sure it's Kosher."

Swifty wrote down his full legal name, address, telephone number, and *twenty percent* on the back of a chit, then handed it to Gordon, who gave it a quick glance, and made a mental note about how to structure a fair deal.

"You gonna need that for our contract, GH. Then I'm gonna

officially offer my resignation. I guess they're gonna be some people upset with me, cause I been totin' bags forever at this damn place, and I seen them come and go. All these people been dependin' on me to give em the right club, to rake the traps smooth, to find them balls that they hit into the woods, to read their putts, to fix them divots so the grass grows back right, to clean their clubs and put on their head covers before they get lost. That's why they nicknamed me Swifty, cause I take what I do real seriously, and I don't waste any time during the round."

Swifty turned silent, just nursed his drink, and stared out into space. "And I ain't eatin' in this fancy place again. Please don't take offense. It's just better that way. We can't afford any distractions."

They shook hands and clanged their glasses.

Swifty signed the agreement a week later and then, after forty some years toting bags at Old Point Country Club, he resigned for good. But nobody seemed to care that he was gone, as if he never mattered, and he spent that evening alone comforted by a friend, a bottle of cheap bourbon.

Chapter 19

WHITCOMB PHARMACEUTICAL WAS HUMMING ahead of schedule like a finely tuned Swiss watch.

In late October, ten transgenic rats harboring a mutant human gene developed ALS like phenotypes, including motor neuron degeneration in the spinal cord.

The brainiacs, with the rats under anesthesia, dissected specific regions of the nervous system. The chemical composition of the rat tissue samples was uncannily similar to historical studies on corpses of ALS victims, in most cases identical.

All the rodents were moved into Norman's private lab, each placed into a locked cage and fed with food and water through an intravenous drip.

After one month, the rats exhibited ALS type symptoms; muscular twitching, abnormal gait in their hind limbs, reflex impairment, and bronchial shortness of breath. After two months, these symptoms had regressed to complete paralysis in both limbs and paws, with extreme difficulty in breathing.

The brainiacs were given a well-deserved three-day respite. They bolted out of town, except for Victoria Chang, who sensed that Norman was working on something super important, and let him know she would be in on Friday and around for the weekend, all but screaming in his ear that she was available.

Norman administered the medicine through the intravenous drip. Now all he could do was to wait until Monday morning, the requisite time for the cure to either take effect, or the rats would be stone cold dead.

HE WASN'T SURPRISED SHE accepted his dinner invitation, although couched as, "we need to go over some details about your rat," was not exactly brimming with romance. It wasn't such a big deal for the boss to take out a valued employee. Besides, he was entitled to a few hours of relaxation, to forget about the rodents, and who better to spend it with than the woman who fired up his twisted fantasies.

Triangle Café, the only decent Italian restaurant in the complex, was her suggestion. It catered to an older clientele, with its soft lighting, mood music, colorful posters, friendly ambience, and modest prices. A small and intimate setting, people could talk and get to know each other over a leisurely dinner with a bottle of Italian wine.

Norman sat at a corner table, wearing a black turtle neck sweater and black dungarees, new for the occasion, trying to look somewhat high tech or conservative cool, his hunched back flush against the wall.

She arrived twenty minutes late. "Sorry, Dr. Berger, I wasn't sure about the perfume. Here, do you like it?"

Victoria Chang bent down close to him to expose her soft neck, allowing Norman to sample her scent, her blouse half unbuttoned, the light thankfully adequate for him to admire her perky breasts.

"Call me Norman, please." He felt a stirring in his loins.

"Well, Norman?" she asked playfully.

"Well what, Miss Chang?"

"Vicky, please," she smiled, his mind racing.

"OK, Vicky," he responded, forgetting the question.

"I'm waiting, Norman," she glanced at her watch, "shouldn't take you this long to make up your mind."

"Waiting for what?" His mind was mush.

"My perfume, silly," she pouted coyly, "do you like it?"

"Sorry, Vicky, I was thinking about the rats."

She signaled for the waiter, who handed them the menu.

"A bottle of Chianti, please, this one here." She pointed to the Chianti Classico, $24.95, good enough to get started.

"Do brilliant scientists ever indulge?"

"Once in a while, do you really think I'm brilliant?"

"I know you are!" she quickly answered him. "You swept me off my feet the first time I met you. To work under you is a privilege; it gets me excited to see you every day."

The waiter brought over two wine glasses. She filled each to the brim and took a few healthy sips, while Norman drank his nervously, a portion of which gushed down his chin onto his new turtleneck sweater.

"So you do indulge," she laughed, "let me tidy you up." She carefully wiped his chin with her napkin, rubbing it against his sweater, dropping it into his lap.

"I'm so darn clumsy," she pouted, grabbing the napkin, making sure he felt her hand in the right spot.

"Let's order, Norman. I'm starved, you work me too hard. Anything you won't eat?"

"What?" He didn't hear a word she said.

"I mean like are you kosher, that type of thing."

"Not glatt kosher, just kosher style."

"What's that mean, something to do with a rabbi making a special blessing over the food, right? You know me, Norman, always like to learn."

Her curiosity was a turn on, no doubt, but he had zero interest in discussing the Talmudic interpretations of kosher. "It's a long story, Vicky."

"Then next time, OK?"

"Sure, Vicky," Norman replied, trying to decipher if this was all for real.

They chatted while they ate. There was never a moment of silence.

She volunteered she didn't have a boyfriend, a blatant lie.

He lied to her about his past relationships. There weren't any.

"So, Norman, you wanted to talk to me about my rat? I tried to follow your instructions and keep you abreast."

"I guess so," he responded half heartedly, not totally focused.
"Well?"

"Well what?"

"My rat, Norman," she again pouted, as if she really cared.

And then he spilled the beans.

"So Monday morning these rats will show fewer signs of neuro-degenerative motor disease?" she asked forthrightly, only too aware of the possible implications.

"I hope so," he answered, somewhat pensive.

"I would do *anything* to know the cure, sworn to secrecy, cross my heart and hope to die."

He fantasized about all the kinky things they could do to each other.

"Kiss me and I'll tell you."

Thoroughly prepared, she puckered her lips, met him halfway and closed her eyes, then pictured her boyfriend as their lips met. *One for the troops,* she thought. *Ugh!*

"C'mon Norman," she moved her chair next to him. "I'm sitting on pins and needles."

He spoke slowly and deliberately. "ALS is a disorder of motor neurons, which send messages, via nerve projections, to direct the motion of all muscles, our respiratory system, bladder functions, arms, legs—you get the point."

"Sure, classic neurodegenerative disease, similar to Parkinson's, correct?"

Norman nodded as he continued. "It's all about artificial intelligence, Vicky, specifically mirror neurons, which are located throughout the cortex. Think of them as copy cats, as neurons that mirror other behavior. Some say they don't exist, but guess what?"

"What?"

"They're wrong. They form the basis of what we call common coding theory, which emanates from cognitive psychology, a theory which claims an association between what we see and how we perform what we see."

Victoria was visibly excited, just the way she fidgeted with her hair, as Norman continued.

"The nerves that mediate motor function require very specific messaging from motor neurons located throughout the length of the spinal cord. My cure for ALS is the ability to enhance these mirror neurons to such an extent that they can develop their own intelligence, to the point where they actually teach the brain how to memorize near term coordinated and complex motor functions."

"That is so totally outrageous!"

Her exuberance, spoken in the lingo of her generation, reinforced their age difference, which was another turn on.

"It gets better," Norman continued. "ALS patients who were incapacitated with the disease can now develop a superior ability to reproduce complex motor functions, with far greater coordination and agility. My cure actually generates a super human ability to lay down complex neural circuits in the brain, so that the patient can generate faster and more reproducible motor functions, as if the muscles remember on their own, without thinking."

"Will your cure work on Parkinson's? The market for that is gargantuan, right?"

"The answer is yes and yes, but first we attack ALS."

"Wow, that's amazing, Jeremy...."

"Jeremy?"

"You sound jealous," she replied coyly, trying to defuse a potential time bomb, "just an old boyfriend."

Norman glossed over it.

Victoria grabbed Norman's hand, her eyes penetrating his, her countenance beguilingly sincere.

"Thank you, Norman," she whispered softly, and signaled for the check, which she insisted on paying. Grabbing a cab, she dropped him off. Her next stop was her boyfriend's apartment, where she made love, intensely.

Norman got into bed, naked, wrote *Jeremy* on the pad he kept on his nightstand, fantasized about Victoria Chang, and fell asleep.

HE AWOKE WITH A headache, trying to recall all of the things they discussed the night before. He brewed some coffee, opened his front door, and picked up the Sunday *New York Times*. It was nice and thick, wrapped in a plastic bag. He would read it leisurely, section by section, as he did every week, lying in bed, saving the crossword puzzle for last. It was one of the few pleasures he had, other than his rats and his new menu of fantasies.

The weather was unusually nasty for December. A cold, biting rain pelted against the windows. He placed the hot coffee mug on his night stand and tucked himself into bed, cuddling up with his newspaper. The bag kept it dry. "Nothing worse than a soaking wet newspaper," he muttered to himself. *Where were his reading glasses?* "Damnit," he said aloud. There was always something to annoy him. He got out of bed and grabbed the coffee mug, which was sitting on his note pad. He had written something on the top sheet, but couldn't read it. *Where were his glasses?*

He remembered. He had taken them off last night to appear younger, and stuffed them in their case in the back pocket of his new black trousers. "That's better," he mumbled. He was now able to read his precious newspaper, as well as the name on the pad.

AT 6:00 A.M. THE following Monday morning, Norman Berger inserted the key into the door lock of his private laboratory. It wouldn't go in. He jiggled it delicately, then more forcibly, back and forth, up and down, with no luck.

"You're an idiot!" he hollered, realizing he had left the key in his apartment.

He placed his ear next to the door, hoping to hear some vestige of life—chittering and bruxing of the rats chattering their teeth, a sign they are happy, squealing and squeaking when they are startled.

Not a peep, only dead silence.

Goddamnit! He thought the Gods were punishing him? What Gods? He was an atheist. His mind swirled. *Were they meting out justice for the protocols he had heisted from Merck?* He was convinced by his guilty conscience that his rats were dead.

He scurried home, returned with the key, and unlocked the door.

The windowless lab was eerily dark. He switched on the lights and cautiously approached the cages, thinking the unthinkable. And then he heard the sounds, at first one, then another, until the room was filled with a cacophony of squeals and chitters, its dissonance sounding like a beautiful concerto, ringing with life. At that moment, Norman knew, and he cried.

He opened the cages and unhooked the intravenous tubes, letting the rats free, picking them up in his arms, cuddling them, his babies. Some hobbled, others crawled, their movements uncoordinated, but there was no doubt the ALS had been reversed. They gently nibbled at Norman's beaming face, licking away his tears, a sign that they accepted him as part of their family, purring like kittens.

Chapter 20

First thing that morning, Norman called in the brainiacs. They sat around the conference table, guzzling their first jolt of morning Joe, curious as to the reason for an early Monday meeting.

He recapped the last few month's events; how he watched the rats sequestered in his lab quickly deteriorate into ALS life threatening symptoms, the intravenous injection last Friday, his 6:00 a.m. morning debacle with the locked door, and then the stunning results.

A deafening roar filled the room, as Norman beamed to a hero's welcome, a prolonged standing ovation.

During her lunch break, Victoria Chang walked over to the nearby Starbucks and called her brother, who answered his phone.

"Jeremy Chang."

"You wanted information, I have information."

"Are you serious?"

"I told you I would call you with my decision, remember?"

"I knew there was a God!"

"Blood is thicker than water, Jeremy, never forget that." She gave her brother an up to the minute briefing.

"Listen, sis, he's got a thing for you. You need to turn on the charm. We're talking about a huge score if he receives FDA approval for human trials. And with an initial public offering done, add in Parkinson's, and this is worth billions. The goddamn stock will be in the stratosphere!"

"If you think I'm going to screw him, Jeremy, you're crazy. Not for all the bullion in Fort Knox, no way, no how, no chance. Have you ever seen what he looks like?"

"OK, OK, relax. I know-Alan clued me in. Just do the best you can. I'm counting on you."

"I'll be in touch." She hung up and tossed the prepaid cell phone into the trash.

NORMAN ORDERED AN ALL out onslaught to prepare the painstakingly tedious application for the FDA clinical review board to approve the drug for human testing.

The Obama administration had been able to speed up the approval process at the FDA on promising cures for the most heinous fatal diseases; pancreatic cancer, small cell lung cancer, advanced colorectal and prostate cancer, intrahepatic bile duct cancer, stage four metastatic breast cancers, acute myelogenous leukemia, Non-Hodgkin lymphoma, and amyotrophic lateral sclerosis.

Dr. Julius Freiberg, seventy-four, a wealthy retired oncologist, headed the FDA review board, not for the token salary, but to keep his curious mind active. A philosophy major at Yale, he was caught up early in the intellectual pursuit of human understanding, engrossed in the great thinkers on ethics, morality, and justice. Had he his druthers, he would have pursued his PhD and spent his life teaching, living a Spartan existence, until his parents reminded him they were forking out the hefty Yale tuition. For Freiberg, it was medical school or no school.

Norman called Ken Mintz, who orchestrated some behind the scenes prodding, which jiggled Whitcomb's paperwork to the top of the stack, and confirmed a post haste face to face meeting. Two weeks later, Norman took an early morning flight to Washington DC. The panel conducted an in depth interrogation, a rigorous drill Norman had been through countless times. *How was this managed? What about placebos? Who verified the data?*

"Dr. Berger, you do understand the implications of this protocol," Freiberg inquired.

"ALS is first, and then Parkinson's."

"Do you have patent protection? If the human trials pass muster, you're looking at a miracle drug, and the wolves will reverse engineer your formula, try to knock you off."

Norman thought Freiberg's question about patent protection was odd, not something in the FDA's jurisdiction.

"Received our preliminary approval last week; my attorney is working on an amended application, just a formality on some of the processes."

"That's impressive," Freiberg continued, "considering you've only been working on this protocol since you left Merck, what, two years?"

Norman sensed more than a hint of sarcasm in Freiberg's voice. He was paranoid that Freiberg knew something. "I've been thinking about it a lot longer, just got lucky; you know how these things work, hit or miss."

The five person panel huddled together as Norman left the room. They called him back after a thirty-minute interlude, unusually brief for a process that typically exceeded a few hours. Freiberg proffered him a copy of the approved application for human testing, convincing the panel to further accelerate the human trials to two years.

Norman wasn't surprised. He had done his homework. He knew Freiberg was a somewhat compassionate human being, who probably wanted to be known as the guy who bucked convention for the sake of ameliorating human suffering.

Chapter 21

"Delivery from Italian Village," the concierge squawked into the intercom.

"Thanks, Frank," Liz replied. "Please send him up."

It was another *lets order up* evening; fettuccini Bolognese, vegetable lasagna, two tossed green salads, some semi-stale bread, a small container of parmesan cheese, and plastic silverware. It wasn't Mario's, but for $12.95 each, not bad.

The buzzer rang. Liz opened the door to a young man carrying a hot assortment of orders. He handed her the receipt and she fished through her wallet, pulled out thirty dollars, and told him to keep the change.

Liz had a flair for creating a more elegant atmosphere to an otherwise mundane dining experience. She laid out two place settings and a ceramic spout brimming with her homemade Dijon mustard and tarragon vinaigrette salad dressing. Uncorking a bottle of inexpensive Pinot Noir, she filled the wine glasses and tapped a spoon against them, imitating the chiming sound of a dinner bell, as she announced in a not so shabby aristocratic English accent, "dinner is now being served in the main dining room."

"Be right in, hon, just washing up." He always got a kick out of her spontaneous playfulness, but tonight was not in the mood.

Gordon kissed her on the lips before he sat down, a nightly ritual, followed by, "so how was your day?"

"How did *you* do today?" She got right to the point.

"I hit it super, hon" Gordon replied. "I played against Jon Doppelt."

Liz looked at him quizzically, not immediately recognizing the name.

Remember I told you about him," Gordon reminded her. "He's a top amateur, won a bunch of tournaments. No doubt he could have turned pro after college-he hits it as good as anyone on tour. His family is big in the diamond district."

"Were you shopping for an engagement ring?"

"No, wise guy," Gordon sensed her sarcasm.

"Well?"

"I was leading by two after sixteen."

"And then what happened?"

Gordon sighed and looked away. "I blew it; double bogeyed seventeen, and knocked it out of bounds on eighteen."

Liz was tired of asking the same question, getting the same sorrowful answer. She picked at her food, nursing her wine, silent.

"Well, any pearls of wisdom, or is this another evening of 'I'm gonna give Gordon the cold shoulder?'"

In a huff, she slugged down the wine and pounded the table, causing the fettuccini to slide over the edge, deftly saved by Gordon's swift reflexes.

"Screw you, Gordon! Don't blame me for your deficiencies. Yeah, I have some pearls of wisdom for you, if you really want to hear them."

"Sure, why not, get it all out now, Liz. You've been dying to tell me, so start shooting. Hope you don't mind if I eat while you psychoanalyze me."

Gordon twirled the pasta around his fork and soaked some bread in the Bolognese sauce, smacking his lips as he devoured it.

"You're clueless, Gordon. You sold yourself a bill of goods, and I bought into it. Every week brings another story while you blow through your savings. Do you have any idea what it costs us to live?"

Gordon shook his head and attacked the salad. "I have no clue."

"How does fourteen thousand a month taste to you?"

"This salad dressing is super; what's in it, mustard and—"

"Don't ignore me, you dickhead!"

She pushed the table, sprang from her chair and pounced on him, as the dinner special from Italian Village went hurtling onto the floor, as did he, the glasses shattering, the wine flowing indiscriminately, soaking the food.

Sabby meowed as she lunged for the treats, finicky about what to attack first, licking and nibbling at the vegetable lasagna until Liz shooed her away.

"I'm sorry, I deserved it."

"I'm not," she shot back, "and I don't deserve the way you've been behaving, treating me like a used dishtowel."

"I know," Gordon replied sheepishly. "Do you still love me?"

She didn't answer him. Gordon stood up, his jeans and golf shirt stained with the remnants of the short lived dinner. He took her in his arms. "Tell me you still love me." His voice was quivering.

"Of course I do, you big jerk. If I didn't I wouldn't have flown off the handle." Liz wiped away a stream of tears.

They held each other in a long embrace.

"We need to talk, Gordon. I've been giving this a lot of thought."

"How about next Wednesday," he teased with a straight face, trying to lighten up the atmosphere.

"No, Gordon, right now," she replied, sounding very serious.

Gordon suddenly lost his appetite.

She swept up the food and the broken glass and wiped the floor clean with a soapy sponge, her demeanor all business. "Pour yourself a double vodka, you're gonna need it." She hustled to the upstairs bedroom, opened her nightstand drawer, and removed the indisputable evidence, which she shoved into her back pocket.

THEY SAT TOGETHER ON the living room couch.

"You ready to discuss our monthly expenses?"

"Yep," Gordon replied, holding his drink for comfort, as if the numbers would change.

Liz pulled out the folded paper from her pocket and laid it down flat on the coffee table. He wasn't surprised she had gone through this exercise, expecting it sooner or later.

"OK, round numbers, the mortgage is $3,600, coop maintenance $2,900, country club $2,500, Swifty $2,000, health insurance $1,200, car insurance $450, food $1,500; so far that's $14,000 a month. We haven't even discussed a vacation, some clothes, car maintenance, gas, tolls, electricity, household necessities, Christmas gifts for the building staff, some odds and ends…."

"The interest on my mortgage is a deduction, so…."

"Listen, Einstein, you have zero income, there's nothing to deduct *from*."

"Correctamundo, good point," he acknowledged, fidgeting with his vodka glass.

"Gordon, we have to be realistic. It's been close to two years since you left Alan, and you've burned through three hundred thousand dollars. Add back the check you wrote to that ridiculous country club, and the number is three hundred and fifty. Whatever I contribute out of my meager salary doesn't make a dent. I'm an old fashioned girl who believes in saving as much as I can. A nest egg gives me some peace of mind. And I'm scared. Business is terrible, and my job isn't secure."

Gordon thought it decent of her to say he left his father, as if it was purely voluntary.

"At this rate you'll be broke in two years, unless you win the lottery. I know what you have in savings; you never kept it a secret. So then what? OK, you can sell the apartment. What's it worth today, maybe two million in this market, but if you believe the pundits, we're in for a rough ride, and Manhattan real estate could drop fifteen, twenty percent. So let's figure a million six hundred thousand, less the mortgage, broker commissions, flip tax, legal fees, what's left?"

"Not that much, maybe a half million?"

"Less than that, Gordon, don't forget income taxes. You told me what the place cost; you'll be lucky to have three hundred thousand in the bank."

"That really sucks," he slurred, "you sure about this?"

He wasn't expecting an answer. Liz, a glutton for detail, never discussed an important issue until thoroughly researched.

"'That really sucks' doesn't solve our problem, Gordon!"

"I know." He sipped his vodka, which numbed the pain.

"You gonna survive this? If you're thinking about doing something stupid, there are a few things I'd like you to leave for me."

"Very funny," Gordon responded soberly, taken aback by her comment.

His eyes welled up and his head drooped, fixated on the scar.

"You do understand that unless we drastically cut our expenses, you have just about two years to turn things around?"

"I got it, one hundred percent."

"You're at a crossroads, Gordon, a time when most men are set on a career path and know who they are; married, children- the whole bit. And you need to be brutally honest with yourself about this dream that you were put on this earth to play professional golf."

Gordon just nodded, his eyes staring downward.

"Sure, you can hit it on any given day with the best of them. But so can hundreds of others; twenty-year olds right out of college, bigger, stronger, with amazing short games. As good as they are, statistically the odds are one in a thousand they get their tour card. They live in their cars, driving hundreds of miles between tournaments, scurrying to rinky-dinky courses, hoping to make expenses. And these kids can kick your butt spotting you two shots a side every day of the week."

He looked up, sullen.

"They have something you never had, the ability to perform under pressure, all about the way you were raised. Why do you think you screw up all these tournaments? Because deep down inside you don't believe in yourself; you always had Alan and his money to fall back on, and were never tested when the chips were down. I knew it when I met you, but figured you would find your own battles to conquer, and gain some self-respect. But you need to be a realist. You're living in a world of make believe, and fantasies won't pay our bills. I know all about your amateur accomplishments. So what? That was years ago. Times have changed. The pros today are phenoms, almost inhuman, like robots programmed to bring the toughest courses to its knees, with massive galleries and a hundred million people tuned in to every shot. You know their names, and you're hallucinating if you think you have a whisper of a chance against them, even if they played blindfolded."

"Good point, I'll drink to that."

"Don't be so flippant, Gordon. The truth is you can't win some half-assed local event, where the competition has real jobs, and play for kicks and a plastic trophy with a blurb in the local paper."

"So what should I do, kill myself?" He wasn't completely joking.

"Stop the melodrama and grow up. Use your talents and work for a hedge fund raising capital, no different than what you did for Alan."

"What, for a lousy draw and a maybe bonus?"

"That's life, Gordon, accept it. If you're half as good as you think you are, you'll be earning a hell of a lot more than what your father paid you. Some of these guys make a million plus a year, and if you have to kiss ass, so be it. Everybody has a boss, up and down the line; that's how the world works."

"And Swifty, just toss him out in the streets? He's my friend."

"And who am I, the wicked witch of the north? I'm your significant other, remember, maybe your future wife. We can't afford him, Gordon, so don't lay a guilt trip on me. I'm just as much a champion for the underprivileged as you are, maybe more so, but let's not mix up morality with survival. You've been more than generous. He'll understand, if he doesn't already."

Her threat, "maybe your future wife," was unexpected.

"I want you to give me a time frame, a promise that when you realize you're just chasing a rainbow, all bets are off. You get a real job, sell the apartment, and start fresh."

"Ten more years," he joked, which she didn't find funny.

"Two more years, Gordon, and not a day more, take it or leave it."

"OK, deal, and you promise to switch from significant other to significant wife."

"Let me think about it," she smiled coyly.

"Screw you!"

"You could if you had a dynamite penthouse on Park Avenue."

They kissed, hurried upstairs and had torrid make up sex.

But Gordon heard the clock ticking. He had to start winning tournaments, no more excuses, as Liz, for certain, was at the end of her rope.

Chapter 22

SWIFTY SAT ACROSS FROM Gordon at the Seven Seas Diner just a few blocks from Old Point. They had just finished a practice session and were having lunch while Gordon recapped his conversation with Liz.

"So she put her foot down, can't say I blame her."

"Yep, she gave me an ultimatum. And two years will go quickly," Gordon said with a heavy sigh.

"Well, I was gettin' ready to tell you the same damn thing."

"So you also have doubts about me?" Gordon sounded annoyed.

"Listen, GH, facts are facts. You been bustin' hump since you left your father, doin' a great job, practicin' all winter and gettin' yourself in shape. You ain't missed a day. But when the seasons came around, and you played in all those tournaments…."

"Ok, Swifty, I get the point."

"I ain't done, GH. You teed it up thirty-one times and the best you ever finished was second place. Cussin' and slammin' your clubs ain't gonna make your scorin' any better. You get yourself into contention and then somethin' happens in your head. And funny thing is that you got more talent in your pinky than these guys who are beatin' you every week. I did my best to get you to believe in yourself, but I ain't a shrink."

"Yeah I know, Swifty," Gordon said disconsolately. "It's eating me up that I can't take the pressure."

"Well maybe you gotta just call it quits and move on. I'm fine with that, GH. It makes no sense in tearin' yourself apart and gettin' Liz all riled up-you agree?" Swifty was just testing him.

Gordon slumped back in his seat and stared into space.

"What you thinkin' about GH, your father?" Swifty needled him.

I'm absolutely not," Gordon flat out lied, although his tone suggested otherwise. Swifty saw right through it. "And no way am I packing it in, Swifty. It's too important to me. Sooner or later I'm gonna figure it out and play to my potential, be a winner."

"OK, GH, whatever you say. I like what I'm hearin'. But understand- it ain't sooner or later. We got two more years, and I'm with you one hundred percent."

Gordon ruminated over Swifty's comment about his father while his stomach knotted, thinking *two more years, just two more years.*

Chapter 23

NORMAN TACKLED THE DAUNTING task of administering the human test trials in accordance with a litany of FDA procedures and regulations. The clinical trial protocol had been completed. It was their bible, a robust set of detailed procedures to be religiously adhered to, which insured the integrity of the results

The brainiacs handled the unglamorous grunt work, travelling to one horse towns, big cities, and places in between, recruiting volunteers stricken with ALS. They set up test locations, coordinated with local site investigators, hired nurses, and analyzed urine, stool, and blood samples. They labored with little rest, chained to an endless, prohibitively expensive to do list.

With the test sites fully operational, the nurses prepared to administer the first dosages of the drug.

The human trials ramped up quickly while the company burned through its cash. Norman needed a solid report detailing the human trials with irrefutable testing data before he could approach the investment bankers.

The results spoke for themselves. In each and every case, the progression of the disease was neutralized and then reversed, leading to an improvement in muscle control, the degree dependent upon the severity of the symptoms.

THE BLURB APPEARED IN *The Wall Street Journal* and major business newswires.

Biotech ALS Start-up Inks Deal For Initial Public Offering

Norman Berger, a pioneer in the study of neurodegenerative diseases, and CEO of Whitcomb Pharmaceutical Inc., based in Triangle Research Park, North Carolina, announced today a definitive agreement with Stifel Nicholas Corp., a St. Louis based investment bank, to underwrite an initial public offering.

The funds will be used to finance Whitcomb's FDA approved human trial studies currently testing a possible cure for ALS, or amyotrophic lateral sclerosis, commonly known as Lou Gehrig's disease.

According to Dr. Berger, "The initial human testing on ALS volunteers has yielded encouraging results."

A spokesman for Stifel Nicholas, which has underwritten several biotech startups, commented on the agreement. "We are pleased to have been chosen by Whitcomb as their lead underwriter. ALS is a devastating disease and we are equally encouraged that Dr. Berger is on the right path."

Whitcomb Pharmaceutical was initially funded with twenty million dollars by Merck, the pharmaceutical conglomerate, which had a long standing relationship with Dr. Berger.

JEREMY CHANG WASN'T SURPRISED to see the press release, having received the heads up from his sister two nights before, after one of her rendezvous evenings with Norman Berger.

As he expected, the announcement was low key, although he knew considerably more. Norman had boasted to Victoria that Whitcomb would be worth north of a billion dollars, smugly confident he would get FDA approval, already secretly writing the clinical trial protocol for an attack on Parkinson's.

Jeremy placed a call to Eric Sewickley, managing director of investment banking at Stifel Nicholas, the guy who had negotiated the deal with Norman and his attorney, and responsible for the success of every initial public offering.

They had spoken on occasion, with Sewickley pitching his company, trying to woo AH Advisors as a client. Alan didn't know the firm, and preferred to keep his fund's money with the big New York banks.

"Jeremy Chang, I'm surprised to hear from you. I threw in the towel trying to land your account a long time ago." Sewickley had a good sense of humor and a reputation for fair dealing.

"How are you, Eric? I figured I'd check in and see what you guys in St. Louis are up to these days."

"Hope you didn't load up on those toxic CDO's or the subprime CMO's, all the crap your friendly New York investment banks invented to enrich themselves at their clients' expense."

"Yeah, we got hurt a little, lost some assets. We need to diversify our banking relationships. I'm looking out west, so I decided to give you a call."

Jeremy knew it wasn't true; AH Advisors got slaughtered.

Eric snickered; *the chicken was finally coming home to roost.*

"What are you guys running now in that fund?"

"We had it up to six billion, but now with this lousy market, about three billion and change. It's tough to raise assets."

"You need better product, Jeremy, some good solid research. Our guys dominate in technology and healthcare, just that St. Louis doesn't have the fancy steak houses, the twenty dollar martinis, or the fifty million dollar condos with the drop dead views."

"Or the drop dead gorgeous women."

"OK, Jeremy, I'll drink to that."

"We want to open an account, Eric, start doing some business. If things pan out, I'll stick more capital with you guys."

"How much are we talking about, Jeremy? You know our minimums have gone way the hell up since we last spoke. We're not such a regional bank anymore."

Jeremy expected this negotiation. Eric wasn't stupid, and knew why he was calling.

"I was thinking ten million, just to get our feet wet."

"Not gonna work, Jeremy, for that kind of money call Charles Schwab."

"OK, give me a number." Jeremy hated to cow tow to anyone, but Alan wanted this done.

"Two percent of assets, that's sixty million bucks; two year lock-up, account is fully insured. We're competitive with your New York buddies on all fees."

Jeremy could hear Eric tapping his pen against his desk.

"Done, send me the paperwork, but with one proviso."

"Is that proviso called Whitcomb Pharmaceutical by chance?" Eric let out a good, hearty, in your face roar.

It was common knowledge on the street that Whitcomb was a hot deal, with all the big investment banks competing to do the underwriting. Eric had been bombarded with calls as soon as the article hit *The Journal.*

"Alan wants a significant allocation."

"You guys must know something I don't know. Biotech can be a treacherous business, all in the hands of the FDA."

"Let's just say Alan is a degenerate gambler."

"Off the record, we're pricing Whitcomb at five bucks a share, selling twenty million shares, raising a hundred million."

"OK, we'll take ten percent of the deal, two million shares."

"We haven't even sent out the red herring, it's at the printer as we speak. I'll overnight the package with wiring instructions. Read through the prospectus with all the usual bullshit risk disclaimers, and shoot me an email with a firm order and we'll get it done."

"Thanks, Eric, let me know the next time you're in the city, I'll buy you a steak."

"You got it, Jeremy, medium rare." Eric hung up, all hopped up, and headed straight to the CEO's office, anxious to crow about his huge score.

Norman Berger and Eric Sewickley rang the bell at the podium of the NASDAQ stock exchange, as Whitcomb Pharmaceutical opened for trading, under the symbol WHIT. Those fortunate investors who received an initial allocation saw the stock gap open at ten dollars a share, five points higher, doubling their money.

Norman Berger's stake in the company was worth, on paper, close to one hundred million dollars. Other than receiving a heftier salary, he was restricted by the investment bankers from selling any shares until six months after the final FDA approval, which insured he kept his nose to the grindstone, assuaging antsy investors.

The brainiacs all received stock options with the same restrictions, making them all paper multi-millionaires. Victoria Chang's performance earned her substantially more. Norman felt compelled to do it, not that she deserved it, as he thought her work was mediocre at best.

Blair Whitcomb cashed out at the IPO price, pocketing some fifty million. He quit medicine for the golf course, chasing that elusive muscle memory. Merck added to their stake, increasing their ownership percentage.

Eric Sewickley honored his agreement with AH Advisors, which gave them a tidy ten million dollar paper profit.

Chapter 24

ALAN HOWARD WAS WHOLEHEARTEDLY convinced that Victoria Chang's inside information was right on the money.

Assets under management at AH Advisors were dwindling quickly. Alan needed a home run to entice back his investors, to save his company and his reputation.

WHIT traded considerably higher during the six months after the initial public offering, along with most biogenetic stocks.

AH Advisors added to their position until they owned some seven million shares, trading at forty dollars. With their average cost at twenty-six, the fund's paper profit in WHIT stood just shy of a hundred million dollars.

ERIC SEWICKLEY PUT IN an urgent call to Norman Berger, who still answered his own phone.

"Norman Berger."

"Dr. Berger, its Eric Sewickley, got a minute?"

"Very busy, is this important?"

"It could be, yes sir."

"What is it?"

"Do you know AH Advisors, a hedge fund run by an Alan Howard?"

"Never heard of him," he lied, "why?"

"Just that he's buying with two fists, taking out the sellers, pushing the stock higher, as if he knows something. Last thing we need is an SEC inquiry, even if everything is aboveboard. With them, you're guilty until proven innocent, worse than the Gestapo, thanks to that Raj guy, SAC Capital, and all the inside information prosecutions."

"So what do we do?"

"Not much we can do, just want to cover my ass, that's all."

"OK." Norman hung up.

He thought that Victoria Chang had mentioned she had a brother who worked in New York City. It took the Google search engine just 4.3 seconds from the time he clicked *enter* to display twenty-three line items for a Jeremy Chang, most just referencing Linked In and Facebook. Scrolling down; a basketball player, an author, a painter, a Congressman from California, an appraiser of rare Chinese artifacts, a celebrity chef, ...a Chief Information Officer of a hedge fund based in New York City, Alan Howard, Managing Director.

That evening they met for another dinner rendezvous. Norman never mentioned the call from the underwriter, or what he had uncovered about her brother. He just gave her what she wanted, and received her undivided attention, his quid pro quo, in return.

Chapter 25

As soon as she returned home, Victoria Chang called Jeremy with an update.

"Listen, it's getting freaky with him, he's perverted, I mean *really* weird."

"You're kidding me."

"I'm not a prude, Jeremy, but some of this stuff is too much for me to handle."

"Like what?"

"Like he wants me to tie him up and talk dirty to him, hand-cuffs, it's the whole sado-masochism routine."

"Sounds like fun," Jeremy laughed.

"Well, why don't you hop on a plane and play bad boy games with him. For all I know he'll find you attractive."

"I'm just teasing, Vicky. So how did you handle it?"

"Told him I'd consider it, which got him all lathered up. Why do you think he gives me all this info? I know how to push the right buttons; I'm in a relationship of sorts."

Jeremy laughed, but she didn't find it humorous, worried that sooner or later she would have to go the extra mile if she wanted this relationship to continue.

"So any new info, or is this just a courtesy call?"

"I only call you with info, bro."

"Like Bud Fox, when Gordon Gekko tells him, and I quote, 'the most valuable commodity I know of is information.'"

"You love that *Wall Street* movie, don't you?"

"Every second of it; if I watched it once I watched it fifty times. I know every line, just brilliant."

"Blue horseshoe loves Whitcomb Pharmaceutical," Victoria said playfully.

"Now that's the kind of information I'm looking for."

"Put the phone real close to your ear, Mr. Gekko."

"OK, buddy boy, speak to me."

Victoria loved the histrionics, as did he, and knew exactly what got her brother all juiced up.

"And congrats by the way, you guys scored a hundred million dollars. You must have done some badass research on this company."

"OK, stop with the sarcasm. I told you what we own and you're getting your share. Alan won't stiff you. I'll make sure of it. And besides, they're just paper profits. What are your options worth, a couple of million bucks?"

"They're worth zero if the FDA thumbs down the drug."

Jeremy knew that Victoria was too savvy to be placated. "OK, give."

"If that big shot Alan Howard screws me I swear—"

"I'm your brother, Vicky, stop worrying!"

"Norman is issuing a press release this Friday to bring everyone up to speed on the human trials, and just mention, without too much hoopla, that he believes the drug—"

"Can work with Parkinson's, right?" Jeremy excitedly finished her thought.

"You hit the nail on the head, bro."

"Later, sis, good work, and don't forget to deep six the phone."

"Yeah, yeah, I know, I may be crazy, but I'm not stupid."

THE PRESS RELEASE FROM Whitcomb hit the major news wires after the Friday market close.

> Dr. Norman Berger, CEO of Whitcomb Pharmaceutical, WHIT, announced today as follows.
>
> We are ramping up our human trials, which have consistently shown positive results. This will preliminarily indicate the effectiveness of the drug as a

cure for ALS. The results will be submitted to the FDA for approval, and the patients monitored for any adverse reactions before the drug is approved for use.

There can be no certainty at this point as to possible unforeseen ramifications of the drug therapy, which may require more extensive testing and additional capital. This is cutting edge science, the brain is a complex organ and only time will tell.

I remain guardedly optimistic that we will conquer ALS, and that the protocol, with some modification of the chemical composition, will be equally effective in other neurodegenerative disorders, particularly Parkinson's.

ALAN HOWARD AND JEREMY Chang spent the evening celebrating at Mario's.

"Mister Alan, buongiorno, so nice to see you, I have your favorite table. By the way, how is your son, Mister Gordon, he doesn't come by much anymore."

Alan sloughed off the question, shook Mario's hand slipping him a fifty dollar bill, and walked inside to the last table on the left, the banquette with the two seats side by side and picture window view of Madison Avenue.

Chapter 26

WHIT OPENED STRONG THE following Monday morning, up another five dollars by the end of the day on volume of fifteen million shares, as hysterical buyers buoyed by the news jumped into the market.

Alan Howard's trading desk sold into the frenzy, liquidating his position and booking a profit of one hundred and forty million dollars, which settled into the fund's account three days later.

Alan was now flush with cash for what he told Jeremy would be "the mother of all trades." The FDA would soon decide the fate of Norman's drug, and Victoria, he prayed to God, would know their decision in advance.

NORMAN AND THE BRAINIACS feverishly completed the required New Drug Application, a two thousand page detailed account of the drug's history from inception. It contained the results of the animal studies, the clinical trials, the ingredients of the drug formulation, the manufacturing process, and how the drug actually functions in humans to cure the disease.

The document was submitted to Dr. Julius Frieberg. The brainiacs were dismissed with their precious options, without a celebratory parting dinner or a champagne toast to a job well done, just a handshake—typical Norman Berger.

Victoria Chang made her presence known, stopping by the office, keeping herself in the loop, waiting for the blockbuster news.

The field inspectors kept close contact with the volunteers. There was no doubt that the drug reversed the ALS in every patient. Many were symptom free; some regaining motor control more slowly, but able to function. Freiberg's hands quivered as he read through the results, his soul shaken by the enormity of Norman's achievement.

But he was only too aware that scientific miracles can be fleeting, and the complexity of Norman's protocol, delving into the deepest recesses of the brain, and meddling with the fabric of molecular DNA and RNA, the essence of life, was riddled with the risk of unforeseen and deadly consequences.

NORMAN COULD ONLY WAIT as the weeks and months passed. WHIT drifted lower, and then higher, buoyed by the usual rumor mills, as nervous investors anxiously awaited the FDA decision.

He spent his days analyzing the cards he was dealt, some aces and some jokers, and how he had played them under the circumstances, smugly certain that the cold, hard, empirical data would be proof that *he* had discovered a once in a lifetime miracle drug.

The FDA had an unspoken rule, allowing a heads up on a major announcement, with the SEC on alert that the information remained private, watching the trading tape for unusual activity.

It was late Thursday afternoon, a day before the start of the Labor Day weekend, when the call finally came through.

Norman just listened as Freiberg spoke, a fait accompli, his mind deluged with too many thoughts, trying to grasp the ramifications of what he had just been told.

The FDA would make the announcement Friday after the market closed.

He called Victoria Chang and made arrangements for an *important* dinner rendezvous.

Chapter 27

"HE SAID IT WAS important, Jeremy."

"I hear you, sis. This could be huge. Listen, if you have to sling a few off the wall suggestions, grit your teeth and do it."

"Do it?"

"No, just lead him on. Perverts like to fantasize, but when push comes to shove, they can't pull the trigger."

"So now you're a sex therapist and the CIO of a recently successful hedge fund?"

"No, I just happen to know a bunch of perverted men."

"Very funny, but I'm not in a humorous mood, can't stand the sight of him anymore. This is my swan song, bro. You guys made enough off my backside. After tonight we finalize our deal, or else what I drag out of him stays with me."

"Vicky, you have nothing to—"

"Worry about, fear, be concerned with? You're not writing the checks, Alan is. For all I know you'll wind up on the short end of the stick. If he has the balls to trade on inside information, then he'd toss you to the wolves in a heartbeat. And what are you going to do, bro, rat him out? You're just as involved as he is."

"As are you," Jeremy reminded her.

"So we're playing a game of brinkmanship, which one of us blinks first?"

Jeremy knew his sister; she was getting hot under the collar, and could be real stubborn if she wanted to. "What kind of assurances do you want, a written agreement that AH Advisors will pay you a 5% finder's fee for supplying inside information?"

"Very funny, Jeremy, and it's 10%, remember?"

"I was just making a point."

"I want Alan to hear it from the horse's mouth."

"OK, Vicky, I get the picture."

Jeremy wasn't surprised it was coming to a head. Sister or no sister, when you're talking this kind of money, people get paranoid.

THEY MET IN THEIR usual place and sat at their usual table, with Norman still in his work clothing, not trying to dress up.

He was early, and ordered a bottle of wine, starting without her.

She arrived twenty minutes late, which she always did, part of their routine, something that turned him on. She wore white short shorts, a tight powder blue tee shirt, no bra, and sandals. It was the perfect outfit for the summer heat, and exposed as much silky smooth skin as possible.

"Did you just come from the office, Norman?"

He nodded, unusually quiet, and filled her glass.

"Cheers, good to see you." She sampled the wine. She wondered why he wasn't in his usual "try to look cool" outfit. "White wine, nice and chilled, fruity," she said, smacking her lips, the one's he loved to kiss.

She went through the same routine as all the other rendezvous.

They talked as they ate, although she controlled the conversation, vivacious and alluring, touching him to make her point, whispering in his ear what he wanted to hear, pressing her breasts against his shoulder, juicing up her act.

"And look, sweetie," she opened her knapsack and pulled out a set of handcuffs, which she slid onto the appropriate spot in his lap.

She prayed to God that her brother was right about perverts, that Norman wouldn't hold back the important information until the handcuffs were put to good use.

Norman smiled, a deranged sort of smile, his eyes bulging.

"I'll be at the Triangle Motel, meet me there in half an hour."

And then he left.

Fuck!

She dialed Jeremy and got his voice mail, then tried him at home and got his answering machine. She left two frantic messages.

Now what? What if there was no information? Her gut told her otherwise. He hadn't lied to her before. He said it was important.

She downed two full glasses of wine, paid the check, and hopped a taxi back to her apartment. She fumbled through her medicine chest for the Vicodin prescription, a narcotic pain killer she used for excruciating back spasms. The motel was a good twenty minute walk. It would give her time to think. *Maybe her brother would call her back?*

He didn't.

Norman played out his weirdest fantasies, knowing this rendez-vous would be his last, as she wouldn't need him anymore.

Chapter 28

VICTORIA INGESTED A BUNCH of sleeping pills later that evening. She awoke late and called Jeremy, armed with a treasure trove of information. He answered the phone, and put Alan Howard on speaker.

"OK, sis, I'm here with Alan."

She needed to keep her composure and tried not to think about last night, although between the alcohol and the drugs she was so wacked out she couldn't swear to all of the details.

She could hear them talking in the background, muffled but audible.

"I hear you have a problem with me, Vicky."

"I sure do, Mr. Howard, and my name is Victoria."

"Well get it off your chest, Victoria, I'm all ears."

"I'm miffed that you never took the time to thank me for being your mole. Put yourself in my position, I think you get the point."

Again she could hear them, with Jeremy coaching him what to say.

"Sorry you feel that way, Victoria. I thought your brother told you how much I valued what you were doing."

"It's simple, Mr. Howard. You guys made a hundred million plus so far on my info, and—"

"Wait one second, sis," Jeremy jumped in. "The fund made the money, the investors. Alan gets a percentage. I kept you in the loop, been totally candid, never held anything back."

"Twenty percent, correct?"

"Exactly," Alan answered.

"So twenty million, what's my cut?"

"We agreed on ten percent, Vicky," Jeremy chimed in. "We discussed it before you called."

"Plus ten percent of any more you make on Whitcomb from my new info, right."

"Nothing in writing, Victoria," Alan interjected, "but you have my word, as does your brother. You'll have to invoice the fund for consulting services. I'll have my attorney draft something up that passes the sniff test."

"Mr. Howard, put the phone close to your ear. Don't screw me! My first call is to the SEC. You and Jeremy have a helluva lot more to lose than me. Norman's in my back pocket; he'll swear up and down he never told me a thing."

She knew she made a damn good point. She could hear Alan rant as clear as day, "that goddamn little bitch!"

"We understand," Jeremy tried to assuage her.

And then she told them.

"The FDA called him. He has a friend there; they approved the drug for ALS. The announcement will be made Friday after the market closes. They want to start animal trials on Parkinson's as quickly as possible."

"You did well, Bud Fox. I'm proud of you." Jeremy tried to contain his exuberance with some private humor.

"Thanks, Mr. Gekko." She hung up and tossed the cell phone into the garbage.

Chapter 29

THEY HAD ONLY A few hours before the announcement. Alan instructed Jeremy to have the trading desk start building a position in WHIT.

"What's the float, Jeremy?"

"Thirty million shares, trading closed yesterday at thirty-six, volume picking up over the last month. The wolves probably smell something."

"Better to know something than just smell it, don't you think?" Alan smirked as they high fived each other.

"I already went through the numbers, Alan. I figure on ALS alone the company is worth north of a billion. Add in Parkinson's, especially in a hot biotech market, and you can expect ten times that number, say ten billion. Just to be safe, let's discount it by thirty percent, since animal trials take time, with no assurances of the results."

Alan was lucky to have Jeremy as his Chief Investment Officer, who possessed a good solid understanding of valuations, and a not so shabby sister.

"So you figure the market values it at seven billion?"

"More or less, and when I do the math, the shares should trade, over time, at just shy of two hundred, adjusted for splits."

"Where do you think it pops when the announcement becomes public?"

"I think the institutions take the weekend to do the math, and it opens Monday at ninety bucks, minimum."

"OK, good work; let's accumulate twenty million shares, use the floor brokers, nice and quiet. If we can average in at sixty, and unload half at ninety, it's a three hundred million dollar payday. Let the other half ride. My gut tells me that Merck comes in and offers to buy the whole damn thing, and with our percentage, we have some negotiating muscle for a higher price."

By 3:30 p.m. on Friday, AH Advisors owned some twenty million plus shares of WHIT, at an average cost of fifty-six dollars, discreetly acquiring a position worth just north of a billion dollars, investing more than one third of the fund's total capital, which prompted a frantic call from the head honcho risk manager at the fund's prime broker, JP Morgan.

"Jeremy, its Fred Miller, you guys blew through our risk parameters. We want your position cut in half. Tell your boss that if he wants to shoot his load on an FDA approval, he's in the wrong business."

"Kind of late for that, market closes in a half hour."

"That's not my problem, Jeremy. You know our agreement, and if you don't do it, we will!"

"Better read the fine print, Freddy, we're way below our threshold. You bastards have been gouging us for years. If you sell one goddamn share you can kiss our account sayonara."

"Jeremy, it's coming from high up, you gotta do me a favor—"

"Forget it!" He slammed down the phone and ran to Alan's office, who was reclined back in his desk chair, sobbing, staring at the ceiling. The television, tuned to CNBC, was faintly audible in the background.

"What's wrong, Mr. Howard- is it something about Whitcomb?" Jeremy spoke frantically as he sat down in the club chair in front of Alan's desk.

"I knew it" Jeremy ranted on. "Stupid sister- too goddamn late to unload the stock, the market's about to close. We're married to it!"

"Calm down," Alan said, trying to sound reassuring, as he wiped his eyes, looked at Jeremy, and held up a handwritten letter.

"Everything's under control. I'm just feeling .... sentimental, jotting down some thoughts-haven't seen him in two years."

Jeremy recognized the tell tale signs that Alan had been drinking; just how he occasionally slurred his words, and the iced empty cocktail glass sitting on his desk.

"It's Gordon, huh?" Jeremy said with a sympathetic voice.

Alan nodded as he silently read through the letter, signed it and inserted it into an envelope. He addressed it to William Steinman, Esq. and left it in his outgoing mail tray.

He poured two double Grey Goose on the rocks and turned up the TV with the remote. They sat back, sipping their vodka, munching on some pretzels, waiting for the news of the FDA announcement.

Chapter 30

GORDON SULLENLY HAULED HIS sorry ass onto his living room couch. It was another aggravating day, losing in the finals to some fifty-year-old attorney that entered the tournament on a lark. Gordon hit it sixty yards past him and had an easy five iron into eighteen, which he snap-hooked into the weeds and carded a double bogey. The rest was history.

He hated to admit it, but Liz was dead right about him; *a classic choke artist.*

As much as Swifty worked on his head, and tried to build up his confidence, it was fruitless. He could see it in Swifty's demeanor, not as upbeat as he used to be, a few telling comments here and there. Every tournament had been increasingly frustrating, and he was running out of time. He felt ready to call it quits, no sense in beating a dead horse.

Now he had to face the Labor Day weekend with a bad head and a worse attitude. But for certain, there would be no golf. He would be content to just languish in the apartment, wander through the park, chill out, channel surf with a slew of beers, and take a brutal reassessment.

It was a few minutes shy of 6:00 p.m. when Liz got home, and saw him lying on the couch, watching CNBC, slurping on a cold Heineken.

"Hey, how was your day? Mine sucked."

"You want to talk about it?"

"Want to listen? You've heard it a thousand times."

"So make it a thousand and one," she smiled, trying to sound comforting.

161

"How about we watch the news and check out the next hedge fund superstar, considering I'll be working for one soon. I'll give you the blow by blow over dinner." She thought he sounded terrible, down in the dumps. She would go easy on him.

"Sure, let me grab a beer. And turn up the TV; you muted it, silly."

He thought about his father and the last time they spoke. Life was easy back then, unfulfilling, but infinitely better than where he was now. At least he wasn't depressed or burning through his savings, torturing himself over a game that required a lot more than just a great swing if you dreamed of making it your livelihood.

Gordon turned up the volume on the remote. Liz planted her usual hello kiss, then plopped herself onto the couch.

Maria Bartiromo was finishing up her daily show, *The Closing Bell*.

"I like her," Liz remarked. "She worked hard to make herself a household name. She's feisty, gets in your face, and tells it like it is."

Bartiromo pushed in her earphone, and waited until she got all the details.

"I have breaking news! I've just been advised that the FDA has *rejected* Whitcomb Pharmaceutical's bid to market their much ballyhooed cure for ALS. This will certainly be a death knell for the young biotechnology firm and its founder and CEO, Dr. Norman Berger. WHIT, which closed at sixty-two, traded down below ten dollars in the aftermarket, as investors dumped their holdings, until NASDAQ halted the stock."

Gordon jumped off the couch, approached the TV, and cranked up the volume.

"That's the guy I spoke with, Liz, remember?"

"Totally, he helped your father cheat his way into Columbia, right?"

"Yep, wait, there's more."

"According to my sources, Alan Howard, the brusque and hard driving hedge fund manager, had accumulated a humongous position in Whitcomb stock through his hedge fund, AH Advisors, placing a huge bet on FDA approval. Mr. Howard has suffered a massive heart attack and was rushed by helicopter to North Shore Hospital, where he has been a major benefactor. I have no further word on his condition. Additionally, Mr. Howard's top lieutenant, Jeremy Chang, was discovered by his wife with a rope around his neck, hanging from an exposed pipe in the basement of their Westchester home. Police are investigating the apparent suicide. This is Maria Bartiromo reporting."

"Holy Christ, Jeremy committed suicide! This is heavy stuff, a real mind blower. I always thought that guy had a dark side, had all his money in the firm. Alan knew Norman Berger. It wouldn't surprise me if Jeremy hounded someone at Whitcomb for information, and paid up for it, but someone got their signals crossed. Guess we'll read about it in the paper."

"Gordon, he's your father for Christ sake, what if he dies? You guys need some kind of closure."

"Why is that, Liz? Where does it say I have to come crawling back on my hands and knees just because—"

"I never told you that, you're still your own man!"

"How about I just call the hospital to see how he's doing?"

"Talk about spineless! Either you get out there immediately like a human being or—"

"I hear you Liz, loud and clear," as he grabbed his car keys.

Chapter 31

GORDON GRAPPLED WITH MIXED emotions as he drove out to North Shore Hospital.

With the rush hour traffic, it took a good hour until he pulled in front of the hospital complex. A policeman came over and motioned to roll down his window.

"Admissions or are you picking someone up?"

"My father is Alan Howard. They just helicoptered him from the city."

"Got any ID?"

He fumbled through his wallet and proffered his license along with the gold and silver badge he had shown to Sergeant Riley.

"No worries, Mr. Howard, I heard about it. I hope your father pulls through, he's a great man. Just park up against the curb, I'll watch it."

"Thanks, I appreciate it."

"Good luck." The policeman attended to the long line of awaiting cars amidst a cacophony of honking horns as Gordon made his way to the information desk

"I'm looking for Alan Howard, a patient, just admitted."

A woman scrolled through her computer.

"Can't seem to find him, not in any room; was it for surgery?"

"No, emergency, had a stroke and…."

"OK, got it, he's in ICU."

Gordon stood silently with a blank look as if to say- *what does ICU mean?*

"Sorry, intensive care unit, off limits except for immediate family and clergy."

"What do you mean by clergy?"

"You know, rabbis, priests, last rites, people ready to kick, that sort of stuff."

"He's my father."

"Got ID?"

Gordon fished through his wallet, gave her his license and the gold and silver badge.

"Sign here," she uttered insensitively, pointing to a register, "elevators in the back, eighth floor," handing him back the identification and a time stamped printed voucher. "Show this to the guard upstairs."

Gordon's heart fluttered as he made his way to the elevators, oblivious to the hustle and bustle of the hospital; people laughing, some sobbing, ecstatic parents of wailing newborns cherishing their deafening sounds as if it was sweet dulcet music. There was life, death and hope, doctors and nurses, wheel-chaired invalids, the frail and the aged struggling on walking canes, the very sick, the feeble and the cured.

He flashed his pass to the attendant at the entrance to the intensive care unit.

"Room 814, it's the last one on the right, end of the hall. Gotta sign in first, sign out when you leave, patient likes to know." The attendant pointed to a log book and went back to flipping through the *New York Daily News*.

Gordon noticed a Sgt. D. Riley had been there an hour before and left just ten minutes ago.

He walked to the end of the hall and stood in the doorway, watching.

Alan Howard lay attended by a cadre of physicians, enslaved to a life support machine, which controlled his vital functions. A ventilator had been pushed into his trachea to control his breathing, a nasogastric feeding tube passed down through the nostrils into his esophagus and stomach, a catheter drained the urine freely from his bladder; a menagerie of intravenous drips and electrical shock sensors, reprieved from a coffin only by the occasional thumping of his fragile heart.

A man with a stethoscope around his neck greeted him. Donned in a white physician's coat, his long curly locks and boyish face defied his age.

"I'm Doctor David Segal." He could see Gordon was upset.

"Gordon Howard," They shook hands.

"You're Alan's son?"

Gordon nodded.

"It must be tough for you. I'm sorry. He's a lucky man; by all rights it should be curtains."

"What happened? The news said a massive heart attack."

"Yep, but we have the heart pumping. He should pull through. Problem is the stroke, bluntly a brain attack, which morphed into cerebromedullospinal disconnection. It's what's commonly called locked-in syndrome, a total paralysis of the muscles. They can't move or speak, except blink their eyes, which is how they communicate."

"Is there a cure?"

"Not to pull any punches, but only one percent of stroke victims acquire it. It's rare, often misunderstood, and the prognosis is for the birds. Most never regain motor control, and within the first four or five months, well…."

Dr. David Segal, a compassionate guy, liked to temper things that were difficult to swallow.

"Go ahead, I need to know."

"The majority die, some live a few years longer, but their quality of life…."

"Not good, right?"

"Depends how you look at it. It's a helluva lot better than a goddamn coma, where you have to consider the alternative. At least he's alive, aware, and you guys can communicate, which isn't so bad."

"Thanks."

Gordon stayed for a few minutes, engulfed in a quagmire of dizzying emotion, and then quietly left, unable to go over to his father, who found out later that he had been there.

Chapter 32

NORMAN RETURNED TO HIS apartment from his last day in the office, still reeling from the devastating news, as Julius Freiberg's quick and to the point telephone call echoed over and over in his head.

There were a slew of voice messages from Victoria Chang, none of them particularly romantic. He knew about Alan Howard's stroke, and her brother's suicide.

Ken Mintz had called, which he expected. He returned the call.

"Hey Norman, thanks for getting back to me."

"Freiberg said you guys would be calling."

"We have a proposition."

"I'm listening."

"Just for the record, it was a damn good try. You almost got away with it."

"Got away with what?" Norman replied, trying to hide his nervousness. .

"There's a big difference between not signing an NDA and stealing corporate proprietary information, or so my legal eagles tell me."

"What are you talking about?"

"Like mirror neurons, mono-amino oxidae inhibitors, catechol…."

"Big deal, my patents are all public information."

"Public information now, Dr. Berger, but we took a peek at your patent submission, and don't think Freiberg wasn't privy to the whole story. We made sure of it."

"That's strictly confidential, how the hell—"

"We have our sources," Mintz interrupted, "and what's good for the goose...you know the rest."

Now it made sense to Norman, why Freiberg had asked him those two misplaced questions at the FDA meeting in Washington, DC.

"And considering you filed your patent application less than a week after you quit Merck, unless you had a divine intervention, it will be a no-brainer proving you stole our information."

"Then why did you invest twenty million with—"

"A criminal," Mintz interjected matter-of-factly.

Norman cringed at the characterization, which made his blood boil.

"You mean my life's work; where people with death warrants can toss away their wheelchairs and feeding tubes, walk, talk, and play with their kids, go to a movie, and live normal lives. Amyotrophic Lateral Sclerosis is a neurological nightmare of thousands of biological permutations. Who else on the planet could have analyzed and combined those protocols? You know it, I know it, and Freiberg knows it. You should kiss the ground I walk on!"

"C'mon, Norman, we trusted you, poured a fortune of money into that project. And you just stalled us, gave us bits and pieces, until you found what you were looking for, and then left us high and dry. I knew you would come to us for capital, and for a lousy twenty million more, we bet you already had the cure."

Norman felt trapped.

"You duped us, plain and simple. Freiberg saw right through it. You're a fraudster, Norman, an arrogant bloodsucker, as if somehow, in your twisted mind, you were entitled."

"So you knew the FDA was going to turn me down?"

"We sure did," Mintz replied haughtily.

"But the FDA was concerned with mutation risk, and said they needed time to study it?"

Norman remembered what Freiberg told him during that fateful telephone call.

"Officially, we were always concerned you were sailing in uncharted territory, afraid the mirror neurons could develop DNA or RNA mutations,

inducing convulsive shock and instant death, even after the patient's neuro-degenerative symptoms were eradicated. This affected close to five percent of the test group. We need more time to sort this out, and make sure it doesn't morph into an epidemic."

"That was the official party line, what was fed to the public," Mintz conceded. "The results were mind boggling, a one hundred percent cure rate. A handful croaked from convulsive shock. So what? Freiberg purposely never even looked for a common link. He had enough arrows in his quill to shoot it down, especially with Merck coming in as the white knight."

Norman suddenly realized why Freiberg told him to expect a call from Merck.

"Pretty cozy arrangement, and I get screwed?"

"Depends how you see it. Freiberg's an ethical guy who likes to look at these things with an open mind, up to a point. He actually negotiated a damn good deal for you, all things considered."

"Go ahead."

"Merck buys your stock for a million bucks, the same number in your retirement account."

"Are you crazy? After taxes I get what, half a million dollars? It's an insult, Ken."

"You're not exactly negotiating from a position of strength," Mintz reminded him. "It's your life, Norman. You can fight the lawsuits or we can cut you a check. Our attorneys are itching to litigate. They'll crush you and go after your patents. Of course, if you have a couple of million lying around, it might be worth a shot."

"It's worth twenty, thirty million, maybe more. I'm handing you a multi-billion dollar business on a goddamn silver platter!" Norman spoke with the desperation of a man with no options, trying to salvage whatever was salvageable.

"C'mon, Norman, I'm just the messenger, it's not my call."

"Cut the crap, Ken. Make it five million and we're done."

Norman was prepared to take less.

"I'll call you back."

It wasn't more than ten minutes when the phone rang.

"Norman Berger."

"You low life, scumbag, perverted, four-eyed hunchback!"

"You must have the wrong number."

"I've got your number. How could you do this to me?"

"Victoria Chang, sorry, didn't recognize the voice. I got your messages but was in Washington all day with the SEC, and by the way, this line is tapped, so...."

The phone went dead. Their relationship was officially over, fun while it lasted.

The phone rang again. "Norman Berger."

"No can do; I begged them, take it or leave it."

It was a crock, all too obvious. Mintz never spoke to anyone. Norman knew him for what he was, a heartless, greedy bastard who stood to make a mint on this deal-no different than him.

"Email me the documents and a copy of the press release for my attorney to review. Any problems he'll get back to you. If he's comfortable, I'll see you tomorrow in my office."

"Done, they're on their way." Mintz hung up.

WHIT REMAINED HALTED FOR the next few days until the FDA made their decision public. Merck announced the deal, issuing a press release, honoring Norman as "a pioneer in the fight against ALS, a man who dedicated his life to finding a cure for this heinous disease."

WHIT tanked to less than a dollar, which Merck furtively scooped up at bargain basement prices, as investors, spooked by the FDA action and Norman's departure, dumped their holdings. A month later Merck made a tender offer for the remaining shares in a swap for Merck stock, effectively buying Whitcomb Pharmaceutical for pennies on the dollar, which rendered the options granted to Norman's braniacs worthless.

Norman packed his bags and grabbed a flight to New York City.

He didn't know that Victoria Chang's boyfriend had found her rambling letter along with her worthless WHIT options, which were torn and scattered helter skelter around her apartment. She blamed Norman for everything that had gone wrong in her life, and left for parts unknown, alone.

He went straight to his mother's apartment in the Bronx, who had just turned ninety, beset with Alzheimer's, and moved back into his same puny bedroom. Nothing had been touched. His precious Gilbert microscope from junior high school was still in good working order.

He had come full circle, a fifty-year journey.

Chapter 33

It was a few weeks later.

"Hey, Liz, guess who just emailed me?"

"Tiger Woods, he's revamping his swing again, heard you're tearing it up with that unorthodox reverse wrist cock. Or better yet, he's looking for a new caddie."

"Very funny, smart ass, try Norman Berger."

"The guy from Whitcomb, how did he get your email address?"

"We exchanged our contact info when I spoke to him, right when he was getting started, remember?"

"I think so. What do you suppose he wants?"

"Don't have a clue. He wants to meet ASAP, said he has some important information to share. Funny, he asked me about my golf, wanted to know how I was doing. I know what you know, what we read in the papers. I mean the FDA decision to turn down his ALS drug cost him a fortune, the news is still fresh."

"Maybe it's got something to do with Alan, that's your only common link, right?"

"Good thinking, Sherlock Holmes," he teasingly applauded.

"So did you tell him your golf career is almost over?"

"Something along those lines," he snapped. "You need to rub it in my face?"

"Sorry, you're right, it was uncalled for. When are you guys meeting?"

"He sounded anxious, so Thursday night. Next week is the qualifying round for the Richardson; some top touring pros won that tournament as amateurs. I need a few days practice. They're playing it at Friar's Head, out east. The course is off the charts. I shot four under par there in a charity event when I was working with Alan."

Liz just took it in stride. She'd heard the same story dozens of times, all his sub-par rounds, his bragging, which meant nothing. She would be supportive, thankful that in a few months he would bag this crazy game and start bringing home a paycheck.

Chapter 34

Thursday came quickly.

Gordon had never been to the Bronx, not intentionally. He had always considered it a crime infested foreign country. He double checked that his doors were locked as he drove up Arthur Avenue to East One Hundred and Eighty-Seventh Street. Forenzo's was Norman's suggestion. Liz checked it out on Zagat's. The reviews were stellar. *At least he would eat well*, she thought, even if Norman's information wasn't worth the expedition. A valet greeted him, a kid in dungarees wearing a black tee emblazoned with *Forenzo's* on the front in large white lettering. There was no indication he was anything but a car thief, no receipt or claim check, just "I got you covered," as he drove away.

Gordon walked inside to the cool rhythm of Tony Bennett crooning through the speakers, the restaurant awash with the locals, tables of six, eight, and ten, men who spoke with their hands, women decked out in faux designer outfits, all with their undistinguished and indistinguishable thick Bronx accents, laughing and carrying on, dining family style.

Bow-tied waiters delivered humongous plates of food and baskets of hot bread; antipasto salad, veal pizzaiola, chicken scarparello, linguine with white clam sauce, shrimps oreganata, steak alla Forenzo, (the house signature dish). Famished diners stuffed their faces with hefty portions, guzzling down bottles of cheap house wine, clanging their glasses with a hearty "Salute," somehow finding room for cappuccino and dessert, then leaving with their cherished doggy bags and well deserved cases of heartburn.

Gordon scouted the premises. "Not exactly a Mario's clientele," he murmured sarcastically under his breath. He was looking for a "four-eyed bald hunchback," as Norman described himself, eyeing him in the corner.

"Dr. Livingston, I presume?"

"At least you have a sense of humor," Norman replied, as they shook hands and Gordon slid into the booth. "You have your father's looks."

"So I've been told." Gordon silently thanked God he didn't look like his dinner companion.

"You know my beef with him, we discussed it." Norman got right to the point.

"And I have my own issues, remember?"

"Just to set the record straight, he paid me the ten thousand, plus interest, and sent me an apology, the usual stuff."

"Knowing him, he wanted to keep his foot in the door. He has a reason for everything he does."

"I agree. Have you been to the hospital?"

"Yeah, he's in the intensive care unit, ironically the one he donated. He's pretty much on life support. He made a huge bet on FDA approval, not like him."

"Maybe he had inside information?" Norman raised his eyebrows, his tone suggestively accusatory.

Gordon sat perplexed. Insider trading was a serious matter. It panged him to believe that his father was an out and out criminal. He thought that perhaps Jeremy was the culprit.

"And his right hand man, Jeremy Chang. Did you know him?"

"Yeah, I knew him; he's one of the reasons I quit the firm."

"I thought you told me Alan fired you, right before Labor Day weekend?"

"I deserved it, egged him on. Either way I needed to leave and do my own thing."

"Then you know Chang hung himself?"

"It's unbelievable. He had all his money in the firm, lost it all. Maybe it was Jeremy who orchestrated the whole thing?"

"He did."

"What happened?"

"One of my best researchers had my total confidence. Somehow Chang got to him and paid cash for the information. I found out about it, and knew the FDA decision a few days early. The rest was simple. I told this rat in strict confidence that the drug was approved. He got to Chang with the information. They loaded up on the stock, and when the news hit the tape, bang!" Norman pounded the table.

"And I guess if the drug was approved, you would have told this mole just the opposite?"

"That's exactly right. They would have put on a massive short position, thinking the stock would tank. When the news hits, the stock goes to the moon, and they're caught in a massive short squeeze. Either way they lose a fortune."

Norman made sure Gordon thought the stool pigeon was a man, seeing no sense in bringing up Victoria Chang, wary that he could track her down through Jeremy's family. There was no telling what she was capable of. He wondered how she was doing.

Gordon let the information seep in, trying to believe Norman wasn't somehow responsible for Jeremy's suicide, or his father's massive stroke.

"Hope you're not blaming me—sorry it had to be your father. But it was his choice."

"You could've said nothing," Gordon reminded him, "and then whatever happened has nothing to do with you, right?"

"I never thought about it that way. The way I saw it, they took advantage and had to pay the price. Besides, they bet the ranch, and were greedy. Funny how people usually get what they deserve, don't you think?"

Gordon just nodded, not sure he agreed or disagreed. But he couldn't deny that having dinner with the guy who probably caused his father's stroke and all but ended his life was difficult to swallow.

"Let's order, we have a lot more to discuss. Anything you don't like?"

"Yeah, stomach aches," as Gordon pointed to the rowdy table shoveling down their food with two hands.

Norman laughed; he liked that type of quick witted humor.

"These people come here to eat, not to banter politics, current events, or cures for ALS. We can go light."

"Fine, that sounds good."

Over dinner, Norman spoon-fed Gordon a condensed version of his autobiography.

"I knew early on I was different. My IQ tests confirmed it. But with this," Norman turned around to expose his deformity, "it was a mixed blessing. Somehow I found a way to accept what I look like, and spent my life in science. ALS killed my father. I made up my mind to find a cure, or die trying. Merck gave me a shot, and tossed in a fortune for research. I ran the group and thought I was close, until they lost their patience and killed the undertaking. I could've stayed and gone through the motions with a salary and fat pension, but I would've been miserable. I knew I was onto something. They wanted me to sign my life away, afraid I would use what I learned. So I left, which caused quite a ruckus. I forfeited my retirement, a million dollars, but didn't give a damn. I had something to prove."

"Seems like a pretty risky move, especially at your age." Gordon was impressed with Norman's moxie.

"Anything worthwhile entails risk. What's that saying- nothing ventured, nothing gained? Sounds simple, but most people cower at their own shadow, at least that's what I've learned from this crazy life."

The conversation took a respite, while Gordon mulled over Norman's telling statement, which hit home, and gnawed at him.

"And then what happened, how did you find the cure?"

"Next stop was North Carolina, Triangle Research Institute, a place swarming with cutting edge biotech companies. I felt alive, optimistic, a real shot in the arm."

"That's where you found Whitcomb?"

"A match made in heaven. They had what I needed and I had what they wanted."

"And you bought the company? I thought you were down and out?"

"I knew enough about Blair Whitcomb, the CEO, to pull off a coup." Norman beamed, proud of the way he had taken a sick puppy and made it healthy.

"Sounds interesting, tell me about it."

"Whitcomb was working on a drug to give ALS patients more time. It wasn't a cure, just a method to reduce the severity of their symptoms and extend their lives. Has to do with what we call protein chaperone therapy. They were burning through their money, and Blair Whitcomb was at the end of his rope. It was obvious, but entrepreneurs sometimes refuse to admit they're barking up the wrong tree. It happens all the time in biotech, just the nature of the beast."

"He's a sitting duck for a guy like you."

"At first I think he resented me, but after a candid discussion he had a change of heart. They had cash, at least enough to get me started. He left. I took over, but he kept a nice chunk of the business."

"Where did he go? He must have been upset?"

"Blair was a neurologist. He returned to private practice and felt a helluva better about the incident, figuring I was a better horse to bet on."

"I guess he was right?"

"More than you can imagine. I quickly raised twenty million from Merck. They also knew I was the right horse. I hired a team of researchers. We busted our humps. Long story short, I figured out what makes ALS tick and proved it in my animal studies. The FDA was so impressed with our documentation they pretty much gave me carte blanche with human trials."

"Jesus, that's incredible!"

"The early results were as I had hoped. Next step was a public offering. We needed the capital to finish the trials and submit our findings to the FDA for approval. It was a hot issue, everyone wanted in."

"I can imagine-did Blair sell his shares?"

"Every last one, he walked away with fifty million."

"Nice payday, how about you?"

"I was locked up, which means I couldn't sell until the FDA approved the drug. That's how these deals work."

"Yeah, I know- they don't want the head honcho to take his money and run. Alan taught me that, it makes total sense."

"You know the next scene; no sense in crying over spilt milk."

"Why did they turn down the drug? Did something happen to those patients?"

"You want the whole story or the condensed version?"

Norman looked pained, just the way he frowned. Gordon would cut him some slack.

"Just enough so I understand, you look bummed out."

"I am."

"I can see it. Go ahead, I'm all ears."

Norman ran through the episode with Julius Freiberg, including Ken Mintz's accusations of how he had misappropriated Merck's proprietary information, the threatened litigation, and his eventual deal.

"Are you serious? You found the cure and Merck steps in for a million bucks?"

"Yes," Norman answered dispiritedly, which played on Gordon's sympathies.

"That's totally unfair; all that time and effort and you wind up with—"

"Stop it!"

"Sorry, didn't mean to upset you."

Gordon changed the subject. "What happened to Blair Whitcomb?"

"Whitcomb is a golf nut. He thinks he's a professional, or could be. That's his whole life, dreaming about winning the US Open.

He would carry on for hours with me, ranting and raving. Basically he's a super rich golf addict obsessed with muscle memory."

"You and I talked about muscle memory, remember?"

"Sure do, when you first called me, a few years ago. Who do you think told me about it?"

"Can't blame this Blair guy," Gordon replied, "every pro on the planet would give anything to have perfect muscle memory, not even close."

"And you thought it was impossible, remember?"

"You reamed me out, said it's difficult, unlikely, farfetched, but never impossible."

"You have a good memory, Gordon, that's exactly what I said."

"That's some story, Dr. Berger."

"Let's cut the formality, I'm not into titles. Call me Norman."

Gordon hoped there was more to discuss, and that Norman hadn't baited him to the Bronx just to bash Alan and regurgitate his life's story.

There was.

Chapter 35

"REMEMBER YOU TOLD ME about this Tiger guy, how much money he makes, like a hundred million a year?"

"He makes more than that if we include endorsements and prize money" Gordon answered matter-of-factly. "He gets two million bucks just for showing up, but nobody's in his league, everyone is playing for second place."

"What's so special about him?" Norman asked.

"What's not? He practices six hours a day, on a mission to stick the club in the same slot every swing. His mind is rock solid and has total confidence in his mechanics, if not perfect, then damn close."

"You mean he tries to place his arms in the backswing in the same position relative to his body and shoulders so his club is always on the same plane, correct?"

Gordon remembered from their phone conversation that Norman knew more than the basics of the golf swing.

"Yeah, pretty much, but he went through some swing changes recently. It's tough to do, but he's a perfectionist and never gives up."

"Does he win every time he plays?"

"No. He's got flaws that creep up and throw his game off for a few holes. But he's always in the hunt, cool as a cucumber, never buckles under pressure."

"What kind of flaws?"

"It could be anything, but usually with him he gets stuck, that's what he tells the press."

"Which means what?"

"There was a really cool article in *The New York Times,* which explained what he was working on. I still have it, probably read it fifty times."

"What was it?"

Gordon stood up, gripped a butter knife as if it were a golf club, and went through the club and body positions to demonstrate his Tiger Woods tutorial. "It has to do with the plane angle of his backswing, which used to be above his shoulder. His body rotation was so fast that they outraced his arms coming down, so they weren't in sync. It caused either a push to the right or he flips his hands at impact, and then it's anyone's guess where the ball ends up."

"How did he fix it?"

"Kind of complicated, but he tried to match the plane of his backswing with the position of the club at address, looking for a more consistent swing plane that mirrors his arms and body. It's called a one plane swing, as opposed to a two plane swing. The club is flatter and not as steep, which allows him to swing without thinking about his timing. It's pretty technical stuff."

Gordon wondered why Norman was so interested in Tiger Woods.

Norman leaned forward and folded his arms, his eyes fixated on Gordon's. "What if someone were able to repeat their swing with the precision of a finely tuned machine, with the shaft always on plane and the club head pointing directly to their target? The rotation of their torso would be perfectly in sync with their hands, arms, and the path of their downswing, the point of impact never wavering, as if they were a robot."

"Jesus Christ, its Iron Byron! That's beyond sick, I mean that's ridiculous, like science fiction, totally awesome, mind boggling, I mean...."

"What's an Iron Byron?" Norman asked curiously.

"He's a golf machine!"

"Sorry, never heard of him; what does he do?"

"He hits golf balls, I mean he tests golf balls, no, he simulates a golfer. I mean he looks like a golfer, but he's really a machine. Wait, let me explain, give me a minute."

He fumbled for his cell phone, opened the browser, and typed "Iron Byron" into the Google search box.

"Here it is!" He handed Norman the phone and hovered over his shoulder while he watched a three minute slow motion tutorial on Iron Byron, a machine developed by the USGA to test clubs and balls for conformity to their equipment standards.

"So?" Gordon asked excitedly as Norman calmly returned the phone, having seen enough.

"Who's Byron Nelson in this video?"

"He played back in the 40s and 50s, won like eleven straight tournaments, eighteen in one year, including the Masters. He retired young, around thirty-four. The story is that his swing was so close to perfect only a robot could duplicate it."

"So Iron Byron's mechanical swing was fashioned after this Byron Nelson's swing?"

"Almost, but has to do more so with efficiency, tough to explain if you don't play."

"No, I got it, efficiency is a function of physics, not to bore you with formulas, but basically it's how much effort one expends to achieve a desired result. I can see it in the video. The machine is built with hinges and levers, same as our wrists, arms and elbows. A good golf swing employs what we call the conservation of angular momentum, basically—"

"I understand it," Gordon jumped in. "I've read every golf instructional book on the planet. It's all about stored power, rotation, and release."

"That's correct," Norman responded. "Remember what you told me about what makes Woods so unique."

"He's just phenomenal, not sure what you're driving at."

"Swinging without thinking, mind rock solid, never buckles under pressure, total confidence in his mechanics. Does that sound familiar?"

"Yeah, I guess, never really thought about it like that."

"Does that remind you of someone?" Norman smiled, arching his eyebrows.

"You mean Iron Byron, no brain or bad thoughts, right?"

"Correct, having no flaws, getting stuck, flipping your hands, or any of the infinite variables that can sabotage a perfect swing. It's all about centrifugal force, centripetal force, longitudinal acceleration, and radial acceleration. The slightest imperfection in the swing interferes with these natural laws of physics. It's why the game can never be mastered except by robots, not by human beings, who are by nature imperfect."

"That's exactly what Hogan said!" Gordon added excitedly. "On any given day he hits one, maybe two perfect shots; all the rest are just good misses."

"Who's Hogan?" Norman thought Blair Whitcomb had mentioned him.

"Just the greatest ball striker ever, that's all."

"What happened to Byron and Woods?"

Gordon needed to stop with the name dropping, as it only confused things. "Good question, unless you have a couple of hours to kill."

"Forget it, it's not that important."

Norman reached into his pocket, took out a vial containing two white capsules, and handed it to Gordon.

"These will turn you into an Iron Byron; an effortlessly efficient robot, all of your God given golfing talent coupled with the genius of the laws of physics."

The freakish looking scientist had just uttered the most outrageously outlandish statement Gordon had ever heard, bar none.

"Imagine being totally ignorant to whatever it is that plays with your head, your own psychological bugaboos; fear of winning, self-doubt, issues with your father, the list is endless and complicated. Only you or your shrink know the reason. Nothing to be ashamed of, we all have issues, some more than others. It's what makes us human, and different, makes life interesting and worth living."

Gordon just listened, speechless.

"Don't get the wrong impression. All I'm doing is making a

superlative swing bulletproof, not a fix for the rank amateur available at your local pharmacy."

"How do these work?" Gordon's hand was trembling, which shook the vial, the magic capsules rattling back and forth.

Norman went through the same layman's explanation on his cure for ALS he gave to Victoria Chang.

"But I don't have ALS?" Gordon looked at him quizzically.

"The capsules work in a similar fashion, although the dosage is much lower, the chemical composition considerably less potent. Remember I said that the drug allows the mirror neurons to develop their own intelligence, to teach the brain how to memorize both simple and complicated motor functions?"

"Yes."

"And remember what else I said?"

"I sure do, something about your drug giving the ALS patients the ability to develop new brain circuits so their muscles can remember how to act on their own, almost like they had artificial intelligence."

"Exactly, Gordon, muscle memory without thinking, that's the key—critical in golf. Do you remember your good swings?"

"Totally!" he replied. "I can almost feel my best swings weeks later. It's weird; never understood it, but for sure it's true."

"And your bad swings, do they linger in your memory?"

Gordon thought about it for a moment. It was a good question. "No, actually they don't." He wondered why it worked that way.

"And these good swings, how do they feel?"

"Like everything is firing in the exact perfect sequence, my hips, arms, legs and hands. The club is so light I can't feel it. It's effortless, but powerful, almost as if I...."

"Like a well oiled machine, is that the feeling?"

"Exactly, smooth as silk."

"Right; has to do with the part of the brain known as the cerebellum, something you probably learned in high school biology. We tend to remember pleasant things and forget unpleasant ones, just the body's way of healing itself."

"That makes sense," Gordon replied. "If I hit a bad shot, I'll curse and throw my club, and then it's forgotten."

Norman jumped at the chance to pontificate. "The cerebellum controls memory and motor functions. Different types of motor neurons in the spinal cord affect coordination, precision and the accurate timing of muscle movement. Technically, Purkinje cells, granule cells, synaptic plasticity, and climbing fibers send out super strong signals that act as teaching mechanisms for changes in sensorimotor relationships, the effect of—"

"How about giving me the two minute version?"

"OK, Gordon, sometimes I get carried away. Long story short, what we're doing is creating a series of intelligent neural motor messaging pathways, allowing you to consistently repeat your best swing, instinctively. These heightened and pleasurable experiences continuously reinforce themselves through the mechanisms in your cerebellum, further bolstering your confidence, building upon itself, over and over, swing after swing, until you become a human golfing machine."

"That's amazing! How long does this take?"

"It depends, but generally people with superior memories can perfect it quicker, it lasts longer, and requires a smaller dosage."

One thing Gordon was sure of was his photographic memory. "Let's say I'm interested, what's the next step."

"There's something you need to know first."

"Like what?"

"Like five percent of the test volunteers who were cured eventually developed mutations of the mirror neurons, went into convulsive shock, and died."

"Are you kidding?"

"I never saw the data, but would bet my last nickel there's some common link. That's usually how these things work. My best guess is the patients who died were all older, probably sixty-five or more, which is when we naturally start losing our memory. We had a hundred percent cure rate, and with ALS that's beyond remarkable. The five percent is well worth it, considering they would have died anyway. And if that's the reason, they can fix it. There's no shortage of remedies on the market to boost memory capacity."

Gordon suddenly stood up and paced back and forth, holding his head.

"It sounds a lot worse than it is," Norman continued. "The FDA didn't want me in the picture and railroaded me, just as I explained. Their official statement was their concern that the number could be higher, and they needed more time. They'll be issuing a detailed report in a few weeks. Besides, the potency and the dosage of what you're holding in your hand are infinitesimal compared to what was pumped through their systems."

"How the hell can you be so sure, for Christ sake? Do you understand what you're saying? Have these been tested, or am I your guinea pig? What if something horrible happens to me? Is there an antidote? Just the *thought* of dying gives me the creeps, and it's not a priority, not something on Gordon Howard's to do list." His voice boomed throughout the restaurant as startled patrons looked over to see what the fuss was all about.

NORMAN BERGER HAD ALWAYS suspected that his cure for ALS, with some tinkering, would imbue the Blair Whitcombs and the Gordon Howards of the world with that elusive muscle memory.

True, that was a whole different business, operated in the clandestine underworld of mercenary voodoo doctors, steroidal injections, performance enhancement drugs, baseball sluggers and Tour de France cyclists, although his magic capsule would be invisible in urine or blood samples.

Nor was he ever opposed to it, if push came to shove, and he was up against the ropes. His drug could be sold to the highest bidder, who would pay through the nose for a fix.

"RELAX, GORDON, AND SIT down, you're overreacting."

"Answer me, Goddamnit!" Gordon replied angrily.

Norman waited until things calmed down and Gordon sat back down at the table. "It's never been tested other than it's derived from my ALS cure," Norman replied matter-of-factly. "It's your decision. If you're nervous, or doubt me, then wait and read their findings for yourself. There's no rush. If not you, there are others. I have no shortage of candidates."

Norman spoke with that take it or leave it haughtiness.

Gordon thought about the Richardson out at Friar's Head, just one week away, his last tournament before crying uncle to Liz and joining the ranks of the nine to fivers. *Those freaking tie and jacket interviews!* Just the thought of it gave him the sweats.

Yet if he won, everything would change, overnight. But without the luxury of reading the FDA report, he would have to walk or bite the bullet. *Damnit!* He berated himself for winding up in this do or die situation.

"What's next?"

"It's strictly business, a partnership. I supply the capsules for a percentage of your winnings."

"What did you have in mind?"

"We can keep it simple, Gordon. I'm getting older and don't need much. You have a whole life ahead of you. But I have an axe to grind, something to prove, and would rather do it with you, considering our ALS camaraderie. And if your father pulls through, you can shove your trophies up his backside, which should give you some sense of satisfaction. So whatever percentage you think is fair is fine with me."

Gordon knew his father would never get better. He shuddered as he pictured him lying in the hospital room, hooked up to the life support machine.

"Nice to know you trust me."

"Why shouldn't I, just because your Alan's son?"

"The thought crossed my mind."

"I always give someone the benefit of the doubt until they prove otherwise."

"Don't worry, that's not how I do business."

Norman acknowledged that with a nod, as Gordon continued, sounding anxious.

"And nobody else gets the capsule, just our secret?"

"A hundred percent; and by the way, in case you're concerned, it can't be traced."

"How long will it take for us to know the capsules work?"

"No more than an hour, maybe less, everybody is different."

"Let me think about it, I might have an idea."

Gordon called for the check, and made arrangements to meet at Old Point the next day, the two of them, Swifty, and a couple of magic capsules.

LIZ WAS ASLEEP WHEN Gordon got undressed in the dark and quietly slipped into bed, trying to avoid awakening her.

"Jesus Christ, it's one in the morning, where the hell did you guys go, to a strip club?"

"Yeah, it was a hot spot on Arthur Avenue, with naked women rubbing spaghetti and meatballs all over their bodies. All you could eat for twenty bucks, tips not included. It wasn't exactly Mario's, but the price was right, and the girls a bit hefty."

"Sounds like fun. Give me the details in the morning on this Norman guy. Was it at least worthwhile?"

"Nah, he ran an hour late, and the service took forever. He's an interesting guy but scary looking, all stooped over like Quasimodo, with some choice words for Alan. I'm bushed, sorry to wake you. I'm going to the club tomorrow to practice."

"OK, hon, goodnight."

He reached over to his night table, opened the drawer and fished around for the vial. He shook it and heard the pills rattle. *Thank God!* He downed four milligrams of Clonazepam, twice the prescribed dosage, a potent anti-anxiety drug he used only for emergencies, of which this ranked number one.

He drifted off into a narcotic induced sleep.

Chapter 36

GORDON STOOD ON THE putting green in front of the clubhouse, waiting for his two distinguished guests to arrive, practicing his short game, hugging the shaft of his Odyssey mallet head long putter against his sternum, rolling in a bunch of ten-foot putts, automatic, one after another.

A few minutes past noon, a taxi pulled up underneath the portico. The valet opened the back door for Norman, who was decked out in rumpled black trousers, a white short sleeved shirt speckled with yellow perspiration stains under the armpits, a half knotted green tie, and scuffed black shoes.

Norman traipsed over to the putting green. Gordon had made it a point to dress appropriately.

"You're putting?" Norman said, recalling the Blair Whitcomb exhibition.

Gordon looked at him as if he were from Mars. What the hell was wrong with this guy? There was no hello, thanks for dinner last night, nice place you have here. *What did he think he was doing, duck hunting?*

"I'm just practicing my stroke, trying to keep it consistent, back and forth like a pendulum. You know what they say about putting?"

Norman remembered Blair Whitcomb had a similar looking putter.

"A hundred percent of the putts that don't reach the hole don't go in."

"Whoa, that's right!"

"It's just logical," Norman quipped, while Gordon pondered

how on earth he knew that. "My formula won't help you with putting. That requires a different set of skills, small muscle control, nothing that can be ingrained."

"Not to brag, but my short game is as good as any pro, even Woods."

"How about chipping?" Norman asked, another Blair reference, having no idea what it was, other than Blair's comment about how players with the best short games make the most money.

Gordon walked over to his bag, removed his fifty-six degree sand wedge, and tossed down a half dozen Titleists onto the short grass. Ignoring the *No Chipping* sign, he had Norman remove the flag from the hole some fifty feet away, and waved him aside to give him a clear look at the break.

"Check this out." He deftly plopped each ball onto the green. Norman watched them roll along the slope line, breaking left to right. Gordon holed out three, the others narrowly missing.

"You make it look so simple."

"Come next to me. I want to show you something totally cool."

Gordon loved to show off with his sixty-four degree wedge. He dropped a new Titleist onto the fringe, addressed the ball off of his left foot with a wide open blade, open stance, and took a full swing, as the ball skied upward some twenty-five feet in the air, and then landed softly, three feet from the hole, stopping dead.

"That's my Phil shot," Gordon grinned, "it comes in handy sometimes."

"Who's Phil?" Norman asked.

Before Gordon could get all pumped up over his hero, Phil Mickelson, his other distinguished guest arrived.

"Hey, GH, sorry I'm late." Swifty hustled onto the putting green. "The damn car wouldn't start, had to have my buddy juice up the battery."

Gordon hoped Bruce Haberman, who was recently appointed head of the grievance committee, wasn't snooping around. A perfect candidate for a miserable job, he would have a field day with Gordon's two eminent invitees.

Gordon introduced Norman to Swifty and vice-versa. He referred to him as Dr. Berger, a sports psychologist, who would be spending a few hours working on Gordon's confidence.

Swifty wasn't quite sure what a sports psychologist did. "He's one strange lookin dude," he whispered. "I hope he knows what he's talkin' about, but it's real late in the game, GH."

FRIDAYS WERE ALWAYS CROWDED with the men's weekly golf games. The upstairs range was packed with all the usual suspects, guys more interested in their side bets than their scores, with nicknames like Pele, who would kick the ball out of the rough, Pencil, who always kept score and never lost any money, Two Balls, who cut a hole in his pants pocket, allowing a seemingly lost ball to magically appear in a convenient spot, and Mr. Gimme, Dr. Bruce Haberman, who took every putt three feet or less.

Gordon quickly hustled Norman down the stairs, with Swifty right behind, avoiding accidentally flaunting them in Haberman's face, then over to the extreme left side of the range, where Swifty set down the bag and some bottles of cold water.

"Hey, Swifty, grab the Sony for us."

"Sure thing, GH," He scampered off to Charlie's teaching facility, making one brief unscheduled stop at the inside foot of the stairwell. Surreptitiously peering back at them, his cell phone camera in hand, Swifty noticed Norman took something out of an opaque bag, which he handed to Gordon, who fumbled it, and quickly dropped to his knees, hastily sifting through the grass until he found what he was looking for and stuffed it into his pocket.

Swifty continued to watch as Norman spoke to Gordon out of earshot.

"I want you to do whatever you normally do, nothing different. Watch your ball flight. You'll know when it's your best swing, the way you explained it to me; effortless, smooth as silk, every muscle firing in perfect sequence. Then stop, concentrate on that feeling, and swallow the capsules."

"I understand; and then what do we do?"

"We wait, at least an hour. You'll need to eat something, remain fixated on that feeling, and let the muscles relax. Then we come back, and we'll know, one way or the other."

Swifty returned with the Sony, set it and adjusted the focus. Gordon loosened up, prepared to bang out another large bucket of balls and analyze his swing, like any other practice day.

"OK," Norman continued, "all I want you to do is to imagine each shot is a do or die situation, to build up the pressure in your mind, and challenge yourself."

"I understand, Doctor Berger."

The repartee was all an act for Swifty's benefit, who didn't understand what this Berger guy offered any different than what he had been continually pounding into Gordon's head. Swifty had no illusions that today would be any different. The past few years together had so far been an exercise in abject futility.

Norman sat to the side and watched as Gordon went through his routine. Swifty recorded each swing, capturing different angles, as he always did, but today noticed an unusual calm in Gordon's demeanor. There were no profanities, no anger, and no clubs hurled into the bushes; he seemed to have made peace with himself and had come to grips with reality, that he just wasn't good enough, not even close.

"That's it, perfect," Gordon murmured halfway through the bucket, after he blistered a five iron, which started off low, then rose, boring against the wind, higher and higher, landing softly onto the artificial green. It took one bounce, and then stopped a foot from the hole, carrying some two hundred and ten yards in the air.

Gordon suddenly scampered away. "I'll be right back, I'm thirsty."

"I gotcha water, GH, nice and cold," Swifty yelled.

"I mean, I gotta take a leak," he hollered back.

He hustled to the indoor shed and went into the bathroom. His mind raced amidst a phantasm of *what if* scenarios, with the specter of some horrific unintended consequences, befuddled whether placing his fate in the hands of a strange man he met only a day before was bravery, desperation, stupidity or a smattering of each.

A good hard look in the mirror prompted more than a hesitation. *How had his life come down to this one defining moment?*

He took a deep breath and a leap of faith, swallowing the two capsules with a few gulps of water, still fixated on that feeling.

"HEY GUYS, HOW ABOUT a quick lunch, we can walk over to the halfway house."

They sat silently, each in their own thoughts.

Swifty had a strange feeling about Norman Berger, not quite sure who he was, or what he really did, or why Gordon never mentioned him before. *And what did Gordon drop and shove into his pocket? And then they were talking, about what?*

But one thing was for sure; the Old Point oversized kosher hot dog, grilled to perfection, heaping with mustard, ketchup, onions and chili, with a side order of cottage fries, tasted a helluva lot better than the baloney sandwich stuffed into his back pocket.

Norman took just a few bites of a sandwich, but had trouble getting the food down. He felt a knot in his stomach as he sipped some water to irrigate his parched mouth. He tried to control his angst that the capsules would not work as he envisioned, or that something couldn't go devastatingly awry. He shuddered at the thought as his eyes fixated on Gordon, who appeared calm, as he chowed down a medium rare gruyere cheeseburger, still hooked on that feeling, as instructed.

THEY RETURNED TO THE range. Swifty focused the Sony as Gordon banged out four dozen balls, exact carbon copies of the five- iron he crushed before he ingested the capsules.

Swifty glanced over at Norman, who just watched with his arms folded, nodding smugly after each shot.

"Those are a sight for sore eyes, GH. I don't know what you

guys been discussin', but I never seen you hit it like that before. Lemme see you work the ball."

Gordon had already figured out over lunch how to attack the pin from the left or the right.

To hit a cut, he set the clubhead behind the ball, turned his hands and closed the face; for a draw, just the opposite, with an open face. He knew most professionals changed their alignment, altered their swing planes and their grips, but his unorthodox method worked flawlessly, allowing him to maintain his ingrained swing, while his hands naturally opened or closed the clubhead at impact.

"OK, Swifty, roll the Sony." Gordon struck a dozen fades, then a dozen draws, each landing on the green, then spinning toward the hole, some gimmes, even for Bruce Haberman. "I'm done, Swifty. We don't need to study the films. I think I figured it out, so let's call it a day." Gordon and Norman left together.

Swifty waited on the range an hour or so, and then made his way down a path through the adjacent brush to Charlie's teaching facility, coming up from behind, wary of being detected. Well past five o'clock, the door was locked, but he snuck in through the back window.

As he always did, Swifty set the video machine to slow motion and turned on the monitor, which was synched to any audio captured by the microphone. Swifty studied the first bucket of swings, each of which was imperfect; the club slightly off plane, or crossing the line, the backswing a few degrees too vertical or flat, the takeaway a bit inside the hands. There were all in all a myriad of flaws which would creep up more so than not, not unlike any touring pro.

And then he heard it, for the first time, "that's it, perfect," uttered with the last swing Gordon made, an awesome five iron, before bolting to the bathroom.

He watched the next set, the ones taken after lunch. The swings were flawless, with the club moving perfectly along the lines and angles superimposed on the monitor, each swing an exact carbon copy of the one before it. He replayed them, astonished by what he was witnessing, wondering if Gordon was in some kind of hypnotic trance, and Norman Berger some sort of voodoo doctor.

But whatever it was, something smelled, and Swifty wasn't sure the aroma was sweet, foul, or a whiff of both.

Chapter 37

THERE WAS NO SENSE in giving Norman the grand tour of the clubhouse. Gordon didn't want to scare the members or risk a run in with Bruce Haberman.

"They work," Gordon opened the conversation as he drove Norman to the railroad station. "But everybody hits it great on the range where there's no pressure to perform. It's a whole different ball game on the course. They say this game is played mostly between the ears."

"You said you had an idea," Norman responded, getting right to the point.

"It's been too many years, almost four, and I'm at the end of my rope. Sure I have talent, but so what. The truth is I choke under pressure. You got to me at the right time." Gordon appeared jittery, nervously tapping his thumbs against the steering wheel as he drove. "There's a major amateur tournament next week, Friday through Sunday. It's the last one this year. The best players will be there. I promised my girlfriend that if I don't win, I'd find a real job, and start bringing home a paycheck. She's been supportive; I really can't blame her."

"And if you do win, then what?"

"If my swing holds up," Gordon looked over at Norman, "then you and I are gonna make a lot of money together. The next stop is competing for my card to turn professional. Then I hit the tour, and should win everything in sight."

"Sounds like a plan, partner."

As they arrived at the station, Norman counted out exactly

eighteen capsules from the bag, loaded them into a vial, and handed it to Gordon.

"Starting tomorrow, take two each day for five days before you start your practice sessions, concentrating on the feeling, and then two before each day of competition. I threw in two extras, better be safe than sorry, in case you lose a few."

Gordon wondered why Norman was so anal about the capsules.

"Understood—I have one last question."

"Quick, the train is here."

"Eventually I won't need these, once my swing is permanently ingrained. At least that's what I thought you meant."

"Maybe, it depends," Norman answered curtly as he hopped out and boarded the train, back to his mother's hovel in the Bronx.

Chapter 38

"HEY, YOU'RE IN A good mood, win the lottery or something?"

Gordon had just returned home after the first day of the Richardson.

"Why shouldn't I be? I was low qualifier with a sixty-two. Every iron was a pin seeker. I missed a downhill five-footer for a sixty-one- would have tied the course record. There could be a blurb in tomorrow's Times if you're interested, definitely on Monday. The Richardson gets plenty of press."

It was the last thing in the world she wanted to hear.

She knew his modus operandi; this was going to be his break-through, just like the other forty or so tournaments he never won over the past four years. She would have to listen to him describe every hole and every shot, which would just get him all hyped up, only to bang it in the water or into the parking lot when the chips were down, cracking under the pressure.

What the hell, she thought, this was his last tournament, and his next stop was gainful employment.

"Go ahead, let's hear the post-mortem, I'm all ears."

"Nah, not too exciting, I just played to my potential, hitting every green, making a bunch of putts, and knocking in a wedge for an eagle. I was in total control of my swing. Let's see what happens tomorrow; if I win in the morning I play again in the afternoon, then the finals are on Sunday."

She noticed it immediately; he was too nonchalant, as if carding a sixty-three was no big deal, especially at this stage of the game.

"How about we have an early dinner? I gotta pick up Swifty and head east early tomorrow; first match is at 9:10."

"Is Italian Village OK, Mr. Woods?"

"Yep, order the usual, linguine Bolognese and a house salad," he said, reaching into his pocket.

"Nope, it's on me, my treat; it's not every evening that Tiger Woods joins us for dinner."

"You're gonna eat those words, wise guy, try them with some Parmesan cheese."

Liz smiled as she called in their order, although her stomach was churning with a gnawing feeling that he would take tomorrow's loss really hard, and possibly go off the deep end.

"LIZ SPEAKING," SHE ANSWERED her office phone.

"Hey, it's Tiger."

"So?"

"Just closed out my morning match on twelve; beat this top amateur, a total blue blood WASP, Baxter Cummings III. He belongs to all the men only restricted clubs. You know what they are; dues are cheap, the locker rooms with the original steam pipes hanging below the ceiling, and the food from hunger. But the tracts are super. He speaks with that Locust Valley lockjaw, like he has cotton stuffed in his mouth. He was really ticked off and stormed off the course. I think he underestimated me. Gonna grab a bite with Swifty. Not sure who I play this afternoon, but I booked a room; easier for us to stay out here for the finals tomorrow."

"Aren't you being a bit presumptuous?"

"No!" he shot back, miffed at her comment.

She wasn't going to start an argument, rain on his parade, or give him reason to make her his scapegoat. The two year grace period they agreed upon was coming to an abrupt end. If he needed to reserve the room to bolster his confidence, then so be it. But unless he flips out, no way was she going to capitulate on their agreement, and if he hemmed and hawed, she would come down on him hard.

"OK, whatever you think is best, good luck." She hung up, dreading the finale to this four year nightmare.

Chapter 39

JACK RICHARDS, FREELANCE WRITER and recipient of a host of journalistic awards, stood numero uno amongst golf aficionados who read his columns as if they were gospel. He had been following Gordon Howard since he split from his father and went out on his own, supplying *The New York Times* with not so flattering articles about the rich kid who had more talent than gumption.

After Gordon won the Richardson, Richards gave him a sneak preview of the article, entitled *Gordon Howard Captures Richardson in Stunning Fashion*, slated to appear next day in *The NY Times'* Monday edition.

> I admit it; I never particularly cared for him, his arrogance, hurling his clubs, temper tantrums and profanities, blaming everyone but himself for whatever prevented him from winning. But the Gordon Howard I watched for the past three days is a whole different animal, and to say I witnessed one of the most remarkable displays of amateur golf would be a gross understatement.
>
> In a cool, calm, almost elevated state of consciousness, the thirty-five-year-old punished the difficult 7,250 yard Friar's Head tract as if it were a pitch and putt course, boasting low medalist by seven shots in the Thursday qualifying round. He carded a brilliant sixty-two on Friday, missing a tricky downhill six-footer to tie the course record of sixty-one held by the uber-talented Mid-Amateur champion and

Master's qualifier, Kenneth Bakst. He played as if he were cruising on auto-pilot. Oh, forgot to mention the sweet eagle on fourteen, holing out a wedge on a slam dunk fly.

OK, maybe it was a fluke round. One swallow doesn't make a spring. Let's see how he fared head to head against guys who know how to win.

Well, he took them down with the brutality of a Mike Tyson right hand, pummeling out prodigious drives, delivering razor sharp irons into defenseless greens, negotiating a howling wind whipping off the Long Island Sound as if it were a summer breeze, until they cried uncle, with no match going past twelve holes.

So what's next for Gordon Howard? I asked him that very question after he received the prestigious Richardson trophy, and he just smiled, shook my hand, and walked into the twilight with Swifty, his longtime caddie, carrying his bag and trudging alongside.

THEY HEADED BACK TO the city.

"I ain't ever seen you hit it like you did these last three days, GH, not even close."

"Yep, I finally got it together, Swifty. It took me four years, with all that practice."

"Hey GH, that Norman guy, what he tell you? You didn't feel no pressure, never tightened up, loose as a goose."

"He just got my head straight, that's all. A bunch of pros have guys like Dr. Berger who teach them how to win and not fold in the stretch."

"Yeah, I guess so, but you gotta have the goods, because without them, it makes no difference if your head is screwed on right."

"You got doubts?" Gordon speed dialed Liz.

"No doubts, GH, no doubts at all." He didn't notice Swifty's tinge of sarcasm.

"Hey, how did it go?" She was surprised to hear from him so soon. He always broke the bad news at home.

"Not bad; I'm driving back, dropping Swifty off first."

"You want to talk about it now? Why don't we wait till later? I'm here for you. There's no sense in going through it alone. I'm happy to be your punching bag."

"We must have a bad connection," Gordon replied glibly. "I won the damn tournament, wasn't even close. The story will be in tomorrow's *Times*. This trophy is huge, so think about a good spot for it in the apartment."

"You're joking, right?"

"Never been more serious, Liz. Next stop is West Palm Beach, trying to earn my tour card. I'll give you the gory details later. How about Italian Village tonight? I'm famished; see you around eight, the traffic's lightening up."

Chapter 40

"YOU SAID HOW MANY months?" Liz choked on a mouthful of vegetable lasagna.

He laid out the PGA Qualifying School for her. Two dozen tournaments played over two months with the finals in early December. Twelve hundred of the best amateurs and once upon a time professionals battling for twenty-five coveted spots, all under unbearable pressure; unable to eat or sleep, sweating, dry heaving, trembling over a one-foot putt. Routine pars would become disastrous triple bogeys, and grown men would sob uncontrollably, as if a loved one had suddenly dropped dead.

Gordon scoffed down his linguine Bolognese and tossed green salad, avoiding the bread, and limited himself to one glass of wine, part of his staying in shape routine.

"Sorry, Tiger, it's not happening. I'm putting my foot down. It's another wild goose chase. If you think I'm stupid enough to—"

"That's bull!" Gordon pounded on the table. "For someone who likes to play by the rules you quickly forget when it's convenient. We had a deal, right?"

Liz sat silently.

"Do I need to remind you?"

"No, that's not necessary," her tone somber and her eyes moist.

"Yeah it is, verbatim. 'I want you to give me a time frame, a promise that when you realize you're just chasing a rainbow, all bets are off. You get a real job, sell the apartment, and start fresh.' Does that sound familiar?"

"C'mon, Gordon, I'm not in the mood for a brawl."

"No brawl, let's just set the record straight. Because deep down inside you never wanted me to make it, hoped I would fail, and bomb out. Well, you were dead wrong. Pretty sorry state of affairs when you can't count on the woman who supposedly loves you, but a guy named Swifty is in my corner one thousand percent. See that trophy? There's a bunch more coming, and a barrel full of money. So how about you start acting like my partner, and give me some respect, not that I didn't earn it."

Gordon bolted from the table and grabbed his jacket.

"Where are you going?"

"Out for a walk, I need to sort a few things out."

He slammed the door behind him, which rattled the dining table. Whatever was left of the dinner from Italian Village found its way to the floor, soaked in a half bottle of inexpensive red wine.

"So what time did you haul your royal ass into bed?" He was sound asleep, responding with a series of snores. Liz poked him. "C'mon Gordon, wake up, WAKE UP!" She poked him harder until he came to life, groggy, with one eye open.

"Sorry to disturb you, Mr. Woods. I know you need your eight hours, but I work for a living, and we have some unfinished business."

Gordon propped himself up against his pillow and took a long swig of the Poland Spring water he kept on his nightstand. His mouth was bone dry from an overabundance of alcohol.

"I know," he replied, smiling sheepishly. "I got home around two in the morning, and didn't want to wake you."

"I'll make coffee."

"Don't forget—milk, two sugars, and a hot blueberry muffin with a pat of butter."

"Sorry Tiger, that's too fattening and not on your regimen." *At least he was in a good mood*, she thought, not the same angry guy who upset her last night.

She returned to bed with two hot mugs of coffee, greeted by

the Monday *New York Times'* sports section, placed conspicuously on her pillow.

"What's this?"

"It's no big deal, just a blurb about *moi*. I picked it up after midnight. Funny how hot downtown women get all turned on to aspiring golf pros, especially with their picture in the paper."

"OK, I get it Romeo, let me read it."

"Then you can give me your journalistic two cents."

"You knew about this?"

Gordon nodded. "Richards has been covering me since I left Alan. He loved to bust my chops and lambast me whenever he could. It was always the same old stuff; great talent but no work ethic, trust fund baby, the whole nine yards. I never showed you the articles, didn't want to upset you. But he was all over me at the Richardson. He figured he would try to patch things up, and get some inside scoop for his readers. He pretty much told me the article would be a home run."

"Yeah, and what did this home run happen to cost?"

"Not a bloody nickel!"

She smirked as if she didn't believe him.

"And you think I found the trophy as the prize in the bottom of a Cracker Jack box?"

"You've got plenty of speech all of a sudden, don't you? One lucky win in God knows how many tournaments and the man has moxie."

"Funny how I figured you would say that."

"This isn't working for me anymore, Gordon. I want, no, I'm *entitled* to a normal life, like most couples. Instead I watch all those years go up in smoke, poof, just like that, with what to show for it?" She snapped her fingers to illustrate the point.

Gordon let her emote.

"Unfortunately," she touched his face, her voice suddenly subdued, "I'm very much in love with you."

"Well that's a rousing endorsement if I ever heard one," he tried to inject some humor into an otherwise emotional encounter.

She was shuddering as he held her; he could feel her tremor, as she unabashedly cried.

"What's this qualifying school or whatever you call it going to cost us?" She wiped away her tears with some tissues she kept on her nightstand.

"Peanuts hon, maybe twelve grand," Gordon replied, relieved she showed an interest. "I'm loading up the Land Rover and staying in flea bag hotels. I figure spending a couple of bucks at strip joints when I get bored with Swifty's company."

"Just make sure it stays in your pants, or in your hand, understand Tiger?"

"C'mon, Liz, you know me better than that, I would never cheat on you."

At least he was travelling cheap, which she thought showed responsibility, but twelve thousand dollars was anything but peanuts. With a pittance in the bank, he'd be close to broke after this trip, except for the duplex, which she prayed he would put up for sale.

"You need to promise me something."

"What?"

"You'll call me every day, rain or shine, win or lose."

"Lose? It's not in my vocabulary anymore, Liz. And here's the deal. If I flunk Q school, it's over. I call it quits and become a bona fide member of the human race. Nine to five, whatever it takes, clawing my way up the ladder, just like the other couple of million animals in the concrete jungle."

"C'mon, Gordon, you make it sound like a death sentence. You'll hook up with a hedge fund and—"

"I'm not finished yet," he cut her short.

"Sorry."

"Assuming I get my card, that's *assuming,* I hit the pro tour and stay out there as long as I make the cut, which guarantees us a paycheck."

"So I sit home and rot, get to see you on the boob tube with an occasional phone call. Maybe you'll come visit me once in a while?"

"I'm glad you're so confident, considering I've won only one tournament in four years, and don't even have my card yet. And you said I was lucky, remember? Maybe you know something I don't?"

"You're right, but I'm thinking the worst and would rather have you home, with me."

"Don't freak, Liz. I'm gunning for the US Open, in it to win it, pure and simple, and then I'm done, promise."

"What? You can't be serious."

"I'm more than serious. It's out at Bethpage Black next June. I love that tract. They're toughening the course up, growing the rough and adding a few hundred yards. The greens will be like concrete. Anything under par should be a winner, and if it rains, or the wind kicks up, these guys will unravel at the seams under the pressure."

"Doesn't that sound familiar, Tiger?"

"It used to, but I'm hoping those days are over. And let's sell the damn duplex. Better to rent a place and have cash in the bank; it'll take some pressure off of me out there."

"OK, hon, I agree!" Liz was proud of the way he was handling the apartment, which was an albatross around their necks.

She couldn't put her finger on it, but something had changed, just in the manner he spoke. But he was taking the bull by the horns. She liked that manliness, which aroused her, and made her feel like a woman.

"Let's have a look at that long putter," she cooed seductively, as she rubbed her hands between his legs, pulled her tee shirt over her head, slipped out of her panties and let her hair down. Her wicked smile was stirringly inviting.

Gordon relished make up sex—that hot, steamy, almost anything goes act of pure passion. He lay back, letting her undress him, as she pulled down his boxers with her teeth, her hair dangling back and forth over his testicles. She started to caress them, just the way he liked it.

Under any other circumstances he would be a raging bull, pounding into her, holding her as she would move up and down, until they exploded in unison. But inexplicably he showed little interest, sheepishly apologizing for his flaccidness.

"It's OK, hon, no worries. I understand. You've got tons on your mind, and I'm very proud of you, more important than a romp in the hay."

His anxiety was assuaged by her explanation, but something bothered him, more than just a passing thought.

GORDON CONTACTED NORMAN BERGER and gave him the information on the Qualifying School tournaments. Two days later, he received a FedEx package containing a vial with the requisite amount of capsules.

Chapter 41

THE PRE-OWNED LAND ROVER LR3 was in road worthy shape for the drive down to West Palm Beach. Liz put it through a head to toe physical, pestering the mechanics with her endless list of items. Most were covered by the extended warranty; all in all she delivered as perfect a vehicle as $1,252.61 would permit, somehow wangling new tires and brakes, a $3,500 expense anywhere else.

"It's my treat, hon."

Gordon laughed when she proudly showed him the bill.

"So you slept with Roberto, that handsome salesman who's a double for Brad Pitt?"

"Nope, just told him I would for the right price, and somehow he believed me."

As they held each other, and he kissed her goodbye, he grappled with the guilt of hiding the truth from the one person in this world he genuinely loved without reservation.

GORDON AND SWIFTY DIDN'T speak much about golf, mostly listened to music on the radio, casual conversation and a few laughs as they headed south along the New Jersey Turnpike onto I-95. Each was alone in their thoughts, munching on an assortment of heart healthy sandwiches and snacks Liz had prepared, all kept fresh in an iced cooler.

Ten hours into the trip, as they crossed into South Carolina, the music was interrupted by an urgent weather bulletin, calling for a violent thunderstorm accompanied by high winds and hail. Dusk settled. The storm hit fifteen minutes later, making driving impossible.

Gordon cautiously crept into the far right lane, flashing his emergency lights as he slowed down to a crawl. Golf ball sized hailstones pelted against the car as the wind howled in a torrential downpour.

"Hey, Swifty, keep your eyes open for Lyman, should be coming up soon."

"OK, GH, we gonna stay there tonight?"

"Yep, it's the halfway point. I'm beat. We'll check into a motel, grab some grub, then up and out first thing in the morning."

And then it happened, out of nowhere; the siren, the flashing lights, the state trooper right up his ass, the "pull over" warning.

Gordon inched over to the side of the interstate with his emergency lights still flashing. The rain poured down in buckets. Three knocks on his window accompanied a familiar circular hand signal. Opening the window, he was now face to face with the black state trooper, his badge, holster and gun protected by a rain poncho.

"You all need some help?"

"Yes Sir, I mean no Sir, I mean...." Gordon just sat there, getting sopping wet.

"What you nervous about, boy? Can I see your license and registration?"

"Yes Sir." Gordon proffered the information to the trooper, who examined it with his flashlight, handed it back, and peered into the car, shining the light on Swifty.

"Hey brother, you lost?"

"We were lookin' for Lyman, on our way to Florida. My man here gonna be a golf professional. I'm his official caddy, name's Swifty."

"Well nice to meet you brother, I'm Clarence." He reached in and shook Swifty's hand. His oversized, muscular arms resembled tree trunks, and his giant face was so close that Gordon could almost taste the dank perspiration that covered his pocked skin.

"Y'all follow me. I'll keep my flashers on. Lyman's about ten minutes, but be careful and ..... Good luck."

Gordon shut the window, grabbed some napkins, and wiped

off the mixture of sweat and rain from his sopping wet face. He followed Clarence down the interstate, thinking it was cool to be escorted by an official state trooper, lights flashing, as if he was somebody important.

Clarence slowed down as they approached the exit, then honked and sped off. Gordon entered into Lyman, a bustling metropolis of four square miles, the population around two thousand, ninety-five percent white. He pulled into the Highway Mini Motel, a favorite with the truckers, which Liz had checked out on Expedia.

Swifty purposely waited in the Land Rover, rifling through Gordon's luggage until he found the vial stuffed with white un-marked Tylenol looking capsules, which was hidden in Gordon's leather Dopp kit amongst his personal items. It confirmed his suspicions, which more than perturbed him, and made his wonder. *What the hell was GH doing?*

"Need a room for one night," Gordon addressed the "manager," a teenager, maybe seventeen, who was lounging back with his feet up on the counter, sucking on a no filter Lucky Strike cigarette, blowing smoke rings, while acid rock blared through the radio.

A total skin head type, bald as a cue ball and donning a nose ring, he was dressed in skin tight black jeans, a black tee shirt and militia boots. Every inch of his arms was decorated with the tattoos of hate; swastikas, white power fists, Aryan Nation, all a mélange of repugnance, not the type Gordon had any simpatico with, or vice versa.

"You wanna single or double?"

"One room with two beds; my wife found you on Expedia, quoted $19.95."

"I don't know what the hell you're talking about." He blew three perfect smoke rings in Gordon's face.

"Doesn't matter, how much for the room?"

"It's $19.95, just like you said, dude." He cranked up the radio and lit another Lucky Strike.

"Be right back."

"Whatever dude, it's a free country, you come back, you don't come back, don't really give a fuck, nothin' else round here."

Were it not for the flooded streets, Gordon would have high-tailed out of there and traipsed around for more hospitable accommodations, with no assurance he'd find much better.

"Who's he?" The skinhead pointed to Swifty as they lugged their baggage into the entrance, both of them drenched from the downpour.

"He's my friend. We're sharing the room, two beds, remember?"

"Listen dude, two beds for two people gonna be $29.95."

"That's crazy! What's the difference? I told you one room with two beds, and you agreed on $19.95."

"You mother fuckers are always tryin' to Jew us down, like we're stupid. Take it or leave it."

Gordon was champing at the bit to hang this despicable excuse for a human being from his balls. Swifty knew he was hot, and nudged him to cool down.

"We'll take it, $19.95," Swifty piped in, as he tossed two ten dollar bills on the counter, then shoved his left hand underneath his sweater, extending his index finger straight out.

"Keep the damn change, gimme our key, and no fuckin' lip!"

The skinhead, taken aback to be spoken to so insolently, especially by some old black guy packing a gun, suddenly lost his bluster and handed over the key along with two somewhat clean white bath towels.

"Yes Sir, upstairs, number eleven, best room we got. It takes a while for the water to get hot in the morning, but at least it's wet."

"Hey, you saved my ass, great job." Gordon followed Swifty into the room, which was one grade above a flea bag, boasting a dead on view of a host of eighteen wheelers parked for the evening.

"Nope, GH, I saved *our* ass, we in this together, remember?"

They skipped dinner, sacked out, and fell sound asleep. The next morning they were awoken at 6:00 a.m. by Gordon's alarm. They cold showered, dressed, and hit the road.

Chapter 42

"GORDON HOWARD, I HAD a funny feeling you'd be carousing around here. How did you like my piece in *The Times*?"

"Mr. Jack Richards, reporter extraordinaire, you staying here?"

"Yep, I'm covering the Q school qualifiers. It's a really strong field this year, should be exciting."

"Hey, thanks for the kudos."

"Nothing you didn't deserve, I hope we can patch things up. I gave you a rough time over the years, not the most flattering of articles."

"Bag it; maybe I deserved it. You called it right; trust fund baby, choker under pressure…."

"Talented, gifted, hits it as pure as the touring pros, has all the shots, can get up and down from the parking lot. It's all true, good and bad. I give my readers what they want to know."

"Thanks Jack, did you know I left my father?" Richards had heard a different version through the grapevine.

"How's he doing? He took quite a hit, I hope he pulls through."

Gordon glossed over the comment and just nodded. He had no idea, and felt guilty.

"Gotta check in and get settled, Jack. I tee off at 8:05 tomorrow. It's supposed to be warm but not too windy. I played the course in a pro-am. It's long but pretty easy if you keep it on the short grass."

Jack pulled out a pen and pad. "Any predictions for my readers, something I can sink my teeth into?"

Just then Swifty joined them in the motel lobby, pushing a trolley cart with their bags and Gordon's clubs.

"Yep, here's a scoop Jack, straight from the horse's mouth. I've been working hard on a new move and finally honed it. Old habits die hard, but I got it down pat. I'm totally in control of my swing. What you saw at the Richardson was half throttle. If I don't blow away the field by ten shots then I'm done, and will get a real job."

"Can I print that?" Jack hurriedly wrote down each word.

"You better," Gordon smiled, "but after the first round."

"Thanks Gordon!" Richards whipped out his cell phone, called his editor at *The New York Times*, and told him to stop the presses.

"Hey GH, he's that newspaper guy, been around us forever, right?"

"Yeah, it's Jack Richards, he's covering the tournaments, just came over to shoot the breeze."

"Why'd you tell him all that bullshit?"

"What?"

"C'mon, I ain't deaf yet, that you gonna win by ten or else you quittin' the game?"

"I'm dead serious."

"And he's gonna write that in the newspaper?"

"Hope so."

"And if it ain't true, you gonna have a whole bunch of egg on that pretty boy face, unless there's something you ain't tellin me."

"Like what?" Gordon sounded nervous.

"C'mon, GH, just cause you won the damn Richardson-that don't make you a superstar."

"Hey, if I'm not confidant in my game, then—"

"Hold on, GH, no quarrelin' a man's gotta have confidence. But unless that Berger guy gave you somethin' more than just a pep talk, I think you're playin' with fire."

Gordon wondered about Swifty's subtle sarcasms. *Could he possibly know something?*

"Listen, Swifty, I need you to trust me on this. How many times did they laugh behind my back, called me a choke artist and a loser? Maybe I didn't show it, but it played with my head and tore my frickin' guts out."

Gordon stopped to wipe his eyes; Swifty watched real tears trickle down his cheek.

"I've got something going. I can feel it in my swing, finally playing to my potential. Don't ask me to explain it; but it's there, it's working, and it's good for both of us. Let's just leave it alone, and see what happens, deal?"

Swifty thought about the capsules he found.

"Deal, GH."

He tossed Swifty the key. "I'm checked in. Why don't you bring our stuff up to the room and we'll walk the course, check out the pin placements."

"OK, GH, be right down."

JACK RICHARD'S ARTICLE APPEARED in the sports section of *The New York Times*.

Gordon Howard Predicts Runaway Q School Victory

In the sixth inning of game three of the 1932 World Series, Babe Ruth, the great Bambino, took two balls and two strikes from Chicago Cubs pitcher, Charlie Root, as the Chicago fans cheered wildly for a third strike. And, as the story goes, Ruth then pointed his bat straight out to the center field bleachers, ostensibly a declaration he would hit a home run to that exact spot.

On Root's next pitch, a curveball, Ruth pummeled the ball some 440 feet, way out past the flagpole in the deepest part of center field, landing over the wall into some temporary seats behind the stadium. According to what I read scouring the internet, Ruth's blast was announced over the radio by Cub's broadcaster Tom Manning. "The ball is going,

going, going, high into the center field stands…and it is a home run!

Well, whether he truly called the shot has been fodder for sportswriters, historians, pundits and baseball fans who want to believe, and unless the Babe is somehow resurrected, it will remain just that, somewhere betwixt fact and fiction, between fantasy and reality.

Just the other day I witnessed a similar brazen prognostication, not by a professional baseball player, but by an amateur golfer, Gordon Scott Howard, the recent runaway winner of the prestigious Richardson, one of some twelve hundred aspiring Qualifying School candidates, brutally competing for two dozen coveted PGA tour cards.

And in no uncertain terms, here is what he said to me when I asked him for his prediction.

"Yep, here's a scoop Jack, straight from the horse's mouth. I've been working hard on a new move and finally honed it. Old habits die hard, but I got it down pat. I'm totally in control of my swing. What you saw at the Richardson was half throttle. If I don't blow away the field by ten shots then I'm done, and will get a real job."

Gordon Howard put on a clinic at his opening round down here in sunny West Palm Beach, a relatively long and well bunkered tract over at golf haven and resort PGA National, the Palmer Course.

He cruised to a six under sixty-four, hitting fourteen fairways center cut, getting up and down twice from the deep greenside bunkers. He carded six birdies with no bogeys, his longest putt fifteen feet. Most of the field faltered, with only a handful at one under par, with the cut at a mind boggling seventy-six, to be expected in this pressure cooker competition.

Is he still comfortable with his prediction? I caught him after the round. He was unusually calm, hanging out with his longtime caddie Swifty, as if he played a friendly two dollar Nassau with his buddies. I asked him that same question, to which he answered me, matter-of-factly, "All the hard work is coming together. I feel I can do what I want with the ball, fade it, draw it and distance control. Let's up the ante to fifteen shots."

And then he flashed that mischievous smile, all but saying that the competition is a bunch of rank amateurs.

Stay tuned, folks.

Chapter 43

THE GRUELING FINAL QUALIFYING School tournament was normally a non-event, hosting a few reporters, friends and family, except for the appearance of one brash out of the blue upstart, who publicly put his ballsy predictions on the line, and made the game look easy, almost too easy.

He had trounced the field by sixteen shots, shooting twenty-three under par, prompting a frenetic scene, with reporters pushing, shoving, and clamoring for an interview, or just a few words, while microphones from *The Golf Channel* dangled from every which way.

"Sorry folks, not today," Gordon reiterated. "I'm only speaking with Jack Richards."

Nobody except Gordon Howard paid any attention to another amateur who also qualified for the tour, a man considerably older than the competition. Gordon was paired with him in an early round, impressed with his flawlessly repeatable Ben Hogan swing, although his chipping and putting had not been razor sharp. He couldn't quite put his finger on it, but something about that guy just didn't sit right.

THEY SAT AROUND THE room, eating sandwiches and drinking cold beers.

"Hey Gordon, thanks for the exclusive, I never expected it."

"No problem Jack; would rather speak to you than a stranger."

"How about I give you the podium to field some questions and answers? You can edit it before we print."

"OK," Gordon replied, taking a swig of a Heineken.

"So your prediction was spot on, you beat the field by sixteen shots; congrats on an incredible performance."

"Thanks."

"Are you surprised?"

"Nope, should I be?"

"Sounds a bit arrogant, Gordon, don't you think?"

"Confident Jack, big difference; let's not misread me."

"Good point, I agree."

Gordon wolfed down half of a tuna salad sandwich.

"Sitting here, you seem so nonchalant, as if it were no great shakes."

"Why shouldn't I be? I just played my game and never worried about what the other guys were doing."

"Right, you told me you were working hard on some swing changes."

"Yep, real hard, it wasn't easy."

"How about some insight into what you were trying to change; my readers would love that. Was it something technical?"

Swifty sat silent, munching down lunch while he listened to Gordon's malarkey.

"C'mon, Jack; don't ask me to kiss and tell. It's a difficult game. We all have flaws. Nobody hits it perfect all the time. Once in a while it all clicks. Tomorrow I can hit it sideways."

"That look on your face tells me that you're not serious."

"You're right Jack, I'm not." Gordon's smirk morphed into a wide smile.

"So what's the secret, Gordon? I watched you. It looked so effortless, with only a few errant shots, the rest dead on at the flags."

"OK, Jack, it has to do with my takeaway, but you'll need a high tech camera to see it. Basically I'm presetting my wrists. The clubface is always square, which lets my body control my hands, but that's all you're gonna get."

"What's your agenda, now that you have your card? I guess the Nationwide Tour? You'll get some experience, then—"

"Not even close, Jack. I'm gunning for the US Open next June out at Bethpage."

Jack roared, a derisive, who are you kidding, what are you smoking kind of laugh.

"What's so funny?"

"C'mon, Gordon, not that you didn't tear this place apart, but hell, one swallow doesn't make a spring. Don't you think you need some seasoning first, to compete against guys ten years younger and fifty yards longer, where a sixty-six is a ho hum round, with real money on the line, guys who didn't grow up with...."

"If you mention my father or a silver spoon we're done!"

Swifty heard it, loud and clear.

"Sorry Gordon-I didn't mean to upset you. I'm on your side, just trying to be objective."

"OK Jack, forget it. I apologize for losing my cool. Send me a draft. I'm grabbing a flight tonight back to New York. I haven't been home in two months, and need to spend some time with my wife to be. Hopefully she remembers who I am."

Swifty knew nothing about these travel arrangements, and approached Gordon as Jack Richards left the room.

"Hey GH, since when are we flyin' to New York?"

"Liz called, all freaked out. She lost her job and we're trying to sell my co-op. I need you to drive back alone."

"Didn't you tell her you won the damn tournament?"

"Yeah, but she'd be happier if I got knocked out. She thinks I'm just wasting my time out here."

"But ain't we goin forward GH?"

"Like I told the man, I'm gonna win the US Open."

"You mean *we* gonna win, right?"

"Correct."

Swifty saw right through it. He was not the same Gordon Howard he shook hands with back in the men's grill at Old Point; humble, partners, a team. Now it was all about him, and that voodoo doctor, he was convinced, was more than involved.

"OK, GH, I'll drive it up north, but I ain't doin it for free; that wasn't part of our deal."

"No problem." Gordon reached into his pocket and pulled out a fat wad of hundred dollar bills which Liz had wired him. "How's five hundred?"

"C'mon, GH, I got gas, tolls, motel, food, how I gonna make any money on five hundred? That ain't any way to treat—"

"Here's a grand, fair enough?"

"Fifteen hundred, GH," Swifty replied forcefully. "With all you gonna pocket with that new swing, and voodoo doctor in your corner, it ain't worth gettin' me all riled up."

Gordon calmly peeled off fifteen one hundred dollar bills as his mind raced. *Was Swifty's veiled threat for real, or just a figment of his imagination?*

Chapter 44

LIZ STRUGGLED WITH MIXED emotions despite the onslaught of telephone calls as the news went viral, barraged by sports agents hounding Gordon for a meeting and magazine editors clamoring for a featured article, until finally they opted for an unlisted number.

December came on with an early winter blizzard, but despite the frigid nights, he had no interest in sweating it up between the sheets.

"I'm scared, Gordon, everything is so unclear." She broke down and cried after another unsuccessful attempt to arouse him in bed.

"C'mon, Liz, I'm solid as a rock. Now's not the time for second guessing."

"There's more to our relationship than you're obsession with golf, in case you haven't noticed." She kicked away the down blanket and rolled into his arms, exposing her long shapely legs and firm breasts, in all their glorious nakedness.

"I know, I know, don't think it hasn't been bugging the hell out of me." He held her firmly, not quite sure what to say next.

"Is it me?"

"Don't be silly."

"I can only imagine what goes on out there, all those sex starved women who would find you irresistible, must be tempting...."

"There's no way! Perfect I'm not, but I swear to you on my grandfather's grave that—"

"OK, calm down, I wasn't accusing you. But put yourself in my position. All of a sudden everyone wants a piece of you. You've been away from me for three months, only normal I would be...."

"Suspicious?"

"I guess," she replied sheepishly.

He was becoming more suspicious that Norman's elixir was responsible for his impotence.

"Why don't you come along to my first tournament? We can make it a vacation. How does Kapalua, Hawaii sound? Qualifying is Monday and Tuesday. I'm competing with fifty other guys for one spot on a sponsor's exemption."

"Hawaii?"

"Sunny, warm breezes, the course right on the ocean, snorkeling, surfing, and—"

"Are you crazy? I'm out of work, you've got a few thousand left in your account, and this place just sits and gathers dust!"

"You're overreacting for Christ sake; you only see the glass as half empty. The trip is ten grand, no way around it, and that's on the cheap. I'm going, Liz, do or die, just like I promised you. First prize is eight hundred thousand."

He reached over to his night stand, flicked on the reading lamp, and grabbed the newspaper articles.

"I know what they say, Gordon Howard this and Gordon Howard that. Maybe you can convince this Jack Richards guy to pay our mortgage. He seems to fawn all over you, like you guys have a thing going." She nestled up against him and buried her head in his chest while guiding his arms around her. "Just hold me, I'm shivering."

He could feel her trembling, guilt ridden he had caused her such angst.

"I've got a confession, something you need to know."

"Don't tell me, not yet." She looked at him; her eyes welled up, thinking the unthinkable.

"How could you, Gordon, to lie and to cheat. Bedroom problems; ha! Who is she?"

He knew it the moment he said it. He was in too deep. She would never condone the magic capsules, and would leave him in a heartbeat.

"Hey, chill out, who said anything about cheating?"

"You did! What do you think *confession* means?"

"Sorry, bad choice of words, it's more a revelation than a confession."

"Go ahead, I'm listening." Her arms were folded, still in a huff.

"I busted my ass for four years. And I just had a gnawing feeling that I was this close," his thumb and index finger ever so slightly apart.

She tapped her forehead impatiently, waiting for this confession, or revelation, as he called it.

"And then it all came together, first at the Richardson, and then at Q school in Florida. Maybe it was divine intervention, or something mystical, like I took a couple of magic pills. But I own my swing. It's second nature, automatic, like brushing my teeth, or walking one foot in front of the other, with no bad thoughts, no doubts, and no second guesses. And it's not arrogance, or chutzpah, or a fantasy. But I'm unbeatable, and its mind boggling, almost scary."

"Maybe you've finally earned their blessing?"

"Whose?"

"The Golf Gods, silly, that's your divine intervention. You better make hay while the sun shines."

At least he mentioned the magic pills, and hadn't lied to her, or so he conveniently convinced himself. He again wondered about these Golf Gods.

"But I do have a confession."

"What is it now?" She sounded annoyed.

"I just want you to know how important you are to me. I realize it's been an uphill battle, and I'm not the easiest guy to get along with, and I know you think it's all a pipedream. But I'm doing this for us, and whatever happens, I love you more than you could ever imagine."

She broke down and cried a watershed of tears. They kissed. He could taste the salty teardrops, and he welled up as they held a quiet embrace.

Liz broke the silence while he rubbed the back of her neck, something she had always liked. "So you'll need a loan?"

"Yes."

"The trip is on me. I'll take it from my savings, fair enough?"

"Fair enough," he echoed, as she fell asleep in his arms, while he struggled awake all night, confused, trying to make sense out of everything.

Chapter 45

"NORMAN BERGER."

"Hey, it's Gordon, just checking in."

"I was expecting to hear from you."

"Have you been reading the papers?"

"Sure, I have an investment in you, remember? Articles were quite flattering. You must be on cloud nine."

"Nothing I didn't earn, Norman."

"You mean *we* didn't earn."

Gordon glossed over the comment; something about it was disturbing. "I have to ask you something" he said sheepishly, "but it's kind of personal."

"You have my full attention."

"Liz and I, well, I mean I'm not, uh, for some reason it's...."

"I'm not a mind reader, just spit it out."

"OK, my sex drive is like zero. I first noticed it before I left for Florida. Maybe it's just a coincidence, not sure, but it's freaking me out."

"Relax Gordon; it happens to men all the time. It could be something physical, like a low testosterone count, or maybe something psychological."

"It's nothing to do with the capsule?"

"Absolutely zero," Norman replied reassuringly. "In all the test data from our clinical trials, libidinal suppression was not one of the contraindications."

"I'm not a doctor, Norman, speak to me in English!" Gordon sounded scared.

"Sorry, we had no evidence that the drug reduced any patient's sex drive, male or female."

Norman knew just the opposite. Some ninety percent of the men suffered erectile dysfunction of varying degrees. But more seriously, almost fifty percent of those men had a low sperm count, and were infertile, although the FDA considered it a small price to pay for curing ALS. He had no reason to be straight with Gordon and possibly upset the apple cart and derail his plan. Besides, Gordon's dysfunction was probably reversible once he stopped ingesting the potion, although there was no guarantee he would be fertile, not that he gave a damn, one way or the other.

"I was just hoping there was some connection, that's all, it's tough to keep on second guessing what's wrong."

"Wish I could help, but I'm not a sex therapist."

Gordon found it uncomfortable discussing his sex life with this weirdo scientist. The mere thought of Norman Berger having sex with a woman was enough to make any man impotent.

"I'm also running low. I have just two capsules left."

"So what's the problem?"

"No problem, just figured I would stock up. I plan to be on the road for a while."

"Sorry, Gordon, it doesn't work that way."

He sensed a definite arrogance in Norman's voice. "What do you mean?"

"Next week is Hawaii, right?"

"Correct, first prize is eight hundred thousand."

"And my percentage is a handshake, whatever you think is fair?"

"That's our agreement."

"Let's not complicate things. I'll send you enough to get you through the tournament, and you compensate me from your winnings, a nice, cozy symbiotic relationship. You have my wiring instructions?"

"Yeah I got it," Gordon answered disconsolately. He more than suspected something had changed, but didn't want to confront it, not yet.

Chapter 46

DR. BRUCE HABERMAN MADE his weekly visit to the ICU unit at North Shore Hospital, where he hunted down Dr. David Siegel, who was making his rounds.

"How's the patient doing?"

"Not bad, considering."

"Considering what?"

"You know the score with cerebromedullospinal disconnection. These things get progressively worse. I'm surprised he lasted this long. He must be one tough sonafabitch. But he's still aware and cognizant, he just can't speak. Some studies were done, pretty interesting stuff. Seems that these unfortunate patients live considerably longer the more contact they have with a loved one; a spouse, a sibling, even a pet, somebody they have an emotional relationship with."

"You mean his son, Gordon?"

"Not my business, but you'd think he'd be camped outside. Funny, I'm always running around with a crazy schedule, so I checked the log book, thinking maybe we just missed each other."

"And what did you find?"

"He was only here once, the night Alan was admitted. He stayed five minutes, if that."

"It's been four months, but I'm not shocked. He's always been a big headache for his father."

"Whatever, I've seen it all up here. It's not a fun place to visit. People do weird things, especially family, so nothing surprises me anymore."

ALAN HOWARD REMAINED PARALYZED with locked-in syndrome, his vital functions controlled by a machine. He was staring at CNBC on the television, listening to the constant financial updates and interviews with hedge fund managers, none of which mattered anymore.

"I have something I want to read to you." Bruce Haberman stood by the side of his bed, holding the Jack Richard's newspaper articles, slowly articulating each word aloud, dramatically emphasizing all of the wonderful accolades about his son, Gordon. The more he read, the more rapidly Alan blinked, unable to beam, or cry.

As he left he dropped the articles on Alan's paralytic lap, which he gratefully acknowledged with his eyes.

Chapter 47

"GOLF FANS, IF YOU'RE watching what I am, don't, I repeat, do not turn off your television sets! We've got a new kid in town, maybe an alien from another planet; who on earth is this Gordon Howard?"

Troy Blake, the irascible and outspoken golf professional turned golf announcer for NBC sports, was having a field day with Gordon Howard. "Some local amateur from Long Island who couldn't win a two dollar Nassau, ready to throw in the towel when he remarkably wins The Richardson, a respectable amateur tournament, but not exactly the US Open. Then he blows away the field at Q school in West Palm like these mega talents had a few too many before teeing it up. And now, if you can believe it, after beating out fifty jack rabbits for one sponsor's exemption spot, he's got a five shot lead going into the final round of the Sony Invitational against none other than Phil Mickelson! I mean talk about a swing? This guy hits it like a machine, scary, almost too good. I've never seen anything like it, and I've been around this game too long. His short game is magical, and whatever he's smoking I want some, legal or otherwise!"

JACK RICHARDS WAITED PATIENTLY by the players' entrance to the clubhouse for Gordon to arrive.

He was walking with Swifty, who was lugging his Wilson Staff bag with *Gordon Howard* emblazoned on the side, white with red lettering.

"Hey Gordon, got a few minutes."

"You're like a fungus, can't get rid of you."

Swifty cringed when he heard the putdown.

"So it's the old Gordon Howard. I thought you buried him? Guess I was wrong, will let my readers know that...."

"OK, I hear you. I'm just teasing, but only two minutes, gotta warm up."

"Thanks, Gordon. So you're a Wilson Staff guy? You're in good company if you have an endorsement deal-bunch of top pros are on their roster."

"Not yet, just carrying the bag and still hitting their irons, but keeping my options open."

"It must be awesome banging balls on the range next to these guys."

"Not really, everybody works on their swings; a few come over, small talk, that's about it."

"Really, like who?" Jack was all excited; it would make for good copy, hoping it was Tiger.

"C'mon, Jack, this isn't kindergarten."

"Nervous?"

"No."

"You can't be serious? Look at your playing partner. Mickelson is a legend, the best in the business, or damn close to it. This is a huge tournament, the pressure has—"

"No pressure, Jack, none whatsoever, anything else?"

"Yeah, how about giving my readers a prediction?"

Gordon looked Jack straight in the eye, and without flinching, told him what he wanted to hear. "No way am I blowing a five shot lead."

"Can I print that?" Jack Richards was all hopped up over the scoop.

"Absolutely," Gordon replied with a wink, and followed Swifty to the players' locker room, where he changed into his golf shoes, walked over to the water cooler, and swallowed two capsules.

Chapter 48

THE TV CAMERAS, BOOM microphones, reporters, and a throng of fans five deep encircled the first tee, as the official announced the last pairing.

"And our final twosome, from Rancho Santa California, winner of forty two PGA Tournaments, the 2005 PGA, the 2004, 2006 and 2010 Masters, the 2013 British open, multiple Ryder Cup and President's Cup appearances, esteemed member of the Golf Hall of fame, Phil Mickelson!"

The crowd ignited in a deafening round of applause.

Phil, always the statesman, acknowledged the cheers. A genuine good guy despite his celebrity, with that boyish smile, he stood resplendent in black and white pinstriped trousers, black shirt, sporting the logos of Callaway, Barclay's, and Accenture, donning a black visor with KPMG printed boldly in white.

He went through his routine, took a few practice swings with his Callaway Razr Hawk Tour Driver, teed up his Callaway Hex Black tour ball, adjusted his visor, and ripped a high fade some 320 yards down the hill, landing on a flat area, 230 yards from the green, an opening par five.

The crowd was all pumped up, as Phil nodded in approval, and handed his driver back to Jim Mackay, his long-time caddie, nicknamed Bones.

"And next, from New York City, in his first professional tournament, boasting the record for the lowest medalist score in the PGA Qualifying School, Gordon Howard!"

Swifty was so nervous that he mistakenly handed Gordon his three wood. The spectators clapped respectfully. Word of his brazen predictions at Q school had spread, with everyone curious whether he was half as good as he boasted, not quite sure if this upstart was for real or a one hit wonder.

Gordon swaggered onto the tee, his outfit devoid of any logos except the Izod alligator on his shirt. He tipped his cap and addressed his Titleist ProV1.

The crowd stood dead silent until he stepped away, walked over to Swifty, and tossed him his three- wood. "What the fuck is wrong with you?"

Troy Blake wisecracked to the TV audience, "I didn't hear that."

"Sorry," Swifty apologized sheepishly, looking embarrassed, as Gordon reached into his bag and pulled out his three-year-old Taylor Made eight degree driver with its stock stiff shaft. Expressionless, he settled into his stance, took one look down the fairway, and pummeled his drive down the right side, drawing it toward the center of the fairway, while he nonchalantly picked up his tee with the ball still in flight. Marching down the fairway, Swifty scurried behind him as his ball landed a few yards shy of Mickelson's.

The television audience would be treated to some good natured banter between Troy Blake and Bruce Kazin, the internationally known instructor turned swing analyst who supplied all the technical jargon to the golf crazed TV fans.

"Hey, Bruce, what's your take on this guy? He's solid as a rock. I figured the chokes would have come in by now. I collared him on the range before, but nothing doing, quiet as a church mouse. He stays to himself, just goes about his business. I peeked into his bag, and would you believe he's hitting Wilson Staff X-31 blades? Are those even made anymore? Now how cool is that? It's tough to get a read on him, but I heard through the grapevine he's got an attitude. Maybe it's his nerves, which is understandable. You gotta be a shrink to figure some of these guys out."

"Well, Troy, I think I noticed something. Let's look at Gordon Howard's swing through the Sony Super Slow Motion sports camera. We took these with Gordon hitting his driver on four different holes, using the same camera angle."

"Ok great," Troy Blake said, as Kazin continued.

"Notice he has a very early reverse wrist set right off the ball, which squares the face. It's quite unorthodox, but he's honed it. With his legs solidly planted, he just turns his shoulders, keeping everything else dead still. At the top he's perfectly on plane with his left wrist bowed, a very strong position. I'm fine with his backswing; whatever works consistently. He starts his downswing with a slight bump of his left hip, and then a violent move to the left, which clears his hips, while his head stays behind the ball. There is zero lateral movement, with the club perfectly square at impact, his weight spent onto his left toe, and his right shoulder left of his body as the arms fall gracefully onto his back."

"Looks like ninety percent of the guys out here, Bruce, me included on a good day."

"Yeah, Troy, but watch this. We superimposed each swing on top of each other, and here's what we got."

Troy Blake stared at the four images which were seamlessly combined into one, with every swing exactly the same, not varying one millimeter.

"Whoa, partner, let me see that again!" Blake sounded dumbfounded. "Gordon looks like a wind up doll."

Bruce Kazin replayed the tape, slower, then faster, as Blake scrutinized it with a magnifying glass.

"What are you thinking, Bruce? You're the expert. I'm just trying to scratch out a living up here in the tower, but that's downright incredible. It's amazing what technology can uncover."

"I'm not sure, Troy. I've taught the best in the business. Nobody on the planet is that consistent, not Hogan, not Jack, not Tiger, not even close. It's impossible, like this guy is some kind of automaton."

"Might be good for the game to give these guys a run for their money," Troy Blake quipped. "I can see the headlines now- humanoid buries competition at Sony Invitational."

Chapter 49

Gordon maintained his five shot lead through the first six holes, matching birdies with Mickelson on one and four. He then bogeyed seven, eight and nine, three putting twice and flubbing an easy chip, which prompted a roar from the crowd as the official scoreboard was updated.

"Here we go folks. If I've seen it once, then I've seen it a thousand times." Troy Blake revved up his audience. "The pressure out here is enormous, especially for some unknown first timer. With thousands of Mickelson's entourage cheering him on, this poor guy just can't take the heat. He needs to catch his breath, put the last three holes out of his mind, and just play his game. I don't want to use the choke word, but it's gonna be tough, especially when Phil smells blood."

"Hey, GH, you OK?"

"Yeah, fine- why?"

"You serious, sure you ain't cavin' in? There's a whole lot of pressure out here."

"Me? Caving? I'm just making this a little more interesting. Let's lose a few more holes on the back."

"Are you crazy, GH?"

"Crazy as a fox, Swifty-gotta give the announcers something to crow about."

"OK, GH, I hear you. Maybe that voodoo doctor gave you what you needed."

Gordon didn't want to discuss Norman Berger, and wondered why Swifty brought him up again.

"I'm sorry about that first hole, Swifty. I shouldn't have spoken to you that way."

"We win this thing, GH, and I got big money comin' to me, no problem you wanna cuss me out."

"Don't worry, Swifty," Gordon replied comfortingly, "just don't worry."

"It looks like a meltdown, folks" Troy Blake commented. "Hot shot Gordon Howard has blown another two strokes on the back nine, just as I predicted. He and Phil are now all even. Funny thing is, he looks cool as a cucumber, yacking it up with his caddie, Swifty, as if eight hundred thousand is no big deal. And the par four eighteenth is playing ridiculously tough, four hundred eighty-two yards into a brutal wind, the green guarded by a huge lake, and the pin tucked in tight just over the water. It's been a three shot hole for a lot of the guys; too many perfectly struck second shots have drowned into double bogeys, but either way we're looking at one nail biting finish, which could go extra holes."

"Hey, GH, you gonna give me a heart attack." They walked up to the eighteenth tee.

"Relax, Swifty; enjoy the scenery, everything's cool."

Mickelson teed-off first, a low draw, which hit the hard fairway dead center and bounded forward another twenty yards, leaving himself two hundred twenty yards to the middle of the green. Amidst the cacophony of oohs and ahs, Mickelson respectfully signaled for the crowd to calm down.

Gordon took one look down the fairway, and launched the Titleist, which started low and then rose, pushing against the wind, until it landed and just stopped, some twenty yards behind Mickelson.

"You do that on purpose, GH?" Swifty already knew the answer.

"Sure did, better to hit first and put the pressure on him."

Phil's loyal entourage surrounded the green as they arrived at

Gordon's drive. Swifty threw up some grass, walked off the yardage and checked the pin placement sheet.

"We got two forty-seven to the center, two forty to the flag, two thirty to clear them rocks if you're thinkin' of goin for the pin."

"What's the wind doing?"

"She's dead into us until you clear that lake, then left to right. I can tell by them ripples in the water. We gotta figure it's a three club wind."

"How do you like a five wood? I start it for the center, and let her drift in left of the pin."

Swifty threw up another batch of grass, watching the flags on top of the clubhouse. "Yep, but start it low, she's gonna climb. This way you ain't messin' with that wind up there, cause no tellin' what it gonna do."

"OK." Swifty handed Gordon the club, then moved out of his periphery.

"Gordon is going for the green, he has a wood in his hands," squawked Troy Blake. "If he's smart he plays for the center, leaving him a long two putt for par, and force Phil to make birdie for the win. But with Mickelson, we've seen it too many times, he's fearless, and can pull off the miraculous."

Gordon motioned to Swifty, who came over to wipe off the moisture on the club's handle and then stepped away.

He took a practice swing and addressed the ball; the only sounds were of the howling wind, the splashing of the whitecaps against the rocks, and the low murmur of the biased crowd. He launched it left of the green, dead into the wind. It veered to the right, over the middle of the lake.

"C'mon baby, be right, be right!" Swifty pleaded, watching the white spectacle as it seemed to momentarily hover over the water below.

Gordon just stared, emotionless, as the Titleist began its descent, clearing the rocks, then hit upon the green and spun toward the flag, stopping fifteen feet below the pin.

Phil Mickelson smiled and flashed thumbs up. He walked to his ball as the crowd politely clapped.

"What a shot, Bruce, this man has ice in his veins!" Troy Blake said excitedly. "What do you think Phil does now?"

"If I were Phil," Kazin replied, "my play is for the center of the green, two putts for par, and put the pressure on Gordon Howard. It's a miracle he made it this far. He's missed a bunch of easy putts today, the first sign of nerves. The chances of him knocking in a birdie from fifteen feet are slim. Now we're talking a sudden death playoff, and the battle tough veteran has a huge advantage in handling the pressure."

Mickelson and Bones surveyed the situation and chose a utility club. He took a few practice swings and addressed the ball, ready to pull the trigger. A spectator yelled, "C'mon Phil, stick it!"

Suddenly he stepped away, appearing unsure. Bones walked over and threw up some grass. The wind was playing games. They collaborated, each pointing to different parts of the green, until they switched clubs, while Bones uttered "trust it."

"Phil has two twenty-seven to the middle," Troy Blake announced. "It looks like he was thinking of attacking the pin, and then changed his mind. He's going for the fat part of the green, playing smart, no sense in trying to be a hero with the wind so unpredictable."

Mickelson drilled a four iron, which carried the water, and landed softly, some thirty-five feet from the hole.

The crowd cheered, "Phil, Phil!" as the players approached the green, He gratefully acknowledged the warm welcome, tipping his cap, while Gordon appeared stoically indifferent, marking his ball and stepping aside next to Swifty, out of Mickelson's sight.

They worked in tandem, examining the slope, deciding the line was just outside the left edge of the cup. Bones pulled the flag as Phil crouched into his familiar putting stance, took a few practice strokes, and addressed the ball with one final look.

It rolled perfectly along its intended path, never veering, with the fans rooting in unison, closer and closer, now some five feet from the cup, as Mickelson pumped his left fist.

Swifty shut his eyes, unable to witness what was about to happen, until he heard the collective moaning of the crowd and saw Mickelson on his knees, his arms cradling his head in disbelief.

"That had birdie written all over it," Troy Blake announced. "Phil knew it, his fans knew it, and for certain Gordon Howard knew it."

Phil tapped in the six inch comeback putt, giving Gordon center stage.

Swifty stalked Gordon's putt from every angle.

"I see it inside left, GH, slightly uphill, but it's late in the day, grass growin' toward the sun, gonna make the putt slower. You can't leave it short."

Gordon knelt down, checked the line, replaced the marker with his Titleist, and nodded to Swifty.

"This putt is worth eight hundred thousand, folks," Troy Blake whispered into the microphone, "and that hole just got a lot smaller. Gordon's gotta be shaking like a leaf, I know I am."

He didn't hesitate as he anchored the long putter against his chest and stroked the putt, watching calmly as the ball nose-dived into the hole, never a doubt.

Chapter 50

THE PRESS CONFERENCE WAS mobbed, standing room only. Gordon sat at the winner's table, the trophy on his right, bottles of cold Evian to his left, the microphone in front, waiting for the buzz and chatter to subside as the executive VP of Sony USA made the introduction.

"Ladies and Gentlemen, on behalf of Sony USA, I would like to present to Gordon Howard, the winner of this year's Sony Invitational, with the first prize of eight hundred thousand dollars."

Gordon stood up as they shook hands to a burst of applause. He stuffed the check into his pocket, then sat back down and opened a bottle of water. Sony was rooting for Phil, not particularly pleased associating themselves with this unknown upstart cocky winner of such a prestigious tournament, notwithstanding the impressiveness of his accomplishment.

"Gordon will take your questions. I would appreciate you keeping it organized. He's got a half hour, needs to catch a flight."

The venue was suddenly overwhelmed with waving arms and nearly hysterical shouts. Gordon held court, picking and choosing from the sea of hungry reporters.

"Congrats on your win, very impressive, tell us how you pulled off that last shot into eighteen."

"That was all Swifty, my caddie. He knows my game, gave me the yardage with the wind, and I just put on a good swing with a five wood. I never considered playing safe, not against Mickelson."

"How was it playing with Phil, knowing the fans were pulling for him?"

"It was cool, ask him how he liked playing with me," his tone humorous with a tinge of sarcasm.

"Great win. Was there any time during the round you pinched yourself, making sure this wasn't a dream?"

"When I missed the five-foot putt on eight, more a nightmare than a dream."

The crowd laughed. Sipping some water, Gordon exuded a cool detachment.

"How does it feel to win your first tournament as a professional? Most guys are out here for a few years before they break through."

"The pros today start in their early twenties. I'm thirty-five, and figured I have to make up for lost time."

"Rumor has it you're cold hearted, at least on the golf course. How do you turn it on and off, or is that your real personality?"

"Good question. I'm seeing my shrink next week, let me get back to you," which elicited another burst of laughter. "The truth is that I get into a zone out here, a higher state of consciousness, nothing religious, probably some sort of Eastern philosophy."

"So you've studied Buddha?"

"If he wrote a golf instruction book, definitely," his tongue in cheek sense of humor gobbled up by the attendees.

"Jack Richards, *New York Times*. An amazing performance Gordon, considering the odds maker had you at a hundred to one. Where do you think you'll rank going into next week's Desert Classic?"

"I haven't thought about it, Jack, but I'm definitely not the favorite. Have a lot more work in front of me competing with these guys."

"Any misgivings between the split with your famous father, that he's not able to share this victory with you?"

Gordon was taken aback at the sudden jolt of reality; his father, all in all, a human vegetable. Not that he feared him anymore, or wished this on him. He wanted to make amends, but just wasn't sure how, or when.

He glared at Richards, holding back a mouthful of expletives, as this was something personal, dirty laundry, and not for public consumption.

"No comment!"

A deluge of questions were followed by Gordon's supercilious answers. The reporters weren't sure if this was some sort of show, or for real, but entertaining for certain, and great for golf. There was no denying that this thirty-five-year-old had injected the game with a freakishly superior talent and a brazen set of balls.

"One more question please!"

A woman, thirtyish, pretty, tall and lean, appropriately dressed for the Hawaiian heat in khaki shorts and a white tank top, stood up in the back row, waving her hand furiously, determined to get noticed.

"OK, your name?"

"Catherine Connors, Miami Herald."

"You prefer Catherine or Cathy?" Gordon couldn't help but turn on the charm. With his ruggedly handsome looks, it caused a noticeable rustling in the audience.

"Whatever you like," she replied coyly, eliciting more stirs.

"Nice to meet you Catherine, nothing too difficult I hope."

"They say you're able to repeat your swing like a robot. Care to comment?"

"Who are *they*?"

"Bruce Kazin, the announcer with that fancy camera that analyzes all the pro swings. He knows what he's talking about, and I quote," as she turned to her notes. "I've taught the best in the business. Nobody on the planet is that consistent, not Hogan, not Jack, not Tiger, not even close. It's impossible, like this guy is some kind of automaton."

Gordon would have to defuse this as deftly as possible; hopefully she wasn't another too smart for her own good journalist, like Liz.

"Sorry to disappoint you, but we're not dealing with science fiction. Last automaton I saw was named Gort, in a great flick, *The Day the Earth Stood Still*, but Gort wasn't into golf."

"Very funny," she smiled, amidst the laughter. "I saw the movie, but seriously, any comment?"

"Actually it's not that much different than SyberVision."

"What's that?" she replied curiously.

"It was developed at the Stanford Neuropsychology research lab, based upon a mathematical process, the Fourier Algorithm. It has to do with numerical frequencies, nerve impulses, and matching waveforms, how the brain functions in storing mental images. I can't explain it scientifically, but basically you just sit and watch a DVD of thousands of perfectly executed golf swings. It's transformed to your brain, which converts those images to muscle memory, repeatable, hopefully at will."

"That's amazing. It seems you're into this hot and heavy, which algorithm?"

"Fourier, spelled like it sounds. I just have a good memory, don't take it to heart."

"So for the record, is this SyberVision your key to swinging like a robot?"

Gordon checked his watch. He stood up and faced her directly, peering over everyone's head. They spoke as if they were completely alone.

"Bruce Kazin wrote the book on the golf swing. He knows it as well as anyone on the planet, but don't take him literally. He was just being flattering to a new guy on the tour. I worked hard on my swing and tried different things, nothing you can't find on the internet. Through trial and error it just clicked. SyberVision is another tool, that's all. Golf's a difficult game, and for all I know, next week I could suck and miss the cut."

"Good story, but I highly doubt that." She took his semi-vulgarity in stride.

"Doubt what, about my swing?"

"No, that you suck."

There wasn't a person in that room who couldn't feel the sexual tension between them.

And then it hit him. *Idiot! What if this press conference was live on TV? And just his luck that Liz was watching.*

The laughter subsided. Gordon grabbed his trophy, thanked the attendees, and made his way outside, ready to pack up and head for the airport.

Attached to his locker was Catherine Conner's business card, with a handwritten note-*call me!*-scrawled on the back. Gordon wasn't surprised.

"About time you called me, Mr. Big Shot."

"C'mon, Liz, like you weren't transfixed to the boob tube with the rest of my golf fans?" She heard the boasting loud and clear, *my* golf fans, not the time or place to get into a tussle.

"I am so proud of you, all that hard work, I knew it would pay off, just knew it." Gordon laughed to himself. If she wanted some credit for his success, so be it, whatever worked to keep her on board.

"Getting ready to fly to Palm Springs, six hour trip, we arrive close to midnight, call that idiot broker and—"

"Already did, hon, the apartment is officially off the market. By the way, I watched the press conference. Don't get too big for your britches, humility goes a long way. It was pretty serendipitous; that newspaper journalist kind of looked like me, don't you think?"

"Goddamnit!" he muttered aloud.

"What?" Liz asked

"Sorry, hard to hear, gotta hop, love you."

Chapter 51

AFTER THEY LANDED, SWIFTY picked up their Hertz Ford and drove the five miles to a La Quinta Motor Lodge, where Liz had reserved a room. It was close to one in the morning when they sacked out, exhausted, with no need for the early morning alarm.

They awoke late and drove directly to Chase Bank.

"I'm gonna deposit my $800,000 check into my account and then we can settle up."

"OK, GH,"

"How many days will it take for this to clear?" Gordon handed the teller the check.

"You're lucky. Both accounts are at Chase, your money will be available in the morning."

Gordon sat with one of the account executives and filled out the paperwork for the wire to Norman Berger.

"A wire isn't necessary, Mr. Howard. I can transfer the funds to Mr. Berger's account at Chase, and save you the wiring fees. Just fill out this transfer form, and I'll do it in the morning after your deposit clears."

"Let's not transfer anything until I call you."

"No problem, here's my card."

Gordon sent Norman an email: *transferring $80K to your account tomorrow.* He thanked the woman for her help and hustled out to the car.

"I'm waitin' for this a long time, GH, a hundred sixty thousand. That's more than I made past ten years loopin' at the club."

Gordon opened his wallet and handed Swifty a check for eighty thousand dollars, payable to Johnson William Franklin.

"This ain't our deal, GH, supposed to be twenty percent; I got our contract right here." Swifty reached into his back pocket, unfolded the paper, and handed Gordon the document.

"Remember I told you to read it?"

"Yeah, I sure do."

"And did you?"

"Sort of, GH."

"You asked me for twenty percent, and that's what the contract says. What's the problem?"

Swifty cast a blank stare, puzzled at the comment, as Gordon read him the salient language.

"Johnson William Franklin, acting in the capacity of a full-time caddy for Gordon Howard, shall receive, in addition to his monthly stipend, a bonus of twenty percent of any tournament prize money paid to Gordon Howard as a member of the PGA...."

"See, like I said, GH, twenty percent."

Gordon held up his right palm to say he wasn't finished. "With fifty percent held in reserve until terminated."

"Say what, GH?"

Gordon repeated it, very slowly.

"Can I see that again?"

Swifty held it up against his face, his finger touching every word as he scoured the document until he came to the poison language, and his dated signature.

"I never bothered with it, GH. As soon as I seen the twenty percent I was OK, just like we shook on. A man gotta trust his partner, right, me and you got a lot a history together."

"Yep, we sure do," Gordon responded sincerely.

"What's it mean, reserve, like you added to my contract, GH?"

"Nothing was added, you just didn't read it. You're getting what you wanted, half now, and the rest later."

"Later than what, GH," checking his watch, "dinner time?"

Gordon laughed, although Swifty didn't find it funny.

"And terminated, what's that mean?"

"When I quit golf, the contract expires, and you get your money."

"So I'm your slave, GH, that what you're sayin' to me?"

"Of course not, Swifty, you got it all wrong."

"I don't think so, GH, you tryin' to own me, and this ain't what we shook on."

"Not true, Swifty," Gordon raised his voice. "And let's be honest. There's a helluva lot more to being a caddy out here than just hauling the bag. A pro and his caddy are a team. They need to know the exact yardages to the green, front, pin and back, what club to hit, fade or draw, high or low, what the wind is doing, where's the trouble, what's the smart shot. Then he has to read the putt. A caddy gives his man confidence, and keeps him calm, like a damn shrink."

"So sounds like me, GH."

"Exactly, and I don't want to lose you, because you're much too important to me. Besides, the normal rate for tour caddies is ten percent, you're getting double."

Swifty glossed over the comment; he didn't see its relevancy.

"Well if I'm so damn important, GH, why ain't you paying me? That's bass ackwards."

"You mean ass backwards," Gordon corrected him.

"Same difference, I got it. You figurin' I won't leave you holdin' the bag so long as you got my money."

"I don't look at it that way." Gordon wasn't sure what Swifty was thinking, or where this discussion was going.

Swifty turned quiet, fiddling with the contract.

"After you won the Sony, I was fixin' to leave you, GH, turnin' sixty-five next year. I wanna slow down, take my money and put my feet up, maybe do some learnin' and educate myself, get me a decent place to live. Shame on me to waste the time I got left. Your bag gettin' heavier every day, courses are too long, huffin' and puffin' up them hills. I did my time, just ain't fun no more."

"Bad move, Swifty, we have another few months. I'll be raking in the cash every week. Besides, after the US Open, I'm through, you'll have a half million in reserve, maybe more."

"That ain't my real reason, GH."

"What do you mean?"

"Voodoo doctor have the same deal as me?"

"What?"

"Don't be playin' dumb, GH, I don't appreciate it."

"Sorry man, you're imagining things."

"I ain't imagining these, GH, two before every round!" Swifty reached into his pocket and slammed two of Norman's magic pills hard against the dashboard, the capsules miraculously remaining intact.

Fuck! Gordon racked his brain. *How did Swifty find them, or know the dosage?*

"Just something to calm my nerves, that's all."

"Bullshit GH! I know exactly what those pills do. After you left the range, I snuck into Charlie's shack, put your swings on the projector. Ain't no question you took them when you hustled to the bathroom, right after you smoked that five iron. I heard you, and the damn camera can't lie. Ain't a man alive who can repeat his swing exactly like you did, unless he was a damn machine?"

"So, you went through my personal items, didn't you? We had a deal, and you went behind my back."

"Stop it, GH. Ain't that the kettle callin' the pot black? Here, take a look." Swifty pulled out his cell phone, scrolled down, and handed Gordon the evidence, clear as day, the snapshot of him on his hands and knees fishing for the dropped capsules at the practice range.

"Don't try to turn it around on me, GH, feedin' me that bull how you got your swing under control, playin' to your potential. Make no difference how I found out, but I know where you keep 'em, and I don't need to be no math wizard to count. You wanna mess around with them clients at the club is one thing, but out here is no game. People got dreams, breakin' their backs just for a chance, followin' the rules, competin' fair and square. It's one tough sonafabitch way to earn a livin', just like life, up one day, down the next, beatin' balls till their hands bleed."

Gordon was speechless.

"Truth is you ain't got what it takes, plain and simple. You just lucky, born right, otherwise you'd be totin' bags like me, or waitin' tables, deliverin' groceries from the damn supermarket. So you go and sell your soul to the devil, that voodoo doctor, like a Houdini, some hocus pocus magic trick, pulling the wool over everyone's eyes. What you did, all them bullshit stories, takin' that money, same as stealin'; made me sick to my stomach just listenin' to you. And lemme tell you somethin'. You ain't any different than the junkies, waitin' for your next fix from your voodoo dealer. I lived with them addicts all my life. And the price is gonna go higher and higher, cause without them pills, you gonna crash hard."

Gordon cringed at the sudden realization. *No wonder Norman was so stingy with the capsules!* He knew Swifty was right. He'd have to face the music and come clean.

HE ADMITTED EVERYTHING, a running commentary of his meeting with Norman Berger that fateful evening in the Bronx, recounting how his exuberance was tempered by his trepidation, spooked by the possibility of sudden death, until he succumbed to temptation, threw caution to the wind, and swallowed the capsules. He never mentioned Blair Whitcomb, didn't think it was important at the time.

"ALS is one nasty disease, seems he didn't get his due. But the way I see it, from what you said, voodoo man put your father on his death bed. Gettin' all involved with him like you did just ain't sittin' right with me, GH."

"Yeah I know, Swifty, it was a difficult decision."

"Well, maybe he got a raw deal, and sounds like you had some doubts, GH. But desperate people are hard to figure. They gonna do anything to survive. Voodoo doctor is still the pusher man and you just as desperate as him, both in the same boat."

"You think I'm desperate?" Gordon asked, sounding as if he had never entertained the thought before. "What happened to confident and mentally tough; a guy who will go head to head with the best in the business without batting an eyelash?"

"Is that who you think you are, GH?"

Gordon pensively thought about the question. "I'm not sure, Swifty, but I'd like to think so, more than you can imagine."

"Does Liz know about this, GH?"

"No way, she's too honest, and would cut my balls off."

"Ain't nothin' wrong with that, gotta respect her."

"Yeah, Swifty, I do. But I sold her a bill of goods, and it bothers the hell out of me."

"Like what, GH?"

Gordon then forayed into their contentious battles about him turning professional, and the confession turned revelation.

"So you almost spilled the beans?"

Gordon nodded.

"Maybe you gotta sit her down and explain your situation. A good woman is hard to find, not worth losin' her. Besides, she's no fool. Sooner or later you gonna slip up, make a mistake, and she gonna figure the whole thing out. Then you is fucked, GH!"

"Yeah I know, already thought about it." Gordon drifted off, playing out the scenario in his mind, wondering what she would do.

"Why are you out here, GH? You ever really think about it?" It wasn't the first time Swifty had questioned his motives. Gordon suddenly perked up.

"C'mon Swifty, did you forget? I'm gunning for the US Open."

"That ain't your real reason, GH," Swifty smirked. "There a lot more to it than a bunch a golf tournaments, even the damn US Open."

Swifty was just about to bring up Gordon's father, but held his tongue. He knew it was a sensitive subject.

Gordon mused about Swifty's comment. "It's complicated. I can't explain it, almost like it was supposed to happen this way."

"C'mon, GH, it ain't that difficult. All you gotta do is to look deep down inside and you gonna figure it out. But lemme tell you somethin', whatever the reason, you're just foolin' yourself."

"What are you talking about?"

"What the fuck you talkin' about, GH! Who you gonna beat out here without them damn voodoo pills?"

The vibrating cell phone from his back pocket allowed Gordon to avoid Swifty's question. He checked the incoming email; *Twenty percent, $160k or no deal*. He banged his fist against the steering wheel, repeatedly, harder and harder, impervious to the pain, accompanied by a barrage of expletives.

"So the voodoo pusher man upped the ante?" Swifty needled him with that *I told you so* comeuppance. "You bust that hand and voodoo man ain't gonna be your problem."

Gordon slumped in his seat, his head down, funereal.

"Might as well fess up, GH, I'm the only real friend you got."

Gordon didn't answer him. His head hung low, his eyes cast downward.

"C'mon, we ain't got time feelin' sorry for ourselves, tournament starts Thursday. Just gimme the damn deal you made, I'll fix it."

Gordon looked up at Swifty with a silent stare, his eyes casting a despondent look.

"Answer me, GH!"

"Just a handshake," Gordon muttered, his tone morose, fighting to contain his composure. "I figured ten percent was fair, he wants double."

"Least I got me a contract!" Swifty let out a good, hearty appreciative laugh, which lightened up the heaviness.

"I thought about it, but too dangerous. If our deal was in writing, he could use it against me."

"I understand, GH, smart move. Now you gotta play him, tell him eighty thousand on this one or you gonna walk."

"And if he says no, I'm fucked."

"So is he. You're sittin' on eight hundred thousand, less my cut.

What's he got? Squat! He's the dealer and you the junkie, plain and simple. You can't let him know you desperate."

Gordon thought Swifty made sense. He composed the email. *10% is fair, 80k, take it or leave it.* He took a deep breath and hit the send button.

Chapter 52

As soon as Gordon had secured the one qualifying spot for the Sony Invitational, he called Norman with the good news, who hopped an early morning plane to Las Vegas the Wednesday before the start of the Thursday tournament. He checked into the Double Seven Motel and wagered $10,000 that Gordon Howard would win, getting 100 to 1 odds on a no name long shot.

Norman was celebrating his million dollar payday chained to the bed in his Las Vegas motel room. He was naked, engaged in sado-masochistic role playing with an expensive prostitute who bore a striking resemblance to Victoria Chang, when he heard his cell phone chime.

"Would you mind? I'm kind of tied up, could be important." Norman thought he was the cat's meow with his little play on words.

"Not a problem, Norman." She laughed, grabbing his cell phone off of the night stand.

He liked that, addressing him by his first name, like Victoria used to do.

"There's a new email. Read it to me." Norman instructed her.

"Hey, we have the same phone," she said excitedly, as if he cared. "It's great for texting. My clients are paranoid, and their wives can't trace the conversations once they're deleted."

"Are you deaf? Read it to me!" She apologized, pulled up his emails, and relayed Gordon's response.

"Norman mused and then said "so he called my bluff," as if she weren't there.

"Is it bad news, Norman?" She sounded concerned, but he

wasn't listening, grappling with Gordon's chutzpah, contemplating whether or not to play brinkmanship, and how much it would cost him if his patsy walked.

"Just hit reply, and type in; 'Ok, will FedEx capsules after receipt, need address', and then send it."

Supposedly a graduate student working her way through school, she was reasonably intelligent and able to follow Norman's instructions. But she wasn't in Victoria Chang's league, except a helluva lot more fun.

Gordon received the email and immediately called the woman at Chase, who transferred the eighty thousand dollars to Norman Berger's account.

Chapter 53

IT WAS WEDNESDAY, THE day before the start of the Humana Challenge, formerly the Bob Hope Desert classic, with a total purse of $5,600,000, which meant plenty of money to be divvied up.

The FedEx envelope containing the capsules was delivered to the motel that day.

Swifty noticed the sender of the package printed on the FedEx form—Norman Berger, Double Seven Motel, 415 Cherokee Avenue, Las Vegas, Nevada, including the zip code and telephone number. He made a mental note to do more investigating, as something didn't quite make sense.

"Great job, Swifty, saved my life, what can't you do?"

"I can't hit it like you, GH, and don't think I'll be livin' on Park Avenue in a fancy building, less you got some pull with the owners." They cracked up, a good, hearty well deserved laugh.

GORDON HAD A GNAWING fear that trumping the next twenty or so tournaments before the US Open would be a disaster waiting to happen. Not that owning the most recognized face on the planet, endorsement deals up the ying yang, rewriting the record books, being worshipped by ecstatic fans, and jet setting with the rich and famous was punishment.

But the cost would be incalculable, with everyone and anyone screaming foul play; the press, the players, the rebel rousing Troy Blake, Bruce Kazin with his pluperfect Sony Super Slow Motion sports camera, right on up to the Commissioner. There could likely be a Senate investigation, which would ignite a brouhaha making the uproar over illegal steroidal drugs seem like child's play.

Over lunch Gordon expressed his concerns.

"I agree, GH, you start blowin' away these guys every week gonna look suspicious, ain't no doubt. I think you gotta take a back seat, aim too far right, left, miss a bunch of greens, get up and down, and make yourself a check. There ain't nothin' wrong with finishin' in the top ten, and stayin' away from them fuckin' press conferences."

"And you're OK working for me? You gave me a hard time before, called me a thief, and said I made you sick to your stomach."

"A man's gotta do what he's gotta do to survive. I never told you I was a saint, and besides, I signed a contract, right? I'm stickin' with you until you quit, always a man of my word."

Gordon nodded appreciatively.

"But there's somethin' else you gotta do, GH."

"I'm all ears."

"When you're out there, you gotta bury your attitude and play up to the people, make them root for you, build up your followin', get me?"

"Yeah, but that's all an act. We agreed I would just go through the motions, enough for a payday. Then after we win the Open, I won't care anymore."

"What the hell ain't an act, GH? We're actin' every day, each in our own particular way. You wanna see honesty then go on down to the damn church, but be careful, cause even them priests are messin' around with those youngsters. Or them bullshit politicians lyin' about them weapons of mass destruction cause they got their own personal reasons to send them troops into Iraq. I knew these kids—they were my friends and some got themselves killed. The ones who come back with no arms or legs are too fucked up to wanna see me. So if you gonna do somethin', then do it right, cause guess what? You ain't gonna be a favorite at the Open, and everybody likes rootin' for an underdog. They don't know about them pills. But you still want them pullin' for you; it makes them feel good seein' their man make a charge and gettin' their money's worth. We all need someone to be rootin' for, and better they're in your corner than somebody else's."

Gordon thought through Swifty's pretzel logic. So far he had been spot on with everything else.

"OK, let's do it your way."

"Good move, GH, you gotta trust me on this one."

There was a lot more to it than Swifty was prepared to divulge.

"How about Norman, he expects me to win."

"He's still gettin' his piece; we just gotta deal with him."

"You still have to deal with him; you're the drug dealer expert."

"No expert, GH, just more experience than you. I know how these people think. You be born on my side of the tracks, brought up on my turf, you could too. Besides, a man ain't a dealer unless he got customers, know what I mean?" Swifty arched up his eyebrows, as if to remind Gordon that nobody put a gun to his head, certainly not Norman Berger.

The brutal honesty spoke volumes about the man. Gordon looked at him; the gray Pima cotton turtleneck, ripped dungarees, a man decidedly older than when they started. He was lucky to have him, anguished over how he had treated him and determined to make amends, starting immediately.

"Got a pen?"

"Yep," proffering a cheap plastic Bic pen, slightly chewed with its cap missing. "What you gonna do, sign me your autograph?"

"It's not worth much," his tone sorrowful, as Gordon reached into his back pocket and pulled out his wallet.

"Here you go, everything is fair and square." Gordon handed Swifty the additional check for eighty thousand dollars.

They reached across the table, a long, striking pose, more than just a handshake.

"You did me right, GH," his eyes moist.

"I love you, Swifty," wiping away a tear, "like a brother."

LATER THAT DAY GORDON called Norman's cell, got his voice mail, and left him a detailed message about his plan to take a back seat until his last tournament, the US Open in the middle of June, where first prize was $1,800,000. That, he thought, should keep Norman pacified, along with a continuous supply of capsules.

He mentioned the call to Swifty, making sure he gave him all the salient details. Swifty didn't say anything, at least not then.

Chapter 54

GORDON PURPOSELY FINISHED IN a tie for sixth at the Humana, pocketing a cool two hundred thousand dollars. It took an additional five tour stops before his star lost its luster; he didn't play poorly, finishing in the top ten through the Northern Trust at Riviera Country Club in Los Angeles. But he was sharpening his act and taking home a nice paycheck, just as Swifty suggested.

At times he would challenge for the lead, honing his own unique brand of histrionics; a solo fist pump after a birdie, hanging his head disconsolately after a bogie, tossing in an eagle or two followed by a barrage of double handed fist pumps.

He had unwittingly given the fans something they sorely needed, a populist hero, acting more than approachable to the increasing swarm of loyalists that felt his pain and shared his elation. He would ignite the crowd, high fiving, tipping his cap, shaking hands and signing autographs, just like he was one of them.

All of which was fodder for the jokester Troy Blake, who coined them *Gordon's Groupies,* remarking, "folks, with all due deference to Mr. Palmer, the King, these fans remind me of Arnie's Army on steroids."

MEANWHILE, NORMAN CONTINUED TO languish in Las Vegas in the Double Seven motel, letting his share of Gordon's winnings accumulate, content with the ten percent. He was finally enjoying his life, spending more time with his expensive Victoria Chang substitute, dining in fine restaurants, reading, watching the tournaments, and patiently waiting for the US Open, where he planned on making a killing.

LIZ FINALLY LANDED A job as director of a public relations firm. Other than the long hours and her six figure salary, it allowed her to utilize her journalistic skills. She loved to work, abhorring those women who lunched with the girls and spent oodles of hard earned money at the nail salon and beauty parlor, on facials, masseuses, personal trainers and shopping, which she considered vacuous and a waste of precious time.

Not that money was an issue anymore. Gordon had earned close to three million dollars. They were getting along just fine, each immersed in their own thing, she counting on his promise that the US Open in June would be his final tournament, win or lose. Then they would become a normal working couple, raising a family, eventually moving to the burbs. She imagined an old Victorian style home, with large picture windows and yellow shutters, maybe green, nothing showy or garish, set back on a healthy piece of property, with a couple of kids and a dog or two.

Chapter 55

THE BYRON NELSON CLASSIC marked the first tour stop in the final leg before the US Open, played in honor of the man who inspired the name Iron Byron, known as Lord Byron for his elegant swing and unassuming manner.

Gordon's groupies were there in droves.

"Folks," Troy Blake announced, "do you remember Gordon Howard, the rank amateur from New York City who somehow got his act together and blew away the brutal Q school best of the best by some sixteen shots, and then pockets $800k winning his first pro gig, the Sony Open, like it was just a walk in the park? I was convinced this guy was from another planet. His swing was as close to perfect as the Sports Illustrated swimsuit cover, like watching a well oiled machine that never broke down.

"Well, Mr. Machine may have a few defective parts because he has faded into relative obscurity since his phenomenal debut. Not that some dozen finishes in the top ten is anything to sneeze at, pocketing some three million large. I was over on the range yesterday watching him warm up, when his longtime caddie Swifty fed me some confidential information, that Gordon has this cool nickname, *GH*, kind of a secret, only for his closest friends.

"But guess what? He started yesterday's third round ten shots back of the leader, a journeyman named Dirk Mathew. And then Gordon cards a sizzling sixty-one. Now he's only four back of Mathew going into today's final round, and his fans are going berserk!"

Gordon knew Dirk Mathew's story, having played one round with him at Q school.

Reared modestly in Dothan, Alabama, the son of a high school football coach, Dirk played varsity everything, attending Oklahoma State on a golf scholarship.

Superbly talented, he spent eight grueling years on the Nationwide Tour, financed by some wealthy investors who owned fifty percent of him, lock, stock, and barrel. He lived with his wife and twin boys, Tyler and Taylor, in a used RV, which he drove to tour events.

Barely making expenses, he had faith in himself and the Lord Jesus Christ. He never smoked, drank, cursed, peeked at pornography, or inhaled a joint. He listened to Christian music, said grace before dinner, and practiced until his hands bled. After five futile attempts, he finally obtained his PGA card, finishing fourteen shots behind Gordon Howard.

Quiet and reserved, downright boring, Dirk just went about his business. Pictures of his twin boys encased in a transparent button were permanently attached to his cap, with his wife Suzie always in the gallery with the kids, praying for a good finish, a breakthrough, a decent paycheck.

All that hard work finally paid off. First prize at the Nelson paid $800,000. That Sunday morning, Dirk Mathew and his family attended a church service and prayed like they had never prayed before.

Gordon picked up two more shots through fifteen holes, prompting Tory Blake to comment; "It's a classic meltdown folks, and Dirk Mathews looks like he is on suicide watch. His lead has dwindled to two shots, and now it's up for grabs."

The sixteenth hole measured 546 yards, a reachable par five, provided you kept your drive on the short grass. Gordon bombed his tee shot, dead center cut, leaving him some two hundred plus yards to the pin, which was tucked right behind a yawning green-side front bunker.

After a mediocre drive, Dirk hit a decent three wood, leaving himself a wedge into the green.

"What do we have to the pin, Swifty?"

"We got 215 to the flag, 209 to clear the trap."

"Four iron."

"Too much, GH, I like five."

Gordon threw up some grass, which swept right back into his face.

"Got wind against me, it's a four iron."

"Look up at them treetops, GH." Swifty pointed to a row of tall stately oaks lining the right side of the fairway. "They're dead quiet; all the wind is down below. You hit that four and you gonna wind up on Fungolina Avenue."

It was something Swifty had picked up from his tough brethren in the hood. Fungolina Avenue didn't exist, but had a dire sort of sound, it meant a bad place; arrested, incarcerated, strung out, over the green, out of bounds, *dead.*

Gordon played with the grass again, looking up at the trees, hands on his hips, with the crowd respectfully silent.

"Hit your five, same way you blistered it with voodoo man on the driving range, slight left to right. She's gonna clear the bunk and nestle on up to the pin, wind ain't a factor."

"OK."

Swifty pulled out his Wilson X31 five iron, handed it to him, grip first, and then stepped aside and behind, out of Gordon's periphery.

The ball was launched low, and then rose higher and higher above the treetops in a missile like trajectory. It veered ever so slightly to the right and descended just beyond the bunker, carrying exactly 210 yards, as it hit the green, took two bounces, and rolled toward the pin, stopping some fifteen feet past the hole.

The roar from Gordon's groupies was electrifying; "GH! GH! GH!" Gordon raised his arms to quiet them down, allowing Dirk to execute the shot, which he knocked three feet from the hole. The crowd half-heartedly applauded, as he walked dejectedly to the green, knowing he had squandered an easy victory, with his wife Suzie in tears.

The spectators erupted as Gordon marched toward the green, thrusting his club as if it were a sword, and he a gladiator. Swifty scurried up next to him, high fiving Gordon, which evoked another round of hoots and hollers, as the two walked side by side, acknowledging the applause.

He marked his ball and tossed it to Swifty for a good cleaning, fixed his ball mark and grabbed his putter.

"What do you think?"

Swifty got down on his hands and knees and studied the break, stalking the putt from every direction.

"You wanna make this, GH?"

"Gotta give my fans their money's worth, right?"

"Yep, left to right, a little downhill but against the grain, I see it this far outside," holding his thumb and forefinger a good six inches apart. "She's gonna break hard right here." Swifty walked over, pulled the flag, and pointed to a spot two feet before the hole, careful not to touch the green and incur a penalty.

The marshals held up QUIET signs as Gordon replaced his ball, picked up his marker, and crouched down for a quick study of Swifty's read. He assumed his stance, anchored the long putter against his chest, took one final look, and stroked the putt.

It slowly traversed the line, picked up speed, closer and closer, while Gordon dropped his putter and stared it down, until it rolled over Swifty's spot and broke sharply left, dive bombing into the bottom of the hole. Gordon's groupies went wild, intoxicated by their hero's two handed triple fist pump.

The throng bolted en masse to the seventeenth tee, forgetting about Dirk, who sat sullenly alone with his head in his hands. Gordon and Swifty politely waited for him to finish out, an easy three-footer, almost a gimme, which he missed, and flung his putter in disgust, murmuring what sounded like a few choice profanities.

Chapter 56

"THIS IS UNBELIEVABLE," TROY Blake squawked into the microphone. "Gordon Howard ties the course record and comes back from a ten stroke deficit, and with that spectacular eagle on sixteen, he finds himself tied for the lead. Wow, and this guy makes it look easy, like it's no big deal. Hey, Bruce, does Gordon have a new swing guru? It looks like he figured something out."

"Doesn't have one," Kazin replied, "never did as far as I know. His local pro got him going, but he has some really unconventional moves."

"Enlighten us. Listening to you dissect a player's swing is like poetry."

"OK, Troy," Kazin laughed, "let's analyze Gordon's bad swings, pulled left or pushed right, something really interesting, just noticed it the other day."

"Cool, got the Sony Super Slow Motion all set?"

"Absolutely, let's take a look. Unlike all touring pros, Gordon plays every single shot from the same position, whether a hook, draw, or fade. You can see it on his last swing. For a high fade, he aims dead straight and then realigns his hands, which closes the clubface, and then takes his regular swing, just the opposite if he wants to hit a draw. It works because the hands naturally want to get back to square. With a draw, imagine closed to square to open, with a fade just the opposite. Look at these pictures—I've slowed them down, clear as day."

"You're right. I can see it, that's highly unorthodox. Most of us change our alignment, take the club more outside, or inside, but our hands remain intact as does the clubhead. What's the deal with this?"

"Check out these four swings, Troy. The first two went left, and the next two went right. Do you see anything?"

Kazin drew a set of yellow perpendicular lines superimposed on the images. "He's aiming like he needs a new pair of eyes. I wonder why his caddy doesn't say something."

"Don't know, Troy, but for sure he plays one swing and one swing only. The club path is always identical. His push or pull is a no brainer to fix. He should win everything out here. It's almost as if he's...."

"Got the perfect swing, Bruce, just like...."

"Lord Iron Byron." Kazin finished Blake's thought. "But there's more to it, Troy. It's strange; he's always hemming and hawing to discuss his mechanics with me. He becomes evasive, like it's an invasion of his privacy, or some secret, or maybe he's discovered golf's Holy Grail?"

"The plot thickens, folks," Troy Blake quipped, in his usual jocular mood. "Stay tuned."

THEY MARCHED DOWN THE roped off path. Gordon stopping to autograph whatever was thrust at him, shaking hands, "thanks, appreciate it," all the usual niceties.

He looked over at Dirk Mathew, who was walking slouched over, his wife and twins trudging alongside just outside the ropes. Every so often he would wave to them, forcing a smile, not wanting to make them feel worse than he already did. Gordon knew hands down that Dirk Mathew was a far superior player, as were the rest of his competitors, all in a different league, hard-working guys who didn't come from money and who earned their tour card legitimately.

"You not thinkin' of winnin', GH, are you?"

Gordon, entrenched in some painful soul searching, didn't answer him immediately.

"Course not; it's time to back off. I was just having fun, making it exciting, getting my troops all revved up for Bethpage."

"Good move, now you're thinkin' the right way. The US Open comin' up next month."

"Don't worry, Swifty. Second place pays four hundred thousand. It's enough."

It's more than enough, Gordon reflected pensively, panged with guilt, *much more than enough.*

"WELL BRUCE, WHO WOULD have believed it? Gordon Howard needed just two putts on eighteen for a win, and then he three jacks it from ten feet for a bogey. It looked like he just wanted to hand Dirk the victory on a silver platter. I'm speechless!"

"Yeah, and it's a real breakthrough for Dirk Mathews, who somehow held it together under all that pressure."

"I agree Troy; you gotta feel good for the guy. But Gordon must be sick to his stomach. He's been out here five months without a break. Money isn't an issue. If I was his mentor, I'd send him back home to New York, have him relax and get ready for the US Open at Bethpage. It's his home turf. I have to believe he wants that one really badly."

Chapter 57

Eight grueling months on the road since Q school with only a brief respite was punishingly exhaustive, although Swifty, who considered his commitments sacrosanct, was not one to quit. Gordon could see it in the way he carried his bag, more of a burden than an honor. He wheezed as he walked, finding it difficult to catch his breath. The grunts and groans from the pain in his joints were impossible to camouflage.

They were sitting at the bar in their hotel, unwinding with a few cold brews, rehashing the day.

"Are you feeling OK, Swifty? You look like something the cat dragged in."

Gordon was being kind. He thought Swifty looked a lot worse.

"Yeah, GH, I'm one hundred percent, where we goin' next?"

"Back to New York, get some rest and prepare for Bethpage."

"Are you sure, GH? Don't do it on my account."

"I'm positive. We're done out here, it's enough. How much more money do you need to call it a day? I didn't forget what you told me, want me to remind you?"

"That ain't necessary GH, I know, think about it every damn day."

Gordon beckoned for the bartender and ordered another round of Heineken drafts with a bowl of unsalted peanuts. He brought over two frosty mugs, foamed right to the top.

"C'mon dig in, Swifty, peanuts are healthy." Gordon grabbed a handful, reminding him of the bar at Old Point; nicely wood paneled, chilled beer steins, TV, padded stools, Grey Goose vodka in all their vibrant flavors.

"Here you go Swifty, twenty percent, another eighty thousand." Gordon folded the check and shoved it into Swifty's shirt pocket. "Got any idea how much that makes?"

"Yup," he answered curtly, working on the peanuts while guzzling down the beer.

"So six hundred eighty thousand is just chump change?"

"No GH, I appreciate it, don't get the wrong idea. I'm just thinkin', got a lot on my mind, maybe too much."

Gordon called American Airlines and booked two first class seats to LaGuardia, while Swifty went up to their room and packed their bags. An unexpected phone call lasted some fifteen minutes. Had it been anyone else, Swifty would have hung up immediately.

"Thought you fell asleep on me up there, what took so long?"

"Almost did, hard to get my ass in gear, made sure I got everything."

"Need to stop at a Chase branch, deposit the check, and send Norman his cut." Gordon maneuvered the rental car out of the hotel lot.

"Yep, gotta pay the dealer if you want the goods, right GH?"

"You got an alternative wise guy?"

"Nope," Swifty conveniently lied, unable to hold back a self-satisfying grin, "but sure wish I did." He wondered how Gordon would react when he gave him the news about what he had planned for him.

"Be right back." Gordon pulled into the Chase branch lot.

"I'm comin' with you, GH, got some important business to attend to."

"Like what?" He looked at Swifty quizzically.

Swifty reached into his pocket and pulled out a wad of checks, all neatly folded and secured by a rubber band.

"Like a bank account, GH, never needed one before."

Gordon sent Norman an email, as he did after every tournament; *Taking some time off to prepare for US Open, send last eight capsules FedEx to Johnson Franklin (Swifty),* supplying his home address and telephone number. The last thing he needed was for Liz to intercept the shipment and start barraging him with questions.

Within the hour, Norman Berger received another forty thousand dollars, while Swifty, with his hefty deposit, became the proud owner of a Chase Gold Executive checking account, complete with overdraft protection, a debit/ATM card, and a complementary Chase brass key ring and coffee mug.

SWIFTY HAD NEVER FLOWN first class, which was Gordon's treat. After a few bourbons before takeoff and a couple more with the steak a poivre dinner, he conked out, snoring occasionally, all curled up against the window. Gordon gingerly slid his pillow under Swifty's head and draped him with his blanket. He looked at him affectionately, letting him sleep for the duration of the flight.

They waited by the baggage claim. Gordon's cell phone rang. He recognized the incoming number.

"Hey, just got in, where are you?"

"Traffic, hon, I'm furious. I left a half hour earlier. Looks like an accident; I can see the damn flashing lights."

"Relax Liz; it's just another few minutes. Come around to arrivals, I'll be outside with Swifty."

"OK, thanks, can't wait to see you, so glad it's your last tournament."

"Me too," he replied, choked up, his eyes moistened.

Swifty noticed it immediately. "You OK, GH?"

"I'm fine, there she is." Gordon waved and got Liz's attention. She pulled up to the curb and popped open the trunk as Swifty loaded Gordon's bags and clubs. They embraced until a police officer flashed his lights, warning them to move on.

"C'mon Swifty, let me take you home, get in."

"No thanks, Miss Liz, I catch me a bus."

"What, at this hour? I insist, let's go, the cop is hounding me."

"It's OK, appreciate the worry about me. You two go on home, got a lot to discuss, don't need me interferin'."

Gordon nudged Liz. He knew Swifty was embarrassed of where he lived.

"Now your upsetting me, Swifty, I won't take no for an answer."

"Hon, don't be a nag, get it!" Gordon turned to face her with a stern look until she understood.

She pulled into the garage underneath the duplex; the attendant came out and loaded his luggage onto a cart.

"Whoa, look at you, and who's springing for this luxury, not like I'm a millionaire." Gordon chuckled.

It was a welcome relief for Gordon to get home and sleep in their bed, knowing it would all be over soon.

Chapter 58

FIRST THINGS FIRST, HE went through the stack of business cards that Swifty had organized for him; a potpourri of sports agents, equipment manufacturers, and iconic clothing brands, all the usual suspects clamoring to capitalize on his fame, betting he would eventually break through to number one in the world.

Each quickly found its way into the garbage. He came across Catherine Connolly's card, with the suggestive handwritten note. She was hot, no doubt, and willing.

It had crossed his mind at the time, but he couldn't, even if the impotency had suddenly disappeared. He thought it ironic that he had no compunction in selling out to the devil, but just one indiscretion with no strings attached, miles from home, *never*.

He lit a match and watched the card disintegrate. It felt good.

He had no reason to visit the club. Why chat with a bunch of fair weather friends vying for his attention, congratulating him on his successes, which were all totally bogus? As much as he wanted to speak to Charlie, his guilty conscience wouldn't let him.

THE CITY WAS DRENCHED with a vicious rainstorm. Liz called to say she was running late, working on a presentation for a new client. She suggested Italian Village, which was fine with him. It would be better to be at home when he told her, no telling what she would do.

"OK, the usual, maybe we spring for a better bottle of vino. I can call the liquor store."

"Fine, but don't go crazy, plenty of great wines for less than twenty dollars."

Swifty was dead on. Liz was a real find. She still watched every nickel, almost impossible to find in a city of insipid implanted women just chasing Daddy Bigbucks.

"Hey, hon, sorry," she traipsed into the apartment, "subway was flooded, had to wait for a bus. Let me ditch these wet clothes. The food smells yummy, I'm really hungry."

He had elegantly prepared the table with their best linen tablecloth and chinaware. A centerpiece vase held a bouquet of the assorted flowers he purchased at the overpriced flower stand on Madison Avenue. He popped the lasagna and linguine Bolognese in the microwave, set the salads out, opened the Argentinean Malbec, dimmed the lights, and lit two candles.

"So what's the occasion, you win the US Open?"

"I just thought I would show my appreciation to the most important person in my life, an incredible woman who comes along once every lifetime; beautiful inside and out, smart, caring, funny, practical—the list is endless, and I was the lucky guy who met her."

"OK, Gordon, you're buttering me up, let's hear it."

Just then the microwave beeped. Liz beat him to the punch and served them both, while Gordon filled their wine glasses and dug into dinner.

"There's something you need to know; no joke, no affairs or anything like that."

From the timbre of his voice, she knew he was serious.

"I'm listening."

He told her everything; start to finish, in living color, condensing eight months of the most egregious ignominy into two hours; everything he schemed, thought, pondered, anguished and planned, a story of such inglorious details that it couldn't be concocted. His journey was an open book, and she was privy to every word.

She remained stone silent.

"Well?" he asked sheepishly.

She stood up and paced around the room, her head down. "Well what?"

"Were you listening to me?"

"Totally," she quickly answered.

"You don't hate me for this?"

She glared at him with an incredulous stare. "Are you kidding? I'm furious! After all these years together, you have the unmitigated gall to undermine everything I stand for, as if I didn't matter, just an afterthought that got in the way of your precious golf. I despise cheaters! And you're the worst kind. Did you forget what I told you about what golf means to me? What you did is no different than stealing from the blind! What planet are you on? How did you think I would react? You have no idea who I am, do you? And if you do, you don't give a damn! It's over Gordon." She frantically walked back and forth, not sure what she would do next.

"Liz, please, you can't leave me, just listen!"

He approached her, but she ran away screaming as he chased her to the upstairs bedroom. She fought to escape, pounding on his chest, kicking him, sobbing hysterically until the emotional trauma exhausted her.

"Just calm down and let me explain a few things. I'm begging you, please!"

She sat on the side of the bed, her head buried in her lap. He nestled next to her and lifted her chin, trying to make eye contact. She had stopped crying, but her eyes showed her grief. She looked away.

"Don't ever think I don't respect who you are. I knew it the moment we met and I've known it ever since. It's just one of a thousand reasons I'm hopelessly in love with you. I would never ask you to compromise your values under any circumstances. And don't for a moment think I don't thank God that you've stayed with me. Sure, I screwed up my life and made some bad choices. But I've tried to rectify them; you know what I've been through. It hasn't been easy, not for me, not for us. Maybe you think I take you for granted sometimes, but nothing could be further from the truth."

She turned to him. "But Gordon, how could you be so stupid, putting your life on the line with some unproven drug from a mad scientist who you didn't know from Adam? What on earth were you thinking? Who knows if your sperm is poisoned? How can I even *consider* marriage? What if I give birth to a deformed child with no hands, or no feet—or God knows whatever else."

"C'mon Liz, you're blowing this out of proportion, thinking the worst. There are ways of testing—"

"Am I? It's easy for you to say, but put yourself in my position!"

"I understand." Gordon let out a huge sigh.

"Remember what I told you after your father booted you out?"

"I forgot. What?" He immediately noticed it; *your father booted you out,* not the more sanguine *when you left your father.*

"How about, and I quote, 'with your rolodex, tons of hedge funds would hire you in a heartbeat.' Does that ring a bell?"

"Yes."

"And that's all you had to do. I would have supported you one thousand percent. But you let me know immediately with your smug attitude that the great Gordon Howard doesn't answer to anybody but himself, with the chutzpah to think you could make a living playing golf. And I stupidly allowed you to believe it. I should have put my foot down then and there, and none of this would ever have happened. Pity on me, maybe I deserved what I got, but it's not too late, it's never too late."

Gordon absorbed every word, thinking.

"It's comical how you had the guts to swallow those pills, but never had the moxie to go out into the world and make your own life instead of hiding under your father's skirt and getting abused for the privilege. Or maybe you're just petrified of working for a stranger, scared to death you won't be able to produce."

"So you're going for the jugular, no holding back. Why don't you tell me how you really feel?"

"Cut the *woe is me* routine, Gordon. You have nobody to blame but yourself. Maybe the truth hurts, but no way will I mollycoddle you so your fragile ego isn't wounded."

She had calmed down somewhat, not as frantic. He was formulating what he would say while trying to maintain some semblance of dignity.

"You're right. I'm not afraid to admit it. And what's totally screwed up is that I knew it when I signed on with him. For some reason I was sucked in, like I was some sort of masochist. And don't think I didn't pay for it."

He rolled up his sleeve and exposed the scar on his left wrist, shoving the wound up against her face, making sure she got a close up view.

"You're entitled to know what really happened."

"It wasn't from a boating accident?"

Gordon shook his head. She knew from the look in his eyes.

"Oh, my God, you tried to kill yourself?"

"Sort of, it's pretty twisted." Gordon displayed a panged look, hoping to quickly defuse a stunning admission and garner a little sympathy.

"Jesus, Gordon, what happened?"

"I'm not really sure, other than I wanted to punish my father, or needed his attention. At least that's what the shrink told me. It was a few months after I started working there. You know he was pretty rough on me as a kid, but I always spared you the gory details."

"So you slit your wrist all to get back at your father? You could have bled to death!"

"I had it under control. I made sure the cut wasn't deep."

"Did your father know about this?"

"I'm not sure," Gordon replied, somewhat lamentably. "Does it really matter at this point?"

"I would think you would have wanted some closure," she said, which gave Gordon an idea. "Was that the only incident, or is there more you want to tell me?"

Gordon ran through the episode at Creedmoor. He never mentioned the suicide note or the incident with the broken glass when he was cleaning out his office.

"So you went through this whole bogus suicide attempt without a goodbye letter? Pretty poor planning if you ask me."

He figured her journalistic curiosity would have picked up on it.

"Sorry, I forgot to mention that."

"And what did the letter say?"

"I was pretty wacked out when I wrote it. It was just a rambling cathartic stream of consciousness, things I couldn't say to him in person, trying to let him know that I hated him as much as I loved him, if that makes any sense. All in all I wanted him to be proud of me, wanted the chance to prove myself."

Liz saw that Gordon's eyes welled with tears.

"I understand Gordon, must have been very painful." Her voice was soothing.

"Yep, it was the lowest point in my life."

"So you had something to prove to your father. I can understand that. And I guess you thought your magic pill charade winning all those tournaments would do the trick."

"For certain Liz, but I'm sure there are other reasons. It's very complicated. I also had something to prove to you and to myself, that I wasn't a loser. And in some crazy way, I figured it would all work out, and never considered the consequences. And believe me; I anguished terribly over it. I swear to God I was ready to tell you the truth, that's how much it killed me. But deep down in my gut I was afraid you would leave me, so I copped out and kind of told you about the pills, in a roundabout way, enough for me to deal with it."

"You're so called confession?"

Gordon nodded.

"I discussed the whole story with Swifty. I told him that I owed you an explanation, that what I did was wrong, not just cheating with the pills, but not coming clean with you. Sometimes you just get caught up in a mess and it takes time to unravel."

"OK, I hear you. But you need to rectify this. An apology isn't enough."

"I already did, last night, on my own."

He reached into his pocket and handed her a check made out to the Alan Howard Foundation of North Shore Hospital.

"I can't believe this Gordon!"

"It's the right thing to do, Liz."

She ripped up the check.

"What are you doing?"

"This isn't necessary, and it's not enough. I made the pledge yesterday in your name. You'll get a bill in the mail. You didn't think I would let you keep any of that tainted money, less what you paid out to Swifty and that Berger creep. We have just enough left to pay the bills, including what I bring home."

"You knew about it?"

"I had a sneaky suspicion. I did my homework, and something didn't add up."

"Swifty told you?"

"Just the opposite, Gordon; emails can be traced, text messaging is totally discreet. I knew Berger was supplying you with capsules, although for what purpose was a mystery. That was your first mistake. And don't forget who balances your bank statements. I didn't have to be a genius to figure out something was going on; all the transfers to the same account, all Norman Berger, all ten percent of whatever you won. You filled in all the blanks, it was obvious."

And then he realized his fatal mistake. Swifty was right. Sooner or later he would screw up, and she would find out. "And you made me get down on my hands and knees?"

"You got away easy, I didn't want to totally castrate you."

"Well, I'm thinking about pulling out of the Open."

"That's between you, your agent, and the Golf Gods."

"What agent?" He again wondered about the Golf Gods.

"Johnson William Franklin; agent, psychiatrist, confidant, and caddie, all packed into one. You can't get better than that."

"What are you talking about? You think I can win this thing on my own? I'll be lucky to break 80."

"Yes I do and so does Mr. Franklin. You guys need to sit down and talk. I think he's got a plan."

He needed to meet up with Swifty anyway, to get a few things off of his chest. He wondered about this *plan*.

"So do you forgive me?" Gordon asked, flashing that boyish grin.

THEY HAD PASSIONATE MAKE up sex. There was no reason for Liz to mention his impotence anymore. Nor was there any reason to mention then what she had uncovered in the FDA official report on ALS, that there was a fifty-fifty chance that he was infertile. After the US Open, they would have a heart to heart, and he would have to get tested. And then, when she had all the facts, she would make her decision.

"You know the old saying hon," Liz whispered as she lied in his arms, both spent.

"I'm all ears," Gordon replied.

"The truth shall set you free."

"Well said, Liz," Gordon answered, letting out a huge sigh, "well said."

Chapter 59

NORMAN BERGER, STILL LIVING in Las Vegas, had signed up an enthusiastic new magic capsule client who he fleeced for a forty percent cut of his earnings, four times more than what Gordon was paying. Ironically, he qualified for his tour card at Q school in the same pack with Gordon Howard. He had been burning up the Nationwide Tour, honing his short game.

He started off shaky, and then went on fire, as the voodoo capsules took time to work their magic, winning his last six tournaments by huge margins and getting all the hyped publicity from the news starved sportswriters.

The purses were skimpy compared to the PGA tournaments, but with his client's total winnings of just over a million dollars, Norman collected a not too shabby four hundred thousand.

The client was on his way to New York City for a week of sightseeing, accompanied by his newest indiscretion—a woman half his age. They would take in a few Broadway shows, hit some expensive restaurants, and do a little lingerie shopping. He reserved a suite in the Garden City Hotel, close to Bethpage. A FedEx package of voodoo capsules from Norman awaited his arrival.

Chapter 60

"SHE KNOWS EVERYTHING NOW."

They sat in a booth at the Seven Seas Diner, their usual lunch spot.

Swifty didn't answer, immersed in his cheeseburger and French fries. Gordon wasn't hungry.

"Are you deaf?"

"Almost, tell you the truth. Heart ain't great either, but my eyes are perfect, help you read them slick greens this week."

Gordon wasn't ready to discuss the US Open.

"She donated everything I made to my father's charity."

"I ain't surprised. She's a good woman, figured you don't deserve keepin' anything if you didn't earn it fair and square."

"OK Swifty, stop messing with me."

"She called me, asked me a bunch of questions."

"When was this?"

"Right when I was packin' up after the Nelson."

"She had your cell number?"

"Said she called the club, caddy master gave it to her."

"What kind of questions?"

"Listen, GH, she's one crafty woman. Said she smelled somethin' wasn't kosher, checked out Berger, did a whole lot of readin' about his cure, knew you went to see him. Didn't make sense that all of a sudden you this golf superstar. Then she saw the emails on your computer and checked your bank statements, saw all them wires to him. I played dumb as best I could, told her you were my boss, whatever's goin' on was between the two of you. But she wouldn't stop, kept on grillin' me, and wouldn't let me off the phone."

"Yep, that's her, like a pit bull. Once she gets her jaws into something, she'll never let go."

"Yeah, she kinda dragged it out of me. I just told her you were all upset and was gonna make it right."

"Why didn't you give me a heads up?"

"Cause I promised her, and I'm a man of my word, GH."

"Anything else I need to know?"

"Yep, a lot more," Swifty answered, his eyes fixed on Gordon.

"This sounds serious."

"Depends how you look at it, GH."

"Go ahead."

"You wanna win the Open?"

Gordon looked at him like he was crazy. "What kind of question is that? Of course I do."

"Are you sure, GH?"

"Jesus Christ, I'm positive! But without those capsules I'm toast. Liz almost left me last night. I came clean, and I'm keeping it that way."

"Now you listen to me" Swifty retorted, thumping his tightly clenched fist against his frail chest. "There's no way in hell would I let you play with them pills. You'll piss off the Golf Gods, and then anything can happen. This got nothin to do with your woman. You wanna win; it got to be on the up and up, no cheatin', just your God given talent. I got my principles too, GH. Sure I sacrificed them out there, needed the money. But the US Open is sacred, it's everything the damn game stands for, and I'm not messin' with it for any amount of money."

"So what's our plan, Swifty? Without the capsules, I'll make a fool of myself out there. Maybe I'm better off just skipping it, finished." Gordon again thought about these Golf Gods.

"I don't wanna hear this, GH, not gonna stand for it. Where's that fightin' spirit? You think you're addicted to them pills, right? Well listen up, because you ain't-don't need the pusher man

anymore. He's gonna find somebody else, and as long as I'm involved, we gonna win straight, I got no doubts."

"Maybe you should clue me in, the guy who's swinging the
damn clubs."

"Check this out, GH, I did my homework." Swifty reached into
his pocket and pulled out a folded oversized sheet of paper, then
spread it on the table, displaying a handwritten spreadsheet.

"I figured you played exactly eighty-nine rounds with the voodoo pill, listed them right here, shows the date and your scores. It
adds up to total 11,926 swings, includin' a practice swing before
each shot. I always wrote down which club you hit and the yardage
to the pin, so we know how many times you hit five iron, or eight
iron, or driver, you get it?"

Swifty was proud of his statistical analysis, you could see it in
his demeanor.

"Plus, I didn't include all them practice balls you hit on the
range."

"Didn't know you were a mathematical whiz; big deal, it proves
nothing."

"That's where you're wrong, GH," Swifty shot back, pounding
the table, "because you own your swing, repeated it so many times
exactly the same way. Those voodoo pills made it a part of you,
do it with your eyes closed. Your muscles are trained, like a prize
fighter spendin' hours in the gym, perfectin' his jab, left hook, and
uppercut. He gets in that ring and its automatic, no thinkin' or
second guessin', like he ain't human."

"You think so?"

"I know so, Goddamnit!"

Gordon slumped back into the booth, closed his eyes and took
a deep breath, wanting to believe his friend with all of his heart
and soul.

"You gotta trust me, GH. You know you got major talent,
always did, but never worked at it, took it for granted. Game is
too hard; tour players all separated by half a shot, maybe less.
Difference between winnin' and second place is out there on the

range, workin' on their swings, hittin' thousands of balls, until its *boom, boom, boom*, all the same." Swifty banged hard on the table to make his point.

"And guess what?"

"What?" Gordon answered, stuck in the same contemplative position against the booth, his eyes shut and head discombobulated.

"You're already there! You paid your dues! Voodoo man did you a big favor and you don't even know it! You got tons of fans waitin for you, can't let them down now, you're their hero!"

Gordon exhaled a huge sigh, frowning, troubled, mired in questions, uncertain whether his romance with the magic capsules, although a dead issue, was not so egregiously dishonest that his swing was permanently tainted. He wasn't sure. But then again, it was his swing, nothing manufactured, or put together like an erector set. Would it break down, buckling under the pressure, as it always had? And if he did happen to win, by some miracle, would it be an authentic victory?

But one thing was for certain. His short game was magical, and nobody, not even Norman Berger, could undermine it.

"Liz told me you had a plan." Gordon sat up, sounding uplifted.

"I tried to tell her about it when we spoke, but she was so mad I ain't sure she was listenin'. Besides, you really got no choice, because these are goin' where they belong."

Swifty held out his fist, opened his hand, and displayed the eight magic capsules from Norman's last shipment. He placed them on the table and smashed each one with the butt end of the ketchup bottle. All of the capsules were exposed for what they were, just empty shells, worthless. Swifty didn't look at all surprised.

"Take a look, GH. Voodoo man is placin' his bets on another horse."

"What are you talking about?" Gordon examined the empty capsules, rolling them between his fingers.

"Do you know where voodoo man been livin'?"

"Sure, in the Bronx," Gordon replied.

"No, GH, that ain't so, unless the Bronx is in Las Vegas?"

Swifty wore a wry grin as he pulled out two FedEx shipping receipts and placed them on the table.

"These here show voodoo man sent you those pills from the Double Seven motel. Look at the damn address. First one was after you beat Mickelson at the Sony. Second one was last week, sent to my house. I did some snoopin' and found out that voodoo man checked into the motel the Wednesday before your first round at the Sony. So somehow he knew you would be playin'. Did you tell him?"

Gordon remembered immediately. "Yep, I called him on Tuesday, right after I qualified for that one spot."

"So looks like voodoo man went out to Vegas the next day so he could get his bet in before the damn tournament started."

Gordon just listened. *What bet?*

"Then I found out that the bookies had you at 100-1 on winnin' the Sony. And my sources tell me that the bookies got their asses handed to 'em, had to come up with a million bucks when you won the damn thing."

Gordon grabbed the FedEx receipts while Swifty continued.

"So you're telling me that...."

"I'm sayin' that why else would voodoo man go to Vegas unless he wanted to place a bet on you? He figured you were goin' to win, especially after you blew them away ay Qualifying School. So he laid down ten grand and made himself a mint."

"Remember I told you that I called Berger after the Sony and left him a message?"

"Sure do, GH. You told him you plannin' on layin' low and just earnin' a check each week until you won the US Open."

"That's right, Swifty. I wanted him to be happy with his ten percent and keep sending me the capsules. But I couldn't imagine in a million years that he pocketed a million bucks betting on me."

"Yeah I know, GH. But it's already done, so forget it. Besides, I think he made a good move bettin' on you, gettin' those odds. Wish I would have thought of it."

"Me and you both," Gordon added.

"Listen, GH, think about what I'm gonna tell you now real carefully."

"Go ahead, I'm listening."

"You messed up big time when you spilled the beans to voodoo man that the US Open was your last tournament. I knew it right away but held my tongue. Voodoo man ain't stupid. He's figurin' that you won't need those capsules anymore after the US Open. So he knows you got no reason to pay him his ten percent after you win. That's a whole lot of money he won't be gettin'. So he probably found himself another junkie just like you. You understand my thinkin', GH?"

Gordon cringed when he heard "junkie."

And then it dawned on him. Swifty made perfect sense. After the US Open he planned on having nothing to do with creepy Norman Berger. And if he won, Berger wouldn't see a red cent of it. What could Berger do, sue him? Gordon laughed to himself at the thought.

"So Berger sent me these bogus capsules figuring without them I had no shot?"

"Exactly, GH," Swiftly replied. "He doesn't want you to win."

"And you think he made a deal with someone else?"

"Yep," Swiftly said confidently. Maybe same time he hooked up with you. And I'm hearin' somebody plunked down two million on some long shot, a 100-1 to win the damn US Open."

Gordon did some quick thinking. He remembered verbatim what Norman told him over dinner at Forenzo's. *If not you, there are others. I have no shortage of candidates.* With whatever he paid to Norman, plus what he collected from this mystery client, and the million dollars from his Merck transaction, Norman probably had the two million dollars. *But was he insane enough to wager all of it on a no name who was hooked on his pills?*

"Do you know this guy's name?"

"I tried GH, but no dice. Besides, gamblers are always exaggeratin'."

"Good work, Swifty. You got any other surprises for me?"

"I got just one more, GH." Swifty displayed an unusually serious visage. "If you're thinkin about takin' the chicken shit easy way out, then go on and do it now, right here."

"What are you talking about?"

Swifty reached into his pocket and tossed Gordon a fresh razor blade still in its packet.

"I'm talkin' bout this!" Swifty reached over and grabbed Gordon's left hand, pounding it down flush against the table, palm up, with the scar clearly visible.

"Who told you?" Gordon could hardly get the words out.

"I got a nurse friend over at Creedmoor. She knows I been caddyin' for you, reads the papers and likes to tell tales. Maybe it was none of my business. She must've got you mixed up with somebody else, because I don't work for the loser guy she was raggin' about last week. Far as I'm concerned you're a winner, a champion, and I ain't never gonna let you forget it."

Gordon stood up, and they hugged each other tightly. Nothing further needed to be said.

Chapter 61

Bethpage Black, a beast, measured 7,468 yards from the back tees, a par seventy-one, a slope of one fifty-two, ranked by *Golf Digest* as the 6th toughest course in America, 26th in the world, 5th in the state of New York, and 5th in its list of America's greatest public golf courses.

With its deep fescue rough, narrow fairways, super slick greens, and windy forecast, the sportswriters and pundits were touting four under to be in the hunt going into the last round on Sunday. Only sixty would make the cut. The total purse was $8,000,000, with $1,800,000 going to the winner.

They were right. The big names, the young guns, the high and the mighty got bitten by the beast. The splendiferous course showed no mercy and played no favorites. The howling winds made club selection a guessing game. Perfectly struck irons rolled off the slick greens into deep, high lipped bunkers. Errant drives a yard off of the fairway required a machete to slash out of the tangled rough. Three and four putts from short distances frayed the nerves of the best in the business.

Their suffering was fodder for Troy Blake's sarcastic swipes and snide snickers, his jocular commentary interspersed with "annihilation, devastation, frustration, ruination," not rapper lyrics, but echoing the sentiments of the helpless professionals whose vulgarities needed to be bleeped off the air by the NBC censors.

Sixty lucky pros made the cut going into the weekend, an embarrassing seven over par seventy-eight.

On Saturday, with the winds unable to make up their minds, par became just an illusion. Except for Gordon Howard, at two under, and Blair Whitcomb, a fifty-year-old unknown multimillionaire neurologist turned golf pro, fresh off the Nationwide Tour, at six under.

The two would play together on Sunday, going mano y mano for the final eighteen holes.

GORDON'S GROUPIES WERE OUT in full force on Sunday, prompting a wisecrack from Blake. "The adulation for this man is so awesome that one would think the Messiah just birdied the first hole," which is exactly what Gordon did, hitting a seven iron to two feet for an easy tap in.

"And who is this Blair Whitcomb, folks? They tell me he was a decent amateur, made a boatload of money in pharmaceuticals, retires and decides to go pro. He had a good stretch on the Nationwide Tour, with a slew of wins under his belt. He swings it like he's on autopilot; maybe he and Gordon Howard use the same coach. Bruce, anything you see in this guy?"

"Thanks, Troy. I was watching him on the range. He doesn't say much, keeps to himself. I tried to ask him a few questions but nothing doing, same as Gordon Howard, like I was invading his privacy."

"Yeah well, people have their quirks, except for me," Blake joked, as they shared some on the air banter, which led into the all too familiar Kazin swing analysis.

"Let's analyze Blair Whitcomb's swing close up, thanks to the Sony Super Sports slow motion camera. These were taken yesterday, two with driver and two with utility clubs."

The four images were flashed onto the television screen as Kazin continued, armed with his yellow magic marker he used to analyze the technical jargon.

"So basically Blair has a traditional takeaway, nothing unorthodox like Gordon Howard. The club goes straight back, and then up, as he turns his shoulders ninety degrees. The club is a bit flat at the top, pointing down the line toward the target, and parallel with his feet. His right and left wrists are cupped, as if he wants to play a fade, so far so good."

"Looks real good right there," Troy Blake interjected.

"As he starts his downswing, initiated by his knees, he rotates his hips to the left while his head stays behind the ball, clearing his body as the club drops down into the slot. His right elbow straightens and tucks against his side. At impact he counter rotates the left wrist, which flattens it, and hits down hard with his hands, which are a good three to four inches ahead of the ball. This creates tremendous lag, preventing an early release, what we call casting."

"It reminds me of Hogan, especially the hand action at impact. From the little I know of this guy, he was a Hogan fanatic, would make sense he copied his swing."

"But watch this" as Kazin superimposed all four swings together and hit the play button, reducing the speed to ultra slow motion. "They're all melded into one motion, Troy, every swing is identical."

"Strange, Bruce, something doesn't jive. Two rank amateurs, supposedly total strangers, suddenly go to Q school at the same time, get their tour cards first attempt, and win all this money. Their swings are both like machines, and neither will give you the time of day, as if it's classified information."

"Two automatons fighting it out for the US Open," Bruce quipped. "It would make a great movie."

"I think we're watching it live and in living color," Troy Blake replied, and then continued, somewhat serendipitously. "Every day brings something new; technology, space travel, experimental drugs. It's amazing."

GORDON PICKED UP TWO shots on the front nine, with birdies at one and the difficult par four sixth, while Blair reeled off a string of nine pars.

And then Gordon's driver started to falter, having to punch out from the knee high rough, as wayward irons left him long par putts between fifteen and twenty-five feet. He holed them on ten, eleven and twelve, pumping his fist, igniting the crowd, while Blair just went about his business; three routine pars, no sweat.

"OK, GH, let's settle down, you're the man, don't be thinkin' about anything. Just take her back and let it rip. Let me do the thinkin' for us, that's my job; gonna ride you in like a jockey."

"OK, got it," Gordon replied, calmed by Swifty's hand holding. Liz was in the gallery, following him for all four days. She suspected he was in trouble, and stayed out of sight, afraid to distract him.

Gordon teed up on the 605 yard thirteenth, which downwind was playing shorter. He could reach it in two, and thinking eagle.

He aimed slightly right for a draw. The narrow fairway was framed with his groupies. He swung hard out of his heels and caught the ball flush, which started low over the fescue, and then rose, beginning to move left over the fairway.

"She's got 350 written all over it!" Swifty exclaimed excitedly as he followed its flight.

Suddenly a huge wind gust from the west pushed hard against the Titleist, forcing it back over the rough. It buried in the fescue, 361 yards from the tee, less than a foot from the safety of the short grass, confirmed by the groans of the spectators.

Blair drilled his drive, getting a good twenty yard roll, and then nailed a three wood, leaving him an eight iron into the green. Gordon hacked at his ball, advancing it some ten yards. He pounded the ground in a rare display of temper, but enough for Blake to comment, "Nerves folks, even automatons have nerves."

"What do we have to the green, Swifty?"

Swifty threw up some grass and looked up at the treetops. "I figure 231 to the flag; wind is across left to right, playin' the number. The pin's tucked right, and there's a bunker behind the mound on the left."

"I'm gonna smoke a four, Swifty. I'll aim for the middle of the mound and cut it toward the front of the green. It should bounce short and run up."

"I agree, GH." Swifty handed him the club, grip first, and then stepped back out of Gordon's peripheral vision, as he always did.

Thwat! The ball started left and hit exactly to the spot, cutting toward the front of the green. It took one bounce and boomeranged off of a round metal sprinkler plate not more than the size of a fist. It accelerated forward, over the mound and into the trap.

"Bad luck, GH, let's get up and down, we'll be fine."

Blair launched an eight iron into the green, which hit eight feet beyond the hole, stopped, and then sucked back, leaving him an easy three-foot putt for a birdie. Other than a few errant claps, the gallery was dead silent.

Gordon waved his cap to his admiring fans as he walked over the mound to assess his lie. Blair marked his ball. Gordon grabbed his sand wedge while Swifty examined the green, walking back and forth around the flagstick, trying to get a feel for the slope.

"How's your lie, GH?"

"She's sitting up, have plenty of green to work with. Where do you like it?"

Swifty took a final look and pointed to a discolored spot just right of Blair's ball mark.

"OK, I see it." Gordon descended into the bunker and dug into the sand. He hesitated, and walked back onto the green, figuring some thirty feet to the spot. He returned to the trap, took his stance, and cocked his wrists up and down. Thump!

The wide flange of his sand wedge moved effortlessly through the sand. The ball exploded from the bunker, hit a foot before the spot, took one bounce, and then spun toward the flag.

Gordon ran onto the green. The ball refused to stop, trickling down the slope, closer and closer, as the crowd stood up in unison, their arms raised, and Swifty urging it to continue. "Be good, honey!" It picked up speed, and then.... bang! It disappeared into the hole, resting flush against the flagstick.

The roar from Gordon's groupies could be heard all the way to North Shore Hospital, some ten miles distant, where Alan Howard was glued to the television, motionless, surrounded by a cadre of nurses, Dr. Alan Segal, and Rabbi Joel Feldstein.

"That," Troy Blake blurted excitedly, "is pure unadulterated genius. It can't be taught; gotta dig deep, comes right from the heart and a whole lot of talent."

Gordon winked at Swifty, who calmly pulled out the flag. He nonchalantly picked the ball out of the hole and tipped his cap, as if it was no big deal, giving Blair Whitcomb something to think about.

Blair had a two and a half foot birdie putt, just inside the left edge. The crowd was respectively quiet. He had switched to the controversial belly putter when he turned pro, which worked wonders with his short game. Anchoring it against his chest, he addressed the putt, and suddenly stepped away, as the crowd moaned.

"Yep, Bruce, the old nerves, it happens all the time. That hole must look smaller than an aspirin tablet," Blake quipped, "and if he jacks this, he's gonna need a bunch of them for a giant migraine. The worst thing he can do now is to reread the damn thing."

Which is exactly what Blair did, while Gordon and Swifty stood shoulder to shoulder, watching with more than a keen interest. Blair readdressed the ball, took a final look and stroked the putt. It rolled perfectly on line, until it stopped short, hanging on the edge of the hole, half in, half out.

"Wow!" Blake uttered, not once, but four or five times. "Rule 16-2 folks," he reminded the nail biting audience. "He's got reasonable time to walk to the ball plus ten seconds. If it drops within that time, the putt is good."

Blair took two steps to the ball and waited for it to fall. It needed just a whisper of wind, which had inexplicably suddenly calmed. Some thirty seconds later a sudden gush pushed the ball forward, as a routine birdie became a gut wrenching par.

Gordon was now only one shot down, as they trudged through fourteen, fifteen and sixteen, where each posted three mundane pars.

Swifty kept Gordon's nerves in check as he intentionally set the pace, with Blair and his caddie traipsing some ten yards behind.

Gordon boldly walked through the roped off pathway, past the rabid fans, holding out his gloved hand for them to touch, drawing strength from his supporters, just as Swifty had predicted.

THE 207 YARD PAR three seventeenth played to a slightly elevated green protected by three wide yawning traps, one left, one right and another back right. The view from the tee box resembled a natural amphitheatre, with grandstands behind the green, corporate tents along the sides, and standing room only in the roped off area. It was, all in all, a circus atmosphere; a humongous semicircle of some 5,000 hooting, hollering, and beer guzzling spectators, all ready to erupt if Gordon stuck it close.

Swifty watched the flag, tossed up blades of grass, examined the direction of the clouds as they drifted over the course, and listened to the rustling of the treetops—deciphering a checklist of too many years of experience. He knew full well that Gordon depended upon him, and that the wrong club selection could spell disaster.

"Wind is playin' against us, GH, but she can't make up her mind. Down low she's left to right and against, but up higher she's dead straight in our face."

Swifty methodically went through his checklist again.

"What do we have?"

"It's 200 to clear those traps. The pin is sittin' 205 front of the green. I'm thinkin' playin' it as 230. Get her up high, wind gonna push her back, and she'll land like a butterfly."

Swifty had no reason to remind Gordon that over the green was Fungolina Avenue.

"Four?"

"Yep, GH, and you need all of it." Swifty shoved the club into his hand, butt end first, and stepped back out of his peripheral vision.

The marshals held up the QUIET signs as Gordon teed his ball and moved it up in his stance. The natural setting of the green was dotted with the colorful shirts of the spectators in full panoply, as if he was hitting into a work of impressionist art.

It was crushed, launched high, clearing the traps before it started its rapid descent. The crowd stood en masse, watching the white spec of the Titleist hover over the green. Their expressions were sullen, certain he had knocked it over everything.

"C'mon wind!" Swifty pleaded.

Gordon watched, expressionless, until the ball suddenly ran out of steam and just dropped, nestling in the short frog's hair between the putting surface and the rough.

Blair just went about his business and played conservatively, hitting a five wood onto the lower tier of the fat part of the green, some twenty feet from the hole.

Gordon walked to the green, tipping his cap while the crowd chanted, "GH! GH! GH!"

Swifty was a few paces behind, wheezing and light headed.

Blair repaired his divot and marked his ball, acknowledged the respectful claps, and moved away to the side with his caddy.

"Sorry, GH, I figured four was the club. I didn't think five would get you there."

"You OK? You sound terrible, breathing really hard."

"Yeah fine, I gotta get you up and down. Lemme take a look."

Gordon had five feet of short grass to negotiate, then another twenty-five feet of green. Swifty got a good read from all angles.

"Don't worry about a break, she's all about speed. The wind is now dead against." Swifty threw up some grass and handed Gordon his putter.

"No, gimme my Phil wedge. I can't take a chance, gotta flop it."

"Are you sure, GH, wanna talk about it?"

"Positive, Swifty, and take the flag out."

"Yes sir!" Swifty handed him the sixty-four degree lob wedge and deftly removed the flag, which prompted a sudden uproar.

Gordon opened his stance, positioned the ball off of his left foot, and fanned the blade wide open. The amphitheater was dead silent as he picked out a spot on the green and took a full swing. The ball flew upward toward the hole, landed ever so softly, and then, as if it had eyes, disappeared.

Gordon's groupies exploded in a collective shout, high fiving, hugging, and some crying, giddy with delight. Gordon just winked at Swifty and tossed him the wedge, both of them nonchalant and poker faced.

"Folks, I am speechless, if that's possible!" Blake was all hopped up. "This man is awesome. What are the odds of making *that* shot, under *these* conditions, at *this* moment, in *this* tournament? Anyone who bets against this guy pulling off the unthinkable needs to have his head examined, he is *that* good!"

Blair pondered the unbelievable turn of events, visibly fidgety, pacing back and forth. His caddy spoke to him, trying to calm him down.

"OK, listen, he got lucky twice. Just take a deep breath and shake it off. She's straight in with no break. Make a nice smooth stroke. If she drops, fine. If not, take your par, and then we win on eighteen."

"I've got it, no sweat" as Blair circled the putt, examining it from every angle, and replaced the marker with his ball. He could feel his hands shaking as he yanked the putter back, his stroke herky-jerky as the ball popped off the head and then slightly off of the ground. It was a double hit, but almost unnoticeable, as the crowd stood up in unison to watch it disappear dead center into the hole.

Gordon and Swifty both saw it as Blair pumped his fist.

"Bingo," Troy Blake uttered, "looks like Blair Whitcomb took a chill pill, great putt!"

"You gonna say somethin to him GH?"

"Not yet, Swifty, just play dumb; I'm on top of it."

It didn't take more than thirty seconds for the switchboard at NBC to be bombarded with calls from angry television viewers who saw the infraction, as the players walked up the hill to the 18th tee, surrounded six deep with Gordon's groupies.

Chapter 62

AT ONLY 411 YARDS, the closing hole was never considered difficult. Most pros kept their drives short of the cluster of bunkers that laced both sides of the narrow fairway, usually hitting a long iron or a three wood, leaving them an easy second shot into the slightly elevated green. Trying to navigate a driver off of the tee offered a low risk reward, as anything off line could bury in one of the bunkers, which would spell trouble.

"Gimme the driver, we're gonna bury this bastard."

"No way, GH, that's suicide. Hit your two iron stinger, play smart."

"Fuck the stinger. Gimme the driver, it's playing straight downwind."

"OK, GH, you the man. I like it." Swifty handed him the driver. He knew it was important to sound supportive.

"It looks like Gordon is going with driver; bombs away, do or die," Blake squawked, as he was handed a note from his producer marked *urgent*.

It was blistered. It started low, then rose and caught the wind. It cruised past the traps, landed center cut, and then bounced forward and rolled to a stop, 366 yards from the tee.

Amidst the hoopla from his hollering groupies, Gordon approached Blair and called him aside. "I have you for a three on seventeen, you agree?"

"How do you figure?"

"Got your rulebook?"

"No."

"Rule 14-4, you double hit that putt. It's a one stroke penalty."

"That's your opinion. I have the final call. It might have looked like it, but no way."

"And by the way, Mr. Muscle Memory," Gordon continued matter-of-factly, "Norman Berger can't help you with your short game. It sucks."

Just then a rules official drove up the fairway toward the tee, waving his arms. The crowd buzzed with anticipation. He approached Blair for a private conversation, which turned into an argument, until the indisputable evidence was displayed to him on the official's laptop, in slow motion, from multiple angles. The official drove away and called Troy Blake in the NBC booth.

"It seems there was a rules infraction by Blair Whitcomb on seventeen, folks. We never saw it, but the phones lit up like Christmas trees. And here it is, thanks to the Sony Super Slow Motion. You can see it for yourself."

Blake broadcast the violation to fifty million anxious viewers, while the official scorer changed Blair's two to a three, and Gordon's groupies went berserk.

GORDON KNEW FROM THE moment they teed off that Blair Whitcomb was in bed with Norman Berger. He remembered him from Q school, where they played in the same foursome. His Ben Hogan swing hadn't changed. He recalled Norman's self-serving condensed autobiography when they first met and his reference to Blair Whitcomb as "a super rich golf addict obsessed with muscle memory." He had done his homework. How else could a fifty-year-old rank amateur qualify for Q school on his first attempt, catapult himself to the top of the Nationwide Tour while beating guys half his age, and then possibly win the US Open in his first appearance?

It was obvious. Swifty was 100% correct.

BLAIR HIT THREE WOOD straight down the middle, seemingly unfazed by Gordon's accusation about Norman Berger, although wondering how he knew, not that it mattered anymore.

"Let's go Swifty, I need you here."

He struggled to keep up with Gordon.

Blair had 181 to the center. Downwind, he played it as 165, striking a full seven iron, which hit two yards short of the green, took one bounce, and rolled toward the flag. The crowd stood up as his ball tracked the pin, barely missing it, while ending up some four feet past.

"Wow!" exclaimed Troy Blake. "Where did that come from? Blair Whitcomb just hit the shot of his career. And Gordon Howard doesn't seem to be the least bit concerned!"

"Hey GH, one thing you gotta tell me." They walked together to Gordon's ball, some 136 yards past Whitcomb.

"What's that?"

"I was listenin'. I told you someone else was hooked up with voodoo man. How did you know it was him?"

"Let's win this thing first and then we'll have plenty of time together, OK?"

"Golf Gods are against him, GH, they ain't gonna let him win. Why you think his putt hung on the lip over on thirteen, or he double jacked it on seventeen? He should have fessed up and taken the penalty. He figured nobody had seen it. But the Golf Gods knew, and they gonna get their revenge, I guarantee it."

"Think so?" He thought about Liz and her Golf Gods.

"I know so, GH. That's why we did the right thing in not winnin' all those tournaments. The Golf Gods were watchin'. And when you gave all your winnings to your father's charity, the Golf Gods took notice, they sure did. Yeah, you got a great short game, always scarin' the hole. But be honest. You think holin' out from the sand on sixteen or your Phil shot on seventeen was all your doin'?"

"What's the distance?"

Swifty methodically went through his paces, checking the

wind, the flag, the clouds, and the tree tops. "You thinkin' halve or you wanna stuff it?"

"Right up his cheating ass."

"We got forty-five to the pin and forty to the front. The wind changed, now she's blowin into us. The green is slopin' down."

"What do you think, partner?" Gordon had already decided. He just wanted Swifty to feel needed.

"Golf Gods changed the wind, just like on seventeen. It's workin' to your advantage now. You gotta clear those traps so choke up on your sand wedge. Play it back in your stance. She's gonna hit, stop and suck back."

"I agree."

Swifty grabbed Gordon's sand wedge, wiped down the grip, handed it to him and started to step away.

"No, I want you to stay here, next to me. We're hitting this one together."

"You sure, GH, don't want to—"

"I'm positive."

Gordon cleaned out the grooves of his sand wedge with a tee, choked up on the club, and made a half dozen practice swings until he felt comfortable. He addressed the ball and took one final look at his target. Gordon's groupies encircled the green ten deep. It was eerily quiet except for the sound of the flag flapping in the wind.

Blake was so nervous he had to whisper into his microphone, his voice cracking. "Folks, this is *the* most important shot of Gordon Howard's life."

Gordon swung the club up steeply and hit down and through, taking a huge thick divot. The ball slid off the clubface and bored against the wind. It cleared the traps and flew directly over Blair's marker, took one hop, grabbed the turf, and stopped on the back of the green, thirty-five feet past the hole.

Gordon's groupies let out a raucous moan. Blair couldn't contain an unsportsmanlike smirk. They both noticed it.

The Titleist was spinning in its own mark until it moved, laggardly rolling down the slope, end over end, inch by inch, taking a full tortuous minute until it nudged Blair's marker and stopped. And then, almost miraculously, a gust of wind pushed it forward toward the flag until it finally settled two feet below the hole.

Gordon winked at Swifty and tipped his cap to the uproarious horde, while Swifty replaced the divot and hoisted the bag onto his shoulder. They walked together to the green, side by side, without any fanfare, although they were busting a gut trying to contain their emotions.

"The Golf Gods were watchin, GH. Did you see how she just stopped, and then the wind picked up?"

"I'm a believer," Gordon replied, patting Swifty on the back. His gesture expressed a whole lot more gratitude than what it seemed. "We've got plenty to talk about, partner."

Swifty didn't answer, unusually silent.

"I couldn't have scripted this any better," the usually jocular Troy Blake announced, clearly broken up. "This is some scene, some scene."

Gordon marked his ball and grabbed his putter. He walked to the back of the green and fixed his ball mark, careful not to step in Blair's line, or make any eye contact.

"I need a drink," Troy Blake quipped. "Maybe Blair Whitcomb could use one as well. This is no gimme."

Gordon's ball trickling down past the hole had shown Blair the line. His four-foot putt broke slightly left to right, just outside the cup. Blair and his caddie studied it from every angle. There was no question it was the correct read.

His caddie pointed to the spot. Blair nodded, addressed the ball, anchored the putter against his chest, and confidently stroked the putt. It rolled perfectly on line directly over the spot. Gordon knew it had to drop as it turned toward the hole.

Suddenly, at the last moment, the ball veered left, stopping just outside the edge of the cup.

"There is no earthly reason how that ball does not drop," Troy Blake blurted in disbelief. "Talk about bad karma? Impossible! I'm just a sportscaster folks, but this is way beyond me. Golf's a crazy game, just a real crazy game."

Blair tapped it in and angrily flung his putter into the front trap, watching disconsolately as Gordon knocked in his victorious birdie.

"See that fuckin' smart-ass grin, GH? Ain't no question Golf Gods seen it."

"Yep, sure did."

And then Swifty collapsed, face up with his eyes closed, right there on the eighteenth green.

Gordon freaked and quickly knelt down beside him. "Swifty! Swifty!"

He didn't respond.

"Blair, you're a doctor, do something!"

Blair rushed over and felt Swifty's pulse. "I need aspirin, quick!"

Gordon tore into his bag. Blair broke two pills into small pieces and shoved them down Swifty's throat, keeping his hand on his pulse, hoping for a sign of life.

"It's faint, but he's still alive. He needs artificial respiration!"

Gordon pounced, placing his mouth on Swifty's, forcing oxygen into his lungs and pushing hard against his chest.

"C'mon, Swifty, I love you man, you can't leave me now," Gordon pleaded between breaths. "Wake up, wake up!" he screamed, pushing harder.

Swifty opened his eyes, looked at Gordon, and spoke in a barely audible whisper.

"You did it, GH, you did it."

"No, Swifty, *we* did it, you and me."

As his eyes closed for the last time, Gordon knelt next to him and held his lifeless body in his arms. He cried, not knowing whether his friend ever heard his parting words.

Liz grabbed Gordon, grief-stricken at the horror that lay before her. "It's your father, the hospital called me, hurry!"

Gordon kissed Swifty a final goodbye. He grabbed his bag, fought his way through the throngs of fans, and sprinted to the Land Rover with Liz alongside.

Chapter 63

GORDON SENT NORMAN AN email while Liz maneuvered the Land Rover through the Sunday traffic, pounding the horn and flashing her bright lights. She crossed onto the service road, and then back onto the Long Island Expressway, zigzagging between entrances and exits, running red lights and stop signs until arriving at the hospital. Gordon jumped out, took the back stairway to the eighth floor and bolted through security. He ran down the hall to Room 814, greeted by Rabbi Feldstein.

Alan lied in bed, unhooked from his life support machines. The television was turned to the US Open. Troy Blake was rambling on while waiting for the press conference to begin, but the winner was nowhere in sight.

"How is he, rabbi?"

"He was glued to that television, and when you won, well, I guess his life was complete. He had no reason to continue."

"Can I have some privacy, please?"

"Of course," as the rabbi left the room and closed the door behind him.

Gordon walked over to his father and started to speak. His eyes were misty with a thousand thoughts, but there was nothing he could say. It was too late.

NORMAN BERGER DIGESTED EVERY word of Gordon's email. *Hope you didn't bet too much on Blair Whitcomb. I'll never forget what you said at dinner about my father and Jeremy. I think it went something like this; "the way I saw it, they took advantage and had to pay the price. Besides, they bet the ranch, and were greedy. Funny how people usually get what they deserve, don't you think?"*

All but dead broke, Norman comatosely trudged three blocks to the Right to Bear Arms gun shop. He showed proper identification and purchased a pre-owned fully loaded Smith and Wesson 357 Magnum. He walked calmly back to his motel room. The television was still blaring with Troy Blake recapping Gordon's incredible victory. His high priced Victoria Chang lookalike hooker was waiting for him, lying in bed, decked out in her finest dominatrix outfit.

"Its Sunday, hon—you know what that means- payday."

Norman ignored her, turned the gun on himself, and fired one bullet into his forehead

Chapter 64

GORDON ARRANGED FOR HIS father's funeral, but not before he drove out to Creedmoor State Psychiatric Hospital and followed the arrows to the patient records office.

"I'd like to see my file, I was a patient here." Gordon proffered his identification to a woman dressed in a white hospital uniform, sitting behind the desk.

"When was that, Mr. Howard?"

"About fifteen years ago, more or less; I was here for a week."

"Those are buried down in the basement." She handed him a printed form. "Just fill this out for me and be sure to sign and date it. It will be a while; we're short staffed here. I can send it to you if you don't feel like hanging around this place."

"No thanks, I'll wait."

Some two hours later he was rifling through his file, which was endlessly detailed with a complete history of his incarceration, all in chronological order. He ran his fingers down each page until he found what he was looking for; "patient requested that father be contacted, attending physician to follow-up after sedation." He went through each successive line item, all of which proved to be fruitless, other than reminding him of the episode.

"Are these files always kept accurately?" Gordon hoped they weren't.

"Oh yes," the woman replied, "almost to a fault. State law requires that we keep a running log, especially conversations with the patient, which helps with the diagnosis."

Gordon returned the file. He had seen enough. The doctor didn't properly follow up. His father never even knew he was there.

Gordon realized his faux pas. He should have gotten the details from Creedmoor before that fateful meeting. He berated himself. *Stupid!* Accusing his father was a first degree blunder. He wondered if things would have been different had he known the truth, but it was too late to apologize.

THE CLOSED COFFIN THAT entombed Alan Howard's body lay prominently near the holy altar in full view. The synagogue chapel was packed, standing room only. Rabbi Feldstein delivered the eulogy, while others spoke, bestowing upon Alan a litany of accolades. Gordon and Liz sat in the first row closest to the coffin. He had planned on speaking, although his emotions were chaotic with feelings he wasn't sure he could articulate. He felt immobilized.

Liz nudged him, whispering, "C'mon Gordon, get up there."

"What would you like me to say, how wonderful my father was?"

"This isn't the time or place to be sarcastic," Liz remarked, pinching him tightly on his leg." It's your father, Gordon. You guys need closure. It's your last chance, for Christ sake."

The murmurs of the congregants echoed throughout the chapel as Gordon approached the pulpit.

He looked out over the sea of mourners and waited until the rustling had silenced. He recognized their faces and he knew what they were, these distinguished members of Old Point, defined by the magnitude of their ostentatious wealth, their grand egos, and their selfish politics, men who were born into the right families, and their dilettante wives who married them for their money. He knew that there were exceptions, self-made men of substance with compassion for the less fortunate, men who he admired, but they were few and far between.

He remembered what Liz had said about the way some members treated the help, like indentured servants.

He thought about Swifty, who had carried their bags and catered to their egocentric whims.

He stood there uncertain whether he deserved his celebrity, or exactly what they expected him to say, but he owed them nothing.

"I appreciate your coming here today to pay your respects to my father. He was a complicated man, and it's no secret to any of you that our relationship was not without a few trying moments."

A brief outburst of laughter lightened the mood although Gordon maintained a serious visage.

"I would like to speak to you about a very special man. He was a man of wisdom despite being deprived of any formal education. He wasn't a Jew or a Catholic or of any religion, but if there is a God, he was always in his heart, and justice was always in his soul. He was not a member of any cushy country club. He didn't drive expensive cars or dine in the best restaurants or drape himself with hand tailored suits or Rolex watches. He wasn't chauffeured in a limousine or live in extravagant homes or spend his summers cavorting in the Hamptons."

Gordon then pointed his finger out toward the audience. His voice became increasingly louder while his tone was suggestively hostile.

"He wasn't a hedge fund billionaire, a partner in a high powered law firm, a business tycoon, a real estate magnate or a bona fide member of the lucky sperm club who happened to be born on the right side of the tracks. But he was a man of more wealth than all your bulging portfolios of stocks and bonds, and unlike many of you, his respect for others was not based upon their personal financial statements."

Gordon waited patiently until the raft of whispers died down. He glanced over at Rabbi Feldstein who rolled his eyes and nervously fidgeted with the ends of his tallit, flummoxed at this brash perversion of a holy service. And then Gordon continued.

"He was the first one to arrive in the morning and the last one to leave at night. He carried your golf bags and raked your traps and hunted down your golf balls and replaced your divots and cleaned your clubs until his hands hurt. He knew your games better than you did. You relied upon him to hand you the right club in the fairways and to read your putts on the greens. He worked for you with dignity and with pride, and you never heard him complain. And then, when he announced his retirement after forty something years of serving you, not one of you had the decency to say thank you, a pat on the back, or a few bucks for a job well done."

Gordon momentarily stopped amidst the dead quiet of the room as he let his words sink in.

"You just cast him off, like a used car with too many miles, a jalopy ready for the scrap heap, and you should hang your heads in shame, because he deserved so much better. Perhaps you should say a prayer for Swifty, Mr. Johnson William Franklin, and hope that the Golf Gods will forgive you, and temper their revenge, but as for me, I never will."

He looked out and saw Bruce Haberman, who cast a glaring stare, stood up, and left the synagogue in a huff. Others out- rightly voiced their contempt. "The nerve of him!"... "Who the hell does he think he is?"... "He gets lucky and wins the US Open and now he's holier than thou!".... "What chutzpah!" .... "This is a funeral, not a goddamn lecture!"..... "No wonder Alan had a problem with him, he's a disrespectful brat!"...... "Who are these Golf Gods?"

Many of the congregants walked out. Others stood up in pro-test. Rabbi Feldstein apologized profusely for Gordon's remarks, urging everyone to remain in their seats, appealing to their sense of the holiness of the event. Gordon didn't care if the synagogue emptied out. He said what he had to say. Swifty deserved to be eulogized. His father would be next.

Gordon called over the rabbi. They spoke in private but by their gestures the onlookers knew there was a disagreement.

"How dare you make a spectacle of your father's funeral!"

"It had to be done, rabbi", Gordon replied testily. "I loved that man."

"Jesus Christ, Gordon, you're missing the point! These people are here to pay their respects to your father. This is a synagogue, not a political forum!"

"Just send me a bill me for the extra time I took from your precious service."

They wrangled back and forth, at times heatedly, until they finally shook hands. Then the rabbi addressed what was left of his congregation.

"Gordon has given me an unusual request. In the Jewish religion, we do not view the deceased in the casket. The Talmudic explanation says that such would be a violation of the deceased's modesty, as we can look at the body but the person cannot look back. But for a family member to view in private has been permitted under certain circumstances. And I believe that this is one of them."

The rabbi opened the casket and chanted the prayer for the dead. From where they were seated, those remaining were unable to see Alan Howard's body.

Gordon pulled out the suicide note from the breast pocket of his dark blue suit while he knelt beside the coffin, and leaned over until he was dead on face to face with his father. A clip-on microphone was attached by the rabbi, allowing his words to reverberate throughout the synagogue. He spoke intimately, as if his father was still alive, and could hear every word. Oblivious to the spectators, Gordon just let the words flow naturally......

"Dad, I remember the last time we were this close to one another. It was in your office, right before the Labor Day weekend. You were pretty rough on me. It wasn't the first time. I deserved it. You were right-I took the cowardly way out. I should have never worked for you. Nepotism was a curse. I always felt like I was in a straightjacket, unable to get out of my own way, walking on eggshells, petrified to say something that might upset you. And it bothered the hell out of me. I just never had the guts to make it on my own. I was afraid of failure, and it was easy to blame you for my shortcomings.

"We had a vicious argument. I stood my ground and you stood yours, nose to nose. I could taste your breath, smell your skin, and see my reflection in the pupils of your eyes. I still hear your voice, baiting me, daring me. And then I punched you as hard as I possibly could. You toppled to the floor. And in that brief moment, standing over you, I felt powerful, almost invincible, brimming with confidence."

Gordon's voice rang with the sincerity of a son yearning for reconciliation from an estranged father.

"I never knew who I was, other than your son. I was floundering, searching for my own identity, to become whatever it was that stirred inside of me. I wanted to fight my own battles, make my own mistakes, and relish my own victories. And I finally figured myself out, and I like what I see, and I think you would too.

"I always got goosebumps reading the glowing articles written about you, or seeing that huge plaque over at North Shore Hospital-the Alan Howard wing. I was just so proud to be your son. Remember when I sarcastically called you a living legend? Well, you were a living legend. I just couldn't deal with it. And that's the truth.

"I'm glad you knew that I won the US Open out at Bethpage. It's a long story but I had plenty of help. Swifty for one-he was on the bag and rode me in like a jockey. He was like.....like a second father to me."

Gordon momentarily choked up, his eyes welled with tears which trickled down into the casket, spotting his father's lifeless, ashen face.

"One night years ago I wrote you this long rambling letter. I was in a dark place. I wanted to hurt myself. Please dad, promise me you will read this, all of it, every single word. There are things about me I could never tell you in person, things....about us."

He deftly placed the suicide letter on his father's chest, and then continued.

"And I owe you an apology," Gordon sputtered, his voice quivering as he stared at this father, his watery eyes cast upon him pleadingly, "because.....because..."

A minute passed slowly. Liz held her breath. The only audible sound in the synagogue was the droning of the air-conditioning.

"Because you didn't lie to me–you told me the truth–you never knew I was at Creedmoor!"

His voice boomed throughout the synagogue, the shocking admission eliciting a collective chorus of gasps from the bewildered congregants.

Gordon caressed his father's face and kissed him on the cheek. He then closed the coffin for the last time.

Hand in hand, Gordon and Liz walked through the chapel and settled into the awaiting black limousine which would take them to the cemetery.

"That was…beautiful," Liz said, as she squeezed Gordon's hand tightly.

Gordon was too chocked up to answer her.

His father was buried in the family plot, next to Gordon's grandfather.

Chapter 65

GORDON WAS NAMED AS executor of Swifty's estate. A handwritten letter was attached to his will

> *Dear GH,*
>
> *If you're readin' this then I know my lawyer called you and I'm up here with the Golf Gods. If you look at the date, you will see this was signed and sealed after our third round of the Open. I knew my time was short, but no sense in getting you all worked up. I had a job to do and you were number one. I didn't want you distracted or scare you.*
>
> *Don't know if I'm gonna make it all the way, but gonna give you whatever I got left. Tomorrow, on Sunday, we gonna win this damn tournament, I got no doubts. And I made myself a note to explain about the Golf Gods, because they're real, and they everywhere, never sleepin', always watchin'. And if you do the right thing in life, then the breaks are gonna go your way. But cheatin' and voodoo doctors is only gonna get the Golf Gods madder than hell, and then you gonna wind up on Fungolina Avenue, no tellin' what can happen, cause the Golf Gods got no mercy.*
>
> *Maybe I'll get lucky and have some time to myself, especially with my twenty percent; that's a whole lot of money.*

You got yourself a great woman. You should get hitched and have your own. I'm sorry I lived my life by myself. At least I got to take care of you for a while, like you was my son, but what you did for me is somethin' I ain't never gonna forget. I hope you feel the same. We were a damn good team.

I want my own plot, a nice coffin, and a decent burial. I'm countin' on you to make the arrangements, with Johnson William Franklin on the tombstone. And one more thing, GH; stick one of them five-iron blades in with me, the one you smoked at the range—somethin' I would deeply appreciate.

And whatever I got left in the bank after I'm gone, I want you to give to the caddie fund they set up over at the club. It provides these young kids with money for education, somethin' I never had; better they should go to college than be totin' a bag.

You gotta promise you gonna visit me once in a while. We gotta stay in touch.

Your friend forever,
Swifty

Gordon cried when he read the letter, he loved that man so much. At the funeral Gordon and Liz went over to the casket and placed his five-iron into Swifty's hand. They were the only ones to pay their respects. He broke down when he watched Swifty lowered into the grave, a whole lot more than when his father was buried, as if every fiber of Gordon's heart and soul grieved. He never had that long talk with his friend, hoping Swifty died contentedly, knowing what was in Gordon's heart, and that he had made a difference.

With the additional $360,000 from Gordon's $1,800,000 first prize, Swifty passed away a millionaire.

THERE WAS NEVER ANY press conference, nor did Gordon grant any interviews. He saw no reason for it, as he had nothing more to say, or to prove.

Epilogue

GORDON OFFICIALLY RESIGNED FROM Old Point Country Club, considering the uproar of the membership over his controversial speech, and with Swifty gone, he had no reason to stay. Charlie pestered him with phone calls and voice messages, jumping out of his skin for the details of his amazing victory.

Gordon wanted to say goodbye to Danny, Laurie and Gus. He thought about what Swifty told him, how the Golf Gods extract their pound of flesh when you don't play by the rules.

He couldn't return Charlie's calls, or look these people in the eye, not with everything that he knew.

It was a price he would have to pay. He wondered if his fame was all worth it.

BLAIR WHITCOMB'S WIFE FOUND out about his extra marital tryst and sued him for everything he was worth, leaving him with a pittance of what he had. His girlfriend moved on to bigger and better things, while Blair turned into a degenerate gambler, losing everything at the Vegas casinos, a few blocks from where Norman Berger killed himself.

NORMAN BERGER'S CURE FOR Amyotrophic Lateral Sclerosis was posthumously approved by the FDA, exactly as he had developed it, and hailed as a "miracle drug." It lined Merck's coffers, and paved the way for conquering Parkinson's and Alzheimer's. Norman Berger never received his just recognition, which history surmised prompted his infamous suicide.

THE OLD POINT CADDIE Fund couldn't scrape together a few thousand dollars, as it hardly qualified as an important ego charity the members used for their tax deductions, or to have their names called out at benefits, or a plaque placed on the wall of a hospital in their honor.

Gordon followed Swifty's instructions and donated his estate to the fund.

But there was one caveat.

Gordon tossed in another $200,000 and dangled the money in front of the greedy board members, who unanimously agreed to change the name of the fund to The Johnson William Franklin Charitable Foundation, which gifted a bunch of deserving caddies a college education.

GORDON SOLD HIS PENTHOUSE for considerably more than the asking price, considering his celebrity, and purchased Liz's Westchester dream house. It had green shutters, just the way she had envisioned it.

Gordon was tested for infertility and his sperm count was totally normal. Liz cried joyously when they received the results.

They were married by Rabbi Feldstein in a private ceremony after Liz went through a conversion, something Gordon somehow in his heart felt compelled to do. They had a son and named him Adam.

His bona fide victory at the US Open opened many doors. Hedge funds vied for his capital raising services. He decided to work for himself, with the golf course his stock and trade, which provided him a very good living.

His name was engraved on the official US Open trophy permanently housed in the USGA Museum and Arnold Palmer Center for Golf History in Far Hills, New Jersey. A replica of the coveted trophy, which each winner receives, was packed away with his other golf memorabilia and remained out of sight, permanently stored in their basement.

He would never go to see that trophy, not without *Johnson William Franklin* etched alongside his name, without which it had no value.

ALMOST TWO MONTHS AFTER moving to Westchester, Gordon received a FedEx from an attorney. It contained a letter and a sealed envelope marked "confidential."

Gordon called Liz into the living room. They read the letter together.

> *Dear Mr. Howard,*
>
> *I am the trustee for the Alan Howard Family Trust, appointed to distribute your father's assets pursuant to the trust document. While most of his assets were invested in AH Advisors, which was liquidated for the benefit of banks and other secured creditors during the bankruptcy proceeding, provisions were made in a separate trust for your benefit. Enclosed please find a check in the amount of five million dollars.*
>
> *Very Truly Yours,*
> *William Steinman, Esq.*

"Oh, my God, your father left you five million dollars?"

Gordon didn't answer her. He was more interested in the sealed envelope, which he tore open, and read the handwritten letter aloud.

> Dear Gordon,
>
> I'm sitting alone in my office at my important captain's desk after a few vodkas too many. When you read this I will be dead and buried, but I owe you some explanations.
>
> I think I'm anebriated. Or is it inebriated or enibriated? I betcha Liz knows how to spell it.
>
> And let me tell you something- you're lucky, because she's smart and special and loves you. I know I called her a shikseh gold digger. Tell her I apologize, please.

Your mother never loved me. It was all about my goddamn money-what I could give her. But she couldn't take the abuse. And she knew about my trysts, I made sure of it, rubbed it in her face. So she did the smart thing, and divorced me.

Remember when you decked me? Was it two years already? Good work, son! That was some beautiful punch, a right hand, as if you were Muhammad Ali. I deserved it. It felt good. I was so damn proud of you that I wore that black and blue cheek like a badge of honor.

I ripped out your picture from the *New York Times* sports section the first time you made All American. I kept it in my desk drawer and I looked at it every day. I bet you didn't know that.

Your grandfather struggled through the Depression and always saw the glass as half empty. He was pretty rough on me in business. God forbid I made a mistake. I can hear him now, screaming in his Yiddish accent. "Alan, that was stupid! Alan, we will go broke! Alan, don't think, just do what I tell you!"

It would be easy to blame my father for how I treated you. It's not something I planned on. It just came with the territory. I am what I am. I tried therapy, but you knew me well enough to know I was too damn stubborn to change.

At Penn I figured my money entitled me, so I slacked off, stayed out late, always partying at the fraternity house. It was all about my grades-my father would have beaten the daylights out of me if I wasn't top of the class. So I made a deal with this brilliant kid from the Bronx, Norman Berger, and paid him to write my papers and take my exams for graduate school. He was deformed, a hunchback, and weird as hell. But I knew he was desperate. And my father couldn't stop bragging that his brilliant son Alan Howard graduated Penn with honors and was admitted to Columbia Business School. If he only knew the truth!

My firm is bleeding and I need a miracle to save it. I ran it poorly-no, not poorly, incompetently. I thank God that my father isn't alive to see how I let his baby crumble, but I curse God for his ALS.

Norman Berger became the CEO of a public company called Whitcomb Pharmaceutical. The stock symbol is WHIT, in case you're interested. He's close to developing a cure for ALS. I have a mole that works for him and tips me off with inside information. I placed a huge bet that the FDA will approve the drug. The announcement will be made within the hour. It will save my fund and my reputation.

If the SEC comes after me, and I'm looking at a prison sentence, I made up my mind to take the cowardly way out. We all have to die sometime.

Don't ever think you couldn't have handled Jeremy's job. I remember how I ranted and raved the last time I saw you in my office. You're smart and damn good with numbers. And you did a terrific job in raising all that capital for my fund. I wanted you to know that.

I swear to you that I never knew about Creedmoor, and if I was responsible for what drove you there, then please find it in your heart to forgive me.

And you should know that you have all the talent in the world to make it on tour, if that's what you want. I read the newspapers, and I know that you're struggling now. It just takes a lot of work and beating balls until your hands bleed.

And I hope you didn't go into a long winded eulogy at my funeral because it was expected of you. Let's be honest, I'm a pathetic excuse for a father.

I'm spinning-have to go and sit with Jeremy- celebrate when the big news hits.

I hope you find happiness and contentment in your life, something which has always eluded me. Nothing else really matters much.

I've been melancholy without you in my life. Your office next to mine is still available, just as you left it. It will always be your office. Sometimes I walk in and I imagine I see you sitting behind your desk, but.......it's only a fantasy from a grieving father.

Just know that I love you Gordon, more than anything else in this world, more than you could possibly fathom, more than all the awards that have honored me, more than all the charitable plaques engraved with my name. One day you too will be a father, and then you will understand what you mean to me. I'm only human, imperfect, flawed and insecure, and tormented by too many demons. Aren't we all? And unfortunately, you had the misfortune of being my son. It's very true-we always hurt the ones we love.

Be well,

Dad

"Can you believe what your father wrote, it's so....I'm speechless!"

"I know, I know" Gordon muttered, mired in thought, as he slowly reread the letter to himself, his lips moving in silence, his demeanor stoic as he digested every word.

"We're not keeping that money, Liz-it's going to Swifty's caddie fund, every last nickel."

"I love you, Gordon Scott Howard, more than you can imagine," she beamed, as they embraced, and held onto each other, tightly.

Gordon lost all interest in competitive golf, becoming totally devoted to his family and his work. He had finally found contentment with everything life had to offer, which gave it meaning and purpose, courtesy of the Golf Gods.

HOWARD JAHRE IS A serial entrepreneur whose business career has included real estate development, musical instrument manufacturing, stock trading, and developing specialized insurance for the financial industry.

Howard is an attorney and a member of the New York State Bar since 1972. He is also of counsel to several NYC law firms which specialize in representing plaintiffs in class action litigation.

This is his first novel.

His interests include golf, tennis, boxing, chess, and playing guitar.

His favorite books are "The American Tragedy" by Theodore Dreiser and "Contact" by Carl Sagan.

His favorite poem is "The Raven" by Edgar Allan Poe.

His favorite movies are "Twelve Angry Men" and "On the Waterfront."

In 1973 he played the lead role of Howie Kaufman in a movie documentary about the Viet Nam war entitled "The POW" which was notably reviewed in the New York Times and the Wall Street Journal.

Howard currently resides in Brooklyn, New York with his wife Elizabeth and Sweden, their loyal white Labrador retriever.

Made in the USA
San Bernardino, CA
03 November 2018